A SOLDIER OF POLODA™

FURTHER ADVENTURES BEYOND
THE FARTHEST STAR™

THE WILD ADVENTURES OF EDGAR RICE BURROUGHS® SERIES

A SOLDIER OF POLODA™

FURTHER ADVENTURES BEYOND THE FARTHEST STAR ™

LEE STRONG

COVER BY CHRIS PEULER

INTERIOR ILLUSTRATIONS BY EARL GEIER

Lee Strong

EDGAR RICE BURROUGHS, Inc.
Publishers
TARZANA   CALIFORNIA

A Soldier of Poloda
Further Adventures Beyond the Farthest Star
First Edition

Trademarks including Edgar Rice Burroughs®, A Solidier of Poloda™ and Beyond The Farthest Star™ owned by Edgar Rice Burroughs, Inc. Front Cover by Chris Peuler and Interior Illustrations by Earl Geier © 2017 Edgar Rice Burroughs, Inc.

Special thanks to Bob Garcia, Gary A. Buckingham, Jim Gerlach, and Tyler Wilbanks for their valuable assistance in producing this novel.

Number 5 in the Series

Library of Congress CIP (Cataloging-in-Publication) Data
ISBN-13: 978-1-945462-09-2

- 9 8 7 6 5 4 3 2 -

Table of Contents

FOREWORD

In April 1940, author Edgar Rice Burroughs, his wife Florence Gilbert, and her two small children moved to Hawaii to start life anew. The war in Europe had all but eliminated the lucrative foreign royalty payments on his novels and Tarzan films, and Burroughs hoped to improve his finances on the islands, where his cost of living was one-third of that on the mainland.

Inspired as much by creativity as by his desire to remain financially secure, Burroughs entered a robust writing period, turning out nearly 300,000 words of prose in eight months, including four 20,000-word novelettes for each of his major fantasy series: Mars, Venus, and Pellucidar. Ray Palmer, editor of Ziff-Davis Publications, proved an eager client, publishing the stories in the pulp magazines *Amazing Stories* and *Fantastic Adventures*. The novellas were later combined into the novels *Llana of Gathol, Escape on Venus,* and *Savage Pellucidar*.

Burroughs began his creative renaissance pecking away at an Underwood typewriter perched on a packing crate in his garage, before relocating to a rented Honolulu office. Having revitalized his existing fantasy universe, he then created one more: the planet Poloda of the Canapa solar system, where eleven planets orbit the sun, Omos, and all are surrounded by a donut-shaped atmosphere band. Always a stickler for detail, Burroughs mapped the planet and created an alphabet for its inhabitants to lend further verisimilitude to his story.

i

Stymied by questions regarding the tides and visibility of the neighboring planets, he wrote to John S. Donagho, professor of mathematics and astronomy at the University of Hawaii. Though Donagho's analysis approved some of Burroughs' theoretical concepts, the notion of a donut-shaped ring of atmosphere was a casualty, about which the author joked, "there are two schools of thought on Poloda: one adheres to the Donaghoan theory, while the other, hopefully anticipating inter-planetary navigation, clings stubbornly to the Burroughsian theory."

Palmer, awash in a backlog of Burroughs stories, declined this newest offering. The fantasy, now titled *Beyond the Farthest Star*, was purchased by editor Donald Kennicott for $400, and appeared in the January 1942 pulp magazine *Blue Book*.

Beyond the Farthest Star details the adventures of an unidentified pilot shot down behind German lines in 1939, who is suddenly transported 450,000 light-years from Earth to Poloda, a mysterious planet in the Globular Cluster NGC 7006. The Polodans are locked in a century-long battle between the free society of Unis and the fascist Kapars, who seek global domination. The patriotic Burroughs' parallel between America's democracy versus the tyranny of both Hitler's Third Reich and the Soviet Union under Stalin is clearly evident. Now named Tangor ("from nothing," due to his inexplicable appearance on the planet), the pilot goes to war for his adopted state, putting his air combat skills to good use.

Six weeks after completing *Beyond the Farthest Star*, Burroughs wrote *Tangor Returns*, a sequel in which Tangor goes behind the lines of the police state of Kapara, to steal a revolutionary power amplifier. *Tangor Returns* remained unpublished until 1964 when both stories appeared in the Canaveral Press hardback anthology *Tales of Three Planets*.

Now, author Lee Strong revisits this faraway world with *A Soldier of Poloda*. In this newest adventure, OSS officer Thomas Randolph is teleported through space and behind enemy lines into the realm of the Kapars, where he seeks to end their evil menace forever.

SCOTT TRACY GRIFFIN
Tarzana, CA

Ghosts in the Machine

The psychiatrist put down the report that he had been reading and looked at his patient. Both were seated in a well-lit office, its walls lined with professional books and certificates. If any room exuded the skill and dignity of the science of psychiatry, this one did.

The patient, a balding elderly man with a still handsome face, looked back. He smiled and asked, "Well, Doc, do I have a normal bean?"

The psychiatrist grinned at the colorful expression and replied. "Yes, Ed, your 'bean' is normal."

His patient relaxed and smiled more brightly, "And the ghosts that are using my typewriter?" His voice was utterly sincere.

The psychiatrist frowned slightly before he smoothed his expression into professional reassurance. "Ed, we've been through this before. There are no 'ghostly fingers' typing stories of life on other planets at midnight."

Ed rebutted forcefully but still courteously. "Doc, I've seen typing paper floating off my desk and inserting itself into my typewriter by itself on several occasions. And I've watched the machine typing by itself faster than mortal hands can type. Maybe whatever or whoever is using my typewriter aren't 'ghosts', but what are they then?"

The psychiatrist exhaled in exasperation. He spoke quietly and firmly, with all the professional authority and persuasiveness that he could muster. "Ed, the so-called 'ghostly fingers' are a series of hallucinations brought on by a mild neurosis."

Ed started. He tensed and shifted uncomfortably in his chair. He opened his mouth to object but his doctor cut him off.

"Ed, there's nothing to be ashamed of. Professionally speaking, your mentality and your ability to deal with the outside world are both normal. You are unusually creative and according to Dr. Rhine's test for psychic abilities —," The psychiatrist tapped the report lying on his desk, "— you score unusually high in that department."

The psychiatrist leaned forward slightly, emphasizing his words. "The problem is that you're under a lot of stress. You're getting on in years. You've had an active stressful life as a soldier, railroad detective, prospector, war correspondent at an age when most men are retired, and, of course, a successful novelist not to mention being a husband and father. These things are very commendable but they are stressful. In addition, Dr. Sprague says that you have heart damage, Parkinson's disease, and other problems that are not uncommon for a man of your age.

"These things take a toll on the best of us. As a result of this pressure, you stay up late, you get sleepy, and then you daydream that 'ghostly fingers' are typing stories rather than you typing them yourself. It's very common for human beings to wish that jobs would do themselves; your daydreams are simply an example of this tendency.

"What you need to do is to relax. Get away from the typewriter; go for walks; visit places that you enjoy visiting; enjoy life rather than locking yourself in an office all day long. And eat and drink moderately."

The office was silent as Ed thought things over. He sighed deeply. "Well, Doc, you're the doctor. Florence said the same thing and I guess that two heads are better than one. I'll, uh…. I'll try to do what you say. At least for a while…!" He grinned and his body language relaxed. The psychiatrist relaxed as well.

After a moment, the psychiatrist asked, "Ed, I do have one question."

"Shoot, doc."

"What brought up the 'ghostly fingers' now? You haven't mentioned them since 1940 or '41. That was quite some time ago. Why now?"

Ed's face scrunched up. He took a deep breath and looked his doctor directly in the eye. "December 1940 was the last time that the ghost (or whatever he is) typed anything. Now he has returned. And he brought a friend."

The patient, a balding, elderly man with a still handsome face, looked back. he smiled and asked, "Well, Doc, do I have a normal bean?"

BOOK ONE:
ARRIVAL ON POLODA

Chapter 1   NO JOKE, THERE I WAS...

MY NAME, rank and serial number are no longer important since I am now dead. I know that I am dead. I saw my body lying against an apple tree in Normandy with my blood pouring out of a gaping hole in my back. You don't get much deader than that. Some German soldier was sharper than I was, and now he would be going home while I went "Somewhere."

In June 1943, my Office of Strategic Services detachment parachuted into France to harass the Nazi regime and gather information on the German armed forces. When the Allies landed at Normandy in 1944 our mission changed to providing information and flank security for the advancing armies. You know what they say about the best-laid plans....

One night in July 1944, my team was moving through an apple orchard overlooking the Sienne River near Pont de la Rocque, Normandy. The American Sixth Armored Division planned to cross the river the following day. The Germans had established an outpost in a windmill overlooking a possible river crossing. We were supposed to chase them out and then scout out the crossings so the Sixth could move across quickly. We never got as far as the windmill.

André's smoker's cough gave us away and some very alert and very lucky German nailed him on the first shot. André went down and stayed down. But he was coloring the air with his vivid French so he wasn't dead yet. The rest of us opened up on where we thought the German position was. We were guessing based on the sound of the Mauser barking because it was too dark to see anything but shadows.

We got lucky; just not lucky enough. In the darkness, someone cried out for his mother in German and the Mauser stopped.

Nobody moved for a while, hoping that someone else would make a mistake. I whispered for Pierre to lead the patrol forward while Suzette and I checked on André. None of us were really doctors but Suzette and I had had some training. He was still cursing when we reached him and I put my hand over his mouth a little too late.

I was kneeling beside André, trying to examine the patient when a sledgehammer hit me in the chest. The force of the blow slammed me backwards into an apple tree of respectable vintage. I collapsed into a heap at the base of the tree.

There was a snapping sound like someone cocking a rifle bolt except that it seemed to come from inside my head. I stood up. I could see my body lying on the ground at my feet. There was a dime-sized hole in my right chest and my left back was a soggy mess. I must have blacked out then.

When I came to, I was still standing up but everything else had changed. It was still night, but the cloud-filtered moonlight was brighter. I was in a shallow valley between unimpressive hills. The apple trees had disappeared somehow, to be replaced with regular rows of what I guessed were crops. Exactly what crops they were was a mystery. They looked like rosebushes in the nighttime darkness but they smelled more like maple syrup.

I took a step forward to get a better look and discovered that I had no boots on. I looked down and discovered that I was stark naked!

I pinched myself a couple of times and decided that I wasn't dreaming. If I was dead, I should be at St. Peter's Desk applying for admission to Heaven. But no theology I had ever heard of described Heaven as smelling like maple syrup. The only theory that seemed to cover all the facts involved a truly magnificent party and a visit to a French experimental farm growing exotic plants. I hoped that I had enjoyed the party.

Well, everything — head, arms, legs, and so forth — seemed to be working properly. There was no hole in my chest or back. All my blood seemed to be where it belonged. So I set off for a walk between rows of the strange smelling bushes. I don't know what I was looking for but I certainly hoped to find it sooner rather than later.

I was following the crops down a slight slope when I spotted lights in the fields ahead. I crept closer and came to a clearing in the rows of whatsits. Crunching footsteps came out of the darkness. I dropped down behind the nearest bush and made myself as inconspicuous as possible.

A German sentry strolled past. I didn't breathe for an eternity or two but he sauntered past, apparently at peace with the world. That seemed odd since the American, British, and Canadian Armies were somewhere nearby, not to mention the French Resistance. D-Day should have dispelled any complacency on the part of German foot soldiers.

Well, never look a gift horse in the mouth. I stuck my head up and looked around for other Germans. Seeing none, I glided forward behind the Kareless Kraut. Being barefoot had its advantages. He didn't hear me until I made his rather impressive knife jump out of its scabbard and whisk across his throat. He gurgled and started on his journey to Valhalla. I caught his body on the way down.

I dragged the Kareless Kraut's body into the bushes and began stripping it. He was clearly the bottom of the barrel as far as the Master Race went. Say what you will about the Nazis, they're sharp dressers. This guy was wearing a gray shirt and coverall outfit rather than tailored field blouse and trousers. His headpiece looked more like a steel football helmet than the "coal scuttle" hat that "G.I. Fritz" usually wore. He had a heavy submachine pistol rather than the usual Mauser rifle or carbine. His face didn't look any too healthy, either.

We'd heard that Hitler was desperate for troops and equipment with the Allies closing in on him. The Kareless Kraut and his nonstandard uniform and weapons seemed to confirm that; an important item to report when I got back in touch with Sixth Armored.

I was examining the machine pistol of unfamiliar make when I heard a droning sound in the sky. An airplane was descending into the farmland. Ah! The lights among the crops outlined a landing strip. Some scout was returning to what I guessed was a temporary forward operating base.

Acting like you belong where you are is usually a better disguise than hiding in the bushes. So I stood up and acted like a German sentry assigned to guard the field. The Kareless Kraut had some papers in one pocket but I hadn't had a chance to read them yet. I decided to be Rupert von Hentzau when someone asked.

The plane taxied to a stop about a hundred feet from me. It was another mystery since its black coloring and bat wings didn't match any aircraft that I had studied. Possibly one of Hitler's alleged wonder weapons, although it landed like any other airplane.

Another gray-clad German got out, looked around and spotted me. He waved and said something that I didn't catch. I waved back and called, "Welcome home, lancer," in soldier's German. Germans love titles. Ordinary soldiers called each other *lancers* as if they were all knights.

He started to say something but a voice from the airplane attracted his attention. Someone inside the plane handed a gold-clad girl out to him.

She was a spitfire. Both hands and both legs were tied and she still hammered his steel pot and chest with everything she had. While he was struggling with her, another gray shirt got out of the airplane and slugged her hard. She went limp. She fell to the ground and lay still.

She had a nice body with beautiful coppery hair and a very tight suit of gold sequins and red plastic boots glinting in the landing field lights. The two goons leered over her. The slugger grabbed her shoulder and flipped her over onto her face. He fumbled with something at her back neckline and moved his hand down her back. I heard a noise like a zipper....

"Hey, lancer," I shouted as I stepped forward. My mouth lives a life of its own. "Save it for your own time. Let's see your orders."

The two thugs looked up, puzzled expressions on their faces. One of them barked something at me. It sounded like a drunken Russian trying to recite Wagner backwards. Possibly some so-called Free Russians in Hitler's service?

Well, the key thing was to maintain the initiative. "Your orders, lancers. Orders. I must see your orders for your mission. What are you doing landing on my airstrip?" I raised my voice and made it as official as I could. Act like you own the world and most people will assume that you do. Especially in military dictatorships like the Third Reich.

These guys stood up and looked at me like I had a lobster on my head. They were dressed and armed like the Kareless Kraut had been. Herr Slugger began shouting at me again, still speaking his not-really-Russian language.

I tried Russian, then French, Portuguese and English before reverting to German. None of them seemed to ring a bell with the gray shirts. They got angrier and angrier. Both of them were barking and gesturing at me. I continued to act like the king of the world who had just found small boys stealing his prize-winning apples. I marched closer and closer, matching their volume.

As I approached, I realized that their insignia didn't match anything in the Axis uniform guides. The Nazis liked skulls, lightning bolts and oak leaves. These guys liked geometric symbols. That was definitely strange. By this time, we were making enough noise to rival the League of Nations session on the Italian invasion of Abyssinia and accomplishing about as much good.

Herr Slugger broke the deadlock by turning to his sideman and giving him some order ending in the word "Kapar." His sideman said something in return and, bending over, picked up the woman's body and raised her to his shoulders.

Just then a loud mechanical clanking broke out behind me. It sounded like a column of tanks starting their engines in unison. I took my eyes off the opposition for a fatal second.

Without warning, Herr Slugger launched a haymaker worthy of Dempsey in his prime. It landed on my chin and rocked my head back. Half stunned, I fell over backwards and crumpled to the dirt of the landing strip.

The shock of a heavy boot crashing into mine woke me up again. Herr Slugger was taking a step to the side, obviously intending to break a few ribs with his next kick. I rolled into his stride. Bracing myself with left arm on the ground, I swung my left leg up, smashing it into the side of his right knee. My right arm grabbed his left ankle and pulled. He crashed to the ground.

I rolled away from Herr Slugger and stood upright. He was fumbling with his unwieldy submachine pistol. I shot first. His shot went wild. Mine didn't.

I was looking at the frozen sideman, still hoisting the girl in a fireman's carry when another shot passed overhead. We both spun around, looking in the direction that I had come from.

A bright rectangle of light filled the lower quarter of the sky. A giant trapdoor had opened in the ground, exposing a tunnel into unknown depths. The Kareless Kraut must have been standing directly on top of the trapdoor when I jumped him.

Human figures were silhouetted against the light. Several of them were more gray shirts carrying tools and heavy pistols. But the center of the group was a pair of obvious of-

"I shot first. His shot went wild. Mine didn't"

ficers, one male and one female, both wearing green rather than gray. The man was tall and muscular, with a hatchet face carved out of granite. The woman was tall, too, a valkyrie rather than a knight. Compared to her, Marlene Dietrich was a boy. But that wasn't what *really* grabbed my attention!

The clouds that had masked the moonlight earlier had moved on. Above and behind the trapdoor, two moons decorated the night sky. One, higher up, was about the right size for Earth's Moon but it was green and white, not silver or gold. The other, lower in the sky and almost resting on the trapdoor, was at least four times the size of the Moon as well as being blue and white. I could see continents and oceans on that one like a child's drawing of Earth as seen from space.

Wherever I was, it wasn't anywhere on Earth. I was still gawking at the light show when someone clobbered me from behind hard. The lights went out again.

Chapter 2 FIRST I DIED AND THEN THINGS GOT WORSE

DESPITE someone's best efforts, I didn't die. I just felt like I had. When I woke up, my first thought was pain. Someone had beaten me rather thoroughly while I was unconscious. They didn't seem to have broken any bones but every muscle in my body ached.

My second thought was to wonder if I was on yet another planet. The last time that I blacked out, I wound up on Two Moon Planet. Now I was naked again but in an obvious prison cell. Poorly poured, cheap, gray concrete above, below, and on three sides; black metal bars and door on the fourth side; and a naked electric light something or other overhead. I say "something or other" because it was spiral rather than spherical. For all I knew, I was now on *Three* Moon Planet somewhere *else*.

That happy thought was interrupted when a green-shirted guard appeared in the corridor on the other side of the bars. He grunted something in that not-really-Russian language at me. I groaned, "Good morning, sergeant. I'd like breakfast in bed today," in German, "and a bed if you don't mind." I was lying on the concrete floor. I repeated it in Russian when he didn't seem to understand German.

He made some comment that I didn't understand, but unlocked the door in the bars and gestured for me to step out of the cage. When I didn't move, he pulled a heavy truncheon out of a holster, slapped his hand menacingly, and gestured again. Well, the obvious threat said what his language skills didn't say. I got up, muscles complaining bitterly, and limped down the corridors that he indicated with grunting and occasional truncheon taps. I noted that his insignia were geometric symbols similar but not identical to what Herr Slugger and the Sideman had worn.

The prison scheme continued for some time before giving way to a different section with a higher-class prison motif. Every cell in the lower class area had at least one prisoner in it, all dressed in black coveralls and rags that had been coveralls. Most of them were sleeping on the bare floors. Some of them stared at me apathetically. Apparently naked prisoners weren't uncommon on Three Moon Planet (or wherever we were). The place stank of too many people enclosed for too long a time without bathing. Periodically, there were control points where guards with guns in fortified cages kept an eye on things. If anyone managed to take a truncheon away from the first guard, the second guard would shoot the troublemaker while being immune to retaliation. Nice.

The higher-class section was separated from the more obvious jail by walls and a checkpoint. The checkpoint's resemblance to a Nazi police station was unmistakable. My guard vouched for my good character and we left the station for the higher-class district.

This section of town wasn't really that much nicer than the jail but the concrete construction was better quality, the light fixtures were shaded, there were doors in the walls rather than bars, and people passed back and forth as they would in a cheap hotel corridor. The people were sallow-faced white men and women dressed either in poison-ivy green or brick-red shirts and coveralls. There were more red shirts than green shirts, but the greens were armed with truncheons, knives and submachine pistols. The reds got out of the greens' way without being told. Two greens shouted at a red and he stopped and produced papers without a word. Green-shirted cops and red-shirted civilians?

There were also posters on the walls that instantly reminded me of Nazi propaganda sheets in Occupied France. Scowling faces and heroic airmen and soldiers exhorted the passers by. All of the military characters wore gray and the scowlers wore green. Perhaps I was still on Two Moon Planet after all. One ugly blue gargoyle feasted on graphically displayed human bodies clad in brick red. The lettering on the posters was mostly geometric symbols. It looked like some math teacher had invented his own alphabet.

My escort and I wandered through corridors and down stairs until we came to an even higher-class jail with two green shirts ostentatiously guarding the place. My guard told them what a swell guy I was. One door guard checked a list and apparently found my name. We went in. The whole procedure reminded me of pompous doormen outside a second-rate nightclub. We picked up more escorts inside the even higher-class jail.

This section of the jail reminded me of some cheesy government office building. There were desks, filing cabinets, and secretaries working with machines that looked like type-writers crossed with Ouija boards. Everyone wore green with silver trim and seemed to know what they were doing. Put everyone in better quality clothes and we could be visiting Dad's office back in Boston.

Eventually, I was ushered into a large office with yet another guard at the door. Inside, the hatchet-faced officer from the trapdoor incident was seated behind a desk suitable for the President of the United States. The valkyrie was seated on the left side of the desk and the gold-costumed redhead to her left.

On the right side of the desk were a double handful of gray shirts and green shirts. Each color coded group stood together but apart from the others. I recognized the Sideman, looking very ill at ease. When he recognized me, his discomfort was replaced with raw hatred. Oh well, I wasn't expecting a Christmas card from him anyway.

I was the only one in the room without clothes on. Everyone looked at me appraisingly. Then the redhead blushed and turned away. I recognized the interrogation techniques from OSS training. Take away a person's clothes and he feels embarrassed and off balance. Subject him to physical discomfort like sleeping on a hard floor and he feels weak and helpless. Surround him with enemies and he feels defenseless and unable to resist his captors' demands.

I certainly didn't appreciate being the object of the floorshow but there wasn't much I could do about it except brazen it out. The officer started to speak but I interrupted and asked for two suits of clothes, one for business, and one for casual travel about town. He cut me off while I was giving him my measurements.

The interview was another League of Nations session. The gray shirts and green shirts all shouted not-really-Russian and pointed at me. I tried my previous selection of languages again, declaimed in Latin, and even recited "Jabberwocky." I also gestured a lot. Nothing seemed to work. At one point, the sideman put his hand on his gun while screaming at me. Another gray shirt restrained him and spoke directly to the officer. The latter seemed to be nodding in agreement. Both green and gray shirts looked at me like I was a Thanksgiving turkey.

Everyone seemed to be in agreement when the valkyrie spoke up. The green shirt officer listened to her and nodded. She spoke to the redhead in a language that sounded like Verdi sung in Japanese. The redhead looked carefully at my face, shook her head, and answered in the same language.

The valkyrie questioned me in not-really-Japanese, not-really-Russian, and what I thought were three other languages. I listened carefully but wound up shaking my head and making helpless gestures again. We reached another impasse.

There was a loud thumping sound somewhere in the distance. Everyone stopped talking, shouting and gesticulating to listen for something. I had no idea what we were listening for but I listened, too. The thumping was repeated several times before it died away.

In the silence that followed, the senior gray shirt spoke up again. One of his gestures included a slashing motion across his own throat. I was pretty sure that he was offering to cut mine rather than the other way around.

The officer was on the verge of agreement when the valkyrie interrupted. Whatever she said, none of the gray shirts or green shirts liked it and they said so. She turned a gorgon stare on them and they fell silent. After a few more words, the officer nodded.

He gave some orders and my personal guard force-marched me out of the office. This time, they locked me up in a different cell, this one in the office building area. The concrete was smoother and better quality, there was a bed, and the last occupant had bathed. After a while, another guard fetched me a set of black coveralls and my dignity. There were white symbols on the chest and back. I was still a prisoner but I had moved up in the world, whatever world I was on.

The next phase of the interrogation was more dignified. Every morning…. I called it "morning" because it was the time after I woke up from a sleeping period that felt like night. The periods of sleeping and activity *felt* like Earth days, but I hadn't actually seen the sun or a clock since I arrived.

Every morning a black-clad servant brought me a bowl of breakfast stew or goulash in my cell. Most of the components seemed to be rubber or lard seasoned with dandruff, but hunger really is the best condiment. A few minutes later, a green-shirted guard came to escort me to the valkyrie's office. If I was slow, he used his truncheon on my shoulders or my stew bowl. Since I had glimpsed a gun-toting guard outside the door, I settled for making a mental note of his face and learning the rules.

The redhead was escorted to the office at the same time. They'd taken away her entertainer's costume of gold sequins and red boots and replaced it with a black coverall. I noticed that her white symbols were identical to mine except for one. I suspected the symbols were prisoner inventory numbers. She was clearly frightened by the whole experience. Nonetheless she had her chin up.

We occasionally had to wait outside the valkyrie's door so I started saying "Good morning" in English. She responded in softly spoken Japanese Verdi. Once I recited a list of Japanese cities and islands on the off chance that she might recognize them, but she wrinkled her brow and shook her head. I introduced myself as Thomas Randolph that she shortened to "Tomas Ran" and then to "Ran." She was Loris Kiri. I started by calling her "Miss Kiri" but quickly learned that Loris was her family name and Kiri her personal name.

The valkyrie was always doing paperwork when we were allowed into her office and into hard plastic chairs in front of her Cabinet officer-sized desk. These people used plastic where Americans would make things out of metal or wood. A green-shirted goon stood quietly behind us.

I recognized more techniques from OSS training. Making us wait while she shuffled papers emphasized that she was The Queen of her little kingdom while Kiri and I were Peasants. But the look on her face when she put the paper down and focused on us caused me to suspect that she was genuinely glad for the break in the administrative routine.

She started off conversationally at first; another trick that OSS trainers warned agents about. The Queen was trying the good cop routine first. If we didn't cooperate, her bad cop goon would give us a truncheon massage to soften us up.

She talked to both of us alternating between her own not-really-Russian and Kiri's native not-really-Japanese. Kiri replied in monosyllables and eventually clammed up entirely. The valkyrie leaned over and casually slapped her prisoner in the face hard. Kiri's head jerked sideways and she fell out of her chair onto the floor.

I jumped up, shouting that there was no need for *that*. As I said before, my mouth lives a life of its own. The guard behind me must have allowed his mind to wander: he didn't catch me in time.

The valkyrie did. Her slapping hand came up and punched me in the mouth hard. I saw it coming and tensed my muscles up. That softened the blow but it still hurt. Then the guard gave my head a short truncheon massage and I blacked out again. This was becoming a bad habit, one that could easily get me killed. It was time for a new strategy; Step One: Don't get killed.

The next day, the valkyrie began teaching Kiri and me the not-really-Russian language, Kapar. She seemed to relish her role as a schoolteacher and we learned quickly. I had the benefit of speaking English and French at home, German and Portuguese while working for Dad, and Latin and Russian in college. It was my facility with languages that got me an invitation to join the OSS and free trips to France and, ultimately, Two Moon Planet. Kiri was originally monolingual but she was both smart and industrious.

School was frequently interrupted by those mysterious thumping sounds but no one else asked any questions so I played dumb for the moment. I noticed that Kiri smiled ever so slightly after the noises ceased but I never got a chance to ask her about them in private.

We learned more than just how to bark and grunt like good little Kapars. Among other things, we learned that our schoolteacher was Sellon Sura. Like Kiri, Sura put her personal name last. She was a Special Assistant to Virrul, the Kapar governor of the city of Gerris in the province of Allos on the continent of Epris on the planet Poloda. We never learned what Virrul's personal name was, or even if he had one.

Since Sura was still trying the good cop routine, I got in a couple of questions before she really started to work on me. "Special Assistant Sellon, who are the Kapars?"

"We Kapars are the Natural Rulers of Poloda," she proclaimed with complete sincerity. "Our society is the most logical and enduring known to mankind."

I nodded sagely, drinking in everything I could. "Why is Kapar society the most logical society?"

"Because it is based on warfare, the natural state of mankind. Unlike lesser societies, we Kapars realize that man is naturally a fighting creature. Therefore, we are a completely military society with no waste or inefficiency to hinder us. We are strong because we have eliminated sentiment and other soft emotions that weaken human beings and cause failure. The validity of the Kapar way of life is proved by the fact that, under the leadership of the Most High Pom Da, we have conquered four of the five continents of Poloda and will soon conquer the remaining one."

"Not while a single Unisan lives!" interrupted Kiri. Her soft voice was edged with steel.

Sura leaned over and slapped Kiri again. The captive woman hit the floor again. Conscious of the guard behind me, I didn't move.

While Kiri was picking herself up off the floor and reseating herself, Sura leaned back and waved her hand as if brushing away flies. "Yes, you Unisans are resisting our inevitable advance for the moment. But tens of other nations said the same thing and where are they now?"

Kiri massaged her cheek silently. The she-wolf went on. "The answer is that they're all under Kapar rule. Zurris, Ithris, Punos – the continents of Epris, Heris, Auris and Karis — disorganized, pleasure-seeking rabble a hundred years ago — Kapar colonies today."

She leaned forward again, a cat eyeing a mouse. "As Unis will be one day. When your weird little technocratic government surrenders, perhaps the Pom Da will name me governor of Unis." Her voice lowered, almost purring. "You can live in your old apartment if you like." She paused, "As my servant, of course." She threw her head back, black mane flying, laughing like Satan.

Kiri clearly wanted to spit in Sura's face but she shrank into her chair. Captivity in the Kapar empire and Sura's boundless confidence were daunting. It was all too easy to imagine Sellon Sura sitting in the Unisan equivalent of the White House.

When her majesty wound down, I ventured another question, "And what will you Kapars do when you've conquered Unis?"

Sura shifted to face me. Her face had the classical beauty of a Greek goddess – and her pale blue eyes a hint of madness. "We will conquer the other planets of Omos, our Sun. We would undoubtedly have flown to Antos or Tonos years ago if the war with Unis had not demanded all our resources."

Well, you couldn't say that the Kapars didn't think big. Even Hitler hadn't made any territorial demands on Mars or Venus. It also meant that, sooner or later, the Kapars would be gunning for Earth. "I don't know the planets by those names. Which one is closer to the Sun and which one further out?"

Sura frowned. "None of them, of course. The eleven planets and the atmosphere belt are all the same distance from Omos." Kiri looked at me with a puzzled expression and nodded her head.*

---

* Dr. Henry Tomino of the International Astronomic Society (IAS) describes the Omos System as an 11 body neo-Klemperer Donaghho rosette in which the planets and atmosphere belt are stabilized by mutual gravitational interactions. Potential perturbations are buffered by the uniform gravitational equipoises and the atmospheric belt. For a partial parallel to the Omos System within Earth's Solar System, see the Lagrangian moons and Phoebe Ring of particles in the Saturn satellite system. Donaghho rosettes were first described by J.S. Donaghho in 1940. Attempts to identify the Omos System by astrometric or radial velocity measurement have not been successful to-date. Dr. Tomino suggests that this is due to the planets' equal distribution around the central star, which causes the planetary gravitational influences to cancel out. As a result, no detectable wobble is imposed on the baseline stellar motion. As a result of recent discoveries, the IAS is currently requesting time on the Kepler space telescope to identify Omos by observations of planetary transits. – Ed.

"Her face had the classical beauty of a Greek goddess – and her pale blue eys a hint of madness."

18

I blinked. I'm no astronomer but I did stay awake in high school science class. I couldn't think of any reason why two women on the opposite sides of a hundred-year long war would both lie about something like this and do so without coordinating ahead of time. My working theory had been that Poloda was one of the nine planets in Earth's solar system. Most likely Mars, which has two moons. But, eleven total planets meant that Poloda was in some other solar system altogether. Ditto the fact that they shared a common orbit. Ditto the fact that they shared an atmosphere belt. Theoretically an *airplane* could fly between Omos' planets much less Robert Goddard's proposed rocket ships. Wow...!

For all I knew, I could be in another *galaxy*...! I wanted to say "Impossible"....

But.... I pinched myself. I still wasn't dreaming. Even if things felt like a nightmare.

Unfortunately, my pause to absorb Polodan astronomy gave Sura time to remember that she was supposed to be interrogating me instead of the other way around. She started in on me personally and then proceeded through Earthly astronomy, geography, history and science. She had a mind like a steel trap and I was the one in the trap. Fortunately, I had had time to get my story straight.

Sellon Sura was clearly a very smart person and she knew it. As the special assistant to the head jailer, she held a lot of power including the power to kill Kiri and me without batting an eyelash. But she had weaknesses as well, including the facts that she was a Kapar and that she wasn't a professional interrogator.

Despite the fact that they'd conquered four-fifths of a planet the size of Earth, the Kapars were about as subtle as so many bricks. They valued strength, military glory, and the rewards of conquest. Ordinary human intelligence seemed to be valued only as it contributed to conquest. The green shirt/gray shirt thought process seemed to run: Tomas Ran is an enemy; therefore kill him; end of problem. Period. End of report.

Sura was smart enough to realize that I must be a special if not extraordinary case. If I wasn't a Unisan super-spy, I might well be something *worse*. Possibly an advance scout for an alien invasion! After all, I'd appeared buck naked in the middle of a military reservation without any apparent means of transportation, killed two of their armed soldiers with their own weapons, and had only been captured by dumb luck. Why was I so confident that I could take on the whole Kapar empire single-handedly, and were there any more at home like me?

It amused me to think of *myself* as the Man From Mars but *from the Kapar point of view* that idea made a lot of sense. So Sura had intervened with Virrul and made it her project to find who or what I was.

Smart girl. Dangerous woman. Very, very dangerous woman.

Unfortunately for her, she didn't have the time or training to do the job right. No professional would have allowed us as much free time as the ice queen did. Every day, Kiri and I were marched back to our cells where we spent afternoons and evenings twiddling our thumbs. I didn't know what the duties of a "Special Assistant" were but they obviously consumed a lot of Sura's time. She should have handed us over to some professionals who would have kept after us without a break until we cracked. As it was, we had time to think....

In OSS training, they try to teach agents that success comes from outthinking the enemy, not just having a bigger and better gun. Dad said pretty much the same thing about business. In OSS, they tell you that, when you talk to the enemy, listen to what they're saying, understand their thinking, give them what they're looking for, and keep your story as simple and as truthful as practical. It makes the story easier to remember and harder for the enemy to unravel. And if they think you're cooperating, they're less likely to torture you until you reveal something important.

If I said that Earth people valued liberty, peace and prosperity, the Kapars would laugh their heads off and begin planning a real life war of the worlds that same day. The only thing that a given Kapar would respect is a bigger and nastier Kapar. So I told Special Assistant to the City Governor Sellon Sura the complete and total truth about Earth. More or less.

I told her that Kiri called me Tomas Ran, which Sura repeated as *Tomas* Ran, and that I had no idea how I got to Poloda. Sura's eyebrows practically climbed off her head but she kept listening.

I told her about how crappy life was on Earth and the other Solar planets. I didn't tell her about dawn over Cape Cod, or hiking in the Berkshires on a summer day, or Currier & Ives snowfalls. I told her about rainstorms, blizzards, hurricanes, ice ages, tidal waves, floods, landslides and earthquakes. I told her about every single one of Earth's nations, states, territories and cities that I could remember. Since Poloda had fought its way down to two rival nations, just listing Earth's fifty or so countries and hundreds of lesser political units boggled the Queen's mind. As it was, after my thirtieth item she gave up trying to memorize everything and started writing notes. Sura had never read "The Purloined Letter."

Kiri sat quietly in her chair, but her eyes kept getting bigger and bigger and bigger....

When we got to Earthly history, I told her about the Roman Republic, the Empire, Christianity.... That led into a discussion of religion. Sura only had a vague notion of what I was talking about since the Kapars had discarded religion along with love, honor and other "sentiments." Very interesting. I dropped the subject.

By the time I got up to the 20th Century, Sura's eyes were glazing over. So I slipped in Orson Welles' Martian attack and Flash Gordon's Mongo invasion as if they were real events. Sura couldn't tell the difference; it was all news to her.

And when I described the Second World War, I mentioned the two hundred division US Army without mentioning that less than half of the authorized divisions were actually manned. I noticed Sura eyeing me carefully when I described numbers and sizes of divisions but I treated it like a weather report. Confidence breeds believability.

I also learned things from the questions she asked. In American military terms, both the Kapars and Unisans had air forces and air defense forces, but no ground armies or navies! They just bombed and strafed each other until someone surrendered!

Oh, ho! I managed to keep my face straight. It was hard to do. I was starting to understand how the Kapar-Unisan war had been going on for a hundred years. I almost choked when I imagined Raymond Massey in a Kapar uniform declaiming, "And now for the rule of the Air Men!" And naturally I dropped the subject of ground armies and ocean navies.

Sura's definition of "science" boiled down to, "military weapons, equipment and supporting technology more powerful than machine guns and cannon." I trotted out every wonder weapon that Hitler's propaganda machine had been claiming since 1933. Since she swallowed one piece of H.G. Wells's science fiction, *which Orson Welles used in his radio broadcast,* I even threw in references to atomic bombs and similar fantasies.

Finally, we were done. Sura had a complete and consistent picture of a violent, heavily armed and incredibly bellicose planet called Earth in a distant solar system. And I hadn't been given a truncheon massage for several days.

I discovered, however, two flies in the ointment. First of all, Kiri wouldn't talk to me. Her face turned into a mask of horror whenever she looked at me. I tried to find out what was wrong but she hid behind her Kapar guard and whimpered for him to protect her. He was startled by the request but more than happy to protect a good-looking young lady from an unarmed man.

I eventually took the hint. And, second of all, Sura declared me insane.

Chapter 3 HARD WORK NEVER KILLED ANYONE

SURA DIDN'T call me to her office for several days. If thumb twiddling was a science, I was now a college graduate. When she did summon me, Kiri wasn't present, which was a shame because I had come to enjoy her company even if she wasn't speaking to me.

Sura gave me the gorgon eye. It was the first time that I had been on the receiving end. I now understood why hardened Kapars shut up when she gave them The Treatment. After a while, I asked if she wanted anything.

"The truth!" she snapped. I started to say something brilliant but she cut me off. She asked me a couple of questions that boiled down to: Was I serious and Did I think she was a fool? I answered Yes to the first and No to the second. Always tell the truth whenever possible.

Unfortunately, Special Assistant Sellon Sura didn't agree with either answer. She accused me of being a *slacker* trying to get special privileges by claiming to be a man from another planet. She sent me to the *question box* for some professional interrogators to get whatever I was hiding out of me. It was almost a pity that I wasn't hiding anything.

Let's just say that Kapar torturers are at least as skillful as their Nazi counterparts and leave it at that. I had two advantages.

24

First, the torturers didn't really know anything about Earth except what I had told Sura. They had copies of her notebooks to work from, but no Earthly newspapers, encyclopedias, tourist guides, telephone directories, reports by secret agents, nothing that might contradict my story. So they attacked the internal consistency of that story. That was my second advantage. No matter what they did – and they did a lot – my story was internally consistent because it was the truth, the whole truth and nothing but the truth.

More or less. Neither Sura nor her thugs were able to spot the discrepancies between my story and real Earthly history and current events.

Eventually they decided that I was telling them what I thought the truth was. Since my planet called Earth didn't match anything in the Omos solar system, they decided that I was making the whole thing up. Once they decided that I was both delusional and lacking any superhuman powers, they got bored and let me go.

More or less. I limped for a long time after I left the question box.

THE ONE REALLY ODD thing about the rough treatment was a visit by City Governor Virrul. He dropped by one day and interrupted some unpleasant experiments with electricity. He exuded sympathy and promises of better treatment if I cooperated. He also claimed to have met another Earthman named Korvan Don or Tangor six years ago in the Kapar capital city of Ergos. Tangor had told everyone there All About Earth. Would I mind confirming a few details about Earthly life?

I was glad for the breather, especially since I recognized yet more techniques from OSS training. Having a "good guy" interrupt torture makes the victim appreciate the "good guy" and cooperate with him. Pretending that you already know everything, and only asking a few questions at a time, eases the victim's conscience because he figures that he's not really revealing anything that you don't already know.

It was easy to see that Virrul was trying to pull the wool over my eyes by pretending to have another witness that could confirm or deny my story. "Korvan Don" *might* be an American name but "Tangor" certainly wasn't. Virrul's alleged expertise was almost certainly a combination of reading Sura's notes and some basic acting. Still, I cooperated with him as much as I could. Unfortunately, he didn't believe me when I said that I had never heard of "Tangor" or the American space program that Tangor had described – one involving flying airplanes to Mars and Venus! I was explaining for the hundredth time how the Martians had used giant cannons to invade New Jersey in 1938, when Virrul cut me off and ordered the voltage doubled.

After a while, he also decided that Sura was right: I was insane.

Being a lunatic in Kapara doesn't get you medical treatment. It gets you beheaded if you're dangerous and worked to death if you're not. Well, at least I kept my head.

WHEN VIRRUL AND THE TORTURERS were through with me, a green shirt marched me upstairs to what I later learned was the seventh underground level of the city of Gerris, where I was handed over to the more ordinary cops. They welcomed me with open truncheons and shoved me into a steel cage about the size of an American rules football field.

There were a couple of hundred black-shirted prisoners milling around when I arrived. The relatively high class Kapars that I had been dealing with didn't look very healthy by American standards and these wretches looked much worse. It was easy to see why. The cage had primitive sanitary facilities at one end and a couple of wooden troughs at the other. One of the latter was full of dubious-looking water. There were no beds or other furniture and a number of bodies were simply lying on the gray concrete floor. I couldn't tell if they were alive or dead. No one had bathed in recent years and the stench was unbelievable at first. After a few minutes, my nose went on strike and just stopped working. Except for the constant electric lights overhead, we might as well have been in Hell.

I was still sizing up the situation when the cage doors opened and a troop of black shirts lugged giant cauldrons in. They were guarded by more cops. The cauldron bearers emptied their burdens into the troughs exactly like Earthly farmhands slopping the hogs. An odor remotely resembling food arose from the troughs. The prisoners eyed the potential meal hungrily but no one moved until a senior green shirt signaled his approval.

Groups of prisoners rushed the troughs and began scooping handfuls of hot slop into their mouths as if it were nectar and ambrosia. The fact that the food was steaming hot didn't seem to matter. I didn't see any plates, bowls or tableware and I doubt that the starving horde would have used them if they had been offered.

I was about to push my way forward when a hideous cackling laughter rose above the grunting and groaning of the starving slaves. The senior green shirt was drinking in the spectacle of human beings reduced to the status of animals and laughing uproariously.

Eventually, the Laughing Hyena got tired of the floor-show and paraded out of the cage. Many eyes followed him but no one stopped scooping up and swallowing as much slop as possible.

"Pleasant fellow," I remarked to no one in particular.

Another prisoner chose to answer me. "You're not from Gerris, are you?" He had a handsome face, a dignified manner, and the first Kapar accent that I had heard. His question sounded more like "Yue aar naut frum Gellis, aar yue?" than Sura's silken tones. I later learned that he was from the colonial continent of Auris. Clearly, the Aurisans had gotten a buy on vowels when they had developed their language.

"What makes you think that?"

"Your face hair and your sarcasm. It is not a good idea to make fun of Kapars regardless of their rank."

I was immediately suspicious of anyone who volunteered to talk to a newcomer and stuck with my story. "Oh, no, I wasn't being sarcastic. Clearly the man enjoys his work and good for him." I looked my newfound friend straight in the eye.

He paused to think and then nodded his head sagely. "I see that you have the true Kapar spirit. Despite your fallen status and your strange face hair."

I stroked my beard and nodded agreement. Polodan males seldom grow beards or moustaches. Very old fellows might have a few whiskers that would embarrass a newborn kitten but younger men's chins are as bare as their palms. My Earthly beard puzzled the prison barbers although they usually managed to hack it into something that could be called neat.

"Yes," I agreed. "I'm from a planet called Earth in another solar system." I smiled serenely as if I was glad to be visiting the garden spot of the universe.

My new friend looked at me searchingly. "Really?" he asked mildly.

"Really; although the authorities have declared me to be insane." I smiled knowingly and pointed in the general direction of the now absent Laughing Hyena.

He nodded his head thoughtfully. "Ah. A man from another planet. And not just any ordinary planet but one orbiting another star entirely. You might fit in very well here indeed. We can use a science fiction storyteller."

I was about to ask about royalties and advance payments when a guard started clanging on a cage bar with his truncheon. Grumbling, the prisoners began forming up into gangs near the main door. Anyone moving too slowly for the guards' taste got a truncheon massage. Other guards with guns kept watch to make sure that no one objected to Kapar ideas of physical therapy.

"Come with me, Prisoner 919V5486," invited my friend, reading the numbers on my black shirt. In turn, I saw that he was Prisoner 886V8953. "Meal time is over. You must go hungry until later. Now we work for the greater glory of the Kapar regime! Afterward, I will introduce you to your fellow philosophers!" He smiled as he steered me forward into formation.

ACCORDING TO PIERRE back on Earth, the finest engineers in France had labored more than ten years to construct the Maginot Line. During that time, they had excavated more than sixty miles of tunnels and used more than 12 million cubic yards of dirt and stone, 1.5 million cubic yards of concrete, and 150,000 tons of steel to construct the greatest fortification of Earth's 20th Century. A typical casement has three underground levels. The Line's deepest point is more than 300 feet below the French countryside.

If the entire Line could be miraculously transported to Poloda, it would be considered nothing more than a small, poorly fortified city. One that would be bombed out of existence in a matter of days.

Gerris had been a small agricultural city before The War. It had been bombed into a ruin when the Kapars conquered the former country of Allos, partially rebuilt, and then bombed into rubble by the Unisan counterattacks. If Gerris valley wasn't perfect for growing the deliciously sweet *garan* fruit that I had smelled on my first night on Poloda, it would have been abandoned. Instead, it was an underground fortress crouching below the fields tended by red-shirted Workers and black-shirted slaves between Unisan raids. The deepest part of the city was 15 levels – more than 600 feet – below the surface. And that was barely deep enough for survival.

At least twice a ten-day week, the Unisan air force dropped by and reminded us that, regardless of Sura's confidence about an eventual Kapar victory, Unis was still fighting. Every time they came, they brought death in each hand.

When they came, sound detectors would usually pick them up 30 to 50 miles away and 12 miles up. Sirens wailed and the city's defense air squadron catapulted out of their hidden hanger exits climbing for altitude. Other Kapar squadrons homed in from all over the continent of Epris.

Mere humans ran for shelter. If you were on the surface, you sprinted for the nearest trapdoor and then climbed down as many levels as the guards would allow you to go. Depth meant safety. Most of us prisoners got no further than the cages on the seventh level. High-ranking green and gray shirts were rushed to the 12th through 14th levels and the red shirts filled in the middle. When the Unisans were almost overhead, a different siren screamed. Door guards slammed the trapdoors shut and dogged them tight. Armored hatches clanged shut throughout the besieged city.

If you were still outside, you died. High overhead, bat-winged Kapar fighter and pursuit planes threw themselves at the bomber streams while sky blue Unisan fighters counter-attacked. Then the bombs came crashing down, followed by the bullet-riddled corpses of men and machines.

Back on Earth, a single raid with one thousand or more bombers against a vital enemy target was a gigantic effort, straining the resources of the Allied economies. On Poloda, a thousand plane raid was a minor attack scarcely worthy of mention.

Unless, of course, you were under it.

The Unisans routinely devoted two-to-five-thousand bombers to a minor target like Gerris. Half or more of them got past the defending aircraft and the antiaircraft guns. The garan fields and — I later discovered — solar energy collectors on the surface marked our general location despite our best efforts to hide.

Each bomber unloaded more than a ton of bombs, blasting and savaging the land. Whenever a secondary explosion or glint of light from some newly excavated crater hinted that the bluecoats had wounded Gerris, spotter planes signaled the oncoming waves of attackers. Every subsequent pilot tried to drop his cargo of death directly into the gaping wounds. Every blast tore its way deeper into the sheltering earth, delivering fire and thunder into the bleeding city.

Huddled in our cages, we prisoners threw ourselves on the floor and clutched the bare concrete as best we could. Explosions crashed overhead. The ground shook and heaved. Human bodies were flung about like toys in a child's tantrum, crashing into the walls and falling back to the floor. Blood and other fluids stained the ground. Steel groaned in agony. Chips of concrete flew, savaging mortal flesh. Dust showered the terrified men and women. More than one slave choked to death. Screams cut through the earthquake roar. And it went on and on and on.

No wonder Kapar propaganda depicted Unisan fighting men as gargoyles feasting on human flesh. After an eternity of fear, the thunder crashes passed. Our lungs sucked in air, dust and relief. Relative silence descended on the seventh circle of Hell. Sometimes someone cracked under the pressure. His screams would go on and on until a guard's gunshot silenced him.

Somewhere above us, Kapar gray-shirt spotters cautiously lifted their man-sized trapdoors and peered into the sky. Sound detectors swiveled on their mounts. If the Unisans were returning to their fortress continent, the All Clear would sound.

When it did, the guards clanged on the bars and the surviving black shirts would rise from the floor and form into work gangs.

"Explosions crashed overhead. The ground shook and heaved. Human bodies were flung about like toys in a child's tantrum, crashing into the walls and falling back to the floor."

32

After a particularly violent attack, I was drafted to help lift and move bodies that would rise no more under their own power. We carried them into a room with steel appliances and left them on table-like slabs of rock. Red-shirted workers converged on them as we left.

"Is this a Kapar hospital or mortuary?" I asked Prisoner 886V8953.

He snorted. "No, a kitchen." He gestured at our recent burdens. "There'll be more meat for the slop tonight."

I started to tell him off for his ghoulish humor but he was perfectly serious. There *was* more meat than usual in that night's slop and I suddenly became a vegetarian.

WHEN THE UNISANS weren't bombing us, the Kapars were trying to work us to death. Red-shirted workers repaired and maintained the city, farmed the crops, built and installed weapons and other machines — all the professional and technical work of a modern industrial civilization. But we black-shirted slaves provided the heavy manual labor. When the All Clear sounded, we formed into gangs, marched to the surface or upper levels, and began the backbreaking work of repairing the damage done in the most recent raid.

Even so, the bright golden sunlight of Omos and cool fresh air of Poloda felt good after the claustrophobic hell that the Kapars had made of Gerris.

A typical day's work might start with searching the garan fields for all of the loose brown fruit that we could find. Even bruised and unripened garan was a delicacy to people eating rubber and lard twice a day. We stole as much as we could get away with. Many guards looked the other way for a percentage. Sura's loudly praised Kapar efficiency had more than a few holes in it.

Then we dug out the bomb craters and smoothed the fields as much as possible so that red-shirted farmers could plant more garan.

The bombs had blasted their way through multiple levels of the underground city. What had once been a relatively civilized place for human beings to shelter and carry on their lives as best they could was now an eerie series of blocky caves filled with smashed debris and ominous sounds. Electric lights strung by red-shirted electricians partially illuminated the strange underworld of broken, tumbled concrete slabs that had been homes, schools and factories. Twisted reinforcement beams groped weird voids like devil's fingers hunting the souls of the damned. And everywhere were shattered machines, corroded cables, broken furniture, burnt pictures, cracked bones, and the hundred and one other things of what had been Allosan and then Kaparan culture.

The Kapars' first priority was trying to hide the city from the next attack. Guided by red-shirted technicians, we hauled stores of metal tubing up from storerooms better protected than our cages and assembled pieces into a kind of super jungle gym filling the former first level. Holes gaping in the floor gave dizzying views into the depths of the earth and complicated our efforts.

One prisoner staggered under the load that she was carrying, lost her balance, and fell four stories into the black void below. Her screams were mercifully short. Her man ran over to the ledge where she had fallen and stared into the darkness. When a guard ordered him to pick up her load, he looked at the guard curiously and then silently jumped after her.

Once we got the framework rigged up to the engineers' satisfaction, we fitted plastic slabs on top of it just below the ceiling of the first level. Then we shoveled dirt on top of the plastic until the crater had been filled in. Farmers planted more garan immediately. Gray-shirt spotter planes surveyed the landscape from the air and reported on our efforts to hide Gerris once more.

If the engineers weren't satisfied with the results, we did everything again. If they were satisfied, we moved on to the next task. There was always a "next task."

The red shirts labored to create new barriers of steel and concrete in the upper levels faster than Unisan bombs could destroy their efforts. We black shirts dug dirt out of the corridors, hauled bags of concrete and stacks of steel, held armor plates in position for welders, pushed flatbed trucks, sorted junk (under the eyes of red-shirted engineers as well as green-shirted guards), swept floors in corridors and homes, washed machines (more often than ourselves), collected and carried garbage to incinerators, ...

The Kapar goal was to work us sixteen hours a day and ultimately to death. In many cases, they succeeded. There was always meat in the slop at night.

Chapter 4 HOW TO WIN FRIENDS AND INFLUENCE PEOPLE

PRISONER 886V8953 did introduce me to my "fellow philosophers." Like most Earthly prisons, the Gerris city slaves were divided into gangs. The largest group was petty criminals – shoplifters, pickpockets, ration cheats, black marketers and so forth. I noticed that there didn't seem to be any "serious" criminals such as robbers, rapists and murderers. 886V8953 explained that anyone that dangerous was beheaded rather than imprisoned. It was clear that the Kapar empire didn't have much trouble with repeat offenders.

The second-largest group was composed of "politicals" that included more or less actual Kapar philosophers. These were people who had expressed some mild dissatisfaction over some aspect of the regime. Again, if the Kapars thought you were really dangerous, heads would roll.

Prisoner 886V8953 had once been Oundurun Tod, an architect in the city of Pud on the continent of Auris north of Epris. (The Aurisans called their homeland "Aud" when Kapar loyalists weren't listening.) He had been drafted to work in Ergos and attracted the wrong kind of attention by grumbling too loudly about it. He might have gotten off with a warning but some of his proposals for a future New Ergos on the surface of the planet were taken as a criticism of the regime's underground building program. Another prisoner was an artist who had drawn a flattering picture of the Pom Da on a scrap of paper that had wound up in a toilet. My sparkling personality made me a natural for this group.

The third group of prisoners was a dozen or so men who held themselves apart from the limited social life of the cage. They always stuck together and the guards seemed to accept the arrangement. Prisoner 886V8953 — we called him Tod when the guards couldn't hear us — identified them as disgraced Kapar soldiers. They apparently held out hope of being reinstated in the Kapar fighting forces. In the meantime, they didn't associate with us "criminals" any more than necessary. The rest of us didn't care to borrow any trouble.

The final group was a gang that Tod solemnly called the Council of Five — a sarcastic reference to the Pom Da's chief political advisors. Our own little Council of Five acted like they owned the cage and everyone in it. They organized the work gangs (subject to red shirt and green shirt approval) and were always first in line for slop.

Tod explained, "They're disgraced police officers. The regular police officers give them a few privileges as long as they keep the rest of us in line. If you object to their orders, they'll gang up on you and beat you bloody. If they can't handle you, they'll report you to the regular police as a troublemaker and...."

"I know. There'll be more meat for the slop tonight."

Tod nodded. "You have the true Kapar spirit." He changed the subject. "Now, however, it is story time. You were telling us about the Gettis City Address when you were interrupted...."

I smiled, stood and asked my fellow politicals to gather around. They shifted positions eagerly and I began the latest installment in my great science fiction epic *The American Civil War*.

In theory Kapar prisoners were either working, eating or sleeping with no time left over to get into trouble. But no human institution is perfect. Occasionally we had some time for ourselves. In the absence of books, sports, cards, dice, pets, or any other constructive outlet, we told each other stories.

The Polodan prisoners had pretty much exhausted their storytelling resources when I arrived. When the Kapars had established their regime and conquered eighty percent of the planet, they had inherited thousands of years of sophisticated Polodan culture, learning and literature. They had burned most of it. Since then, they had ruthlessly suppressed anything that didn't contribute to war, conquest, killing and the glorification of brutal killers. Having too much imagination was especially dangerous because it often led you to question Kapar values, which often led to your head rolling across the floor. The result was a planet full of people starved for fresh entertainment. They latched onto my "science fictional" tales of the exotic planet Earth like starving men and women eating free ice cream. They particularly enjoyed hearing about Abraham Lincoln freeing the slaves.

Unfortunately, the old saying that everyone's a critic is just as true on Poloda as it is on Earth. In my case, two of the Council of Five wandered over in time for the final chapter of *The American Civil War*. Everyone in my audience eyed them nervously. The counselors listened stonily to Lee's surrender. Grant's generous peace terms provoked intense whispering. Lincoln's assassination....

"You! Prisoner 919V5486! Stop that subversive talk!" shouted one.

I trailed off. "What's wrong, Kapar? This is a science fictional story of life on another planet."

"Shut up!" he explained. "It is subversive to discuss the assassination of a Kapar leader!"

My mouth lives a life of its own. I laughed in his face. Abraham Lincoln was as far from being a Kapar leader as I was. Unfortunately, laughing at someone who's already angry was a mistake.

He turned red, wound up and threw a punch. I side-stepped and he went sprawling on the floor. My audience started laughing. The second critic reached for the bleachers and threw his own haymaker. I ducked again. These two stooges weren't used to dealing with people who didn't tremble in their boots at the thought of green-shirted vengeance. He fanned the air and tripped over his buddy, who was trying to get up. Both of them went down in a tangle. My audience was howling.

The critics managed to untangle themselves and slowly got to their feet, murder in their eyes. The laughter died away. I eased into an unarmed fighting stance....

"What in Omys is going on here?!" screamed someone. The two critics whipped around and saw another member of the Council of Five glowering at everyone. They made fists in the Kapar salute and stood at attention.

"You must be Moe," I decided. I pointed at the drama critics. "Curly and Larry here tripped. They were dancing and forgot who was leading. I was about to help them up when you dropped by."

Moe's face darkened and Curly and Larry started screaming at me. The Kapar language is very good for cursing and these guys were taking full advantage of the fact. I noticed that neither of them tried to jump me without Moe's permission. I folded my arms in a way that looked relaxed and non-threatening but is neither.

Moe slapped his fellow stooges across their mouths. They shut up instantly. He pointed to them. "You two, back to the station." They started slinking over to the Council of Five's favorite lounging area. He pointed to me. "You. I'll deal with you later." He stalked off.

It was clear that I had been tried and found guilty of revealing a state secret; thugs pretending to be cops generally make incompetent cops. The court was now in recess to determine the punishment.

Tod stood up, his face downcast. He sighed. "Ran, you are a good man and a great storyteller but you'll be meat in the slop by tonight."

I looked around, at the Council now in session at their favorite station, at the worried faces around me, at the other prisoners scattered around the cage. "Not if we get help." I waved at the political prisoners. "Everyone up. Right now. Follow me or you're meat in the slop tonight."

Once they started following my orders, I led them over to the disgraced soldiers. Change the uniforms to American brown and the former Kapar fighters would look like any class at Fort Benning getting a lecture on dental hygiene.

One of them stood up and challenged me as I approached. He might as well have had "First Sergeant" stamped on his forehead. "What do you want?" he demanded.

"Protection," I answered. "We are loyal Kapars who are being threatened by thugs contrary to law. We request the protection of the Kapar fighting forces." His stony face cracked, briefly revealing a human being. He did what any puzzled junior officer would do. He bucked the decision to his boss.

Company Leader Garrud Kun listened to my story. His face narrowed when I mentioned Lincoln's assassination but lightened up when I described what had happened to John Wilkes Booth and his co-conspirators. You could see the wheels turning in his head. Garrud approved of moral lessons, especially ones that seemed to fit Kapar philosophy. He also approved of people who taught moral lessons (me) and people who learned moral lessons (the political prisoners). He wanted to be reinstated in the fighting forces and therefore he sympathized with people who also wanted to be reinstated in their former roles in the Kapar machine.

He was nodding slowly when the Council of Five arrived en masse. The Council marched up to Garrud and Moe began demanding my head. While the counselors were glaring at Garrud, the ex-soldiers quietly stood up and formed into five-man fighting teams. The politicals grouped up behind their protectors. I'd seen this behavior before — usually just before a bar fight that sent people to the hospital.

We had another League of Nations session until the real guards began clanging on the bars signaling the end of playtime. The Council retreated, blustering threats on the way out. The criminals started forming the usual gangs. Some of them eyed our new group thoughtfully. The politicals stuck with the ex-soldiers.

At first, I thought that nothing had been settled. I was wrong. Company Leader Garrud had settled on his course of action. He spoke quietly to the "First Sergeant."

"Section Leader."

"Yes, Most High?"

"I believe that those overbearing *prisoners*..." He jerked his head towards the retreating Council members, "....are about to suffer an unfortunate series of accidents the next time they are working on the upper levels. We, the fighting forces of Kapara, will organize the work groups in the future and coordinate with the prison guards. In the meantime, I believe that Kapar Tomas Ran should be assigned some duty conspicuously far away so that no one suspects that he had anything to do with the accidents."

"Yes, Most High. The sewers are on the 15th level. I suggest that Kapar Tomas work there for the next few days." The Section Leader quirked his eyebrows at me in an obvious question.

I quickly joined the team. "Company Leader, I volunteer to work in the sewers for as long as needed."

"You have the true Kapar spirit, Tomas." Ouch. I thanked him anyway.

I WAS SHOVELING MUCK when my travel agent called.

Despite the fact that the high ranking Kapars in Gerris *wanted* to live and work on the 15th and presumably safest level of their fortress city, they had to yield to the laws of physics, which work the same way on Poloda as they do on Earth.

Water flows downhill, so the Gerris water treatment plant was in a monumental room on the 15th level where it collected waste water and overflow from the surface and the fourteen higher levels. Giant pipes dumped waterfalls into huge collecting ponds where even more gigantic pumps moved it around. The constant sloshing noise was incredible and the smells were pretty impressive as well. Much of the liquid was simply pumped into a tube that you could sail a midget submarine through and ultimately into the Gerris River at a point several miles downstream in an effort to fool the Unisans as to the city's location.

The rest of the water was pumped into algae farms: huge open tanks with variously colored algae growing under harsh electric lighting. The tanks filtered the water and the resulting liquid was pumped upstairs to slake the thirst of Kapar people and machines. Periodically, the algae were harvested and became the vegetables in the so-called food that sustained the population.

My job was cleaning out the accumulated muck and miscellaneous trash in the bottom of the tanks. Other slaves hauled hand-trucks full of mud upstairs where it became fertilizer in the garan fields. Waste not, want not.

I was quietly catching and eating Polodan snails under the guise of picking trash out of the water when a green shirt with gold trim on his uniform appeared. He walked over to the silver trimmed guard who was more or less watching the slaves slog around in the algae tanks and started talking to him. They shouted over the background noise at each other for a few minutes before Silver Trim began waving to attract my attention.

I dropped the empty snail shells into the water and waded over to Silver Trim. Maybe Gold Trim had some butter and garlic for the snails. I climbed out of the tank, grounded my shovel, and shouted, "Yes, Most High?"

He shouted back, "Go with this agent. He will take you to Ergos."

Uh, oh! In Occupied France, *going to Berlin* was usually a one-way ride. I suspected that going to the capital of the Kapar empire was the same. "Yes, Most High. Shall I return my shovel to the equipment room or will you take it?" I pointed to the equipment storage area to emphasize my question. Gold Trim looked where I was pointing. Silver Trim's answer was automatic. No slave master wants to dirty his hands if he can avoid it. "No, you take it."

I nodded and shouted a request that he explain his order to Gold Trim so there would be no misunderstanding. I then picked the shovel up and swung it up to my shoulder so that I could carry it easily and stood there until the situation was clarified.

Silver Trim and Gold Trim leaned their heads together to make themselves heard. I caught them both with the first blow. The shovel blade smashed in the back of Gold Trim's head and knocked his face into Silver Trim's. They both went down in a tangle. Some more shovel work ensured that they would never get up. As they teach you in OSS school, if you're not cheating, you're not trying.

Discarding my weapon, I stripped Gold Trim of his uniform, pistol and truncheon, and then added Silver Trim's machine pistol. I didn't need two truncheons so I tossed the second one to another slave, who was standing in his algae tank gaping at me. I screamed, "Run!" at him but I doubt that he understood me over the background noise.

I jogged over to the waterworks control room next to the equipment store and stepped inside. The thick plastic walls and glass-like plastic windows muffled the constant roar outside to a bearable level. The room was full of control consoles manned by red shirted technicians. Each one was working with controls that looked like Ouija boards. There was also another silver-trimmed green shirt, one with more trim than my recent sparring partner. They all looked up at me when I entered, obviously wondering about my unscheduled arrival but not unduly

"*The shovel blade smashed in the back of Gold Trim's head and knocked his face into Silver Trim's. They both went down in a tangle.*"

alarmed. I shot the guard while he was opening his mouth to inquire about my presence. That woke *everyone* up.

"Attention to orders!" I bellowed into the shocked relative quiet. "Stop all pumps immediately! Then sound the emergency alarm and leave the city!"

One slow learner tried to argue with me so I shot him as well. After that, the red shirts got busy with their controls. The pumps stopped. Silence hit our ears like so many hammers. Several red shirts looked nervously through the windows at the collecting ponds. Water was already slopping over the edges of the ponds. Black-shirted slaves began running for the exits followed by another silver-trimmed green shirt.

"Highest Most High, may we go?" asked one technician. His voice quavered. He was frozen in position but his brain was still working.

"The emergency alarm," I reminded him.

For a moment, he looked at me as if I had a lobster on my head. Then the spell broke and he grabbed a blood-red lever on his console. He flipped it and a hideous klaxon began whooping.

"Very good, Kapars. You may go." I paused. They seemed welded to their chairs. "Now!" I shouted and waved Silver Trim's machine pistol around but didn't actually shoot anyone else. They bolted.

I was sure that they would spread panic throughout Gerris as they went. I emptied Silver Trim's pistol into the control consoles, looted the guard's body, and then changed into police green – the one with the greatest amount of silver trim. Once again, I had moved up in the world.

I had to splash through rising water on my way to the emergency stairs.

The Gerris River valley was in chaos when I popped out of my trapdoor like Punxsutawney Phil on Groundhog's Day. If the Unisans had attacked at that moment, they could have wiped out the entire city in fifteen minutes flat.

Every trapdoor from the one-man scout holes to the giant aircraft exits was wide open. People were pouring out and scattering in all directions, trampling the precious garan crop underfoot. Some were carrying essentials; others the oddest things. One red shirt was waving something that looked like a key the size of a tuba. When another red shirt offered to take it from him, he swung it like a club and battered the second man to the ground. It broke and he stood stock still looking at it while people ran willy-nilly around him.

Many people bolted out of their holes, ran a few steps and suddenly froze in position. They looked around, eyes bulging, and fell to the ground, shaking like leaves. I guessed that they were agoraphobics who couldn't stand the thought of being out in the open. They, their parents, and their grandparents had lived their entire lives underground. Confronted with the brilliant sunlight and naturally fresh air, they panicked and collapsed.

The mobs were screaming and shouting hysterically. I caught snatches of words, mostly about "the flood." One man claimed that Unisan bombs had destroyed the city. Green shirts were trying to restore order but their chain of command had broken down and their shouted orders contradicted each other. They fired pistols into the air adding to the panic. The whooping of the emergency alarm made the simplest things difficult. Gray shirts had debouched from their aircraft hangar doors in relatively good order but they were eyeing the crowds that were surging back and forth nervously. The guards had their pistols and swords ready and I could see hands surreptitiously easing weapons out of their holsters. One wrong move and a massacre could result.

I glanced around and decided that the unimpressive hills rimming the Gerris Valley were the best place to be. I began jogging toward them, conserving my strength, and doing my best to look like a man with a mission rather than an escapee.

I stopped for a breather and a quick look around when I reached the nearest ridgeline. Down in the shallow valley, some green shirt was imposing order. Lesser thugs were listening to commands and then forcing red and black shirts into more or less orderly formations. The panicky gunfire had stopped, replaced by deliberate shots at fleeing black shirts. I saw a familiar black mane swinging wildly as she turned to survey the situation. I should have known that Sellon Sura would be the one to get things under control. I cursed and ducked behind the ridge.

On the other side of the hill, the garan fields abruptly changed to wild grasses and shrubs. A green and brown Polodan forest loomed a few hundred feet away. Beautiful multicolored flowers decorated the grassland and the treetops.

The heavy hand of war lay on the forest in front of me as well as the farmland behind me. The ground was cratered and trees shattered by bombs that had missed the roof of the hidden city.

Just what the doctor ordered. I stepped forward, starting to jog into the forest's cover. Without warning, a slab of ground swung up in front of me. I tried to stop but slammed into the turf wall that had suddenly erected itself in front of me. It knocked the wind out of me and I had to pause for a minute to catch my breath.

While that was happening, I heard heavy footsteps and a querulous voice issuing orders from the other side of the turf wall. Obviously, someone had opened an emergency escape trapdoor and I had run into it.

I cautiously looked around the door. To my astonishment, I recognized the two escapees. City Governor Virrul's ramrod back was to me. In front of him, Loris Kiri looked fiercely into his hatchet face. His arm came up and his fist hammered her to the ground. My pistol jumped out of its holster into my hand....

I stopped, remembering the last time that I saw Poloda's Thomas Edison. I reholstered my pistol and withdrew my truncheon. "Hey, Kapar, the Man From Mars is here!" I snapped as I swung. He whirled, clawing for his own pistol, but a truncheon to the face put him out of Kiri's misery and mine.

I stripped his body including his better quality, higher ranking uniform and weapons. Then I dropped him headfirst down the escape shaft.

O.K. That last part was petty, vindictive and unbecoming to an officer but it *felt really good*. Kiri was standing up rubbing her cheek when I finished looting the body. Her eyes were the size of dinner plates.

"Come on, Loris Kiri. We need to hide in the forest." I waved Virrul's gun in the general direction of the woods.

"No!" she coughed. Her soft voice was filled with horror. "You're a monster!" She started looking around wildly, clearly seeking escape from the Man From Mars.

Now was not the time for a debate. I scooped her up, throwing her across my left shoulder in a fireman's carry. Her upper body was draped down my back while I held her left leg in my left hand. I started jogging for the tree line.

After a minute, Kiri reacted. She started kicking my chest with her knees and pounding my back with both fists. Whatever lions and tigers and bears the forests of Poloda had in store, those animals would just have to take their chances. I was clearly carrying the most dangerous creature on the planet.

Chapter 5   LIONS AND TIGERS AND BEARS! OH, MY!

ONCE WE WERE in the forest proper, I continued running, changing direction a few times to confuse anyone who had seen us enter the woods.

When we came to a little clearing, I thought we could take a breather. I stopped and hoisted Kiri off my shoulder. After the way she had pounded my chest and back, I wanted to drop her like the proverbial hot potato, but I set her down easily. She alighted like a dancer.

"I see I rescued the wrong person!" I hissed vehemently. Never shout when you're in enemy territory unless absolutely necessary. "I thought Virrul was beating you up. I see now that he was just defending himself from you!"

She gave me a look mingling chagrin, horror and disgust. Disgust won. "You're a horrible monster!" she shouted. "Your planet Urtha is a nightmare of ice and fire! You Urthans are warmongers worse than Kapar Ov himself! You don't have nations on your planet, just a horrible mass of squabbling gangs armed with inhuman weapons! You're some kind of superhuman spy scouting out Poloda for an Urthan invasion! And you stink!"

She had me there so I confessed. "Your Honor, I plead guilty with an explanation. Sure, I stink, but that's because the Kapars assigned me to clean the sewers. And I suppose that Virrul named you his advisor on international relations with a

big office, an enormous salary and three square meals a day!"
Kapar is a wonderful language for sarcasm.

Kiri paled and then flushed. That was saying something
because Polodans didn't get out in the sun very much. My
common American suntan made me stand out like Jesse Owens
in Hitler's Germany.

She whirled around, arms wrapping her body, chin
sinking to her chest. I barely heard her whisper, "No, I was a
slave, too."

Clearly, I had touched a nerve but I wasn't sure what
nerve I had hit. Well, Mama had always insisted that a gentleman should try to settle disputes – even if he didn't start them
and especially if he had.

"Loris Kiri, I am sorry if I offended you. I am not a
monster and Earth is really a nice place — when people like
the Pom Da Adolf Hitler aren't messing things up."

She was still facing away from me but she spoke a little
louder. "Thank you, Tomas." Kiri turned her head and looked
at me over her shoulder. She had the most beautiful green
eyes....

"*Are* you a spy scouting Poloda for 'Operation Overlord'?" The English term translated easily into Kapar.

I smiled at her question. Clearly, she had confused
parts of the story that I had told Sura. And she had certainly
accepted the idea that Earthmen were more Kapar than Kapars.
"No, Loris Kiri. Operation Overlord was a code name for an
invasion *on Earth*. No one on Earth is planning any invasion
of Poloda. I was an army officer assigned to work as an intelligence agent in occupied France. But I am not superhuman.
And I really do not have any idea how I came to Poloda."

Kiri paused to digest my correction of the record. She
partially turned, facing more directly towards me. Her body
language relaxed. Perhaps my smile had helped. She sang
something to herself in her not-really-Japanese native language.
Then she switched briskly back to Kapar. "Tomas Ran, thank

you for rescuing me from City Governor Virrul. And from the Kapars who kidnapped me from Unis. What are your future plans?"

I exhaled. Her change of pace was a bit sudden. "Umm, I haven't had a chance to make any. Yours?"

"I wish to return to Unis," she said simply. She looked around, glancing at Omos overhead and then to the east. "This is Allos. Unis is northeast of here on the other side of Punos and the Talan Strait." She sighed. "It will be a long walk." She squared her shoulders in determination.

My options were pretty limited. As I saw them, they were: (1) invite myself to Unis, (2) live like Tarzan in the woods of Allos, or (3) hunt around for another option. None of them seemed terribly appealing. Kiri might be dead set on walking (and swimming) to her homeland, but I had very little evidence that Unis was any nicer than Kaparland was. Just because the Soviet Union was fighting Hitler's Germany didn't make Stalin's Workers' Paradise a decent place to live. Playing Tarzan was even less appealing. I'd lived in the French *maquis* country with Pierre and the other French résistants, but that wasn't a permanent way of life as it might be in the Kapar empire. And Poloda didn't seem to have a Switzerland where I could grab a hot chocolate and take some time to sort things out. When in Rome...

"May I go to Unis with you?" I asked in my most winning manner.

Kiri twitched and eyed me as if a lobster had crawled out of my ear and waved at her. "I am not certain that is a good idea," she said politely but loftily. Clearly, she was still worried about the Man From Mars.

I was caught between a rock and a hard place. A gentleman doesn't force his company on a lady but I really wanted out of Allos.

Just then, a burst of gunfire cut through the soft sounds of wind stirring the leaves. Both of us spun around and stared at the trees shielding us from the Gerris Valley. All we saw was a flock of greenish birds taking flight. I thought they had the right idea.

"Sura is getting things under control, I see," I commented sourly.

Kiri paled again. "Is Special Assistant Sellon in charge of Gerris now?" she whispered.

"Unless I miss my guess. I saw her getting things organized just before you popped out of the bolt hole and Virrul isn't going to be contradicting her orders."

She stared in the direction of the gunfire. Again, she whispered something to herself in not-really-Japanese. She shook herself. "Tomas Ran, I invite you to accompany me to Unis." Her voice was shaky but clear.

"Thank you, Loris Kiri. Would you like a police uniform and pistol?" I held out Virrul's clothes and equipment.

She frowned at the thought of wearing a Kapar thug's uniform but yielded when I pointed out the camouflage value of green clothes in the brown and green forests of Allos. She suggested I wear Virrul's larger clothes while she took More Silver Trim's smaller uniform. We changed in Nature's dressing rooms (bushes).

When Kiri came out of the Ladies' Room, she checked her machine pistol professionally, including removing the magazine and replacing it. I noticed that she did that in front of me rather than in private. I also noticed that she never pointed the gun at me. I took both hints, complimenting her on her skill handling a gun.

She smiled thinly, "I had home guard training at home in Tuldros." Her face twisted into a grimace. "To protect myself if Kapar infiltrators attacked me in Unis."

I paused to phrase a delicate question diplomatically....

Kiri answered it before I asked it. "I ran out of bullets." She checked the magazine again. "That time."

I closed my mouth and nodded. We heard more gunfire behind us and headed east, quickly.

WE SPENT OUR first night in an oak tree. The forests of Allos in the southern part of the continent of Epris resembled those of New England. The trees looked like pines, maples, oaks, apples, birches, and so forth. They even smelled a lot like home. But they were different in detail. Polodan pine cones were springy balls, lively enough to bounce yards away from the parent tree when they hit the ground. Polodan acorns were the size of my thumb and shaped like curved triangles. When I dropped one, it glided away like the maple seeds back home. Clever tricks to spread seeds throughout the forest.

We made a meal (more or less) out of acorns. They were dry but tasty enough after eating slop twice a day. We settled in on broad branches about ten feet off the ground. Not the most comfortable bed I'd ever had but not the worst ever. Above us, the planets Antos and Rovos lighted the night sky as they had when I first arrived on the planet of perpetual war. The tree's leaves masked the stars. I fell asleep wondering what Poloda's constellations looked like.

THE NEXT MORNING, we had visitors. Some noise penetrated my sleep and I woke up. I pretended to still be asleep. I slitted my eyes and tried to understand what I was hearing and seeing.

About ten feet away, Kiri was still asleep – or nearly so – on her branch. A monkeylike creature was seated above her, its long fingers exploring her hair. It wasn't hurting her. In fact, it seemed enchanted by the morning sunlight glinting off her coppery strands. Kiri made a vague waving motion with her hand as if she were shooing flies away and sang something in Unisan. The monkey "Ooked" in response.

Sleeping Beauty woke up. She opened her eyes fully and saw the monkey's wizened face staring into hers. She felt its hand in her hair. She screamed loudly enough to alert every Kapar forest ranger in Allos and jerked upright, clawing for her machine pistol.

The monkeylike creature jumped off Kiri's branch and flew away. More monkeys leaped out of the nearby foliage and flew away. Startled, Kiri aimed and fired a burst at the departing simians. She caught one solidly but most of the flock of monkeys got away.

I came fully awake, goggling at the flying monkeys. I realized that they were really gliding on flaps of skin between their arms and legs like Earthly flying squirrels but still....

"Now there's something you don't see in Boston," I breathed in English.

Kiri glared at me. Just for a moment, I thought she might shoot me as well. "You were no help!" she screeched. Even her screeching was musical. "They might have... might have... might have hurt me for all you cared!"

Clearly, she didn't believe they were more likely to be curious about us than harmful. "I just woke up myself. What do you call those things?" Sura's Kapar language instruction hadn't included many names for plants or animals.

Kiri looked back in the direction that the monkeys had flown off in, then back at me. She was clearly expecting a second simian attack. "I... I don't know. They look similar to Unisan *kuikols* but kuikols jump from tree to tree. They don't fly."

I mentally pictured Polodan rabbits jumping through Polodan treetops and grinned. That produced another glare from the Unisan. I tried to change the subject. "Very well, we'll call them *ozmonkeys* for now. Are kuikols poisonous?"

"I don't know. Why?" Kiri's voice was normal again, but she was still upset, either at my grin or because she had to blame *someone*. With the ozmonkeys gone, I was clearly in charge of Taking Blame.

I pointed at the carcass. "Because that's meat. I'm tired of nuts and algae. Would you care to join me?" I looked at the ground carefully to be sure that some Polodan lion wasn't waiting for us to drop in for breakfast and climbed down the tree. After a minute, Kiri joined me.

"What does *oz-mong-kee* mean?" she asked.

I told the story of *The Wonderful Wizard of Oz* as I was preparing and cooking the ozmonkey. Kiri was singing a Kapar version of "We're Off To See The Wizard" when we resumed our trek. I smiled at her singing and she smiled back.

WE WERE SOON reminded that The War was still going on. Black bat-winged Kapar airplanes came out of nowhere, roaring overhead, climbing for altitude. Ozmonkeys and birds screamed and flew for cover. We humans froze in place. The bat-wings didn't see us, green shadows in a green environment. When they passed, we hid behind the thickest tree we could find, one with nice sturdy roots. The Unisans had returned.

Hiding under the forest canopy as we were, we didn't get a very good view of the final battle of Gerris. Airplanes would occasionally swoop low overhead but they mostly stayed miles above the ground, dots of death against the brilliant blue sky. From time to time, one hammered into the forest floor nearby. Waves of thunder rumbled through the ground as Unisan bombs smashed into the target city. Two days walk from ground zero, the apocalyptic noises were awe-inspiring. Back on Earth, the Allied air campaign against the German Atlantic Wall defenses had literally driven hardened soldiers insane with the overwhelming noise, the physical punishment, the omnipresence of death. This *routine* Unisan attack, made twice weekly against a minor target, was all that multiplied by ten. That afternoon, the Unisans flew away from what a civic booster might have called "the City of Garans."

In the days that followed, we often saw airplanes of both nations high overhead. But there were no further Unisan attacks on the city behind us. Gerris was dead.

THE DAY FOLLOWING the battle, we found a small clearing smashed into the forest by a falling airplane. Like so many things on Poloda, it was plastic rather than metal. Its sky blue body was crumpled as if Paul Bunyan had swatted it out of the sky and then pounded on it for hours. One propeller blade was lodged in the trunk of a Polodan birch.

A short distance away, we found the pilot. He was hanging a few feet above the forest floor. Apparently, he had bailed out only to have his parachute snag in the branches of a Polodan oak. He rocked gently back and forth in the breeze. A couple of major bullet holes in his sky blue plastic uniform explained why he hadn't gotten himself out of the tree. Polodan birds and insects were enjoying a feast while a circle of *ikhurrs* (Polodan rats) made futile leaps trying to reach his boots. Kiri squealed and fired a burst at the ikhurrs. The survivors scattered frantically, their comical short hops utterly unlike the scrabbling runs of Earthly rats but effective enough. Their tiny piglike bodies vanished into the debris of the forest floor. The birds took the hint without waiting for Kiri to shoot them up. "Now what?" I asked.

"We bury him," responded Kiri simply.

Burial proved to be easier than I first thought. Unisan pilots carried short swords as well as machine pistols. I pulled his body down, confiscated his weapons, and slashed his parachute cords for him. We scooped out a shallow grave and piled tree limbs and rocks high to discourage Poloda's lions and tigers and bears and rats. When we finished, Kiri stood looking at the grave in silence. I murmured a short prayer in English.

Kiri asked me what I had said and I did my best to explain. The prayer translated into Kapar as "Pilot, good luck on your next mission. I ask that the Highest Leader approve your actions."

Her forehead wrinkled. "Are you an Uvalan?"

"I don't know what an 'Uvalan' is."

"Uvala is a planet on the opposite side of the Omos solar system. Before The War, many people believed that the life forces or spirits of good people moved to Uvala when they died. Uvala is supposed to be a paradise without want or suffering. Of course, only astronomers would know what Uvala is truly like. Uvalans are Polodans who still hold this belief. They say prayers to wish spirits a safe and speedy journey to paradise. There are not many Uvalans left."

"Why not?" Had the Unisans purged their Uvalan population as Hitler had murdered Germany's Jews?

"The War," she responded simply. "The War is now in its 107th year. At first, people prayed for an end to The War and a happy life on Poloda. As The War went on and on, people lost hope in prayer, especially when the 'unsentimental' Kapars seemed to be so successful. Most people stopped praying and became unsentimental as well."

Kiri paused and sniffed. "People still curse by Omys, though."

"'Omys'?" I repeated. "People curse by your sun?" I glanced upward at the sunbeams peering through the leaves and branches overhead and then back to Kiri's sad face.

She smiled wanly. "Not quite. 'Omys' is an ancient pronunciation of the name of the sun. Before The War, people believed that the spirits of evil people moved to Omys when they died and were consumed as fuel for the sun, thereby paying for their crimes by providing light and heat to Poloda. Of course, we now know that *Omos* is a ball of hydrogen that is being transformed into helium by natural processes rather than supernatural means. But the old name survives as a curse word."

"Humph," I humphed. "A more constructive use for dead Kapars than I would have imagined. But, getting back to your question, no, I'm not an Uvalan."

"But you moved from Urtha to Poloda when you died." She looked at me thoughtfully.

"I have no idea how or why that happened," I admitted. "There are some passages in our religious books that suggest that the Highest Leader transported people across the face of Earth by supernatural means. Most people interpret those passages as being visionary, though." I looked up at Omos again. "And yet here I am."

Kiri sang something in Unisan that seemed to make her happy. I asked her what she had said.

"It is time to continue our journey," she said primly. A little too primly, I thought, but I didn't challenge her.

AS WE CONTINUED our trek eastward toward the mountains separating the former countries of Allos and Punos, we encountered many more clearings torn out of the forest by falling bombs or crashing airplanes. Neither the Kapars nor the Unisans had targeted the woods but the constant warfare had savaged the landscape nonetheless. Shattered trees lay across our path like barricades. Old fires had scorched the land. Creaking timber and calling birds sounded like hunters' footsteps and challenges. One obnoxious bird sounded *exactly* like a Kapar calling "Hey, you!".... We moved like hunted animals, staying under cover as much as possible, entering clearings only when we had to. Far above us, airplanes cut the sky seeking prey.

When the sky seemed clear, we scavenged the smashed aircraft for supplies. Apparently, the Kapar regime didn't have forest rangers policing the woods. Ikhurrs and other vermin had stripped the flesh and emergency rations from shattered cockpits. But they left canteens, weapons, ammunition, tools and pouches for us to pick over. We stocked up.

Loris Kiri was a delightful companion – witty, informative, entertaining – but she was a city girl. She had no woodcraft. She moved like a dancer but never seemed to pass a dry twig without stepping on it or a rock without kicking it. She wasn't stupid – not by a long shot – but life in Unis' underground cities made natural woodlands a mystery to her. She didn't realize the dangers of the Allosan – or any other – forests until she stepped on a wolf.

We entered a clearing, keeping what we thought was a careful eye out. Omos peered through the forest canopy, striping the ground with light and shadow. Kiri put her foot down on a dark patch of ground. The ground reared up, teeth flashing, savage mouth lunging for her unprotected neck. She squeaked and fumbled for her pistol.

I was off guard as well, guns and swords "safely" in my holsters. I reacted as best I could. I punched it in the side of its head. Probably not the best move in the world but I was going for results, not style. My blow knocked the catlike head aside. Fangs slashed Kiri's shoulder instead of her throat.

I was off balance and just fell on the thing. I knocked Kiri down in the process but she fell backwards, away from the gleaming teeth. The thing tried to stand upright on long, thin legs while whipping its head back to bite me. Dignity was already out the window. I just hit it again, left fist to the jaw and left knee to its snaky neck. My right arm was hunting for a sword but the thing's claws distracted me. It tried to bite my left leg but I punched its head again and it bit down on air. We were all tangled up and it clearly didn't like my fighting style. Oh, well, it could complain to the Boxing Commission later....

Its legs were thrashing around, trying to get purchase on the forest floor and lever its body upright. Its claws were scratching me up pretty badly but it couldn't get enough traction to move a highly irritated Earthman. I looped my left leg over and around its lanky body in a new judo hold I invented for the occasion. I shoved with my right leg and rolled over on top of the thing. Its head thumped the ground, squealing like a New Hampshire hog caught in a fence.

While it was complaining, I hammered its exposed throat as solidly as I could. The thing stopped squealing and

"I reacted as best I could. I punched it in the side of its head..."

began choking. I'd damaged its windpipe. I got both hands on its throat and finished the job.

I rolled off the thing and looked around for Kiri. She was standing a few feet away, gun out, covering the beast and me. When I disengaged, she pointed the pistol at the sky.

"Why didn't you shoot that thing?" I panted.

"I was afraid of killing you by mistake," she replied.

"Thank you for not killing me. What do you call that thing?" It looked like an Earthly cat the size and general shape of a wolf but with legs and neck twice as long as any wolf that I had seen in the Boston Zoo. Its dark, splotchy coloring and sprawling legs had made it look just like a random shadow on the forest floor.

"I... I do not know. It looks somewhat like a *churor* but churors are bigger and bulkier. And churors hunt by stalking, not ambushing." Churors sounded like Polodan lions.

"Very well, it's now a *shadow wolf.* And lunch. But first let's take a look at these bites and scratches." Our wounds proved to be superficial. Kiri's coverall had been slashed but not her skin. The shadow wolf didn't have any poison fangs or claws. I applied clean water and clean living and hoped for the best.

Over lunch, Kiri asked if Earth had a magical land of shadow wolves. She was disappointed when I said that I just made the name up. After that, we both moved more carefully, guns ready. When a green-furred Polodan bear roared its disapproval of our raiding its berry bush, we rebutted its argument with lead. Smoking the *kalidah* steaks — another name imported from the Land of Oz — took the rest of the day but we ate well that week.

GRADUALLY THE LAND rose before us, beginning to form the Hallas Mountains separating the conquered nations of Allos and Punos. Polodan apple trees gave way to birches and aspens. We ate less fruit and more herbs. Small game continued to be plentiful – and welcome. There were fewer and fewer clearings created by bombs and airplanes. We were moving away from the center of Allosan civilization. We hadn't seen another living human being since we escaped from Gerris.

One day, we reached the top of a ridge. Above us the blue sky was free from airplanes for the time being. Behind us, the forests of Allos whispered their secrets. Ahead and below us stretched a broad valley cupped by mountains. A dozen shades of green paved the floor below us while white and brown striped heights slashed the eastern sky. Brilliant dots of color marked flowers adorning the branches of the trees. High above, Omos touched the flowers with fire and turned snow on the Hallas range into a field of diamonds. It also highlighted two streaks of dirty white cream cutting through the valley below.

The planet Poloda was a Garden of Eden run by serpents. Kiri made a soft gasping sound. She was looking at the whitish streaks.

"Do you know what those white lines are?" I asked.

"The Path of the Sun," Kiri said in awed tones. "It was the greatest roadway ever built in Polodan history. It connected the capital cities of Punos, Allos and Zurris in a great east-west route. It was supposed to be a model for a network of super roadways connecting all the major cities of Epris." She smiled bitterly. "The day before the leaders of the three nations were scheduled to inaugurate the road, a relatively new invention — an airplane — flew the same route in one tenth of the time that a motor car would require. The Path was obsolete before it opened." She paused. "We thought that the Kapars had destroyed it."

I searched the sky and landscape before I answered, "Apparently, only some of it. If it goes to Punos, we can use it as a guide." I pointed at the white-capped peaks to our east. "I'd like to avoid those mountains if we can." We scanned the sky for airplanes yet again before we began our descent into the valley.

HITLER'S PROPAGANDA BOYS liked to brag about the *wunderbar* autobahn expressways that tied the New Germany together. The Path of the Sun made Hitler look like a piker.

The super highway was ten lanes wide, five in each direction, with a strip of parkland in the middle separating the eastbound and westbound lanes. Bomb craters had shattered the pavement here and there. Weeds, bushes and not-so-small trees grew where cars and trucks were supposed to speed by. But much of the concrete Path was unbroken, still waiting for a future that never came.

Following the road was easier than navigating through the woods. We changed our routine and followed the white carpet by night and slept by day. Poloda's night sky was a jewel box of stars highlighted by ten neighboring planets in stately orbit around their diminutive sun. There were no city lights to interrupt our view. Kiri lectured on astronomy as we walked. Unisan astronomers had long ago given names to the strange constellations filling the sky and to the continents and oceans on the nearer planets.

Everything *reminded* me of Earth – but nothing I could see *was* Earth. Kiri noticed me studying the night sky intently – perhaps *too* intently – and asked what I was thinking about.

"Home," I whispered. I continued staring upward.

"Are you going back to Urtha when we reach Unis?" Kiri's voice was particularly soft.

"I tried. It didn't work," I said. My voice broke. "I want to go home – my home – as much as you do. You can walk to yours. I've tried prayers and wishing and magic words and clicking my heels three times and cursing. Nothing works."

Kiri took my sleeve in her hand....

High overhead, a squadron of airplanes passed in front of the blue-white disk of the planet Tonos and the mood passed.

Survival trumped emotion. We hid beneath a tree like the hunted animals that we were.

When we first stepped on the Path of the Sun, it was deserted. Vegetation had a hard time getting a grip on the concrete and dangerous animals avoided the manmade desert. As we entered the Hallas Mountains, we began finding wrecked vehicles. Like Polodan trees and flowers, Polodan cars and trucks looked much like their Earthly equivalents. So did the skeletons of their murdered drivers. The cars and trucks were all headed away from Allos toward Punos. It was easy to guess why.

Some of them had crashed into things — bridge abutments, safety rails, rocks and trees along the edge of the road, or simply each other. But most had been strafed or bombed from the air. Ruined machinery of both men and machines littered the highway of hope.

We tried to bury the skeletons but we gave up on the second night. There were just too many of them. We marched stoically onward. We looted when we found something useful but mostly we just kept going, living ghosts on a planet of death.

The walls of the great valley of the Path closed in, creating a natural chokepoint. Gray-brown cliffs loomed overhead on each side. Smashed vehicles became more and more numerous, eventually forming a tortured wall across all ten lanes of the highway. We tried to pick our way through the morass of metal. We were defeated by loose metal underfoot, twisting, rolling and clanging no matter how carefully we moved.

We left the Path when we discovered a side road running upwards into the mountains. We climbed the road, trying to get around the mess on the highway below. From above, we could see the reason for the graveyard of metal. Overlapping bomb craters had blasted the entire width of the Path into a shallow lake fed by melting snows. Dozens of cars and trucks were partially submerged in the stagnant water, preserved by their plastic construction. Other vehicles had piled up behind them, succeeding waves smashing into the earlier ones. Kapar aircraft had had an easy time shooting helpless Allosans in the back. Neither of us said anything for a long time.

SUNRISE FORCED US TO SEEK SHELTER. We could see a gigantic cavern mouth in the mountainside a short distance uphill. It would be a perfect place to hide from airborne Kapar eyes. We thought.

Outside the cave itself were the remains of bombed stone buildings and a parking lot with more wrecked cars. At the edge of the parking lot was a huge stone carved into a sign. The Allosan words were close enough to Kapar for us to read "Cave of the Winds King's Park: A Gift to all Allosans." I barked laughter at the sight.

Kiri looked a question at me and I explained that Earth had tourist caves as well. "For a moment, it seemed as though I was home in New England."

She sang something in Unisan. Before I could ask her what she had said, she switched back to Kapar. "The cave looks like a good place to sleep until nightfall."

Cautiously, we entered the gaping cave mouth. Morning sunbeams over our shoulders lit up a grand ballroom carved by Nature. Near the great doorway, the rocks were blackened by ancient fires.

There were human skeletons on the floor of the great room within. Ikhurrs and Poloda's ten-legged insects had long ago cleaned the flesh away from the bones, but their dining hadn't disturbed the bones themselves very much. One collection of skeletons lay crumpled behind rocks near the entrance. They had badly burnt rifles or carbines, all pointed towards the doorway, a defense against an enemy who had never set foot in the cave. Some of them had small brass globs among their bones. One of them still wore a square Allosan helmet.

Another, tighter group of smaller bones lay in a semi-circle around a natural throne in the center of the room. They were jumbled together, arms embracing each other. We made out the remains of wooden boxes with Allosan writing on them.

There were two skeletons on the majestic chair carved by Nature. The slope of the rock had preserved their human outlines. One was man-sized. He had a golden crown with rubies on his skull and a silvery sword in his lap. His right leg bones were broken below the knee and three brass globs lay in what had been his rib cage. His companion was smaller. I guessed that she had been a young adult, a girl who had not quite lived to be a woman. She had a golden, emerald studded coronet in her lap and the man's hand in hers.

Kiri gasped. I looked at her. She didn't see me. She was very far away.

"Zurrya, the Last Princess of Zurris, and Vollor, the Lost King of Allos," she murmured. "So this is where they died. Kapar Ov, the first Pom Da, overthrew the old kingdom of Zurris and murdered the royal family. He wanted Zurrya for his... woman. But she escaped to Allos where Vollor gave her sanctuary. The Kapars attacked and conquered Allos. The Princess and King fled with their guards. No one knew whatever happened to them...." Her voice trailed off, lost in unspoken sorrow.

I looked around the cavern. "I think we can guess what happened.

"They were trying to reach Punos. The Kapars bombed the Path of the Sun and cut off their escape. They came here to make a last stand."

I looked at the royal skeletons. "The king had at least three bullets in him and a broken leg. He must have been in agony. But he and the princess tried to inspire their troops by personal example. The men prepared to defend the entrance against a ground assault while the women set up a medical station.

"But the Kapars didn't make a ground assault." I pointed to the scorch marks on the rocks. "I think they bombed the entrance with incendiaries. The fire sucked all the oxygen out of this room. The Allosans and Zurrisans smothered to death." Kiri was shaking silently, her body racked with emotion.

"I think their end was peaceful," I said quietly. I was probably lying but I thought that Kiri needed to hear that. Suddenly, her tears broke into the open. She threw herself against my chest and clutched me to her. I was startled, frozen in place. Then I enfolded her in my arms. I whispered impossible assurances that the Kapars would never bother her again. Just then, I meant every word.

If every Kapar on the planet Poloda had shown up armed with cannons in each hand, I would have killed them all to keep Loris Kiri safe. I told myself that I was thinking that because I was a gentleman protecting a lady. We stood there for some time.

As I held her, I reflected on the curse of war: millions upon millions of lives lost, minds and bodies enslaved, billions of dollars worth of property destroyed, books and plays burned, science and culture stunted and twisted.... If anyone deserved to burn in Omys, it was the first Pom Da and his followers.

We must have rocked back and forth a little. A vagrant sunbeam found its way past us and touched the Princess' crown and the King's sword with fire. They hadn't given up. Neither would we.

Chapter 6 IT'S ALL DOWNHILL FROM HERE

PUNOS IS A beautiful country," sang Kiri in Unisan.
"It certainly is," I chanted back in the same language.
Kiri's lectures and my questions had evolved into language lessons. I never learned to sing not-really-Japanese as beautifully as Kiri did but, then, Kiri could make a song out of an iron foundry.

Once again, we stood on a ridge surveying the lowlands ahead and below us. This time, however, we were on the eastern side of the Hallas Mountains, overlooking the tortured landscape of the conquered country of Punos.

The plants were similar to what we had hidden under in Allos – somewhat lusher, perhaps, since Punos got more rain than Allos did. But land and forests alike were scarred by the heavy hand of war. From our elevated vantage point, we could see endlessly overlapping bomb craters. Nature had done her best to clothe the battered planet in green finery but she had only masked the devastation of war, not hidden it or repaired it.

As we surveyed the skies for airplanes, Kiri squealed in delight and pointed southwestward. A river of fire poured over a cliff in the Hallas range, golden in the morning sunlight. As we stood spellbound, the cascade flickered slightly, painting the mountain walls beside it with faerie lights. "Oh, Ran, we must see it close up!" Kiri commanded.

I smiled. It was good to see my brave Unisan happy after the emotional hardships of Allos. The nights were getting a bit crisp as autumn fell across Poloda's southern hemisphere but we could afford a short side trip. Or so I thought. "Sure, let's go," I responded.

WE BEGAN OUR DESCENT into Punos. With the Hallas range to our west and another range running away eastward, we entered into a great upland covered in vegetation. The greenery was trying to be a primitive forest but there were more bomb-shattered clearings; far more than in Allos. Travel was rough because of the uneven ground. We didn't see any shattered cities, airplanes or men. Nor did we see many animals. Those that we did see were small: ikhurrs and the Polodan versions of squirrels and groundhogs. I wondered why the Kapars were punishing a remote wilderness so thoroughly.

Two days travel brought us to the lip of a small canyon. Across the way fire tumbled out of the Hallas Mountains. We camped under some piney trees and sat together watching the sunlight playing on the pillar of flame and the rainbow of minerals on either side. Not much of a vacation but it was all we could afford on our budget. Omos wheeled overhead and the river changed from gold to silver.

It was early afternoon when we realized that we were watching a waterfall, not a "fire fall." The morning sun's Midas touch had changed the water into liquid gold. Now the great magician Omos had worked a further transformation and returned the false fire to silver elixir. We laughed at our mistake, at Omos, at a squirrel chattering overhead, at a dozen little things....

For a moment, Poloda was Eden and the serpents were on some other planet. I leaned towards Kiri; she smiled and lifted her face....

The thunder of bombs shattered the mood. We scrambled for cover, hiding in the trees, cowering from the wrath of Satan.

We hid the rest of the day and the night, eating sparingly and making plans in whispers. No Kapar flying overhead could possibly have heard us if we had shouted at the top of our lungs, but we kept our voices down nonetheless. It was life in Kaparland. It was war.

THE NEXT DAY, we headed northeastward, aiming towards the unnamed mountains running west to east through the center of Punos. Unis was somewhere beyond that range. We had intended to follow the remains of the Path of the Sun as far to the southeast as we could but the bombing had come from that direction. So we headed away from the Devil's tramping ground.

Several days later, the new mountains loomed up ahead of us, lower than the Hallas but still formidable. We were in a relatively level mountain upland pockmarked with ancient bomb craters and shattered trees. We followed a small river flowing down from the new mountains, looking for a place to cross.

We found a shallow ford in a large grassy landscape dotted with clumps of young trees and splashes of brilliantly colored wildflowers. We were debating crossing it in daylight or waiting until nightfall when the decision was yanked out of our hands. Black-winged Kapar aircraft roared out of the innocent seeming sky ahead of us. We froze in place, trusting in our green camouflage.

It worked. The Kapars swept over a particularly handsome stand of trees about two miles ahead. Bombs dropped; fire flashed in the forest; the Devil's voice rolled across the plain. Successive waves of bombers savaged the landscape and punished the innocent seeming trees. Vee formations of flyers orbited overhead, guarding the bombers in case their victims managed some sort of counterattack. I had no idea what the trees had done to offend the Pom Da but they were certainly paying for their mistake...!

Suddenly a group of black dots broke from the flaming forest, frantically racing across the quaking land. They headed towards the ford, apparently aware that it was the only practical river crossing in miles. As they came, the dots resolved themselves into antelope-like creatures with sleek hides of green and brown and single horns projecting from their foreheads.

The unicorns of Poloda didn't make it. Kapar fighters swooped, machine guns blazing. There must have been a hundred fighters, all attacking twenty desperately fleeing animals. The unicorns were shredded into steak tartar in seconds.

When the hapless creatures were dead, I thought that the attack would stop. I was wrong. Succeeding waves of Kapars made pass after pass on the corpses until their guns ran dry. Only then did the mighty Kapar air force fly away. I imagine that the Pom Da gave them all medals for their heroic defeat of a herd of unicorns.

Kiri had dropped to her knees in order to lower her head and get some blood in her brain. I wasn't ashamed to join her.

After a few minutes, we realized that we could salvage some unicorn steaks (or hash). We scanned the sky for repeat offenders and then moved into the open. As we approached the unicorns' last stand, we saw that we were not alone. We froze again.

Figures appeared from behind rocks and clumps of vegetation dotting the upland plain. Heads popped up and down, swiveling, searching for menaces in the air and on the ground. Short rushes from bush to tree or clump of grass brought the figures closer and closer to the antelope bodies and us.

As they approached, we realized what they were. "Human beings," I decided.

"Punosans," amplified Kiri. She relaxed. I didn't.

Whoever these people were, they were human by a generous definition. They all looked like typical reconstructions of Earthly cavemen. They were filthy, with matted head and body hair. Their malnourished bodies were more or less clothed in various animal hides. They had spears and bows and arrows mostly. One old fellow seemed to have a gun holster on a belt although he carried a bow and arrow as he approached the unicorns.

About that time, they raggedly jerked to a halt, staring wildly around at each other. They started shouting and gesticulating. Clearly groups of them were threatening other groups.

At least three separate gangs of "cavemen" had converged on the unicorn café. One group on my left wore tan or brown hides. The bunch in the center had reddish loincloths and the gang on my right wore gray-colored animal skins. I repressed a snort of laughter at the thought of Stone Age fashion plates.

My musing was interrupted. One Tan Team member realized that Kiri and I were watching him. He shouted "Khaparhs!" and pointed to us. That got everyone's attention.

Everyone turned, spotted us, and aimed weapons at us. So much for Punosan hospitality....

Wary of predators, Kiri and I had been carrying one machine pistol apiece but casually, not pointed at anyone. Now we filled our hands. Kiri covered the Gray Gang with two guns; I covered the Tan Team and the Red Shorts with one apiece. I aimed my left-hand pistol directly at the old codger with the gun belt.

That brought the Welcome Wagon to a screeching halt. Clearly they knew what personal weapons could do. There was a moment of awkward silence. The wind whistled through the surviving trees.

"We are not Kapars!" I shouted, first in Unisan and then in Kapar.

They were filthy, with matted head and body hair. Their malnourished bodies were more or less clothed in various animal hides. They had spears and bows and arrows mostly."

73

"We are Unisans traveling home. We mean you no harm," sang Kiri in both languages.

"You wear Kapar uniforms!" cried one Red Short in the latter language. "You must be Kapars!" His fellows nodded in agreement. After a moment, the Gray Gangsters murmured agreement. The Tan Team looked back and forth, apparently hunting for more evidence.

"No!" denied Kiri. "We were Kapar prisoners but we escaped! We wear green clothes to hide in the forests from Kapar bombs! We are Unisans; not Kapars!" She gestured towards her head with one pistol.

Another awkward silence followed. Clearly the Gray Gangsters and the Red Shorts weren't convinced but no one wanted to charge into a firestorm of lead.

The Old Codger looked at me and spoke in halting Kapar. "Are you a Unisan? I have never seen a Unisan with brown hair." His accent made his challenge sound like "¡Oh! ¿Arr yoo ay Oonhisi? Iy haav nhiverr seenh ay Oonhisi wiv brrounh harr."

I articulated as carefully as possible. "This woman is a Unisan. I am an *American* from a planet in another solar system. We are going to Unis so that this woman can go home. Allow us to pass peacefully." I kept him and the Red Shorts covered, in case sweet reason was insufficient.

From his reaction, the lobster that lived in my ear had climbed out on my shoulder and called him "Papa." His mouth dropped open and his arms fell to his sides, bow in one hand and arrow in another. Several of his Tan Teammates shared his reaction.

The Gray Gang seemed to be trying to understand the situation. For that matter, so was I. The Red Shorts seemed to working themselves up to a Charge of the Light Brigade. Kiri shifted her position, aiming one pistol more directly at the head Red Short. He paused to consider his options. He chose Staying Alive.

The Old Codger spoke up, "Are you a friend of *Tang-horr*?" His accent was doing strange things to the Kapar language but he was apparently sincere. Also, he was no longer pointing either bow or arrow at us.

I recalled that name *Tangor* from Virrul's good cop routine, but it still meant nothing to me. "No, sir, I have heard that name but I do not know the man. Why do you ask?" In the United States Army, friendly male civilians are called "sir" and the Old Codger seemed to fit into that category. (Unfriendly males are called "targets.")

"Many years ago, a Unisan pilot named Tangor visited us. He said that he was an Amerhikhan from the planet Urtha."

Now it was my turn to see the lobster. "Urtha" was the common Polodan pronunciation of "Earth" but neither Kiri nor I had mentioned either word to any Punosans. If I could die and be transported to Poloda, why not another...? My head spun.

"The food is getting cold while we argue," pointed out Kiri simply. She gestured towards the unicorn meat between us. "There is enough for all."

"Yes, yes," agreed the head Gray Gangster. "And the insects are beginning to eat our food. Let us each take as much as we can carry and withdraw." After a brief pause, he added "Peacefully." Everyone glanced around and nodded.

We all began grabbing as much as we could carry and then some. The "cavemen" snatched up samples and stuffed their mouths full. When it came to packing food out, Kiri and I had an enormous advantage over the poorly equipped locals with the pouches that we had scavenged in Allos as well as a rucksack that I had made from kalidah hide. The head Red Short purpled when he saw us stocking up, but I looked him in the eye and repeated Kiri's observation about the quantity. After some more posturing, he exhaled and resumed gathering up unicorn chops. As it was, the ikhurrs and insects had a feast after we left.

Kiri and I started to withdraw into the woods when the Old Codger approached.

"Please come to the town of Bhon with us," he invited somewhat timidly. "Our dwellings are very poor compared to the great cities of Unis and Amerhikha but you are welcome to share them with us. We will not harm you. We wish to talk to you."

I was still suspicious but Kiri nodded slowly and I concurred. I was curious to learn more about this *Tangor* fellow who so many Polodans had heard about.

The "town" of Bhon turned out to be a village hidden under a cliff in the Mula range that divided north and south Punos. We followed Tukarr Derru — the Old Codger's real name — and his hunters into the mountains, up a broad canyon, and into a patch of forest crouching under a cliff. The forest was luxuriant, nourished by a waterfall descending from a mesa. The forest on one side and the cliff on the other made Bhon invisible from the air.

The hundred or so Bhonans greeted their returning men folk eagerly, especially when they saw that the hunters were loaded down with meat. It was easy to see why. Everyone in the pathetic "town" was on the ragged edge of starvation. The children looked more like gollywog dolls than real human beings: distorted torsos, stomachs bloated from eating grass, pipe stem legs and arms.... Kiri choked and snuffled at the sight, and I quietly agreed.

That night, the children of Bhon ate real food for a change. Kiri, a beautiful woman from the exotic, free land of Unis, was the center of attention. Happy children swarmed around her, hugging, stroking her red hair, giggling.... She loved it.

Derru and I sat quietly watching the feast and celebration. We talked long into the night. "This is the first time that many of those children have laughed," he commented.

He told me the story of the former republic of Punha, as Punos had been called before the Kapars renamed it. Once it had been a great nation, the breadbasket and fish market of Epris. Then the Kapars had arisen in the former kingdom of Zurris — which they had renamed Kapara — and begun their conquest of the world. The Punosans had fought as long as possible but they were overwhelmed. Their resistance had earned them the undying hatred of each succeeding Pom Da.

Long after the great cities of Punos had been destroyed and their people murdered or enslaved, the Kapars continued to torment the wounded land. For a time, the gray shirts had occupied the new colony and the red shirts had attempted to build grim Kapar fortresses in the ruins their masters had created. But the Unisans had built vast fleets of warplanes as well and bombed the Kapar bases out of existence. The "all-conquering" Kapars had withdrawn to their homeland (and more pliable colonies).

But the gray shirts still maintained aerial patrols and ruthlessly bombed and strafed any hint of Punosan renaissance or any resources that might help the few survivors rebuild. I nodded. That explained the otherwise pointless attacks on the *juthi* unicorns. Neither one of us could understand the attacks on the trees as the bombers had left millions of others intact.

I recognized the psychology of dictators: no one and nothing could be allowed to challenge The Leader. On Earth, the villages of Lidice and Oradour-sur-Glane had paid terrible prices for defying the Nazis.

Derru asked, "What are your plans?"

"To return Loris Kiri to her home in Unis. After that, I'm at loose ends," I paused. "Perhaps I can join the Unisan army. Or start a clothing store. Kapars have abominable taste in clothes," I opined.

Derru made a gargling noise that I decided was a chuckle. He obviously hadn't had much practice at laughing. "You remind me of Tangor. He came to Poloda and joined the

Unisan Fighting Corps. He crash-landed here and visited us for two days. He gave us these guns but we have used up all the ammunition."

Interesting, very interesting; I wanted to meet this Tangor fellow. His name meant 'from nothing' in Unisan. A curious name, but certainly no more curious than the very proper King of Great Britain, George V, officially naming two relatives Helena Victoria of Nothing and Marie Louise of Nothing!

Unfortunately, Derru knew nothing more about Mister Nothing. He had rescued a comrade, repaired his airplane and flown away never to return. He had probably been killed in battle. Based on Virrul's comments, Tangor *might* have visited Ergos at some point but the deceased city governor hadn't been specific about the timing. I filed the issue with a thousand other questions about the planet of perpetual war and dropped the subject.

Derru quietly watched his people eating their fill. Several children had lost their dinners from trying to stuff too much meat into their stomachs. Mothers chided them about wasted food but, for once, there was enough for all. I commented on the fact.

The old fellow was silent for a while. "It is very rare for us to have this much food at one time. The Kapars killed off most game animals when they occupied our land. Now we are killing off all the remaining game faster than it can propagate."

Now I was silent for a time. "There's a great deal of food available in the forests of Allos. Kiri and I encountered several large carnivores. There must be a large population of herbivores to feed the carnivores, with a large plant base to feed the herbivores."

Derru looked at me like the lobster was back. I clarified, "That's basic biology. I stayed awake in high school science class."

He frowned and was silent again. Finally, he said, "The Allosans will never allow us to harvest their food."

"'Allosans?'" I asked. My experience was that Allosans were a subset of Kapars as Poland was supposedly a province of Nazi Germany.

Derru explained. The Red Shorts and Gray Gangsters were descendants of the Allosans and Zurrisans who had fled the Kapar conquest of their homelands. The original refugees had joined with the Punosans in fighting the Kapar tsunami but defeat, national pride, the stress caused by the continuing Kapar threat, and the harsh necessities of life in the ravaged country had driven them apart. Now, gangs with the names of once great nations roamed the Punosan wilderness squabbling with each other and competing for what little food was available. Fortunately, the squabbling was mostly shouting, screaming and waving spears in the air— so far.

"You should fight the Kapars, not each other. And you should trade for resources, not fight." I watched the chief of the hidden village as I opined.

He snorted. He was getting better at laughing. "Oh, yes, my friend Ran. I agree that is what we *should* do. But I fear that the Allosans and Zurrisans will not agree so easily." He thoughtfully looked at the happy children of his village and then at me. "Or do you have a plan to persuade them?"

"I do," I said confidently. "We will convene a session of the Polodan League of Nations."

Chapter 7   *THE ODDS AGAINST US WERE A MILLION TO ONE...*

BOUT A a ten-day Polodan week later, the Polodan League of Nations convened its first plenary session. In other words, the Punosan, Allosan and Zurrisan gangs sat down for a peace conference under a Polodan oak tree not far from Bhon. Also present were one Unisan and one American. Ironically, we spoke in Kapar since that was the only language that we all shared.

The head Red Short seemed to be in a better mood this week. He confined his pigeon puffing to introducing himself as, "Gillan Alle, Hereditary Prime Minister to His Majesty, Vollor, King of Allos."

The Zurrisans and Punosans had heard this before. They tactfully concealed smiles as Gillan pontificated. The head Gray Gangster allowed that he was "Baron Honnol Jannam of the True Kingdom of Zurris."

When it came Derru's turn, he announced that he was the Chief of State of the Republic of Punos and that he led the First Punosan Army of Resistance. He pointed to his Bhonan hunters when he mentioned his army.

"'Chief of State'?" echoed Gillan incredulously. "When did this promotion happen?" Clearly, the hereditary prime minister didn't like being trumped in the one-upmanship contest.

Derru hesitated but plunged gamely onward. "Oh, it happened this past week. The Quorum of Punos elected me

Chief of State and Commander in Chief for the duration of
The War. We intend to take the offensive against the Kapars."
The Punosans, Kiri and I nodded sagely. No one mentioned
the fact that the Punosan Quorum was really just the town
council of Bhon.

The declaration of war brought a hubbub from the
Allosans and Zurrisans that took a while to calm down. "Impossible" was one of the politer comments.

"We think that it is entirely possible provided it is done
the right way," contradicted the new Commander in Chief. "I
have appointed Group Commander Tomas Ran to command
the First Army. Group Commander, please explain the plan
to our allies."

I stood up amid more muttering from the Peanut
Gallery and thanked Derru. In Polodan militaries, a group
commander was the equivalent to a US Army colonel. It was
a nice promotion for a deceased OSS captain.

"Gentlemen, the four nations gathered here are all
victims of the Kapars. Rather than allowing the gray shirts to
continue bombing us whenever they will, Chief of State Tukarr
and the Punosan Quorum propose to unite our forces and
resources, and take the war to the Kapars.

"If you agree, we will unite the fighting forces of Allos,
Zurris and Punos to form a single League Army to maximize
our strength. The Army will attack the Kapars when and where
they are weak and refuse battle when they are strong. This
technique of warfare is commonly known as 'guerrilla warfare'
on Earth, where it can be extremely effective against occupying
forces when intelligently applied.

"To support the League Army in the field, we will also
unite the economies of the three nations and thereby obtain
the necessary food and other resources to support our civilian
populations as well as our fighting forces.

"We will also communicate with the Republic of Unis
at the first opportunity and invite them to join the League.

Since they are already fighting the gray shirts, they should be willing to join and contribute to victory over the Kapars." Kiri, as the only Unisan present, nodded sagely as if her country's adherence was a foregone conclusion.

I spoke as confidently as possible, making it sound like a matter of course. The assembly seemed to be in shock. The Kapars had been pounding on them and their ancestors with great success for 107 years. The idea of deliberately attacking the gray-shirted aggressors was....

"Impossible!" barked Gillan. "We only have four or five hundred free Eprisans among our three nations! Of those, no more than 100 are fighters! In contrast, there are over 400 million Kapars from here to the Northern Pole! And you expect *us* to attack *them*? What else do you expect us to do? Jump over the trees and land on Uvala?" He went on for several minutes before running down.

When Gillan paused to breathe, Honnol raised another issue. "The odds do seem to be against us," he commented wryly. "Especially since most of our fighters are actually hunters who must spend their time searching for food for our families. Assuming that we *choose* to attack the Kapars, how will we feed our people? Especially since food is already scarce throughout Punos."

"We can get both plant and animal food from the forests of Allos," I answered. The Allosans and Zurrisans gaped.

I went on, repeating my previous discussion of high school biology and adding details. "Food is scarce in Punos because the Kapars are destroying as much of it as they can find and a relatively large population — ourselves — is eating the remainder. In Allos, the Kapar population is eating algae and, ah, other things grown inside the Kapar cities. So the natural plants and animals have had a chance to recover from the devastation of The War. What we need to do is establish a system to carefully harvest that food in Allos and to transport it to our people living here in Punos."

There was a moment of stunned silence. As if on signal, a Polodan acorn glided down from the tree above us and landed in Kiri's hand. She smiled and handed it to the nearest Zurrisan. He stared at it as if it were a message from God. All around him, Allosan and Zurrisan faces began lighting up at the thought of all the food that they could eat.

Except for one; Honnol started to say something intelligent when Gillan exploded. The upshot of his remarks was that I wanted to steal Allosan food and that he would never allow that. He went on at some length about what a scoundrel I was.

When he ran down again, storm clouds were visible on every Punosan and Zurrisan face. A new world war was brewing.

I headed it off at the pass. "Prime Minister, you are mistaken. The Kapars stole your land, but no one here is suggesting stealing anything Allosan. Instead, you should *trade* your food to Punos and Zurris...."

"In exchange for what?" he grumped.

"A hundred years' worth of rent on the Punosan land that you and your people are living on?" I suggested. My eyebrow arched knowingly. The Allosans (and Zurrisans) were struck dumb.

Finally, Honnol squeaked, "Do we, too, owe Punos a hundred years' worth of rent?" His face was pale.

Honnol looked at Derru but I answered for the Chief of State, "Of course not." I smiled and gestured grandly, implicitly reducing all Punosan-Zurrisan disputes to the level of which friend would pick up the dinner check. "After all," I continued, "Punos and Zurris are allies – partners in the great alliance established by our ancestors and confirmed at the beginning of the Kapar War by Princess Zurrya, Chief of State Mekarru, and King Vollor."

"Princess Zurrya...!" murmured Honnol.

"King Vollor?!" barked Gillan. "What do you know about our great king?"

"That he gave his life for the alliance of Allos, Zurris and Punos. That he gave sanctuary to Princess Zurrya of Zurris. That Vollor and Zurrya sent their people to Punos where both peoples could live in peace with their allies and fight the Kapar tyranny together. And that he and Zurrya fought a heroic rearguard action to buy time for their people to escape and to fight for the freedom of all Polodans."

Gillan was reduced to silence. A hundred years of defeat and overcompensation took time to overcome. The heroic memory of his gallant king would help him.

Honnol squeaked again, "How do you know these things?"

I spoke Kiri's name. She reached into my kalidah-hide rucksack and extracted the brightly polished crowns of Zurris and Allos and the Sword of Vollor. There was a gasping sound as the Zurrisans and Allosans all sucked in their breaths at once. Even the staunchly republican Punosans were impressed.

Kiri stood up and held Zurrya's crown overhead. Omos' rays peering past the branches overhead turned the diadem to green fire. Kiri solemnly said, "Zurrya, the last ruling Princess of Zurris, refused to bow to Kapar tyranny even at the cost of her life. She died comforting the wounded. We received this crown from her hand. She passes this to you, her loyal Baron, so that you, too, will comfort the injured and never bow to tyranny." She handed it to Honnol. The Zurrisan took the crown reverently. He said nothing but his shining face was more eloquent than a hundred speeches.

Kiri repeated the gesture with the second crown. She said, "Vollor, the great king of Allos, gave sanctuary to the persecuted and fought tyranny until he died in battle for the honor and glory of Allos and the alliance of free peoples. We received this crown from his hand. He passes this to you, his loyal Prime Minister, so that you, too, will uphold the constitu-

"She reached into my kalidah-hide rucksack and extracted the brightly polished crowns of Zurris and Allos and the Sword of Vollor."

85

tion of Allos and the alliance of Epris." She handed it to Gillan. The Allosan took the crown and seemed to freeze in position, his eyes riveted to the emblem of legitimacy.

Kiri then took up the sword and moved it above her head. "Vollor also passes this Sword to his loyal minister so that you will defend his people and defeat the Kapar menace." She handed it to Gillan. The Allosan passed the crown to one of his followers and took up the Sword of history. It was a minute or more before he tore his eyes from the silver blade.

When he looked at us, he was young again. He spoke gently but his voice carried. "Chief of State Tukarr, Baron Honnol, Group Commander Tomas, and Dame Loris, I apologize for my harsh words and past actions. I have not acted as a minister of King Vollor should act. I ask that you accept my apologies and that you accept the Sword of Allos in the fight against Kapar tyranny." Naturally, we did.

WHEN THE DEAL CUTTING and air kissing was over, I thanked God for Mama forcing me to participate in the Brockton Community Theater. I thanked Derru for his briefings on the personalities and interests of the other leaders. And I thanked Kiri for making me lug those stupid medieval trinkets across half a continent because she had "a feeling about them".... If it had just been me, I would have left them in the cave since I must be the worst swordsman on two planets.

Chapter 8   ...AND THEREFORE WE ATTACKED

EARLY IN The War, the Unisans had bombed all of the Kapar colonial cities in Punos out of existence. They'd missed one.

Like classical Gaul, Punos was divided into three parts. Two mighty rivers drained the Hallas and Mula mountains and converged in a great bay on the southern coast. Before The War, the sophisticated city of Nira had encircled the bay. It had been Punos' capital as well as tourist mecca and trading center for Poloda's entire Southern Hemisphere.

Derru could talk for hours about the majestic bridges and sandy beaches of a fairy city that no one now alive had ever seen.

The Kapars had bombed Nira into rubble and then tried to rebuild it as Niros. Then the Unisans had bombed Niros into rubble. What the bluecoats had missed was that the gray shirt garrison had hung on, and managed to excavate a stronghold under the ruins, Fortress Niros. They kept their heads down for fear that the Unisans would realize that they were there and return to finish the job. And they were still there, like so many ten-legged insects burrowed under the skin of Punos.

The Punosans and their allies couldn't understand why the Kapars insisted on maintaining an outpost of so little military value. I could. It was more of the psychology of

87

dictators. As long as some gray shirts occupied the capital, the Pom Da could claim ownership of Punos.

It was time for an eviction notice.

A LONG POLODAN hour* after sunset, a shadow moved in the ruins of Niros. A rocky slab swung upward. A Kapar "Punxsutawney Phil" cautiously stuck his head up, scanning the nighttime sky for Unisan aircraft. Seeing none, he opened his spyhole's trapdoor wider to get a better view of the heavens. Poloda's evening companions, Antos and Rovos looked serenely back. After a few minutes, he picked up an interphone and reported his post number and "All clear." His next report wasn't due for 50 Polodan minutes.

Phil locked the trapdoor in the upright position and climbed out of his hole. A grass-covered mound a few steps away made a more comfortable couch than his official observation post. If he saw a flight of airplanes in the light of the neighboring planets, he'd report it but the Unisans seldom flew this far south. And, even if an enemy scout flew directly overhead, it would be impossible to pick out one gray-shirted blob among the shades of black that had once been the city of Nira.

Phil settled in for 45 minutes of goofing off followed by five minutes of looking alert. Instead, more shadows moved around him. Hands clamped the Kapar's mouth, arms and legs shut. A gun glinted in the planet-light and a face loomed out of the darkness. A voice whispered a demand for surrender in accented but understandable Kapar. Phil slowly blinked acceptance.

The hands holding Phil prisoner were replaced by ropes and a gag. His machine pistol, sword, flashlight and other equipment went one way while he went another. As soon as Phil had departed on his all-expense paid vacation trip to Punos'

---

* The Polodan day is divided into 10 hours which are subdivided into 100 minutes each. Each day officially begins at dawn. Despite the geographic expanses of the nations, Unis, Punos and the Kapar empire all have one time zone each. Dawn and other units of time are measured at the respective capital cities of Orvis, Bhon, and Ergos. – Ed.

new POW camp, Kiri and I climbed down his ladder into the uppermost level of the Kapar city.

Nirosan construction was, if anything, worse than Gerris: cheaper concrete, exposed metal bars, rough-hewn wood panels instead of the plastic sheets Polodans preferred.... Half the electric lights were broken or burnt out. The air conditioning had a bad case of mechanical asthma. And the garbage hadn't been taken out recently.

We began exploring the poorly lit tunnel leading from Phil's post. Since we were wearing high-ranking green police uniforms, we marched into Fortress Niros as if we owned the place. We came out of Phil's tunnel into a larger corridor and confidently turned to our right. Directly ahead, a pair of gray shirts was walking along, looking like they knew what they were doing. They glanced at us and made fists in Kapar salutes. We started to return their salutes when we stepped into a pool of light under an electrical curlicue and things came unstuck.

One gray shirt jerked to a stop, eyes goggling. His buddy stopped a few seconds later. "Zabo?" the first one asked as he stared at my gold trimmed green uniform. "What are Zabo agents doing in Fortress Niros?"

Uh, oh. The Zabo was the high-level Kapar secret police organization. As a practical matter, the Zabo was the government of the Kapar empire. That was logical enough when you remembered that a police state considers every little thing to be a security matter. Nazi Germany had been headed in that direction when I died.

"Surprise inspection," I snapped. "We're checking on guard alertness." I paused, nodded in approval, and added, "You have the true Kapar spirit, airman." Buddy relaxed, saluted and said, "Thank you, Most High." Flattery will get you everywhere. Even on Poloda.

Goggle Eyes almost joined him but not quite. He began hesitantly but picked up steam as he went. "Fortress

Niros is an Iron Gray Level *military* secret. The Zabo doesn't *know* that it exists. How can you be inspecting…?"

I glared at him and interrupted, "Fool. The Zabo Knows Every Thing." I sounded as arrogant and portentous as I could. "Including *military* 'secrets.' Our presence is proof of that. Now, Kapars, what are your names and assignments?"

Buddy started to answer the question like a good little robot but Goggle Eyes cut him off. "Noooo! Something is wrong here. High Command would never reveal the existence of Fortress Niros to the Zabo…!" His voice was half suspicion and half fear.

In other words, he had the true Kapar spirit.

He started to pull his gun out of its holster as he stared at the Man From Mars.…

Kiri's sword came slashing down out of nowhere and separated his gun hand and arm. He gargled in shock and pain. Kiri brought her sword up and around, slicing across Buddy's throat while my haymaker put Goggle Eyes out of his misery. Buddy tried to scream but failed. Another haymaker and he joined his comrade en route to Omys.

One of our instructors at OSS school was a professional stage magician named Jasper Maskelyne. Among other things, he taught us that a magician's charming assistant can rob the audience blind while everyone is concentrating on the magician instead of her. Obviously, the Kapars had missed that lesson.

"What do we do now?" hissed Kiri.

"Grab these guys and go. We're dressed wrong for infiltration," I replied. We could hear people noises coming down the corridor. Kiri tried to lift Buddy's corpse but he weighed too much. "Cover me," I ordered. She nodded, yanked her pistol out and stood guard while I fireman-carried first Buddy, then Goggle Eyes and his hand back to the ladder and out of Niros.

AS THEY TAUGHT us in OSS school, everyone should have a Plan B so good that people will instantly mistake it for your Plan A. We didn't have time to invent a Plan B because the Nirosan Kapars were after us in a matter of hours. Goggle Eyes and Buddy had left a lot of blood in their corridor and Phil didn't answer his interphone calls. By midnight, the forest that had been Nira was boiling with patrols confident that the true Kapar spirit would quickly find and eliminate the problem. However....

Guerilla warfare does not come naturally to airmen trained to bomb and strafe unicorns and other enemies of the Pom Da into death or submission. The Nirosan Kapars made every mistake possible. They were loud and had no sense of communications discipline. They waved flashlights around in the middle of the night. They shot at every odd sound including other Kapars' gunfire. When they moved, they tried to march as if they were on a flat parade ground instead of overgrown rubble. Their curses were truly magnificent. In other words, they made themselves perfect targets for people who had been surviving on stealth for 107 years.

After years of being hunted like ikhurrs, a few members of the League Army wanted to head for the hills when the Kapars came out to play. But they manned up when I reminded them that a *girl* had killed two gray shirts with a *knife*.

We hid in the woods and rubble while Kapars tired themselves out shooting at shadows. After several hours, most of them were out of ammunition.

That's when the arrows started flying. Hunters whose ability to eat depended on the quality of their bow and arrow work were very, very good at hunting exhausted, mistake prone, loudmouthed Kapars lit up by planets and flashlights.

Bows and arrows make almost no noise compared to heavy machine pistols. And the occasional snap of the bow and whish of an arrow was almost entirely drowned out by elephantine crashing through the Punosan undergrowth and endless shouting and cursing. Screams from wounded gray shirts broke through the background noise but we put those fellows out of our misery quickly enough. Nerves jangled and tempers frayed.

When Omos climbed over the edge of the world, the Kapar company leaders called a halt and tried to take stock of the situation. Section leaders assembled their men.

About half of the gray shirts didn't answer the roll for various reasons. Some were lost; some were dogging it; some were dead tired; most were just dead.

Even hardened veterans get shaken by brutal combat losses. It's worse for third-rate troops on easy duty where boredom is a bigger problem than enemy bullets.

Discovering the bodies of fellow airmen littering the woods rattled most of them.

Company leaders bellowed orders and individual scouts fanned out to find answers. They mostly found more bodies – always gray shirts.

The League Army faded into the woods ahead of them. Communications discipline means that you don't shout orders where your enemies can hear them. The Kapars had missed that lesson as well. When the individual scouts were out of sight of their nervous fellows, arrows and spears flew. Scouts disappeared.

Subsequent scouting parties found more bodies but not their weapons and equipment. That made the Kapar airmen even more nervous. People began volunteering to return to Niros for various reasons.

By mid-afternoon of the second day, the garrison of Niros had lost at least a third of its men and the remaining airmen were on the verge of panic. Officers had shot a couple of would-be deserters to encourage the others.

We were taking losses, too. When torrents of gunfire sprayed the woods, a few bullets were bound to find Punosan, Allosan or Zurrisan bodies as well as trees, shrubs, ikhurrs, birds

"When the individual scouts were out of sight of their nervous fellows,
arrows and spears flew. Scouts disappeared..."

93

and squirrels. Songbirds trying to serenade Omos took a particularly heavy toll. We rescued our people when we could and dragged bodies away when we couldn't save them. Kiri had a decent knowledge of first aid and I helped when I could spare the time. A lot of guys owed Kiri their lives.

Balanced against our losses — miniscule compared to a Kapar bombing raid — was the thrill of victory. For the first time in 107 years, Eprisans – Punosans, Allosans and Zurrisans together – were on the offensive against their oppressors! And winning!!

If the Second Battle of Nira had been fought in Europe, the history books would barely have mentioned it. But for each ally who went to Uvala, a dozen Kapars journeyed to Omys – usually leaving his equipment in our hands. My Eprisans couldn't have been more proud if we had won Yorktown, Waterloo and D-Day all on the same day.

When Omos settled below the western horizon that convinced the Kapars to call it a day. They mustered their survivors and started marching back to the safety of their holes. As soon as they were moving in the right direction, our gunfire ripped through the woods and into their retreating gray backs.

Discipline broke. The Kapar airmen – conquerors of unicorns and songbirds – ran like Olympic champions. They piled up at the entrances, fighting and clawing to reach safety underground. One gray shirt, already bleeding from an allied bullet in one arm, began shooting his way to the ladder through his own men. Other Kapars responded in kind.

We stopped firing. I believe it was Napoleon who said, "Never interrupt your enemy when he's destroying himself." As it was, some of our most hardened fighters had to excuse themselves after watching the Kapars savage each other.

NEXT DAY, we noticed the piles of bodies jerking and moving. Gray-shirted engineers were clearing away the trapdoors by pulling corpses out of the bottoms of the piles.

We couldn't do much about that, but things were different when the engineers poked their heads out of their holes to retrieve the Kapars who hadn't made it that far.

Once again, arrows, spears and bullets flew. Eventually, the Niros garrison gave up on that approach and left the remains to feed the ikhurrs. The ikhurrs took advantage of the situation and then moved into Niros looking for more free lunches....

Some bright boy tried to send scouts out of spy holes behind our lines but that didn't work too well. We had spotters scattered around the woods and supposedly sneaky Kapars mostly disappeared without a trace.

We put some of our prisoners to work cutting heavy logs and placing them on top of selected trapdoors. The Kapar engineers tried to force the blockages out of the way but they couldn't get heavy machinery into the narrow corridors connecting the spy holes with the fortress city. Those holes stayed plugged.

We pretended not to find certain other holes. The besieged Kapars quickly came to depend on the unplugged holes for fresh air and occasional reconnaissance — exactly as we planned.

The Kapar High Command had Niros on a regular supply schedule. Every night five or ten airplanes flew into and out of concealed airfields. That stopped when we stationed crack gunmen near the landing strips. Kapar airplanes were made of extremely tough plastic that shed bullets frighteningly well. But the propellers were wood and the engines were metal. Neither of them took dum-dum bullets at all well.

One pilot must have had Satan himself for a co-pilot because he managed to crash-land a plane with both engines masses of fire, and then stagger into the underground hangar. But he was the exception.

The High Command gave up after 20 or so planes hammered into the Punosan landscape, splattering weapons, ammunition, tools, parts, and other supplies through the woods. Naturally, we liberated as much as we could. I never learned to enjoy Kapar cuisine but hardtack and sausage was the nectar of the gods to Eprisans accustomed to living on squirrels and birds.

While the Pom Da was figuring out his next move, we made ours. Nira was downhill from the Hallas and Mula Mountains, and Niros was partly below sea level. We put the prisoners to work digging small canals from the converging rivers to the air holes of Niros.

One cloudy night, knots of Kapars crouching under partially raised trapdoors for a breath of fresh air were suddenly attacked by tree limbs! Teams of volunteers had shoved long poles into the spaces between tunnel rims and hatch covers. While the astonished Kapars were swatting at — and sometimes shooting — tree branches, other workers hacked their way through earthen barriers. Water gushed downhill into a dozen newly opened air holes. Attempts to close the trapdoors and seal the fresh holes were thwarted by tree limbs wedged in the openings.

We heard panicky voices, screams, gunfire, mechanical clamoring, sounds that no human can describe....And what we heard was only the merest fraction of the bedlam erupting beneath our feet.... The entire League Army stood – transfixed – listening to the horror. A troop of Girl Scouts could have wiped us off the face of Poloda in fifteen minutes.

Kapar airmen must have tried to slam internal doors shut to isolate the inrushing waters. Engineers must have tried to rev up pumps and build cofferdams and spillways. Junior officers must have reported the flood and requested orders. Senior officers must have tried to make sense out of the situation and issue coherent orders....

Nothing helped. The flood was rushing into Niros from a dozen directions. Closing one door left men vulnerable to waves approaching behind them.

Kapar maintenance worked against the frantic garrison. The Unisans hadn't attacked Niros since the early days of The War. People had gotten lax; very, very lax.

All too often, machinery had rusted or disappeared completely. Safety procedures had been ignored. Emergency equipment had been stolen for other purposes.

Even the relatively slow speed of the flood did its part to kill the trapped Kapars. If a million gallons of water had smashed into Niros all at once, the struggle would have been over in seconds. The entire garrison would have gone to Omys almost instantly.

Instead, the water level mounted relatively slowly. Men and women had time to absorb the horror — and to panic. Fear-crazed airmen splashed through the rising fluid, desperately seeking escape. With many of the trapdoors plugged, crowds of human animals collided as they sought alternative routes. Some found previously secret bolt holes and clawed their way to the surface. Others popped out the exits we had left for them. There, they encountered the League Army. If they surrendered quickly enough, they lived.

Most, however, perished in savage fighting among themselves. The screaming lasted all night. When Omos rose over Punos the following morning, Niros was dead....

...Along with several hundred Kapars.

Water eventually stopped draining into the hecatombs of Niros and pooled to form a dozen new ponds and lakes. They sparkled in the sunbeams peaking through the forest canopy.

BY MORNING, I was dead tired from lack of sleep. I turned to send a messenger to Derru and discovered him standing directly behind me. His eyes were the size of dinner plates. His arms were hanging limply at his sides.

"Derru, are you well?" I asked.

He shook himself and answered, "Oh, yes, Ran, I am well. I am very, very well." He looked from side to side. "I have never seen such a victory over the Kapars. We have tales of victories during the early years of The War, but nothing such as this...." His voice trailed off as he surveyed the new lakes – and the gray-shirted bodies floating in them.

I smiled grimly and stood up straighter. Omos cast a brilliant spotlight on the victorious Punosan. Songbirds provided a triumphant chorus.

"Chief of State Tukarr, I present the city of Nira to you and the Quorum of Punos," I said formally. "The League Army is still rounding up prisoners and salvaging equipment so it will be a few days before we can submit a final report. I recommend that you appoint a governor for this region but that we evacuate the area as soon as possible. Sooner or later, the Kapars will realize what happened and retaliate. And, in the meantime, I'd like to take a break."

"Oh, yes, yes, Ran. Do whatever you wish to do...." Derru was turning his head back and forth, up and down....

I turned to go. I heard Derru whisper, "Nira is ours again...."

As I walked into the woods, I imagined that he was seeing the Nira of old in his mind's eye: proud towers, arching bridges, millions of happy prosperous people.... We hadn't brought those people back to life, but we had at least avenged them. I smiled as I walked.

Loris Kiri had established a field hospital in a natural cathedral formed by Polodan redwoods and the broken walls of old Nira. Decades of fallen needles carpeted the forest floor and provided mattresses for wounded warriors. They also soaked up sounds and created a feeling of tranquility. The new day's birdsongs were muted. For the moment, Poloda was a planet of peace.

Most of the injured soldiers, Eprisans and Kapars alike, were asleep when I entered. One Zurrisan was awake. He noticed me.

"Commander Tomas! We won! We won, didn't we?!" His face was that of an angel, but the Devil had played hob with his legs. His entire lower body was encased in bandages soaked in blood.

I stepped over to his "bed" and knelt down. "Yes, soldier, we did. You and your brothers beat the Kapars and recaptured an entire city. Thanks to you, Punos is free again." He glowed with pride.

"Now, soldier, you need to get some rest. We'll move you to a better hospital soon and you can heal up. We'll save some Kapars for when you're better." He smiled and closed his eyes. After a minute, I realized that he had left Poloda. I prayed that he made it to Uvala.

When I stood up, Kiri was standing beside me. She had been watching us. She seemed very thoughtful. I said so.

"The human waste of war," she replied. She sighed deeply. "Still, it had to be done. It is war."

She turned to face me more directly.

"You've wrecked two Kapar cities now, Ran. That's more than a million Unisans have accomplished since The War began. The Eprisans are whispering that you're a superhuman warrior from the Time of Legends returned to Poloda."

I shook my head firmly. "*We* wrecked Fortress Niros. Each and every bowman and gunman in the League Army; every engineer who dug canals and moved logs; everyone who found and transported food; every doctor and nurse in our hospital…." I bowed my head to Kiri as I said that. "*We* wrecked Niros." I breathed deeply to clear my head.

"My contribution was things that I learned: enemy analysis, strategy, engineering, communications, some lessons from history, leadership…. Maybe aggressiveness as well."

"And what will you do now, glorious warrior?" She looked up into my face. Her voice was soft and there was a mysterious smile on her lips.

"I came here to help you with the wounded." Some emotion that I couldn't decipher flickered across her face.

"Well then, I suppose that I should help the wounded as well. There are first aid kits there — behind that tree root. Please pick up as many as you can carry and bring them to the worst wounded," she said briskly. She turned back to her patients.

"Yes, ma'am." I walked over to an alcove between the wooden buttresses supporting the redwood. A small store of medical supplies confiscated from captured Kapars was stacked there. I began picking up the plastic boxes...The songbirds had fallen silent. I heard a shrill whistling sound.... I dropped the boxes....

The world exploded around me. A giant's foot kicked me into the wooden wall of the great tree. My back knotted in pain but that was blotted out almost instantly. My face slammed into the tree. Stars blossomed in my brain. The world went black.

WHEN I WOKE UP, I knew I wasn't in Omys because the faces of Derru and Alle were looming over mine, and I knew I wasn't in Uvala because every muscle in my body groaned in pain. I concentrated on focusing my eyes and rasped, "What happened?"

Derru turned away. I wanted to see what he was looking at but turning my head provoked a headache the size of the national debt.

Alle breathed deeply and spoke. "The Kapars bombed Nira just after dawn. You were injured in the first explosion. One of the airplanes that we did not kill must have alerted the enemy to the situation. We are still counting the dead but we lost at least 75 men and women." He winced and his mouth twisted in turmoil. "We also lost our Kapar prisoners. They did not know to dodge from tree to tree when running from airplanes."

I asked, "What happened to Loris Kiri?" Alle started to say something but Derru interrupted.

"Oh my friend Ran, I am very sorry, but your lady Loris Kiri is dead."

I wanted to collapse but I was already lying on the ground, cradled by Polodan pine needles. I started choking. I flailed my arms helplessly. Alle turned me over and slapped me on my back, trying to stop the choking.

His slap sent a wave of pain up my spine. I blacked out again. As unconsciousness claimed me, I realized — *now that it was too late* — that I had loved Loris Kiri.

BOOK TWO: UNIS

Chapter 9 *THE PIRATES OF POLODA*

THE FOLLOWING SPRING found me on the north coast of Punos. I was stalking some wild date-like fruits that grew on a mangrove-like tree when I heard bursts of gunfire nearby. Songbirds fell silent. I froze and then slid my guns out of their holsters. I moved quietly forward.

I reached the edge of the Polodan mangrove forest quickly. Before me was a beach of gleaming white sands and occasional curiously shaped sea shells flung onto the shore by ocean waves. Beyond the beach Omos glinted on the brilliant blue waves of the Talan Strait playfully pounding the shore. The air smelled of salt, rotting seaweed, and stranger odors. Somewhere beyond the Strait was the continent of Unis. Geography wasn't my top priority at the moment.

At the beach's edge, six Kapars surrounded a man in a Unisan pilot's sky blue uniform. Three blue-clad corpses lay at their feet. Beyond them was a sea-blue vessel about the size of a New England whaleboat. Two Kapars were holding the Unisan's arms in a painful position behind his back while another gray shirt shouted insults at him. Another Kapar was inspecting the boat while the last two watched the sky.

After several minutes of browbeating, the head Kapar snapped some orders. The two guards marched their prisoner down the beach toward a large rock projecting out from the shore. When he didn't move quickly enough for them, they pistol-whipped him. The head Kapar followed. They disappeared into a secret door in the rock. Oh, ho! Another Fortress Niros?

The three remaining Kapars tried to drag the boat up the beach and under the trees all the while keeping an eye out for airplanes. They didn't make much progress but three more gray shirts appeared from the rock and joined in. Between the six of them, they got the boat and corpses under the trees.

This brought them quite close to my position but I kept still. The human eye sees motion faster than it distinguishes shapes. In OSS school, they teach you that it's better to let a bad guy walk on you than to reveal yourself unnecessarily. In addition, my green Zabo uniform still provided excellent camouflage in Poloda's green and brown forests (even though it was getting a little tatty from hard use).

The working party began taking blue boxes out of the boat. It had apparently been packed full. After a few minutes, four Kapars picked up about a dozen boxes and headed towards the door in the rock. The other two continued unloading. That made things much more convenient. I re-holstered my guns and drew sword.

Whenever possible, break the job of fighting large numbers of enemies down into smaller tasks so that you outnumber them in any given battle. Based on what I had seen and the Polodan fondness for the number ten, I guessed that I was facing ten enemies. This called for Extra Special Cheating.

The nearest Kapars had their heads down in the whaleboat. I could hear excited comments about "real" food. Apparently the Kapars had the same opinion of their national cuisine as I did. I eased myself upright and then crept up on them, one step at a time and one eye on their rock. When I came up behind Number One, he must have sensed something. He stood up.... And my sword opened his throat.

While One was trying to remember how to breathe, I jumped up on the railing and kicked Number Two in the face.

He crashed backwards. Hauling them into the undergrowth and hiding the bodies was easy.

Two more Kapars were leaving their rock to tote loot home but I was masked by the mangrove trees. I laid a trail of food and boxes into another bush. I then hid myself behind a tree and thought leafy thoughts.

Numbers Three and Four surveyed the scene and decided that One and Two had found some extra special swag to party with. They followed the trail. Three told Four to keep quiet so that their commander wouldn't notice. The door in the rock was still closed so their commander didn't notice me shooting them.

Or Five and Six.

By this time, the commander had noticed that no one was hauling stuff back to the rock. He appeared in the doorway and ordered two more airmen to find out what was going on. By this time, I was still in the woods but about halfway to the door. Never be where the bad guys expect you to be. I continued easing around to his blind side as he watched Numbers Seven and Eight trudge across the beach toward the whaleboat. They had their guns out.

Everyone, including the commander, was watching the trees hiding the whaleboat. Even if they suddenly turned around, the trees and then the rock masked my approach.

I sidled around the rock until I could see the edge of the wide open door and hear the commander talking to someone over his shoulder. Numbers Seven and Eight were cautiously entering the forest. Not being a four armed Martian, I holstered one gun.

Someone inside the rock reminded the commander to watch the sky. He grunted. I gave him a few seconds and then rushed him. I grabbed the door handle with my left hand as I hosed the distracted Kapar's chest. The door swung smoothly shut as I swept the room inside the rock at chest level, catching

Number Ten in the process. The rock walls muffled the gunshots.

When Numbers Seven and Eight came running back to report, they found the door closed. They pounded a code sequence on the rock. Since they obviously knew the secret password, I unlocked the door. While they were pulling it open, they were distracted for the last time.

I THREW MORE WATER into the face of the prisoner. Sputtering, he came to. "Where am I?" he sang in Unisan.

"You're in a Kapar sound detection post on the north coast of Punos," I chanted back. I gestured at the room with one hand. I kept the other hand near a holstered pistol.

He looked around, seeing a largish one room military post carved out of Punosan granite. One side of the room held controls for a sound detector concealed on the far side of the rock. The other side held minimal living arrangements for ten men including bunks, food storage and sanitary facilities. Overhead, electrical curlicues lit the post with the usual sickly pallor.

The prisoner himself was lying on a bunk. I had moved him there after almost tripping over his body lying on the stone floor. Typical Kapar hospitality. I had also removed his makeshift gag and wrist and ankle restraints.

"What's your name, airman?"

"Kaldur Ron, Special Officer, Unisan Fighting Corps." He recited a serial number. The Fighting Corps was the combined air force and army of Kiri's nation. He sat up despite the obvious effort. I'd cleaned the blood off his head, but couldn't do much about the pain.

"What's your mission?"

He breathed deeply before answering, "Scouting Punos." He grimaced and added, "My crew apparently landed right on top of a Kapar post. I think they are dead."

I nodded. "You're correct. Your crewmates are dead. I wrapped them in sheets but we better bury them quickly or the ikhurrs will eat them." I pointed to three human-sized bundles lying on the floor near his bunk.

Kaldur blinked. "Thank you." He paused and asked, "What happened to the Kapars who captured me?"

"They're dead, too. I was planning on leaving them when we evacuate this post." I pointed to four Kapar corpses lying on the other side of the room. The others were outside.

"'Dead'? What happened to them?" Kaldur's face betrayed his confusion.

"I killed them. I would have preferred to take them alive but...."

"You killed them?" Kaldur interrupted sharply. "You and what air force?!" Clearly the lobster that lived in my ear was back.

"Me, myself and I. Plus the fact that Kapar airmen don't expect to be attacked from the ground. I attacked from different angles and caught them by surprise."

"Who Are You?" He enunciated his words very carefully.

"Tomas Ran, Group Commander, Polodan League of Nations Army," I answered. The League Army hadn't issued any serial numbers and my US Army identification would be meaningless to a Polodan. "And speaking of which, I would like to borrow your boat to conduct a diplomatic mission to the Republic of Unis."

"Why?"

"We wish to invite Unis to join the League and our war against the Kapars."

Kaldur Ron took offense to the implication that Unis had somehow not been fighting the Kapars. It took some time before he calmed down. I apologized for the misunderstanding and gave him a brief description of the League of Nations, especially the Second Battle of Niros.

He was stunned for a long minute, but admitted that Unis had been out of contact with Punos for decades. He asked if we could contact the League. I said that they were several days or weeks' travel to the south and could we please take his boat to Unis. He asked what the rush to get to Unis was. I reminded him that the Kapars had a habit of bombing installations captured by their enemies *such as the one that we were sitting in.* Kaldur agreed that getting out of Dodge would be a good idea.

We buried Kaldur's crewmates under the mangrove trees and left the Kapars for the ikhurrs. We rounded up all the paperwork that we could find in the outpost for intelligence analysis, then wrecked the place and sound detector as thoroughly as we could. We threw the excess Kapar weapons into the surf for the salt water to take care of. We stripped the plastic boat's cargo down to essentials and launched.

Among other things, I noticed that Kaldur Ron was in much better physical condition than the Kapars. He modestly passed that off as the result of better diet and exercise. I scratched my head but couldn't remember any Kapars actually exercising.

Once in the water, Kaldur unpacked a small device that looked like a radar dish. He hunted around until a lever moved on a control panel. Then he started the engine. I asked what the "radar set" was. He looked puzzled and replied, "A power receiver. I wish to save the batteries and we are close enough to Unis to make reception possible."

I admitted that we didn't have broadcast power where I came from and he asked where that was. I gave him a condensed version of my life and death on Earth and Poloda. He listened politely but clearly the lobster was back and waving a bottle of tequila at him.

Kaldur Ron loosened up on the way to Unis. A pleasant sea voyage with good companionship will do that. The Strait was several hundred miles wide and it took *Number Nine* three days to purr its way north to the Southern Islands of Unis. *Number Nine* was our boat. I asked Ron about the name and got another blank stare. Apparently, Polodans didn't give their air or water craft cute names. Ron didn't like my suggestion that we rename it the *Good Ship Lollypop*.

We talked a lot on the way. I had already introduced Ron to the concepts of Earth and teleportation to Poloda. As I got to know Ron, I added details, particularly about Earthly culture. Naturally, he had never heard of William Shakespeare or Washington Irving but he liked stories as much as anyone.

In return, Ron talked about life in Unis. Kiri (and Sura) had given me a lot to think about and I was anxious to double-check their accounts.

Ron was fiercely if quietly proud of his nation. In his eyes (and those of Kiri), Unis was a fortress of freedom. Surrounded by Kapar colonies, attacked night and day by massive air fleets, outnumbered and cut off from the world, Unis fought on. Every other nation in the world had bowed down to the Pom Da, but Unis not only resisted but also struck back whenever it could. Each Kapar black-winged aircraft was met with two or more bluecoat planes; every iron gray bomb answered with two or more blue steel explosives. The Kapars had smashed every city in Unis to rubble in the first ten years of The War. The Unisans had repaid the debt tenfold from Pole to Pole.

I had seen the results in Gerris and Niros. I nodded my head in agreement.

But Unis' greatest triumph in Ron's eyes (and those of Kiri) was the preservation of liberty and law. Ron acknowledged the temptation to remake Unis as a tyranny as "efficient" as Kapara. Certainly, Unisans were not as free as their great-grandparents had been in the comparatively carefree days before The War. But Unisans, leaders and followers alike, had drawn back from the abyss into which Pom Da had eagerly dragged eighty percent of the planet. Unisan leaders were chosen by voters, policies were debated rather than dictated, cops had to have probable cause for arrests, buyers and sellers negotiated prices, people went to the church of their choice or not, and so on.

Ron glowed with unmistakable pride. Unis was free because Unisans wanted to be free. Ron had given me a great deal to think about. I found my suspicions melting away. Good companionship works both ways.

Airplanes flew high overhead in both directions every day and night. If any of them had attacked us, we would have slept with the fishes. But *Number Nine* was too small to attract attention, especially since both air forces routinely flew high above sea level. Even if some pilot looked directly at us, our sea blue coloring rendered us effectively invisible. The War passed over us. Other problems were more immediate.

Late in the afternoon of the second day of our journey, a behemoth came over the horizon. A blue-gray vessel about 450 feet long moving east to west cut across our approach to the Southern Islands. Except for having power receivers instead of smokestacks and being made of plastic rather than steel, it might have been some American Liberty ship bound from Los Angeles to Micronesia.

I looked for a national or house flag but didn't see any. Ron cursed as the behemoth approached. "I take it these people aren't your friends?" I said.

He cursed again but explained, "Smugglers! Illegal traders supplying food to Kapara in exchange for rare metals." He looked westward, calculating something. "They are bound for Umars in Ithris." He unholstered his machine pistol and sword.

I kept my eyes on the smuggling ship. There was a glint of light from the quarterdeck. "I think they see us. What are they likely to do, and what should we do?" I asked.

Ron glanced up at the approaching behemoth. He answered, "Sell our lives as dearly as possible."

"Humph," I humphed. "Let's try something else first."
I stood up and waved one arm at the smuggler watching us
through a telescope or binoculars. I put a great big smile on
my face as I did so.

"What in Omys are you doing?" grunted Ron.

"I'm acting like they're our best friends," I explained as
I continued smiling and waving. "Put your gun and sword
down before they decide we're a threat."

The behemoth was now close enough that we could
see individual crewmembers along the south railing. I couldn't
hear anything they were saying but their body language was
relaxed. They were pointing at us, and a couple of them waved
back.

Ron was staring at the sight. His arms hung limply at
his sides, gun and sword still in hands. He really needed to
drop them quickly but at least he wasn't waving them around
like a stereotypical pirate or other threat.

"Why are they not shooting at us? I am an officer in
the Unisan Fighting Corps!"

"Ron, they think we're smugglers as well," I explained
through my smile. "You're wearing a Fighting Corps uniform
and I'm wearing a Zabo uniform. The only time a Zabo and a
Fighting Corpsman would be cooperating is if we're really
smugglers ourselves. The fact that we're waving at them makes
them think that we're part of the fraternity."

The strait-laced fighting man was nonplussed but he
stood quietly while he worked through the logic. In the meantime, the behemoth crew didn't open fire or drop a couple of
whaleboats to round us up. We would have gotten away clean
if the behemoth's cook hadn't dumped the garbage.

The smugglers were directly in front of us now. We
were closing on them at what I estimated was ten knots.
Someone emptied a silver cylinder over the stern. A rain of
debris cascaded twenty feet into the Talan Strait. The waters

came alive as giant fish jumped to snatch mouthfuls of debris out of the air. Clearly, dinner was served.

The behemoth sailed on, leaving both dinner and diners behind. The friendlier members of the crew gave us a final wave and went back to whatever duties smugglers had between swindles. I returned the salutes and breathed a sigh of relief. Professional courtesy among pirates only goes so far. André had told horror stories about dishonor among thieves in wartime Paris....

We were getting close to the garbage café. The fish were still jumping around fighting for choice bits. They looked more shark-like the closer we came. "Ron, steer this boat to the right at least one tenth of a circle. Two-tenths would be better."

The Unisan had been staring after the departing ship, apparently bemused by their failure to attack us. When I raised my voice, he took in the leaping sharks and turned to steer *Number Nine* around them. First, however, he paused to re-holster his gun and sword. He reached for the Ouija board-like steering control....

Too late! We rammed a shark broadside at full speed. Our bow cut into the great fish's side and blood reddened the water. Its body brought our good ship to a halt, electric motors straining to no effect. I tumbled forward into the boat's well. Ron retained his upright posture by virtue of grabbing onto the steering control. The boat wagged back and forth in place as his hand sent random signals to the gear.

In seconds, we were surrounded by sharks. Four or five hacked their wounded comrade to death. Others circled our stern, obviously expecting to find more treats in our wake. One enterprising fellow apparently realized that our gunwales were only a single foot above the water line. He leaped into the air, aiming his powerful body at Ron's presumably succulent flesh.

I had landed on the boxes of food. My hands closed on a couple of them as I tried to regain my footing. I rolled onto my back....As the shark's snout passed overhead. I kicked its lower jaw.

It wasn't a very powerful blow; I was still off balance. But it changed the shark's angle of attack upward. It continued rising instead of leveling off and seizing Ron's body in its mouth. For a moment it was suspended in midair, water falling off its body and on to us. I kicked it again, this time in the midsection.

The great beast's momentary truce with gravity ran out. It collapsed into the boat, smashing Ron into the tiny pilot's seat. But its mouth was hanging over the stern, unable to reach its intended prey. It thrashed wildly trying to dislodge itself.

I still had the boxes of food in my hands. I threw them high over our shark's body and the stern to get rid of them. The other sharks chased them down.

My guns roared at point blank range, and the great predator's midsection disintegrated into a steaming pile of blood and guts. Directly on top of me. Since the designers of the whaleboat had not included a bathtub, I stank of shark guts until we reached Unis. I thought about taking a seawater bath but there always seemed to be a shark nearby.

THE NEXT DAY, a green and yellow tropical island of considerable size rose over the horizon. Ron informed me that it bore the pleasant name of the Island of Despair. Clearly the local chamber of commerce needed a better publicity team.

To me, it looked a great deal like St. Augustine, Florida, as seen from the sea — at least if St. Augustine had 20-foot high ferns interspersed among the palm trees. The latter formed a mysteriously inviting green wall beyond the yellow-white sands of beaches undefiled by tourist footprints or candy wrappers. Brilliant flowers flaunted every color of the rainbow from sunlit treetops and shadowed meadows. Despite its name, the island seemed to be Paradise before the Fall.

Ron steered *Number Nine* along the coast watching various rock formations as we passed them. He explained that

"It collapsed into the boat, smashing Ron into the tiny pilot's seat. But its mouth was hanging over the stern, unable to reach its intended prey."

113

Kapars routinely destroyed obviously manmade markers so Fighting Corps Special Officers learned to navigate by natural landmarks.

Eventually, he found an indentation in the shoreline where a creek emptied into the Talan Strait. He steered through a screen of giant Polodan cattails topped with orange fuzz and into a small natural harbor. We tied up at a dock formed by a carved stone.

"Now what?" I asked once we were ashore.

"Now you explain what you are doing in Unis," sang a strange voice.

I was tempted to whirl around, guns in hand, but stopped myself. Someone clearly had the drop on us and might well fire if rapid motion startled him. Instead, I turned slowly towards the voice.

Five men dressed in red plastic spangles and black boots had materialized out of thin air. They each had a gun aimed in our general direction, ready but keeping the threat level down.

"Honorable police officers, we are dangerous lunatics," responded Kaldur Ron smoothly. "This man believes that he is an alien being from the imaginary planet Urtha and I believe that I am a spy for the Unisan Fighting Corps. You should lock us both up while you investigate our stories." He already had his hands in the air.

Well, there were no flies on the Unisan police force. They disarmed us both and hustled us underground and into a jail cell where they chained us to the bars, on opposite sides of the cell. This was a good thing because otherwise I would have strangled Kaldur Ron.

Chapter 10   GO DIRECTLY TO JAIL; DO NOT PASS GO

I CALMED DOWN soon enough. Ron had done nothing that I wouldn't have done if our situations had been reversed. I said so, and he thanked me – very cautiously. He still thought I was a lunatic pretending to come from an imaginary planet.

The police interrogated us separately. They took Ron away and I never saw him again. I suspected that he gave some secret passwords to someone important and was sent back to spy school for a refresher course.

The differences between Unis and Kapara emerged quickly. The red-uniformed police were suspicious of my claims but they treated me with professional respect. Of course, that included keeping eyes on me to prevent me from stealing their guns, swords and dignity, but they didn't see any need for truncheon massages or electroshock therapy.

I told my story over and over to several ranks of cops including the group commander for the Island of Despair. He scratched his head and bucked the issue up his chain of command to someone in the city of Orvis, the capital of Unis. In the meantime, he had me tell my tale to an elderly gentleman wearing gray plastic sequins and gray boots. This fellow was a judge. Apparently he was a critic as well: he ordered me confined pending a thorough psychiatric examination.

115

Unisans don't waste time doing things. Within an hour of the judge's order (and my insufficiently brilliant rebuttal), I was marched into a red plastic car. The driver got some report on weather conditions — including whether or not Kapar aircraft were raining bombs — over a telephone or interphone setup and we were off. A Unisan trapdoor eased open and we exited the police station guarding the little harbor. After an hour of bouncing through the jungle, we came to an apparent hill where another trapdoor opened.

During the entire hour, there had not been the slightest sign of civilization. Unless you counted the bomb craters left by Kapar air raids on even the most isolated part of Unis.

We went through the second door and down a long ramp. Heavily armored doors opened before us and closed behind us at regular intervals. After descending to a point 100 feet below ground, the car negotiated a heavy metal gate and stopped in a courtyard lit by artificial sunlight. We got out and I was processed into Prison 116.

They confiscated my Zabo uniform and issued me Unisan prison grab: soft boots and a form fitting uniform all composed of bright pink plastic sequins. I couldn't decide if the uniform was an incentive to break jail in order to find a decent set of clothes – or an incentive to stay put in order not to be seen in public.

There were other contrasts with Kaparland. At first glance, Unis seemed to be a Utopian dream world. Everyone seemed to be taller and healthier than the Kapars. People were pale from living underground but the contrast with the unhealthy Kapar complexions was striking.

Most astonishing of all, every man was a natural blonde and every woman was a redhead. Thinking back, I remembered Kiri and Derru commenting on hair color but I hadn't realized the significance at the time.

How this worked genetically I had no idea. When I asked about it, I got a lecture on history and eugenics. About

400 years ago, Unis had been a hereditary monarchy. Inbreeding among the royal and noble families had weakened both to the point where there weren't enough healthy children among the upper classes. The nation might continue but the aristocracy would not.

Ulandu, the last king of Unis and himself a physical grotesque, took drastic action to preserve his nation. He swept aside the remaining legal and social barriers to merit. He provided for the humane treatment of the handicapped and for the education of every citizen. And he instituted drastic eugenic laws to encourage healthy children and reverse the degeneration of the race.

The Unisans had never heard of the Greek ideal of a healthy mind in a healthy body but, for more than 15 generations, they had been working to make that ideal a reality. And judging from what I could see, they had succeeded.

Since I was a suspected lunatic, I spent most of my time taking (and retaking) a battery of tests administered by the prison psychiatrist. Many tests were Polodan versions of questionnaires used by Earthly headshrinkers; others were just weird. What difference did my five most favorite colors and flavors have to do with whether or not my head was screwed on tightly enough?

I had to take several tests over again for reasons my doctor refused to explain. I suspected that he didn't believe the first set of results and was trying to catch me either cheating or making stuff up. He shook his head a lot when he was scoring the answers. He didn't give me a reason for *that* either.

One time I spotted him studying me while I was making a list of English words and their Polodan equivalents. I was using my right hand to write with but I raised my left hand over the table edge like a sea serpent surfacing and waggled my fingers at him in a kids' club greeting. He *really* didn't like that. The next couple of times that I caught him spying on me, I pretended not to see him. That bothered him too for some reason. You just can't please some people....

WHEN I WASN'T contributing to the advancement of Polodan psychology and psychiatry, I talked to the other prisoners. After my experiences with Kapar penology, I was flabbergasted by the amount of free time that we had.

I asked Morga Sal about that. We were seated in a pink-walled recreation room with a hundred or more fellow inmates. Some guards walked around the room while others kept watch from a small room separated from us by transparent plastic. The atmosphere was like night and day compared to Kapar prisons. Most of the prisoners ignored the guards and played simple party games. Other prisoners, including Sal, read books from a surprisingly well-stocked library.

He shrugged. He seemed to take many things philosophically. "Most of us are here because the government suspects our loyalty but does not have sufficient evidence to convict us of treason. So we are locked up 'for the duration of The War' to keep us out of trouble."

He used an elbow to point to a youngish fellow playing the Polodan version of Twenty Questions with his buddies. "Soran Zan there is a good example. He joined the Fighting Corps at an early age in a fit of patriotism but could not stand military discipline. He got into a number of arguments with his superiors and here he is."

Sal sighed. "I think Zan is a good fellow but, like the rest of us, he does not wish to be hypnotized and reeducated into being a good citizen. Since we have not been convicted, we have the right to refuse treatment and here we sit."

At that moment, our attention was attracted to a guard walking up behind a tall, thin man seated at a writing desk and then snapping his fingers. The prisoner jumped in surprise and glowered at the apparition. The guard jerked his thumb at the guard station. The prisoner got up and walked slowly to the station followed by the jailer.

Sal volunteered, "Tunzo Pal there is an exception. He is a counterfeiter rather than a suspected slacker. But he is naturally resistant to hypnosis and therefore cannot be reeducated by conventional means. He was probably forging a certificate of release when the guard caught him."

Sal looked at me thoughtfully. "*You* are another exception. You are almost certainly here because Prison 116 has more advanced psychiatric facilities than the police station where you were captured."

"The prison psychiatrist doesn't seem to know what to make of me."

"You are an unusual case. Most professed aliens are lunatics with fantastic and easily disprovable stories about life on Antos or Rovos." He looked at me for a long minute. "You seem sane to me but I was a general studies student before I was imprisoned, not a psychiatrist." He smiled sadly.

"If I may ask a personal question, why are you here?" I probed gently.

Sal was silent for a long time. I was about to excuse myself and leave when he exhaled loudly. He had apparently come to some difficult decision. "I loved my sister."

"That's not a crime where I came from."

"Well, it is not the official reason why I am a prisoner in 116. My sister, Morga Sagra, was a traitor." I exhaled but didn't interrupt.

"We were orphaned at an early age by a Kapar bombing raid that killed our parents, brothers and sisters. We had no close relatives and Morga, who was several years older than I was, became both mother and father to me. Many Unisans have similar stories, similar burdens, and similar pains. In Sagra's case, our struggles to build a new life warped her. People told her that she had to be emotionally strong to survive and serve our nation. She took that advice too far. She became strong

"We were orphaned at an early age by a Kapar bombing raid that killed our parents, brothers and sisters..."

but lost her conscience along the way. She came to worship strength alone. Ultimately, she became a Kapar."

Sal paused and tears of sorrow filled his eyes. He looked down at his lap. He wiped his face and looked up again.

"We fought bitterly. We still loved each other as family but she no longer loved the people who had helped us survive and grow and thrive. She no longer loved Unis." He paused again.

"We had a final falling out when I volunteered for the Fighting Corps and failed the flying tests. She accused me of failing her. She.... We called each other terrible things. Terrible, horrible, hurtful things. I stormed out of her apartment and lived at school for almost a year. When I finally went back to beg forgiveness, she was gone. She had moved without leaving a forwarding address.

"Several years later, I was celebrating passing my college course in economics when the police came to ask about Sagra's friends and possible accomplices. I discovered that she had flown to Ergos with someone named Tangor — "

I started but Sal didn't notice. He was trying to escape from his own private hell.

"— and she had taken important military secrets with her. Ironically, she was killed in Ergos by a man named Gurrul. He thought she was a Unisan spy.

"At the time that the police questioned me about possible accomplices, I did not... I *could* not believe their statements. My anger had faded away and Morga was again the loving sister who sacrificed so much for me. So I screamed at the police – called *them* names – accused *them* of being traitors.... And here I am," he concluded.

"How long ago was that?"

"Seven or eight years."

"And you're still here? Because you don't want a psychiatrist to hypnotize you?"

"Yes. I... I do not want someone else to control my mind – even for the best of reasons."

"What if there was another way out of Prison 116?"

THE WARDEN'S secretary announced a guard to see him. He gave permission for the jailer to enter his office and placed the thick file that he had been reading on his desk. A few more entries and the file would be five pages long.

The guard marched into the room with his face carefully blank and thumped his chest in a military salute. The Warden asked what the issue was.

"Honorable sir, the prisoners have formed a Loyalty Committee. They request opportunities to prove their patriotism and loyalty to Unis."

The Warden glanced at the file he had just been reading and then at the guard. "Let me guess, the leader of this Committee is Tomas Ran."

The guard nodded.

Chapter 11   WELCOME TO UNIS

I WAS SHOVELING rocks into a hopper when my travel agent arrived. Unisans use giant iron moles to burrow through Poloda's crust, leaving nicely engineered tunnels and caverns in their wake. This particular one was connecting up the underground cities and prisons on the Island of Despair and, eventually, the mainland subterranean train and motorway networks.

The iron moles kiss the cavern wall with electrodes the size of automobile tires and a lightning flash sufficient to level Sodom and Gomorrah pulverizes the rock into gravel. Mechanical jaws catch most of the gravel and feed it into giant, flexible pipes. Somewhere down the road, the spoil is sifted for minerals. The remainder is ground up for fertilizer or dumped into the ocean. A hundred wheels rotate, the mole lurches forward, and the process begins again.

What the mechanical jaws don't catch, I shoveled up. It's always good to have a second career in case the first one doesn't work out.

Another loyalist swept the floor behind me. Kapars are subject to a constant iron discipline and are messy; Unisans are free men and women and are neat.

My guard signaled that he wanted to talk and held out an interphone plug. His hand stayed close to his sword hilt. I nodded and grounded my shovel. Then I plugged his cord into my helmet. Unisan prisoners on work details are issued full-

123

head helmets to protect their ears and eyes; another difference between the Polodan prison systems.

"Come with me, prisoner. A psychiatrist and a fighting man are going to interview you about your claim to come from planet Urtha."

"Yes, honorable guard. What are their names?"

"Harkas Yen and Harkas Tangor."

HARKAS YEN knocked on the door labeled "Prison Psychiatrist." A voice bid him enter, and he did. Two people were seated inside the office: a man behind the expected desk and a woman in a chair in front of it. To his surprise, Harkas recognized her as Sangor Maro, the national Commissioner for Foreign Affairs. She was a older woman with a slightly distracted expression. Her body language suggested a combination of stress and excitement. The man behind the desk was easily interpreted as the prison psychiatrist.

The two men greeted each other simultaneously, "Doctor." The prison psychiatrist gestured Harkas to a chair. The latter sat down and waited for his host to open the conversation.

The latter introduced his two guests to each other. Harkas politely reminded Sangor that they had met before when Tangor had arrived in the capital city of Orvis. She replied noncommittally.

The prison psychiatrist spoke up, "Doctor Harkas, you are Unis' leading expert on persons claiming to be from other planets." The latter smiled serenely and nodded. "How much do you know about Earthmen?"

"A good deal," replied Harkas confidently. "I have studied one at close range for several years. They are physically identical to Polodans and psychologically very similar to Unisans; more individualistic than typical Unisans but cultured and well-mannered."

"And very aggressive?" queried Sangor.

"Yes," confirmed Harkas, "but their aggressiveness is disciplined by character and channeled into socially useful directions much as Unisan aggressiveness is." She nodded in response.

"You base your conclusion on your observations of your son-in-law?"

"Yes," said Harkas carefully. "And, negatively, various lunatics claiming to be from Antos, Tonos and other planets. Since we have not established that 'Tomas Ran' is in fact an Earthman, Tangor is our entire sample of the Earthly population. I and others have always found him honest, forthright, modest, courteous, patriotic, efficient and effective." Sangor nodded again. Harkas asked "Is there a problem with this 'Tomas Ran'?"

The prison psychiatrist looked Harkas directly in the eye. "There may be. Your son-in-law's aggressiveness index is among the highest in the entire Unisan population but still within normal bounds. In contrast, Tomas Ran's aggressiveness is off the charts."

I WAS ESCORTED into a conference room near the Warden's office. Inside, two men, five chairs and a table waited for me. I sized them up and nodded politely. I greeted the elderly man in black spangles and white boots as "Honorable Harkas Yen." I pivoted slightly and greeted his younger partner in blue spangles and boots as "Honorable Harkas Tangor." Both of them looked surprised. The fighting man recovered first.

"How do you know our names?" he inquired.

"A guard mentioned your names and, as far as I know, there's only one person in Unis with black hair. That makes you Tangor the American from the planet Earth. By process of elimination, this gentleman must be Harkas Yen." Tangor glanced upward as if he was trying to see the hair on top of his head. The psychiatrist hid a smile.

"I'm very pleased to meet you. You're a famous man in southern Epris and Unis," I said sincerely......in American English. He frowned without speaking.

In the brief silence, questions flashed through my mind. Did he understand English? Had I caught a faker? I kept my facial expression as politely expressionless as possible.

"Don't tell my family.... My Earthly family. They regard fame as a character flaw." He grimaced, half humorously, half seriously, also in American English.

"I won't tell them," I promised seriously. "Where does your family live?"

"My Polodan family lives in Orvis." He introduced Harkas Yen as his father-in-law.

"Honorable Tomas Ran, I am pleased to meet you," greeted the psychiatrist also in English. He pronounced the English words properly but put them in Unisan grammatical order. His courteous salutation was, "Honorable Tomas Ran, you to meet pleased I am."

"I am pleased to meet you, sir," I replied in English. Then I switched to French. "Do either of you speak the language of Dumas and Voltaire?"

We lost Harkas Yen at that point but Tangor spoke excellent academic Parisian French. We played Tag through several languages. We both spoke German, Kapar and Unisan. He spoke Italian, Herisan and Aurisan while I spoke Latin, Portuguese and Russian; and Jabberwocky.

We switched back to English so that Harkas Yen could follow us and quizzed each other on Earthly geography, history and customs for a couple of hours. Like me, Tangor had taken a German bullet in the heart. Unlike me, he had been a fighter pilot scouting the German Rhineland in September 1939 when he had been jumped by three Messerschmitts. If he was faking being an Earthman, he fooled me.

Tangor was fascinated by the changes on Earth since he died, including Franklin Roosevelt running for a third term of office. He nodded his head sadly when I described how the Axis Powers had plunged Earth into the worldwide war that he had merely tasted. Harkas Yen nodded grimly as well. Both commented morosely that eternal warfare was humanity's natural state whether on Earth, Poloda or planets yet unknown.

I raised my eyebrow and said, "The story's not over."

I told them about the refusal of the Allied Nations to submit to tyranny and the great mobilization of industrial, military and, most importantly, spiritual power. I described the counteroffensives that had liberated North Africa, most of the Pacific, and much of Europe and Asia by the time that I had died in that Normandy apple orchard.

I told them of our nations' determination not to repeat the mistakes of World War I and to build a lasting peace. And, finally, I told them that General Eisenhower and Admiral Nimitz must surely have hung Adolf Hitler and Hideki Tojo by now as object lessons to the next ten generations of aspiring Pom Das. Finally I ran down.

Harkas Yen sat quietly, breathing evenly, his thoughts turned inward, grappling with some unexpected vision. Tangor's face was raised to the ceiling. I imagined that his mind's eye was fixed on distant Earth.

After a long time, Tangor came back from Earth. His breathing was ragged. His voice was strained but understandable. "There is no question about it, Yen," said Tangor.

"A countryman?" asked the psychiatrist.

"Yes, an American," Tangor replied.

"I am almost surprised," Harkas said. "Yet why should I be? You have crossed – there is no reason why others should not." Unis' leading expert on persons claiming to be from other planets looked directly at me. "Tomas Ran, welcome to Unis." He shook my hand American style.

I CHANGED INTO a suit of brown plastic sequins and boots, which signified that I was a citizen of Unis performing civilian service rather than a prisoner. My Zabo uniform and collection of guns and swords were boxed up and sent to Orvis.

I subsequently learned that *every single Unisan* is limited to owning three color-coded plastic uniforms during their entire adult lives. Unmarried boys wore yellow and unmarried girls wore gold. Male members of the Fighting Corps wore blue, members of the civilian service wore brown, and older men wore the black of retired service. Married women wore silver and widows wore purple. Public officials of either sex wore gray like my judge and critic had. There are some exceptions to the system but they are rare indeed.

When I first met Kiri, I had thought that her gold sequins and red boots meant that she was an entertainer — possibly a dancer. Boy, was I wrong! Like Clark Gable and Jimmy Stewart joining the US Army Air Force, Unis' professional entertainers had joined the war effort years ago. Loris Kiri, I later found out, had been a schoolteacher. I also discovered why there are no fat Unisans: there's plenty of food but you can't hide a spare tire in a form fitting plastic uniform.

Americans had made a lot of sacrifices to win World War II but if President Franklin Roosevelt had attempted to enact such a scheme, he would have been impeached and thrown out of office. If his clothes horse wife didn't kill him first.

MOST UNISAN CITIES are connected by underground roadways but the system didn't reach Despair. So, we took an airplane from 116's underground airport to one of Orvis'. It was my first airplane ride on the planet of airmen. I almost didn't go when I met our gold-sequined pilot. She had no arms.

The Harkases and two women dressed in official gray were waiting for me. None of them seemed to notice anything wrong but our pilot spotted my shock. She smiled as if the situation was the funniest joke on Poloda.

"I am Fontan Ianami, Flight Officer, Unisan Courier Service. Yes; I am one of Ulandu's Godchildren," she said cheerfully. She gestured at one shoulder with her head. "There are no nerve endings for surgeons to graft new arms onto and I have found that I do not need prosthetic limbs."

The older of the two women mumbled something that sounded like "So typical of so many young men and women."

I was still focused on our pilot. I swallowed and squeaked, "How do you fly an airplane?"

"With my feet." She elevated one foot and I saw that she was wearing sandals rather than the universal Polodan boots. "Come on; we have to launch soon or wait until the next lull in battle." She pointed the way into her courier plane with her leg.

Bemused, I climbed in after her. The Harkases and the women were already seated in the small passenger compartment. The four of them immediately launched into some deadly serious private discussion. I caught the phase "the fate of the planet" once. There were only four seats in the passenger compartment but Fontan chirped an invitation for me to ride with her. Since I was clearly not invited to the fate of the world discussion, I joined her.

She unsnapped her sandals with her toes and dropped the footwear into a map holder. Then she stood in the pilot's chair, buckled her tensioned seat belt with her toes and slid down into a sitting position.

I'd flown often enough on Earth and Polodan belt buckles were almost identical to American ones. But, somehow I suddenly felt clumsy compared to Fontan Ianami.

She continued the normal routine of a pre-flight check-list with only minimal concessions to her disability.

When a ground controller signaled, Fontan fed power into the engines and taxied into position at the foot of a ramp leading upward. A distant gleam of sunlight flashed down the ramp as the armored gates and trapdoor high overhead opened.

She pushed the planchette-type throttle forward and the courier plane leaped up the ramp and into the air.

The mottled greens of the Island of Despair receded beneath us. The trapdoor closed behind us and the opening disappeared as if it had never been there. Except for the bomb craters scattered across the landscape, Despair looked like an untouched jungle paradise.

We continued climbing for two or three miles before leveling off on a northeasterly course. Fontan remarked that we were high enough to fly through the Mountains of Loras but low enough for the war fleets to pass overhead. She seemed blithely unconcerned about the possibility of being attacked by Kapar blackwings but I noticed that she never stopped checking her instruments and her sky.

Courier planes have a cruising speed of about 500 miles per hour but my Polodan Beatrice opened our chariot up and we were soon making 600 miles per hour. Even so, we had a five-hour trip ahead of us.

I rubbernecked as we flew and talked. I asked about the other passengers and learned that the older woman was Unis' Commissioner of Foreign Affairs. That struck me as odd since there was only one other nation on the planet and Unis was at total war with them. However, I recalled that the US Government seldom abolished bureaus no matter how obsolete they were. When in Rome.... The Commissioner apparently was deeply interested in other planets including Earth. Well, I suppose that other planets are *foreign*....

Below us, Unis' Southern Islands were emeralds edged in gold dust and set in lapis lazuli. If any Florida real estate salesmen made it to Poloda, they would be hawking beachfront property on twenty planets (Omos' eleven and Sol's nine). Soon enough, we left the islands behind and sailed high over a great gulf indenting the southwestern flank of the continent. Omos glinted on cerulean waves highlighted by huge schools of leaping silver fish. But the seas were apparently empty of human life.

Eventually, we crossed the mainland shoreline, passing over creamy waves crashing onto ivory sands and then a bright green jungle belt. A dozen hues from bottle green to olive clothed the land. A few minutes after that, white clouds obscured the view.

"Look forward," suggested Fontan with a mischievous tone. I did.

Below us, the clouds still masked the land. But now they were torn and whipped by unseen winds. The cotton veils shredded, revealing glimpses of tan colored highlands flecked by grass greens and chartreuse tints. The subdued browns yielded to glittering snowcapped mountains, sharp peaks cutting the blue sky into aerial bays and fjords. Overhead arched the vault of heaven with the pale blue crescent of Tonos a ghostly lighthouse marking the way to Orvis.

"The Mountains of Loras," explained my pilot. "Not as impressive as the volcanoes on the east coast but higher. They are the southwestern ramparts of our fortress. There are many cities buried safely below those peaks."

She added softly, "For those who want to be safe."

In a moment, safety was the last thing on our minds. We were flying between sheer mountain walls when some malevolent angel slapped our wing *really* hard. The small airplane spun like a top in midair – far too close to a mountain wall to our right for acrobatics. I realized that the slam had been accompanied by a loud *blanging* noise following by bullets cracking through the air.

Tangor and I shouted, "Can I help?" simultaneously.

Fontan snapped, "Pray," and shoved the speed control forward. Still spinning, we accelerated away from the mountain's savage beauty. I heard distressed noises from the passenger compartment. Someone wanted to throw up but couldn't tell which way was up.

"Ran! Look behind us and above!" commanded Fontan. Her legs were nudging the plane into more or less level flight.

I remembered that leg muscles are more powerful than arm muscles.

There were mirrors on each side of the dashboard. I reported, "Lone Kapar aircraft above and to the left. Swinging to right to line up shot."

"Thank you," she murmured. Our chariot leveled out for a few seconds. Fontan threw us to the right. I paled. If she was any closer to the wall, she could drop our wheels and *drive* across this Mountain of Loras. Seconds later, a hail of machine gun bullets thundered by on our left side.

Fontan continued skimming the unyielding rocks. "Tell me when he swings again."

I didn't say anything until I could see the bat-wing lining up his next shot. "Swinging now."

Fontan yanked our plane violently, turning it ninety degrees to the left and then down. She poured on the remaining power. Someone lost something in the passenger compartment.

Another storm of bullets savaged the mountain wall as we sped away. A cloud of rock chips erupted from the mountain side. Diving to catch us, the Kapar scout flew into the rock storm. His engines convulsed and shook themselves apart. The mountain did not forgive his mistake.

Fontan serenely leveled off and dialed the power back. She straightened out on our original course through the mountain passes. She sighed. "I wish the Fighting Corps would arm our courier planes. We could defend ourselves better from these marauders if we had guns on board."

I was watching the woman-made firefall as the Kapar bat-wing smeared itself down the mountain. I took a breath. "Flight Officer Fontan, the only weapon this airplane needs is the one flying it."

She paused and grinned. "Why, you smooth talking devil, you...."

WE LEFT THE mountains behind and passed high over the central plains of Unis. A city of slender towers on a great river, both made toy-like by our altitude, sped past us. Ianami identified the city as Polan and the river as the Yalivis. Around the city and up and down the river valleys were neat plots of farmland, mostly lime, moss and pea green against the darker shades of the surrounding jungles and savannahs. Neat spaces interrupted by still more bomb craters. From our height, we could barely see tiny dots moving across the landscape. Members of the Labor Corps systematically erased the craters so that farmers and ranchers could feed a nation wholesome food.

Four hundred and fifty Polodan minutes into our flight, we sighted the Plateau of Orvis and its guardian wall of low mountains. Sky blue Unisan Fighting Corps fighter airplanes orbited the mountains constantly — an inner guard against Kapar infiltrators and invaders. Five of them flew over to inspect us. One edged close. Its pilot waved his hand and Ianami waved her leg in return. He flew away.

While I was recovering from that, I raised a suspicion. "He seems rather casual about possible sneak attackers. What if we were Kapars in disguise?"

Ianami snorted derisively. "The sound detectors would spot any Kapars this close to Orvis. Each plane has a signal modulator that changes our basic engine noise to the code of the day. If we did not sound the code, the air patrol and defense guns will shoot us down."

"Ah, what about radio communications?"

"They are not practical outside laboratories. We use the radio spectrum to broadcast power to aircraft and remote locations."

"I've seen Unisans use telephones or interphones."

"They only work on land or inside aircraft where they are insulated from the broadcasts." She pointed her foot toward what Earthlings would call a hand phone. "If you would like to talk to the Harkases—"

"No, thank you, I would rather talk with you." Ianami smiled and we continued chatting until we reached Orvis.

AFTER ANOTHER 40 Polodan minutes, Ianami headed the plane over and we began our descent into the capital of the fortress continent. At first there was nothing to see except more pea green and umber farmlands covering hundreds of square miles. No buildings, no railroads, no highways, and certainly no airports.

"Ah, where's Orvis?" I asked cautiously.

"Straight ahead of us," Ianami pointed to a corrugated green landscape in the near distance. "However, we are landing at Airport Orvis 21." She shifted her leg and pointed at an umber rectangle almost below us.

As we descended, the brownish rectangle split in two. The two halves rose to 45 degree angles and began withdrawing into the ground. In the rapidly enlarging black center, I could see landing strips. Any aircraft carrier in the US Navy could be docked in the artificial canyon with room to spare.

While I was staring at Airport Orvis 21, Ianami tapped me on the shoulder and pointed ahead. The city of Orvis was rising up out of the ground!

We were less than a mile from the corrugated ground. At this distance, it was a vast, beautifully cultivated parkland interrupted by mounds of dirt covered by trees and shrubs every hundred feet or so. As I watched, buildings rose up out of the earth, each one an architectural masterpiece. Most of them were slender towers but there were boxes, spheres and a dozen other shapes. As they rose, each building carried several hundred square feet of garden with it. When they stopped rising, each was capped with a miniature park of surpassing beauty. Doors opened in the lower floors and Unisans of both sexes stepped

"As I watched, buildings rose up out of the earth, each one an architectual masterpiece. Most of them were slender towers but there were boxes, spheres and a dozen other shapes

135

outside to enjoy fresh air and natural scents. All of them scanned the sky before venturing further.

Then we flashed into Airport Orvis 21 and screeched to a stop. Above us, the Emerald City of Poloda gleamed in the sunlight. We disembarked and mechanics towed the little plane into an armored bunker. A messenger was waiting for Commissioner Sangor. She and her aide hurried off. Tangor grinned at me.

"Well, Ran, what did you think of Princess Ianami?"

"'Princess'?" I asked, turning to look at the disappearing aircraft.

"Princess," he affirmed. "Of course, now it's only a courtesy title. King Ulandu abolished the political powers of the old aristocracy. But she is a descendant of the old royal family."

I whistled in admiration. Ianami was a princess in the truest sense of the word; a woman who served her nation without regard to birth or handicap. Unis was indeed a beautiful land. But the true beauty of the land was the courage and dedication of its people.

"Tangor, do Unisan men ask women for their telephone numbers?"

Chapter 12 THE MAN FROM NOTHING

HAVING THE Harkases as sponsors made fitting into Unisan life much easier than it would have been otherwise. Tangor had been drafted into the Labor Corps when he arrived and worked like a dog. I was placed in the hands of the military Bureau of Intelligence and the academic Bureau of Science and treated like a lab rat. After a couple of days of nonstop interviews about Earthly and Polodan League of Nations military and scientific capabilities, cleaning up after iron moles started to look good again.

After hours, I became a Unisan; more or less. Harkas Yen and his wife Juniri (Jun) lived in a house that rode its elevator shaft up and down each day. Other Harkases, including Tangor, his wife Yamoda and their children, lived nearby. When the sky was clear of Kapars, we enjoyed fresh air and natural sunshine or starlight. When the general alert sirens sounded, every building in Orvis dove like so many submarines, coming to rest at least 100 feet underground if not deeper.

I questioned the expense of moving buildings daily but Yen explained that Unisans had not given up on the idea that some day peace would come and they could live on the surface full time. He did admit that almost all of the current construction was at or below the 100 foot level. And electric power from Omos was both unlimited and almost free.

Unisans lived monastic lives with the majority of industrial production devoted to their war effort, their underground cities program, and their culture. Whether in bobbing buildings or permanently buried labyrinths, homes were spartan boxes with movable walls and inflatable furniture to create the illusion of space and property. When I stayed with Yen and Jun overnight, we moved their living room walls to create a guest bedroom. We attached some plastic blocks to the omnipresent air conditioning units and they inflated into a bed, chair and clothes rack. Attaching the same furniture to the exhaust ventilators restored them to their shoebox sizes.

The one element of seeming luxury within each home was the well-stocked library. The Kapars had burned thousands of years of "un-sentimental" Polodan culture. The Unisans dedicated resources to preserve the best of theirs. I read as much as I could.

Jun and Yamoda insisted that I get my head out of Yen's books and meet real people. We visited other homes where we chatted and played simple party games. Any American board game maker could make a mint on Poloda. We visited a zoo where I saw churors, kuikols and a hundred other strange Unisan animals that Kiri had mentioned. We toured a museum where caretakers diligently maintained the cuckoo clocks, stuffed animals, portraits, toys, board games, fashionable clothes, doodads, knickknacks and thingamabobs of pre-war Polodan civilization — "non-essential" things that no one had used in over 100 years.

One night we attended a production of one of Unis' favorite plays, *Five Daughters and a Crown*. "We" were nine Harkases, including five unmarried female cousins of Yamoda, and myself. Fortunately, there is safety in numbers.

The community theater players had no costumes, no scenery, no special effects, nothing but themselves and a small band, but they brought the comic court of legendary good King Orondo to sprightly life. The five princesses bemoaned and beguiled, their suitors wooed and competed, courtiers pontificated and gesticulated, the bombastic chamberlain strutted and stunned, everyone sang and danced, and the audience ate it up. When the pompous chamberlain appeared to announce the end of the play, the normally stoical Unisans drowned him out with the Polodan equivalent of "Encore! Encore!" The cast rescued him by returning to the stage and leading the audience in a joint chorus of the time-honored tribute to love and romance "Maidens Rejoice." After applauding the cast (and themselves) again, the audience finally began to disperse.

Tangor and I had a minute to ourselves as the other Harkases chatted and bid each other farewell. "Interesting," I mused.

"What's 'interesting'?" he asked.

"The Unisans' reaction to the play."

His brow furrowed. "What about it?"

I paused a moment and answered diplomatically, "I observe that Unisans are a very resolute and determined people but also a very sad people. They really came alive when they watched a play that showed folks solving a series of major, if comic, political problems rather than merely enduring the situation."

Tangor didn't seem to understand my point. "It's a comedy. Of course, people are going to laugh and sing. Did you expect them to cry?"

"Umm…. You've lived here for seven Polodan years. What's your impression of Unis?"

"I don't have to tell you that I like Unisans. Our courage and morale are magnificent. I like our form of government, too. It is simple and efficient and has developed a unified people with few criminals or traitors."

I nodded sagely. "But they have no hope of a better future." Just then, the general alert sirens sounded and the school where the play had been held plunged into the earth.

TANGOR WAS DEEPLY thoughtful the day after the play. Then, he disappeared for two days. When he returned, he rescued me from a discussion of the wonders of Earthly science — mostly cameras and movies — and escorted me to a secure conference room in the House of War. Despite its grim name, the House of War was an office building housing Unis' civilian and military leadership. The conference room's library was scientific, logistical and budgetary reports.

Commissioner Sangor and her aide joined us but didn't sit down. "Honorable Tomas, welcome to Unis. I can only give you a few minutes but I wanted to emphasize the importance of what you are about to hear. Millions of lives depend on this and once you hear Flight Officer Harkas' briefing, I am sure that you will support the Zondor Plan."

"Thank you, Honorable Commissioner. I hope to live up to your trust."

She nodded and left the room, trailing her aide like a comet's tail.

I wasn't sure what I was getting into and looked at Tangor expectantly.

He coughed and gestured for me to be seated. "I've been thinking about your comment that Unisans have no hope of a better future," he began. "And I have permission to reveal a top secret project to you and to ask for your comments. This project is classified as Glorious."

I nodded sagely. "Glorious" was apparently the equivalent of an American Top Secret rating. Tangor wore the sky blue uniform of a Unisan airman but I had noticed that he didn't seem to have any definite military duties. Now I learned why.

He had appeared in Orvis seven Polodan years ago. During those years, he had been a fighter pilot, a spy in Ergos, and a space explorer as well as a Labor Corpsman and de facto expert on the exotic planet Earth. Kaldur Ron and other special officers (scouts and spies) had been looking for Bhon and the Punosan resistance at Tangor's insistence.

I whistled in amazement when he modestly described pulling the wool over the Pom Da's eyes, stealing a power amplifier from the Kapar war machine, and escaping with his life. Using the power amplifier to propel their aircraft, Tangor and his crew had flown through Omos' atmosphere belt to the neighboring planet of Tonos. I listened spellbound as he described their adventures among the curious creatures of the atmosphere belt and planet, not to mention the madmen and monsters that ruled the ruins of a cruelly murdered civilization. After years of work, war, exploration and diplomacy, Tangor and the remains of his crew had returned to Unis in triumph.

The flight to Tonos had not been undertaken in a spirit of pure science but to find a new home for the war weary Unisans! Tangor explained that many Unisans, including Commissioner Sangor, were sick of the endless slaughter, the privations of war, and the grinding hopelessness of the future. The courage and resolution of Unis was being worn down into bitter despair. He mentioned in passing that the Fighting Corps averaged a million dead *per year*[*]. Rather than surrendering to the Kapars who showed no signs of abandoning the fight, a previous Eljanhai (chief executive) had proposed establishing a New Unis on Tonos and transporting the entire population of 130 million Unisans to that planet!

The books in this room were Tangor's scientific reports on Tonos and the detailed planning for the migration.

He summarized firmly, "Tonos is the better future that Unisans deserve."

I was silent for a long time absorbing the idea. I had read Jules Verne and other authors who had written about interplanetary exploration and colonization in Earth's solar system, but no one had ever proposed anything like this...!

And yet... how many millions of people had migrated to America...? I looked around the room at the planning documents and whistled again.

Tangor resumed. In a few days, the Janhai, or commission that ruled Unis, would make the final decision to migrate or not. Since the first Earthman to appear on Poloda was all

---

[*]   *The total dead for all American Armed Forces for all of World War II is estimated as 292,131. – Ed.*

in favor of the project, the project sponsors were interested in the opinion of the second.

My mouth lives a life of its own. "With all due respect to you and the Unisan leadership, I think it's a very bad idea."

He looked stunned but rallied. "Why?"

"You would be running away from tyranny rather than defeating it. When the Kapars see you running, they'll be encouraged to finish you off. They'll shoot you in the back as you run and then bomb your depleted rearguard into submission. Once the forlorn hope that you leave behind surrenders, the Pom Da will have control of Unis' resources as well as everyone else's. And, finally, running away to Tonos (or any other planet) won't do you any good because the Kapars will reinvent the power amplifier, follow you and conquer your resource-starved New Unis."

Tangor looked like someone had kicked his dog. He was quiet for a time, looking around the room. I speculated that he was mentally reviewing the massed reports – and their assumptions. Finally he spoke up.

"Unisans won't stand another hundred years of warfare. We can't go on and now we can't go away...." His voice dribbled off into nothingness. He looked at me like a drowning man searching for a lifeline. "Do you have an alternative idea?"

"Yes. Win The War."

A FEW DAYS AFTER THAT, there was another lull in the war. Tangor suggested a picnic on the surface and his family agreed. I cautiously invited Ianami and she cheerfully accepted.

We took a convoy of motorcars to a park on the outskirts of Orvis. Night was approaching and Poloda's evening stars, Antos, Rovos, Vanada and Sanada, looked down through the gathering twilight.

Campfires were not allowed because marauding Kapar aircraft might spot them but Ianami and a dozen Harkases had packed plenty of food in heat-trapping and cold-keeping containers. We ate and talked and played games. Everyone was fascinated by Ianami's version of Polodan Charades.

After nightfall, Tangor invited me to see something. We took flashlights with blue filters to guide ourselves without alerting Kapar night flyers and walked over a small hill. The sounds of the party quickly faded. The chirping and clicking of ten-legged insects filled our ears and strange scents filled our noses. We stopped. Tangor pointed upward. My eyes followed. I gasped in astonishment.

Overhead a hundred million stars twinkled, majestically gazing down on the planet of perpetual war. They formed a vast lens of jewels — mostly blazing diamonds but also sapphires, topazes, carnelians, garnets and rubies. Poloda's winter stars blazed against the black velvet of interstellar space but the grand galaxy overhead painted its portion of the sky with misty light. After a while, I remembered to breathe.

Sometime after that, Tangor clarified, "The Milky Way Galaxy. As seen from outside. Omos is a yellow dwarf star in a small spherical galaxy situated in the Hercules constellation*."

After another time, I choked out, "Where is Earth?"

He pointed to a blazing ball of brilliants relatively nearby, an interstellar island off the coast of the vast continent of light above us. "See that group of stars? Unisan astronomers call it Kanapa. Earthly astronomers call it Globular Star Cluster NGC 7006. Telescopes on Earth can see the cluster in the constellation Delphinus." He moved his hand a short distance to his left. "That's where the constellation Hercules is in Earth's sky.

"Earth is 450 thousand light-years in that direction," he announced. I sank to my knees, overcome by the vastness of the universe and the distance to home.

---

*   The Hercules Dwarf Galaxy was rediscovered in 2006 in the data from the Sloan Digital Sky Survey. – Ed.

"*I sank to my knees, overcome by the vastness of the universe and the distance to home.*"

Tangor stepped towards me, flashlight flickering over my kneeling body. "Ran, are you ill?" His voice was filled with concern.

I looked up at the cosmic vision. I whispered, "Have you tried to teleport home? To Earth?"

Tangor seemed surprised by my question. "No; never. Poloda is our home. We died, Ran. And now we live again. On Poloda. This is our home."

"And you've never even *tried* to communicate with Earth?" He looked up, focused on that part of the sky where our mother planet lay.

"When I first came to Poloda, I dreamed about Earth frequently. And sometimes it seemed as though I was talking to a man — an Earthman — named Ed. But most of my dreams were nightmares of alien sights and sounds. I asked Yen to hypnotize me and those dreams went away.

"I've often wondered whatever happened to Ed." He looked down at me, still kneeling on the moss-like grass of a planet 450 thousand light-years from Earth. He spoke gently.

"Poloda is our home, Ran."

I paused for a long minute as my thoughts whirled. Then, I took a deep breath of Polodan air. I inhaled the fresh clean scents of the Unisan countryside grass and grains, fragrant flowers, a dozen smells with no Earthly equivalents. My mind cleared.

I took a last look at the cosmic spectacle overhead. I stood up and looked at the first man from nothing. Tangor stepped backwards. His face was pale in the starlight.

"Yes, Poloda is our home," I acknowledged. "And therefore I must be a Polodan; and a Unisan. And we Unisans...." I paused.

My voice hardened. "And *we* Unisans *will* win The War and bring peace to *our* planet."

Chapter 13 PARLIAMENTARY
PROCEDURE IN ORVIS

A POLODAN MONTH after Tangor and Yen sprang me from jail, the time came to present our ideas to the Janhai of Unis. King Ulandu assumed that the end of his dynasty would be the beginning of a new one. So he had vested his royal authority in his Cabinet as a collective body, "until such time as a monarch worthy of the Unisan people can be found." And then he had died, so beloved by his subjects that no one could replace him. And so Ulandu's cabinet had evolved into the commission known as the Janhai.

The Janhai as a corporate body possesses the legislative, executive and judicial powers that the American Constitution divides among the Congress, President and Supreme Court, and more. It makes budgets and sets tax rates, appoints judges, provincial governors, high-ranking national military and civil officers, exercises oversight over them, and is the court of last resort. The governors appoint mayors of cities and provincial officers, and the mayors do the same for their cities.

In addition, the Janhai elects one member as the El-janhai, or High Commissioner, for a term of six years. He or she is the chief executive of the whole nation and is eligible for reelection although not consecutively.

We were escorted into the House of the Janhai building currently deep inside downtown Orvis. Lines of citizens filled the outer lobby with requests for action by the Janhai.

Once past the lobby, guards checked our credentials carefully and inspected us to ensure that we weren't carrying

146

any unauthorized motorcars in our pouches. Other guards checked us again outside the Janhai's conference room. We were ushered in exactly on time.

When my civics class visited the Massachusetts State House, I had seen more impressive *closets* than the meeting place of the most powerful people in Unis. Artificial sunshine illuminated unadorned pale blue walls, a heavy plastic table surrounded by 20 chairs, eight people, pens and notebooks. The commissioners were seated along one side, all dressed in the dignified gray of public service. In contrast, their purple-clad secretary, seated at one end of the table, was a peacock among crows.

The Eljanhai and Commissioner of the Interior, Chendin Dol, was seated in the middle of his side of the table rather than at the head. He greeted us courteously and directed us to chairs opposite him. Everyone said "For the honor and glory of Unis," in unison. Air conditioning whispered faintly in the background.

I was worried that parliamentary procedure in Orvis might be controlled by *The Rufus T. Firefly Rules of Order*. Instead, the commissioners stuck to the agenda and kept things moving. Our proposal was the third item.

The first item was a request from Sangor Maro to send a diplomatic message to the Kapars offering an honorable end of The War. The crusty Commissioner of War, Palden Zar, reminded her that Unis had made similar suggestions a hundred times over the years, always unsuccessfully. What good would a 101st offer accomplish? Sangor spoke passionately about not passing up any opportunity to end The War and to stop the waste of human lives. No one bothered to speak further against her motion and it carried by a listless voice vote.

The second item was the Zondor Plan to colonize Tonos. It had originally been introduced by the Commissioner of Commerce, Zondor Von, when he had been Eljanhai six years ago. Now that Tangor had returned, Zondor moved formal adoption of the plan. He agreed with Sangor that war was a terrible waste of lives and property. Since the Kapars refused to end the fighting, the solution was to leave them behind and transport all Unisans to Tonos.

Palden objected that abandoning the real Unis of their ancestors was tantamount to surrendering to the Pom Da. How did Zondor reconcile such abandonment with the honor and glory of Unis?

Commissioner of the Treasury Tondul Misema added that the project would cost immense amounts of money to build the airships to transport people and tools, and to establish new cities, farms and factories on Tonos. She maintained that the taxpayers couldn't finance a New Unis and the current Unis at the same time. The stone-faced Commissioner of Justice Montar Ban tersely agreed with Tondul and Palden.

As the debate continued, it looked like Zondor had a bare majority in favor of transportation. Sangor and he were passionate for the idea and Chendin and Commissioner of Education Denbol leaned in their direction. The others were solidly against the concept but they couldn't persuade a fourth vote.

Deadlocked, Zondor asked Tangor for his opinion as the explorer of Tonos and potential director of the transportation project.

Tangor took the bull by the horns. He spoke clearly and to the point. "Most honorable commissioners, when I first heard of this plan I was astonished; I considered it a heroic migration in search of peace unparalleled in human history. Now, however, I have changed my mind."

That statement exploded with the force of a hand grenade. The commissioners began arguing in surprise until the Eljanhai clapped his hands loudly. That was apparently the Unisan equivalent of pounding a gavel and produced immediate silence.

"What caused you to change your mind?" demanded Zondor harshly. Tangor had said that he was a statesman but clearly we had kicked his pet dog. The other commissioners watched the confrontation intently.

"Tomas Ran and I discussed the plan and realized that some issues had not been fully explored...."

Zondor focused on me, eyes blazing. The lobster that lived in my ear was back and making rude gestures to boot. He snapped, "I would think that an adventurer from another galaxy would support our exploring and colonizing our own solar system."

I didn't know if talking back to commissioners was allowed under Unisan parliamentary procedure, but, as I said before, my mouth leads a life of its own.

"Most honorable commissioners, I certainly support the exploration of the Omos solar system. I, too, would like to see the paradise of Uvala, to explore the ruins of Tonos, and to visit the Kingdom of the Beasts. However, your current plan will lead to the destruction of our current Unis and your proposed New Unis."

There was a stunned silence. Sangor turned as white as the proverbial ghost while Zondor's eyes widened in awe, Then, both faces narrowed in anger. Chendin watched me judiciously. I plunged on.

"The problem that this plan ignores is that the Kapars will not *allow* you to migrate to Tonos or...."

"*Allow*?" interrupted Zondor fiercely. "Do you think that we intend to ask for their *permission*?"

"No," I replied, "but you need to consider their response to your proposed movement." I went on, telling the Commission what I had previously said to Tangor.

"What!" Commissioner Palden exploded like one of his own bombs. His pale white face flashed beet red in fury. His body language tensed as if he was going to jump over the table and strangle me. "And just where do you think our airmen will be when the Kapars attack?"

"I'm sure that your airmen will fight as best they can, but there won't be enough of them."

"What!!" screamed Palden again. This time he did stand bolt upright although the table was still between him and me. "Explain your reasoning, young man, before I...." He coughed violently to regain control and directed, "Explain your reasoning."

"Sir. The proposed migration to Tonos will require vast resources to transport a population of 130 million citizens and then constructing the infrastructure of a new civilization. Where are these resources going to come from? The answer is that they must come out of your existing war effort.

"You will have to divert thousands of planes and millions of airmen and engineers to transport and house your colonists. Since the Kapars are *already* bombing your cities on a daily basis, reducing your defensive air fleet will allow *more* raids on your cities and other infrastructure as well as allowing them to shoot at your transport planes en route to Tonos. And reducing your offensive air fleet will allow the Kapars to build more planes for *their* offensive forces.

"In the meantime, diverting people and other resources to establishing a colony on Tonos means that those people and resources will not be available to maintain your cities, farms and factories in current Unis. Bomb damage won't be repaired or replaced and your infrastructure will break down, especially your farms. Starving people seldom make rational decisions.

"At some point, the bombed, starving citizens that you leave behind will surrender to spare themselves further misery. Your history books say that's how the Kapars conquered the other continents.

"And that's how they can conquer this one – if you give them the opening that they need."

By this time, six of the seven commissioners were on their feet, shouting, screaming, trying to get a word in edgewise.

The exception was Chendin. The man continued to watch the action like a judge.

Palden shouted "Be quiet!!!" in a parade ground roar. The others fell silent. "Sit down," he directed in an icy tone that approximated normality. He did and they did. He turned back to me and asked, "Are you finished?" His voice could have frozen the Talan Strait.

"No, sir. One more point. The Kapars are *already* thinking about expanding their empire to other planets. Even if you do establish a solid colony on Tonos with them shooting you in the back—" Palden, Montar and Sangor flinched, "—they'll simply follow you when they've digested Unis — if not sooner. Think of the misery that they've inflicted on Unis with eighty percent of Poloda's resources; now imagine what they'll do to your New Unis with one hundred percent of those resources."

I took a deep breath and concluded, "I therefore respectfully recommend that you postpone the migration plan until after The War."

There was a pregnant silence broken only by Sangor's harsh breathing. Clearly, *she* was impressed by the thought of an even more horrendous Kapar War spanning two or more planets.

"'Until after The War'," quoted Zondor in a hollow voice. "That is effectively forever." You could practically see his heart breaking.

"Not if you win The War," I responded. "Then your plan becomes perfectly feasible." There was another deafening silence.

Palden spoke up, his voice crisp and clear. "What do you mean 'win The War'? We have been fighting the Kapars for 108 years and we are no closer to victory than we were on the first day."

"Sir, you've been playing the Kapars' game. They bomb you; you bomb them; and repeat over and over. Both nations are too well protected for either air force to force a conclusion to the fighting. You've inflicted heavy damage on the people of Kapara but they don't make decisions for that empire. Until you can strike fear into the heart of the Pom Da, you'll never persuade them to stop. And so The War goes on and on without end.

"You need to cause the Pom Da to agree to your terms because the alternative is that Unisan forces will dig him out of his hole and arrest or kill him and anyone who counsels continued war. I respectfully recommend that Unis form a land army, insert it into Ergos and the other Kapar cities, and force them to surrender. They don't know how to fight on the ground and their airpower will be useless inside their own cities. If you train and use a land army, you can win The War."

Except for the Harkases and the secretary bent over her notebook, everyone in the room was a picture of puzzlement. Even very intelligent people have trouble dealing with concepts outside their experience. Finally, Palden broke the spell.

"And where do we get this land army, young man? You just finished saying that we cannot afford to build a space fleet. Logically, we cannot afford to create a land army."

Sangor and Tondul nodded their heads, the first vigorously, the second thoughtfully. Chendin continued to play the Sphinx of Poloda.

Tangor spoke up. "Sir, we can get them from several sources. First, ask for volunteers from our existing Fighting Corps. That will reduce our defensive and offensive efforts but not as much as the migration plan would, and our Fighting Corps will still be *fighting* the Kapars. Tomas Ran has suggested different weapons and tactics to keep the Kapars off balance.

"Second, we have a pool of people with fighting spirit but who can't fly for various reasons. That was true on Earth and it's bound to be true on Poloda. Those people will jump at the chance to whip the Pom Da.

"And third, call up our reserves. We've been fighting a *sustained* war for decades. I suggest that winning The War would be a good use for them."

I joined back in. "And, you can recruit a good number of people from your prison population in exchange for freedom…."

"Nonsense!" barked Montar. "Criminals belong in jail."

"Why?"

"Punishment," retorted Montar. "I will not have criminals running around the cities of Unis."

"They won't be running around Unis. They'll be under military discipline fighting in Epris for the honor and glory of Unis. Surely a willingness to die for Unis will prove their repentance and their loyalty." I looked at him with a sincere expression that I learned in business school.

Montar pursed his lips thoughtfully. "And if they die for the honor and glory of Unis, they are no longer a problem." A sardonic smile crossed his lower face without getting near his eyes. "Very well, gentlemen, you can ask for volunteers among the prison population."

"And if you cannot find enough men, I will find you a division or more of women." We all turned to look at the secretary, Vondol Varima, in surprise. Like the butler in classic murder mysteries, she had been invisible until she spoke up.

She put her pen down and explained in her clear voice, "Five years ago, Jan — my husband — and his crew crash landed near Hagar. They spotted Kapar fighters approaching and played dead." She paused slightly and continued, her voice still clear if not entirely steady, "The blackwings strafed the apparent corpses out of pure sadism. Jan's tail gunner survived. Jan did not. There are hundreds if not thousands of widows with similar stories. We will fight."

Sangor looked like someone had kicked her in the stomach. "We need to break this cycle of endless vengeance."

Varima looked the Commissioner of Foreign Affairs straight in the eye. "Yes, honorable commissioner. When you make the 101st offer of an honorable end to The War, please inform the Commission of the Kapar response. Our spies say that the Kapar Department of Education and Propaganda publishes our offers to convince their subjects that we are weak and on the verge of surrendering. If the Kapars end The War, I will apologize and withdraw my suggestion. Until then, the women of Unis will fight." Sangor flushed.

Varima paused and added, "I apologize for inserting myself into the Commission's debate." She bowed her head, not in resignation, but as a soldier returning to her duty. Her pen resumed its recording.

Palden answered her, "And I will be proud to lead *all* Unisans in battle." Varima blushed but said nothing more.

Sangor's tortured expression deepened. "You are speaking as if we are already committed to this lunatic strategy and Tomas Ran has been elected Commissioner of War!"

Palden sniffed loudly but Montar answered first. "Nonsense. We are debating a hypothetical strategy to end The War. You yourself said that peace is desirable. Since the Kapars are uninterested in a peace of equals, perhaps a victorious peace is our best strategy. Certainly, Tomas Ran has answered the obvious objections."

"Not all of them," demurred Tondul Misema quietly. "Honorable Tomas, your project sounds very expensive. Where will we get the money to pay for a land army?"

"Land armies are less expensive than air forces because their equipment is less expensive to manufacture."

She nodded thoughtfully. "Assuming that the Janhai approves your proposal." A hint of a smile relieved her stoic expression.

Denbol piped up, "Honorable Tomas, what are the weaknesses of your plan?"

Hmmm.... Polodan schoolteachers use some of the same debaters' techniques as Earthly professors do. Fortunately....

"Sir. The formation of a land army and a counteroffensive into Epris is not a panacea. It will demand great sacrifices from Unis in both blood and treasure. It will be expensive. It will strain your resources and infrastructure. And the fighting on and under the ground in Epris is likely to result in more casualties than your current air battles. According to your news reports, your Fighting Corps suffers an average of one million dead per year. I guesstimate two to three times as many casualties."

"Two to three million dead. Possibly four to five million," interpreted Palden.

"Yes, sir. But balanced against that is the fact that a land army in Ergos will force the Pom Da to make an end to The War on Unisan terms."

There was a long pause. The only sounds were the faint hum of the air conditioning and the scratching of Varima's pen. The room smelled of sweat and something else – something hard to define.

Palden looked at me. "And can you get a land army into Ergos?" Everyone looked at me.

"Yes, sir. There are a number of weaknesses in the Kapar empire, including the fact that they have no garrisons in Punos or eastern Allos. Your Bureau of Intelligence has my report. We can exploit these weaknesses to maximize our strength and minimize theirs. We start by...."

Palden cut me off with a forceful hand gesture. "I read your report. We will work out the details later and bring the proposed grand strategy to the Commission for approval." I nodded, followed by the Harkases.

He turned to the Eljanhai. "Most Honorable High Commissioner, I move that we return Commissioner Zondor's plan to the table and approve the Tomas Plan for development."

There was a moment of silence. Zondor whispered, "I second the move to table the migration plan."

Visibly shaken, Commissioner Sangor demanded that Palden's motion be split in two and Chendin agreed in his capacity as chairman. The Zondor Plan was returned to the table unanimously. Zondor seemed to sink into himself but he said nothing.

The Commissioner of Foreign Affairs then tried to filibuster against the plan to win The War but Chendin cut her off after a few Polodan minutes. There were more remarks and the Eljanhai called for a vote.

The plan carried 5-2, Sangor and Tondul dissenting. The nation of sleepwalkers had awakened.

Tondul Misema sighed and then spoke up. "Very well, if we are going to develop this strategy for possible execution, we will need to prepare a proposed budget. Zar, I need...."

Sangor interrupted, a look of horror on her face. "Misi, what is wrong with you? You just voted against this lunacy!"

Tondul looked at her colleague as if the lobster had transferred its residence. "Yes, Maro, but the commission adopted the Tomas Plan; the same way that we adopted your proposal to offer peace to the Kapars. It is now time for us to support the policy. I need your department to prepare...."

"Never!" screeched Sangor. She reached down and pulled her pouch into her lap. She fumbled for something....

The Harkases and I tensed up. Sangor's body language....

She brought a heavy pistol out of her pouch and drilled Chendin Dol between the eyes. The Sphinx of Poloda fell over backwards without a sound, as neat in death as he had been in life.

Sangor swung her gun towards Tondul Misema....

I threw my holdout knife, and nailed Sangor in the shoulder. Her arm spasmed upward. She got off one shot before the pain hit her. The bullet narrowly missed Tondul's

*"Sangor swung her gun towards Tondul Misema... I threw my holdout
knife, and nailed Sangor in the shoulder. Her arm spasmed upward."*

157

head. Say what you will about her grasp of parliamentary procedure, Sangor Maro had grit. She clenched her teeth and aimed again.

Her next targets, however, were Varima's notebook and Tangor's chair, both flying towards her face. The dum-dum bullets shredded the notebook and knocked the chair out of the air. It crashed onto the center of the table. Once again, the traitor took aim....

My *other* holdout knife appeared in her eye.

She leaned drunkenly over and collapsed onto the table. I heard her whisper "Five million deaths..." and then she went to Omys.

The door crashed open and guards poured into the room, guns drawn. Palden and Montar both shouted for them to stand at ease and they did.

Commissioner Montar looked at me as if I was a particularly ugly insect that might need squashing. "Honorable Tomas, you are a very dangerous person. Zar, I recommend you enlist him immediately so that he is under military discipline and in Epris as soon as possible."

"Good idea," agreed Palden. "Tomas Ran, I hereby draft you for military service and attach you to my office. Your first duty will be to advise Commissioner Montar on improved security. We will discuss the Tomas Plan later."

Montar shook his head. "No. You will advise my deputy as the Acting Commissioner of Justice. The assassination of our Eljanhai during a commission meeting is an unacceptable security breach. I accept full responsibility. I hereby resign my position. I will, of course, provide my successor with a full report and remain ready to serve Unis in whatever capacity the commission finds desirable." He saluted the Janhai.

Wow, a politician who accepts responsibility for failures in his department and resigns to clear the way for a (hopefully) better man or woman. If I didn't know that I wasn't on Earth before, I knew it now.

Tondul Misema became the new Eljanhai by acclamation and the meeting broke up. The Commissioner of War pointed at me. "Tomas Ran, you come with me."

"Yes, sir. By the way, sir, there is the matter of my rank in the Unisan Fighting Corps. I am already a Group Commander in the League of Nations Army." I kept my face as expressionless as possible.

Palden snorted "Very well, Group Commander. You are hereby enlisted in the Fighting Corps with the temporary rank of Division Commander. If your plans work out, we will consider possible promotion to the rank of Wing Commander."

I nodded my head in thanks. In Polodan militaries, division commanders are the equivalent of US Army major generals or lieutenant generals while wing commanders are the equivalent of "full" generals. The Harkases were my first volunteers.

BOOK THREE:
BY AIR, BY LAND, BY SEA

Chapter 14 MAD SCIENCE

I WASN'T PRESENT for many of the changes that followed the Janhai's decision but I learned about the important ones later.

"WHAT IN OMYS is *this*?" demanded the distinguished arms manufacturer. She looked at a series of blueprints that the government contracting officer had unrolled on her desk.

The contracting officer smiled, metal teeth flashing in the artificial sunlight 23 levels below ground. He'd heard variations on that exclamation before but never so often as in recent days.

"Ma'am, these are a series of new weapons for our fighting forces to use. This one —"he pointed to the uppermost document "—is called a 'ry-ful.' Essentially, it's a man portable gun that shoots bullets significantly further than pistols do."

The arms maker's forehead wrinkled. She turned to the next document. "And this is…?"

The contracting officer answered. "A 'gree-nayd.' A *greenayd* is a small bomb that a single man can carry and throw at an enemy."

The arms maker continued leafing through the stack of documents. She paused at one point. "I thought our fighting men already had swords." She pointed to a particular set of specifications.

The contracting officer looked at the blueprints. "That is a special type of short sword that attaches to the muzzle of the ry-fuls. It's called a 'bay-yo-net.'"

The arms maker finished her cursory review of the documents.

"And how many of these new weapons does the Fighting Corps need?"

"Ten million of each. As soon as possible consistent with quality production."

"Omys!!!" exclaimed the arms maker. She struggled to regain control. "Why?"

"That, ma'am, is classified. However, I can say that this production is Essential to The War Effort. If you accept the contracts, you will receive the required production priorities."

Stunned almost speechless, the arms manufacturer did remember to close the conversation with a courteous, "For the honor and glory of Unis." The contracting officer echoed her equally courteously.

"ATTENTION TO ORDERS! The Fifth Force Group is hereby formed and assigned the mission of special offensive operations against Kapara. The 20th, 21st, and 22nd fighting Forces are hereby formed and assigned to the Fifth Force Group."

A UNISAN SQUADRON commander entered his unit's briefing room deep below the Mountains of Loras. The assembled pilots and crews stopped talking and gave him their full attention. On the wall hung a hand drawn plastic poster. The center of the poster showed a handsome antique shield emblazoned with a crossed silver sword and golden lightning bolt. Above the shield was the official title "2016th Bomber Squadron." Below the shield was the very unofficial motto "Ergos Travel Association."

"Listen up, men. The first item on this morning's agenda is a special request from the Department of War." Ears perked up around the room.

"The Department has established a new Fifth Force Group for special offensive operations against the Kapars. They're looking for volunteers…."

"I volunteer Chan!" shouted a voice from the back of the room. The target of the alleged humor rolled his eyes towards the ceiling.

"Very funny. If we have any more comments…." The squadron commander looked around the room. Every face was a picture of innocence. "All candidates for the Fifth Force Group must be physically fit capable fighters. Pilot and parachute qualifications are desired but not required."

That set off a buzz of speculation. The commander heard one voice ask, "How is the Fifth Force Group supposed to attack Kapara without pilots?"

One mechanic stood up. "Yes, Chan?" asked the squadron leader.

"Honorable Commander, are mechanics eligible for transfer to this new Force Group?"

"Yes, they are."

"Then I volunteer." There was a brief round of applause and several squadron mates followed his example.

"ATTENTION TO ORDERS! The 22nd Force is hereby designated as a special operations and weapons force. Its mission…."

SOMEWHERE IN ORVIS, two men sat down at a table with a random book on it. Both of them briefly glanced at the title. If someone else entered the room, they would claim to be playing *kishkin* for an evening's entertainment.

One man tapped his ear and said, "First clue." A doctor might notice that he moved stiffly. If asked, he would truthfully say that he had suffered a war wound.

The other man shook his head and said, "An animal." He then pointed to the various corners of the room and covered his ears.

The first man nodded and asked "A churor? What news?"

The second man said "One wrong; guess again" aloud. Then he whispered, "The Blues are up to something but I can't tell what. A lot of military people are getting new assignments. But the Department of Justice cracked down after the Eljanhai and Commissioner were assassinated. Half my sources are being questioned in the House of Justice and the other half are afraid of their shadows."

"A new air offensive?" speculated the first man.

"Possibly. The new Eljanhai wants to show the workers how tough she is."

"I'll report that to Ergos. Anything else?"

"Nothing worth mentioning. More rumors about spacemen from Tonos landing in Orvis."

The first man snorted derisively. "Keep digging. We need to find out what the bluecoats are planning." The second man nodded.

"Don, where's my steel? We need beams and armor plating and we need them now. Section 45 is a huge cavern supported by temporary bracing. We need to start putting in the permanent supports and roof immediately." The voice on the interphone was all the introduction the speaker needed.

"Gar, I'm sorry. I haven't got any more. The supply chief says that we're not getting any more steel until next month. Somebody in Orvis took them for another project."

"Omys!" Gar cursed. "'Another project'? The underground cities program is supposed to have Honorable priority. Who outranks us?"

"I don't know," responded Don irritably. He'd already had the same frustrating conversation with the supply chief. "I suppose someone with a Glorious priority."

"'Glorious'!" Gar repeated, his voice rising in volume as he spoke into the interphone. "There's nothing 'Glorious' about leaving our citizens living in shallow holes on the surface! We need to get them down here where it's safe as soon as we can!! What am I supposed to tell them the next time the Kapars bomb their families?!!"

"It is war." Gar cursed vigorously but no new steel beams or plates materialized that month. Or for many months thereafter.

"YOU CAN'T *build* ships out of metal. They'll be too *heavy* to float. What's the *point* of building ships that will sink as soon as they leave the dry dock?" The industrialist's face was a picture of confusion. He looked alternately at the official messenger and the thick package of war orders and specifications that the latter had deposited on his desk.

"Sir, read the attached engineering report. Ships made of nickel-steel alloy will float."

The industrialist was not reassured. "I'll read it but I really don't see *how* a metal ship can float. Plastic, yes; metal, no." He shook his head. "And what's the *purpose* of a metal ship??"

The messenger pointed at the package. "Sir, read the mission statement in the contract."

The industrialist started to read the specifications. His eyes bulged. He put down the document. "And *where* are we going to get this amount of steel alloy?"

"Sir, read the production priority schedule. You'll get your steel. This is a Victorious Level War Essential Project."

The industrialist frowned. "'*Victorious*'? There isn't any such classification. '*Glorious*' is as high as the priority system goes."

"It is war!"

"Sir, there is a Victorious priority level now and warships are part of it. Before you go any further, please read the security instructions."

The industrialist looked at the indicated document and read it quickly. His eyes bulged again. The messenger waited patiently until the shipbuilder signed and returned the security agreement.

"ATTENTION TO ORDERS! The 1098th, 1099th, and 1100th Bomber Squadrons are assigned to the 20th Force of the Fifth Force Group for special offensive operations. The 1101st, 1102nd and 1103rd Bomber Squadrons are assigned to the 21st Force for re-equipping and special training in support of special offensive operations."

"BUT WHAT WE really want are these devices. They're called 'bih-nok-ku-lers.' They need to be made to these specifications so that individual soldiers can carry them...."

THE FACTORY MANAGER waited until break time to speak to Vornan Tomada. Officially, the white-haired widow was just one of the girls running Polan Parachutes' weaving machines. Unofficially...? She was the heart and soul of the firm....

The women's jobs didn't seem glamorous but many air crews owed their lives to the workers of Polan Parachutes and the quality of their work. At the moment, most of those women were enjoying cups of *oomm*, a mild stimulant similar to Earthly chocolate. During the break, maintenance girls serviced their machines.

"Most Honorable Manager, how may I help you?" inquired Tomada with old-fashioned courtesy. Her gracious manners set the tone for the entire factory. The fact that she was twice her manager's age lessened the respect she showed not one bit.

"Most Honorable Vornan," began her manager. She paused and started again. "Tomi, we have a difficult request from the War Department." She paused again. "They would like us to double our production."

The normally unflappable Tomada gasped in surprise. She controlled her breathing as she thought. The manager respected her employee's brain.

Finally, Tomada said, "The only way would be to draft more girls out of the school system. We can squeeze a ten or twenty percent increase by using overtime but production of that magnitude…." Her voice trailed away. "That is the only answer that I can see."

"And what about the young women who miss out on their education? We have long said that a stupid Unisan is a dead Unisan."

"It is war," stated Tomada simply.

The manager sighed. "It is war," she echoed. Her voice was brittle with suppressed emotion. Tomada patted the younger woman's hand in reassurance. They shared a cup of oomm before returning to work.

"PRISONER TUNZO PAL reporting to the Warden."

The Warden looked over the tall thin man with delicate fingers and suspicious face standing before him, almost dapper in prison pink. He indicated a chair in front of his desk and then a competent looking man to his side. "Please be seated, Tunzo. This man is an agent of the Department of Justice. He is here to offer you a commutation of your sentence."

Tunzo murmured, "Honor and glory," in lieu of cursing. He seated himself and then looked directly at the Justice agent in his official red spangles and black boots. "Who do I have to kill to win release?" His face radiated cynicism.

"The government doesn't want you to *kill* anyone," responded the agent primly. "However, if you agree to counterfeit documents *for* the government instead of *against* the government, we have a place for you in the war effort. And an early release from prison."

Tunzo's suspicious face flashed instantly into a bright smile. "Honor and glory," he said with sudden patriotism.

A GRAY-SHIRTED Kapar airman cautiously raised the trapdoor covering a particular spy hole leading down to the city of Murrs in northern Epris. The fresh air and breeze felt good but he looked carefully at the surface landscape before opening the trap fully. The sound detectors had reported that the bluecoats were headed back to Unis. Still, it never hurt to be careful....

Suddenly the world went black! Something sticky and clinging slapped onto his face, blotting out his vision and hearing. Startled, he lurched backward, losing his grip on the ladder to the surface. Fortunately for him, his fall was broken as he landed atop another airman. Cursing vigorously, the gray shirts untangled themselves and sat still for a minute trying to catch their breaths.

The first airman pawed his own face. A single sheet of plastic peeled off in his hands. Furiously, he studied the offending sheet, trying to understand why it had attacked him.

He saw two pictures side by side. The first showed two Kapar airmen sitting on benches sharing a typical meal of hard bread, slices of meat, a vegetable, and a flask of beer. A caption read "Comrades in arms share the rewards of a generous nation...." The second caption continued, ".... while Unisans survive on scraps."

The first airman bent over the second picture gawping in disbelief. It showed a Unisan family of ten gathered around a table loaded with enough food to feed twice as many Kapars. Hot food.... Abundant food.... Wine.... Sweets...! All being served and eaten by smiling, attractive women and fit, handsome men. One couple was *kissing!* The first airman couldn't remember the last time that he had seen a Kapar woman *smile...!*

And the clinging plastic garments that Unisans wore made their beauty very, very clear....

"What is it?" growled the second airman.

"Nothing," replied the first as he balled up the sheet and threw it on the floor for some black-shirted slave to pick up. "Just propaganda." He apologized for the fall and the two airmen returned to their duties.

But the first Kapar continued to think about the contrasting pictures as he worked. When the next meal break came, his rations didn't seem as generous as they had been yesterday. Nor did his fellow airman seem as comradely.

The disgruntled gray shirt vented his frustration on his section's black-shirted servant, accusing the latter of stealing food from the fighting men of Kapara.... The second airman tried to stop his comrade's ranting.... Guns were pulled....

"YOUNG MAN, I have been building airplanes since before you were born! This, this thing, this 'gly-dur' doesn't have any engines! How can it possibly get into the air? And what would you do with it if you could get it airborne?"

"YOU CANNOT make a bomb that big! And even if you could make it, you cannot fit it through a bomber's bomb bay doors!"

"Most honorable manufacturer, you make the bombs and the Fighting Corps will get them to the targets."

The All Clear sounded throughout the Kapar city of Umars in southern Ithris. Troops of black-shirted prisoners were assembled, equipped with tools, and force-marched to the surface. Red-shirted engineers and green-shirted guards accompanied them.

The damage was surprisingly light. Rumors had spread through the medium-sized city that the sound detectors had spotted thousands of bluecoat bombers en route to Umars. But only a few hundred tons of bombs had battered the landscape

— an extraordinarily mild punishment. The craters would be easy to fill and repair.

What was odd about the landscape was the thousands upon thousands of pieces of thin plastic littering it, blowing about in the breeze, catching in the few remaining bushes.... A red-shirted engineer picked up a batch and glanced at it irritably. He was about to order a slave to take the mess to a recycling bin when he realized what he was looking at. Food coupons! Tens if not hundreds of them!

Given a choice between a thousand extra food coupons and a ton of pure gold, the engineer would have instantly taken the former. Frantically, he began gathering up the precious documents and stuffing them into his coverall. Other Kapars noticed his behavior, looked more closely at the innocent seeming plastic, and followed suit.

Riots broke out that evening when thousands of workers *and* cops armed with armfuls of extra coupons mobbed the food distribution points and warehouses. Shelves, bins and boxes emptied in less than an hour. Kapars waving coupons besieged hapless clerks demanding their *rights*! Shoving and shouting turned into fistfights; fights turned into battles as green shirts without coupons struggled to regain control; battles turned into an insurrection.

The Police High Command in Ergos clamped a news blackout on the flaming city and poured in three divisions of shock troops. The city was back under control within a month. But Umars' petrochemical factories — including the food factories that fed all of southern Ithris — were out of the war effort for at least a year and thousands of citizens were out permanently.

Across the ocean in Orvis, Tunzo Pal officially changed his garb from prisoner's pink to citizen's brown. Printing presses ran night and day, readying the next attack on the Kapar economy.

"ATTENTION TO ORDERS! The 119th Intelligence Wing is hereby transferred to the 22nd Force of the Fifth Force Group. The Wing's mission...."

AN OFFICIAL MESSENGER entered a modest wine shop on the upper levels of the university city of Siron and asked after a customer. The waitress pointed him out. The messenger stepped over to a table where an elderly man wearing the black spangles and white boots of retired service was reading a book. A cup of wine sat on the table in front of him.

"Professor Nangan Don?"

The customer looked up. "Yes, young man?"

The messenger handed him a folded page of plastic. "Most honorable professor, you are recalled to active military service by order of the Commissioner of War."

The professor made a disbelieving face. He carefully placed his book on the table and enunciated his thoughts. "Young man, you must be joking. I'm retired. I served twenty years in the Fighting Corps and forty years making and install- ing air conditioning equipment. I'm an instructor of history now."

"Yes, most honorable professor. That's exactly why the Commissioner recalled you to duty. The new Fifth Force Group needs your expertise."

"HEY, ANG. We have orders to double our output."

"What for?"

"I don't know. No one ever tells me anything. It is war."

"It is war," sighed Ang.

THE SKY BLUE UNISAN spotter plane eased down- ward, spiraling around a tower of fire-shot black smoke rising from the savaged landscape of the colonial continent of Heris.

At the foot of the pillar of smoke gaped a vast crater freshly blasted into the ground. Flickering lights below announced explosions, fires, electrical arcs — the death knells of a city — made small by distance.

The pilot and third gunner only glimpsed the devastation intermittently. The former was flying the plane through the violent updrafts generated by the burning city while the latter was scanning the sky for enemy planes.

As the plane circled, two intelligence officers searched the new crater with binoculars. "Uvala!" one exclaimed. "The new bombs and tactics really worked! How many planes did we put against this one target?"

"Fifty thousand bombers and twenty-five thousand fighters," replied his partner.

"Did any Kapars get away?"

"Not many. I estimate less than four hundred fighters. Our pilots had a relatively free hand for a change. 'Quantity has a quality all its own,'" the partner quoted.

"The giant bombs really peeled off the city roof and smashed up everything inside." Both intelligence officers stared into the cauldron, their professional detachment shaken by the magnitude of the destruction.

"Looks that way."

The pilot cut in. "Sorry to interrupt, men, but bad guys are coming in from the southwest. Let's call it a day." The plane began a rapid turn and climb. The intelligence officers continued to observe the results of the fifty thousand plane raid as long as they could.

"What's the name of this city again?"

"Sathis. It used to be called Sathis."

SOMEWHERE IN ORVIS, two game players convened for another evening's entertainment. After the preliminaries, the first man said, "Our theory about a new air offense was right. Ergos was pleased by the report."

The second man smiled thinly.

"YES. You'll have to work his job in addition to yours. It is war."

"ATTENTION TO ORDERS! Special maneuvers will be conducted in the West Central Military Region on the following dates...."

"Company Commander Morga."

"Honorable sir?" The new paratrooper officer came to attention facing his squadron commander.

"At ease, Morga. Are your men ready for the exercise?"

"Yes, sir. We will drop on both sides of the Yalivis River, form up and advance towards the 'enemy' city of Tuldros. When we reach Phase Line Ila, we halt and transfer to Training Area Lantor to practice assaulting a city. If the control officers give the Red Signal, we halt and dig in because real Kapars will be overhead."

"Very good, Morga. We jump tomorrow at dawn. Have your men ready. For the honor and glory of Unis."

"For the honor and glory of Unis." Company Commander Morga thumped his chest in salute and briskly departed the squadron commander's office.

As he left, Morga quietly added, "And for our own honor and glory as well."

TWO YEARS RUSHED BY. The War entered its one hundred and tenth year.

THE BRIEFING in the House of the Janhai's new conference room concluded. All eyes turned to the Eljanhai. She breathed deeply and spoke. "Go."

Chapter 15 THE OVERLORD OF POLODA

GODLIKE, War Leader Marran Kun surveyed the conflict as it raged across Poloda. Marran was seated comfortably in the command balcony overlooking a gigantic map of the entire planet. That map was meticulously painted on the floor of a huge cavern in the heart of Kapar Military High Command operational headquarters deep beneath Ergos.

Color coded symbols depicted the locations of Kapar and Unisan cities, bases, factories, food farms, solar farms, motorways, pipelines, all the infrastructure of modern military civilization. Plastic markers showed the current locations of the great air fleets. The walls of the ballroom-sized cavern were covered with more maps, charts, and graphs, all displaying the thousand and one details of a world at war. From his vantage point, Marran could see the war as a whole or drill down on any detail.

Below the command balcony, staff officers received reports, consolidated, analyzed, and passed the flood of information to their superiors. Conversations were quiet but hundreds of voices in a confined space created a muted background roar. Gray clad soldiers, selected for their manual dexterity as well as their loyalty, walked carefully on the map itself, moving markers, placing and replacing note cards, and keeping the map up to date.

Every airman in the Unisan Fighting Corps would have given his life to study the master map and then report his findings to Orvis.

Marran surveyed the great map as his operations briefer droned on and on about yesterday's actions. An estimated hundred thousand bluecoat bombers had hammered targets across Heris while an equal number of fighters dueled with Kapar defenders. For some reason, the Unisans had been pounding Heris ruthlessly while skimping on other targets. Well, he'd reallocated the central reserve fighters to counter their new "avalanche" tactics and that seemed to be working. And "skimping on other targets" was only relative. Twenty thousand bluecoats had ravaged Auris and as many as a hundred thousand were en route back to Unis after repeatedly violating Epris yesterday. Initial casualty reports were grim.

It wasn't all one-sided, though. Fifty thousand Kapars were conducting a fighting retreat across the northern Karagan Ocean after punishing northwestern and central Unis. A fast advance scout plane had reported that the enemy university city of Siron was in flames. *Kapar power had taught those professors a lesson!*

The operations officer concluded his report with two enemy raids on Punos. "Why Punos?" mused Marran aloud. "Since Niros was destroyed, there's nothing there worth bombing."

"Most High, we believe that the Unisans are using Punos as a training ground much as we do," responded the officer. "Our defending forces there are weak precisely because there's nothing worth defending. So their new air crews gain experience with comparatively little risk."

Marran looked over the balcony railing at the map. It was just now midnight in Ergos but dawn in central Punos. Sound detection stations indicated two light raids, only about one thousand bombers and accompanying fighters each. One raid was aimed at the ruins of Niros while the second was headed towards the Hallas Mountains.

"You are probably ri…." Marran broke off abruptly. There was a flurry of activity on the map. Technicians were placing bluecoat air fleet indicators on the southern Karagan Ocean due east of Kapara where none had been earlier.

The War Leader directed, "Find out what that activity is." The operations officer made a fist in salute and ran down the balcony stair to the main floor. More and more air fleet markers were appearing over the Karagan.

And the southern Wudan Ocean as well! Unisan air fleets were passing over southern Heris en route to Kapara from the other side of the planet! Reports were sketchy due to the previous destruction of Herisan sound detection posts and other infrastructure. What in Omys was going on?! Marran leaned forward. Down on the map floor, one senior technician was shouting for more boxes of markers to be brought out.

HOURS LATER, things were clearer. And deadlier. Much, much deadlier.

The Unisans had put their *entire air fleet* into the skies! A twenty thousand plane raid was *nothing* to what was happening on his watch!! A *million* bluecoat airplanes were blackening the skies over the Eastern Hemisphere!!! And half of them were converging on Kapara itself! As gigantic as the attacks on Heris and Auris were, they were merely *diversions*!! The true target was Ergos, the heart of Kapara!!!

Marran shuddered at the thought of the bluecoats' new super bombs smashing into the roof of the capital city. Some of the uppermost levels were unarmored limestone caves. *And he had sent the entire central reserve to fight off the diversionary raids on Heris…!*

He turned to a control officer with ice in his throat. "Sound the general alarm, Kapar. Then call the palace. I will speak with the Pom Da personally. I think that the bluecoats are coming to destroy the Pom Da and the capital."

The controller worked his machine. A sequence of red lights came on. In the city above the command center, sirens wailed. Bone-tired airmen threw water in their faces and staggered back to their hangars. Air defense artillery section leaders kicked their exhausted men awake and drove them back to their guns. The petty Unisan raids on Punos were forgotten.

THE BLUE-SUITED jumpmaster stuck his head into the paratroopers' compartment and shouted, "Five minutes to the drop zone!" over the throbbing propellers.

Company Commander Morga Sal nodded. He clapped his hands and waved to his men. The company Uvalan finished his prayer in a rush, words jumbling together. Everyone stood clumsily in place. Each man checked his own gear and then the gear of his jumping partner.

Morga shuffled into position on the lip of the drop tube that had replaced the conventional bomb hatch. Morga looked up, seeing his men with new eyes. He smiled. It was a shadow wolf's grin, a paratrooper's grin, a grin to make the Pom Da shake in his boots.

The jumpmasters prepared to open the top of the tube. Morga shouted over the engine noise, "For the honor and glory of Unis!"

"Honor and glory!" came the loud chorus.

"And our own," whispered their leader.

His second sentence was inaudible over the propeller noise, but his fellow soldiers — his brothers — knew what the slight movement of his lips meant. They echoed him, "And our own."

He settled into the upper portion of the tube, hands holding his body in place, ready to slide down and out. The men knew their jobs. The senior section commander shuffled forward, ready to follow Morga. The others began working their way forward.

The assistant jumpmaster cranked the exterior hatch open. Air roared into the troop compartment, buffeting the men. They'd practiced this action tens of times over various parts of Unis. No one fell prematurely.

The jumpmaster was watching a clock. After an eternity, he sliced his hand into his chest in salute and whipped his arm forward, pointing to Morga. "Go!"

Morga Sal pushed himself into the tube. He slid down and out of the troop carrier into the air of Poloda's Southern Hemisphere. Over the years, many Unisans had parachuted into Punos – none voluntarily. Until now. Above him, his transport aircraft diminished as he fell towards the captive continent.

Above plane and parachutist alike, the sky rippled with thousands of flakes of blue. A thousand powered airplanes and two thousand gliders marched across Punos' sky in perfect ranks and columns. On the western side of the armada fighters hunted for prey. But they would be disappointed this day; the Kapars who might have ravaged the defenseless transports were in Heris.

Sal counted seconds. For a tenth of a minute, he was alone. Despite his concentration on his task, he briefly savored the sensation of flying without an airplane. He shook himself and focused on his mission.

His senior section commander's body emerged from the tube. And behind him came the first section of the Second Chancers....

Sal was no longer alone. His brothers were with him. *Ergos is there!* He pulled his ripcord to slow his descent. Below him, he saw the Valley of the Path of the Sun, its gray-brown walls glinting in the morning sun. The whitened mountain tops rose past him.

The sky blue parachute caught the air. He jerked violently as his body abruptly slowed its fall. But he'd practiced tens of times over Unis. He shook himself again and watched the ground rise to meet him. Morga Sal descended into the valley of death.

He pulled firmly on the risers, controlling his fall. He wanted to land near the Path of the Sun but not on its concrete surface. The air was still – breathless – waiting....

The ground rushed upward. Company Commander Morga Sal's boots crashed into the soil of Epris. His knees flexed; he rolled to absorb the shock of landing. He forced himself upright, hands busy unstrapping his rifle.

He rotated, quickly but carefully, surveying the Eprisan landscape. Dawn illuminated the off white lanes of the Path of the Sun stretching east and west through the Valley. Beyond the concrete strips, the varied greens of a temperate forest swayed in the breeze. Above him, the morning air was full of descending parachutes. Higher up, the armada of planes and gliders continued their relentless advance. Each left a cargo of men as it passed overhead. Morga slashed himself free of his parachute cords with his sword and began trotting up a small hill cut in half by the Path.

At the peak of the hill, he stabbed his sword into the ground and slung his rifle. Hands temporarily freed, he seized a flag tube from his back. He ripped it open. Brightly colored signal flags fluttered to the ground. He selected a long thin rod wrapped in blue and gold cloth. He whipped it through the air. The rod extended from two to ten feet in length. A twist and the new length locked in. He whipped it back and forth to free the cloth. He speared one end into the hill. The golden sun and blue field of Unis snapped in the breeze of the once conquered continent.

"For the honor and glory of Unis," he breathed. "And for our own." A tear rolled down his face.

Around him, thousands of blue clad parachutists landing in the historic Valley. As he watched, Unisans cut their way free of plastic cords and began gathering into sections. Shouted commands and colorful signal flags began imposing order on the chaos of war. Overhead, the armada had disappeared into the brilliant blue sky.

The nearest unit was commanded by a senior platoon commander who greeted Morga Sal with a touch of relief. He saluted despite their training not to salute in the field. He sang in Unisan, "Most honorable company commander, we have been unable to locate the squadron commander. You appear to be the senior commander on the field. Do you have orders for us?"

Morga sighed quietly and replied, "Yes, honorable platoon commander, you will act as my chief of staff for the time being. Find two fully staffed platoons. Send one to each end of the Valley where they will establish defensive positions as soon as possible. Take another platoon and send scouts out in all directions to locate stragglers and guide them here. Continue to assemble our men. We will leave a small force behind as a local garrison but we will begin moving our forces to the west end of the Valley in one hour. Stragglers will just have to catch up. Get started." The newly minted chief of staff acknowledged his orders and began executing them.

Automatically, Morga scanned the sky. "Unisans, get off the Path."

A sky blue transport plane was descending towards the Path — and them. High in the morning air other flecks of blue were orbiting the Valley, awaiting their turn to approach. Morga could see a dot swinging into position behind the leader. Paratroopers sprinted clear of the makeshift runway.

The first giant transport plane lowered itself gracefully onto the concrete pavement. A sodden thump announced touchdown. Brakes gripped the giant plastic tires with a double squealing sound. The plane slowed to a stop....

Not soon enough. The front tires rolled over the edge of an ancient bomb crater and fell to earth with a thunderous boom. The plane's rear elevated, and came to rest pointing drunkenly at the sky.

Bawling orders, Morga raced to the stricken aircraft followed by a gaggle of bluecoats. As they reached the giant plane, its rear cargo hatch cranked open a few feet, hanging open ten feet or more above the concrete. A round Unisan head poked out. Alert eyes and a worried expression surveyed the situation.

Morga arrived under the hatch and shouted a request for information.

The head answered offhandedly, "Technical Officer Rondor Chan reporting, most honorable sir. Would you please get your honorable self out from under my airplane so I can open the hatch, sir?"

Morga and his followers complied. They could see Rondor speaking forcefully into the airplane's interphone. An electric whine came from within the unseen cargo bay. Rondor shouted something to someone. Slowly, the great aircraft tilted backward. Its rear lowered, its nose raised.

Rondor shouted into the interphone again. The rear hatch dropped, hammering the concrete.

The bluecoats on the ground could see a section of 10 Unisans wedged into the rear of the cargo bay, their weight helping to swing the aircraft into a more normal altitude. At Rondor's command, two tractors drove onto the cargo ramp formed by the lowered hatch. Crewmen attached cables to the small machines. They drove off the ramp, straining to pull the airplane backward.

As the bemused paratroopers watched, ungainly vehicles appeared from the cargo bay, driving up the sloping interior and then down the ramp. They looked a great deal like cars but with metal sheets forming a second skin. Aircraft cannon snouts poked out of the windshield area. As the weight shifted, the cargo plane came to rest in a horizontal position.

Technical Officer Rondor bounded from his perch and raced over to Morga. He saluted and shouted, "Sir, I respectfully ask that you loan me two sections of paratroopers. I need to get the plane unloaded so we can move it to a better spot and get that hole filled in." He paused. "And, sir, what is that doing here?" He pointed to the east.

Morga swung around to see a courier plane just landing on the Path. It screeched to a stop almost under the huge transport. The door thumped open. Out bounded....

"Uvala! Wing Commander Tomas Ran! What are you doing here?"

I smiled. It's always good when the troops are alert.

"Commanding the land invasion, Morga. Walk with me." I headed to the nearest clump of trees. He shouted for the closest platoon to assist Rondor and then followed me. He reported as we moved. Varima and three bluecoated staff officers caught up with us. She was already taking notes on her writing tablet.

The courier taxied past Rondor's cargo plane, accelerated and got the Omys out of Dodge. Behind it, the second of thousands of transports touched down on the other side of the Path.

Morga's acting chief of staff ran up to us and saluted. I reminded him not to do that in the field. It tells the enemy who the officers are and therefore who to shoot first. Including acting chiefs of staff.

"Pardon me, sir. But we have not seen any Kapars. Where in Omys are they?"

"In Kapara, platoon commander." I looked toward the western gap in the Hallas Mountains. "Where thousands of Unisan airmen are keeping them off our backs." I looked back at the kid. "So, let's not waste time chatting. So, let's get the men together and moving. We have an appointment in Ergos."

The kid grinned and nodded.

"APPROACHING ERGOS, Wing Commander."

"Thank you, Ianami."

Tangor was seated in the co-pilot's seat of a fast scout/pursuit plane with the armless angel beside him. The early morning darkness masked the tattered greens and browns of the savaged countryside two miles below them.

Ahead of the small plane, the dawning sun illuminated a sky filling with masses of gnats. Swarms of black-winged fighters were rising from hidden airports. They funneled upward climbing for altitude, aiming themselves at the streams of bombers and escorts high in the sky. The streams whose engine noises were drowning out the whisper of Tangor's command plane.

"Our fighters are diving on the defenders." The after cockpit was occupied by two spotters armed with telescopes. The plane's guns were fully loaded but the ship relied on stealth today rather than firepower.

High above the Pom Da's capital city, fierce firefights were breaking out. Both sides tried to maintain their fighting formations but combat was dissolving into thousands of individual dogfights. Tiny lights twinkled and merged into an eerily beautiful aurora of fire. Individually, the gunshots were invisible at this distance but when thousands of planes were trying to murder each other....

Once, Tangor had been a combat pilot. His place had been *there*, high above the city, fighting and killing to protect the sky blue bombers. The blood red memory of combat rose within him. Duty combined with something more primitive. Sternly, he repressed his own thoughts. Today, his duty was to be a commander. His hands caressed the light signaler, essentially a powerful flashlight, with which he could order men to die for the honor and glory of Unis....

The corpses of men and machines began raining down. Puffs of flame-shot brown, made small by distance, sprouted from the ground.

"Approaching the crater," reported Ianami.

Tangor turned his attention from the grand dogfight to the ground. Ergos had once been a city of a hundred square miles. A century of bombing had torn a hole thirty miles wide and perhaps a mile deep in the soil. He had been *there* as well. In Ergos. He repressed memories of fears and horrors.

"Beginning orbit." Ianami swung the plane into a sweeping circle around the target, a distance chosen as carefully as possible to maximize viewing while minimizing danger.

"Kill ratio analysis?"

His second spotter replied. "Estimated six or seven to one. Airplane sally rate estimated at one every twenty seconds." Unisan airplanes sallied at one every three seconds. Exhausted pilots flew slowly and fought poorly.

Tangor signaled "Press home." Hopefully no Kapar would realize why a light was blinking far below them. And if one did? Ianami jinked the aircraft to avoid a falling blackwing.

"Bomber stream overhead."

Tangor turned his own telescope upward. His trained eye sorted out the masses of gnats. High, high above, swarms of Unisan heavy bombers converged over Ergos. It was an intricate ballet. Lacking radio communication, Polodans depended on scheduling and the judgement of their flying officers to coordinate attacks. Very tiny dots broke away from the bombers. Unisan fighters scattered from the path of the falling packages of death. The Kapar counterparts tried to climb further into Poloda's thinning atmosphere. Some attempted to destroy the bombs in midair. Most attempted to attack the bombers as they donated death to Ergos. More sky blue fighters escorting the bombers dove on the blackwings. Airplanes rained from the sky like leaves blown by a gale.

The crater that had once been the city of Ergos buckled and heaved. Explosions wracked the land, crash after crash after crash. Thousands of tons of conventional bombs smashed into the roof of the city. Dust obscured the target.

Suddenly, the ground convulsed and disappeared. Dirt was sucked downward into a gigantic hole. An earthquake ripple shook the land. Fire continued to rain down.

"City roof collapse," announced the first spotter. "As you predicted, sir."

Tangor's face was taut. "We just smashed open the caves that formed the upper levels of the city." *And killed an unknown number of prisoners who were housed in concentration camps there. Including many Unisan airmen who had survived previous raids.* He breathed, "It is war."

"Air defense gunports opening." The first spotter's voice was coolly professional. He had never been a prisoner in those cavern camps. He had never known those men personally. He merely reported what he saw: the opening of a hundred or more armored turrets, the unmasking of a hundred or more giant cannons.

One Unisan bomber fell from heaven close to the command plane. Tangor saw the insignia of the 2016th Bomber Squadron as it passed. The plane was a mass of flames but the pilot still had some control. He steered across the sky and slammed into an air defense turret. A volcano erupted; the fragments of the giant gunbarrel somersaulted gracefully and crashed to earth a mile from its origin.

"For the honor and glory of Unis," breathed Ianami.

"Light bombers approaching," announced the first spotter.

"Good timing," commented Tangor. "Ianami." He signaled commands upward. Sky blue fighters began scattering again. Freed of their loads, bombers radiated outward. They lingered high, high above Ergos and machine gunned any Kapar who escaped their escorts and approached the "unarmed" warplanes.

"Moving outward," she responded, a beatific smile brightening her face. The plane swung away from the target city.

The air defense cannon began belching fire and death. Giant shells climbed into the sky, straining to reach the bombers' altitude. Most would explode into clouds of shrapnel; others would strew wire nets and other traps across the upper air.

As they fired, light bombers and their escorts appeared an average of three miles above the quaking ground. They, too, were masked by the sounds of the colossal firefight far above them. The surface was still dark but the gun flashes signaled both the location and timing of the targets. The blackwing fighters were out of position high overhead. The bluecoats dove and blasted until more fireballs signaled the end of Ergos' air defense gunnery.

Tangor signaled, and most of the escorts turned upward to savage the belated Kapar response. The light bombers also had machine guns. They formed a perimeter and hosed pests moving in either direction.

Subsquent waves of light bombers attacked the giant trapdoors protecting the Kapar airports.

Tangor sipped some oomm and offered some to Ianami. She scarcely noticed. Her eyes glittered as she watched the unfolding destruction. But her airplane danced lightly away from falling debris.

"Super heavy bombers approaching," observed the emotionless spotter.

Tangor returned his gaze to the sky. With Kapar aircraft raining down on their homeland like an angry thunderstorm, the so called super heavies came in at medium altitudes. They began long glides towards the tortured crater. The "super heavy" name was misleading. The airplanes were almost identical to other bluecoated heavy bombers. But, they towed gliders packed with explosives. Gracefully moving through a sky almost cleared of enemies, the super bombs glided in on their target.

"Super bombs now impacting in the crater. Massive explosions sighted. Secondary explosions sighted."

Tangor watched the ground ripple and jerk. His emotions were under control again. He stated, "We just smashed open their weapons stories. The military airports and other installations are destroyed. Their surviving airplanes have nowhere to land. At least not here."

More bombs glided home.

"Flashes of light smiliar to lightning sighted in the crater. Further ground collapses observed. Visibility decreasing due to rising dust clouds."

"We are smashing into the red shirt sectors of the city. The flashes of light are almost certainly electrical arcing."

"Fires sighted...."

"...food factories being destroyed...."

"Waterspout sighted in the crater!" The previously emotionless spotter's voice shook at the vision of fountains splashing through the thick clouds.

"...plumbing and waterworks breakdown."

"Sir, should we continue?"

"Continue until nightfall or until we run out of bombs."

MARRAN KUN was white with emotion – a mixture of rage and fear. He gazed at the great master map as technicians struggled to compile a coherent picture.

One thing was clear. The heart of the Kapar empire had been savaged as it never had been before.

The bluecoat fighters had attacked the exhausted black-winged defenders with unholy glee. Marran had long known that the Unisans were more skillful opponents than Kapar propaganda gave them credit for. Now, the proof lay before him in constantly mounting casualty lists. The defending air fleet had been slashed, maimed, disemboweled....

And behind the enemy fighters, the bombers and their super bombs.... Fragmentary reports spoke of entire levels blasted open to the sky and then collapsing into other levels. Many military facilities — necessarily located close to the surface — were out of communication. Normally docile red shirt engineers screamed insults into telephone mouthpieces when his officers demanded more information.

There was massive rioting going on in the middle levels as survivors fought their way downward. Marran had heard fragmentary reports that almost an entire wing of police — more than 100,000 green shirts — were battling to regain control of the panicking red shirts. Battling — and not succeeding...!

Worst of all, there *might not be* safety in the lower levels! There was an ominous coating of dust on the great map and the men and machines of command within the vast cavern. The command center was one of the most safely buried installations in the entire empire. Dust sifting downward might signal a collapsing roof, breaking air and water pipes, electrical failures, perhaps many other possible disasters...!

Teams of engineers were inspecting the operations center and the multiple layers of armor above it now. So far, they had nothing constructive to report....

Unconsciously, he glanced at the floor of the great cavern, his mind's eye seeing the Pom Da's palace below. He shuddered.

The telephone connecting the palace to Marran Kun buzzed its demanding tone. Its attention light went directly to red. The War Leader's shaking hand reached out to pick it up.

NOT ALL THE bluecoats were en route back to Unis. There were a handful of markers on Punos. In the chaos gripping the command center, no one paid them any attention.

THE VOICE OF THE Polan Parachutes factory manager interrupted her workers. "Honorable workers, your attention, please. Eljanhai Tondul Misema will speak to the nation about the War. Please turn off your machines and give her your full attention." Puzzled, they did so.

There was a burst of static as the manager connected the factory's speaker system to the nationwide telephone network. Eyes focused on the principal loudspeaker. Some functionary in Orvis introduced the Eljanhai and the latter's solemn voice filled the factory.

"Most Honorable Unisans, I am speaking to you today to announce a new development in the course of The War – potentially the most important development in the one hundred and ten years that we have been at war.

"At noon Unisan time, our Fighting Corps launched a massive invasion of the conquered country of Punos on the continent of Epris." The Eljanhai paused.

Tomada's sudden intake of breath was startlingly loud in the near silence. Eyes filled with questions turned towards her but her own face was rigidly focused on the loudspeaker from which the Eljanhai's voice emanated. The chief executive resumed.

"The purposes of this invasion are to liberate Punos — which has been our ally since the beginning of the Kapar War — to gain a military foothold on the conquered continent of Epris and to force a successful conclusion to The War. We have great hopes of success.

"In addition to the usual methods whereby we have prosecuted The War to date, we have employed revolutionary new weapons and tactics. Operating in necessary secrecy, we have created new land and sea fighting forces. Our gallant soldiers landed in Punos by parachute —"

Other voices in the factory gasped. Several faces turned to look at their parachute spinners as if those machines had suddenly started singing "Maidens Rejoice."

"— and ocean-going vessels. Our conventional and unconventional forces are now engaged in a great battle over Punos to consolidate our foothold and to defeat the Kapar counterattack. Other air forces are engaged in spoiling attacks against Kapara and the other conquered nations.

"I wish to caution each and every Unisan against over-confidence. Great battles in the air *and on the land* lie ahead. Much will be demanded of our fighting forces and of us, the citizens of Unis. We have already sacrificed much in our fight for freedom. Now I must ask you — each of you — to give our nation and our gallant fighters one final unit of support, one final push for freedom, and one final effort to win this terrible war and to win peace for our planet."

There were more words but Tomada heard none of them. She was crying. Four generations had passed since Unisan women had permitted themselves to cry in public. Tomada did not *care*. She was *too happy* to care.

Her fellow factory workers – *her girls!* – crowded around her, asking a hundred questions. "Tomi, are you ill?" "I don't understand!" "Tomi, what does this mean?"

The dignified, always calm, always supportive Vornan Tomada choked back her tears. She snuffled. "It means peace, girls, real peace. At least a possibility of peace that we haven't had since my grandmother's day."

That quieted them. And puzzled them. One girl-woman stepped forward. "Tomi, I don't understand. *What is 'peace'?*"

Tomada looked into the innocent face. She smiled a crooked smile. "Dear one, you don't know...! You've known only war all your life and all your mother's life and all your grandmother's life.... Even I don't remember a time without guns and bombs and hiding in the ground whenever an airplane's shadow passes. But my grandmother told me of the days before The War.

"Dear one, 'peace' is freedom and life and joy. It means no more fighting and killing and dying. It means that men don't have to slaughter each other and women don't have to grieve. It means our children will *live* instead of dying. It means that we can live in the sunlight and starlight *all the time* instead of crouching in caves and tunnels forever and ever.

"It means…. It means…Peace means we can love again."

The girl-woman broke down, her own tears flowing. A dam broke. A river of tears flowed. An entire shift of machine operators and maintenance girls was helpless with joy.

The factory manager came to see why the machines were quiet and joined her girls in tears of happiness. After a time, someone asked "When? When will this happen?"

Tomada shook herself. Steel crept into her voice. "After we have defeated the Kapars. Come on, girls, one last push; the job's not over yet. Back to work. Our men need our parachutes now more than ever."

Tomada turned back to her parachute-weaving machine. Her eyes were glistening with tears but her hands worked steadily through the night and the next day and the next night before she collapsed.

Chapter 16   SURRENDER OR DIE

WAR LEADER Marran Kun stood like a statue on the command balcony of the Kapar war room in front of his own chair. Today, however, he would not sit in his chair. It was occupied by the Pom Da, the supreme leader of the entire Kapar empire, who was staring at Marran Kun as if he were half a worm found in a garan that the dictator had just bitten into.

The War Leader reminded himself that raw hatred was the Pom Da's normal expression. The thought did little to reassure him. Sweat glinted on his forehead.

Around him, the work of the operations center continued. The War had not stopped.... Indeed, its already brutal pace had accelerated. Therefore neither could its direction. But the normal sounds of the center were even more muted than before. Marran barely avoided choking on the stench of fear.

The command balcony was crowded this evening. Not only was the normal military night staff present and standing at rigid attention but the Pom Da had brought twenty of his elite Zabo bodyguards. The latter's guns were still in their holsters but gold encrusted, green-sleeved hands hovered in readiness. Ironically, the gray-shirted military officers had no personal weapons with them. Guns had been thought unnecessary inside the supreme operations center.

After staring at his War Leader for an eternity, the dictator snapped, "So you are Marran Kun, the traitor?"

"With respect, Highest Most High, I am no traitor."

"Then explain to me why you allowed the Unisan *ikhurrs* to destroy half of Ergos! The capital city of Kapara!! *My* city, Marran Kun!!!"

"Most High, the Kapar air force fought as hard as possible. We estimate that we shot down 100,000 bluecoat aircraft of all types. We drove…."

"At the cost of more than twice as many of *our* airplanes! Possibly more!! The casualty reports are still mounting!!!" screamed the Pom Da. "All because you sent the central reserve force to Heris!!!"

"Most High, Heris seemed to be the focus of the bluecoat offensive. I thought it necessary to defend the food factories and rare earth mines…."

"You understand nothing, Marran Kun! You are nothing! No!! You are less than nothing!! You have failed me for the last time!!!"

The Pom Da drew his heavy machine pistol and fired a burst into the chest of the erstwhile War Leader. Marran Kun's body crumpled up and fell backwards. It toppled over the command balcony's railing and disappeared. There was a sodden thumping sound from the lower level.

The Pom Da raised himself from the command chair and walked over to the railing. He looked over. His left hand gripped the railing possessively. His right hand still held his pistol.

Marran Kun's broken body lay on the portion of the great map representing southernmost Epris. The force of the impact had scattered tens of markers and cards. A red lake was coloring the floor.

Technicians buzzed uncertainly around the body. Some stared at the new corpse. Others looked up. When they saw the Pom Da's venomous face staring down at them, they paled.

One senior technician shouted, "Back to work, Kapars! The Most High Pom Da has acted for the Kapar nation!"

Marran Kun's broken body lay on the portion of the great map representing southernmost Epris. The force of the impact had scattered tens of markers and cards. A red lake was coloring the floor.

194

The Pom Da frowned at the sight below him. "What are those?" he growled as he pointed.

There was a brief pause before operations officer Terro Garr cautiously stepped forward and looked. The Pom Da was pointing at a scattering of blue aircraft markers in Punos and eastern Allos. The thickest concentrations were in the Hallas Mountains, at the former site of Fortress Niros, and along the northern coast facing Unis. Other blue spots dotted the entire region.

"Highest Most High, those represent a series of Unisan raids on our eastern colonies."

The Pom Da looked over the remainder of the map. "Terro," he snarled. "All of the other Unisans have fled back to Unis. Why are some attacking our colonies when everyone else has gone home?"

The operations officer quickly read the map. The Pom Da was correct. In the aftermath of the apocalyptic raids, the skies over the Kapar empire were now almost completely clear of the enemy. The bluecoats were streaming home. No doubt they were congratulating themselves on a *superlative* day's work, he thought bitterly. But a small force of several thousand aircraft was still doing *something* over Punos and Allos.

"Most High, I believe that these are Unisan training raids. Alternatively, they may be more diversionary raids intended to distract us from the repair and reconstitution of our forces."

The Pom Da's ugly face furrowed. "You may be right. Chase them off anyway. I do not wish any Unisans in our skies. Now or at any time in the future."

Terro gulped. He spoke delicately, "Most High, our airmen are very tired. May I suggest…."

The Pom Da turned toward the officer. His scowl deepened. He interrupted the suggestion. "Kapar, I have already executed one traitor today. Are there more traitors on your staff?" He pulled his gun into a ready position. His bodyguards stirred expectantly.

"No, Highest Most High! I obey! Every man in this room has the true Kapar spirit!" Terro's face was as white as a cloud but he held himself erect and made a fist in the Kapar salute.

"Very good. You are promoted to the rank of War Leader and will assume command of the Operations Center Night Staff immediately. Prepare an offensive to eliminate the Unisans over Allos and Punos. Immediately!"

The newly promoted officer saluted again. The tyrant made a dismissive gesture that the gray shirts pretended was military courtesy.

The Pom Da snapped, "Back to the palace" at his bodyguard. He and they started to go. The assembled gray shirts carefully made fists in salute. Suddenly, the dictator stopped and turned. He regarded his new War Leader once again. The latter saluted yet again. Every military heart seemed to skip a beat.

"One more thing, Terro Garr."

"Most High?"

"That technician who cleaned up Marran Kun's mess. Give him a promotion. No, give him two promotions. He is the only one in this headquarters who knows what he is doing."

TERRO GARR immediately ordered all of the surviving aircraft on the continent of Epris to investigate the bluecoat activity over Allos and Punos. That done, he moved the central reserve back to Kapara to reestablish the capital defenses. Then, he asked his new operations officer what the Eprisans had found. No one knew. The investigation force was never heard from again. It was only when the garrison of the colonial city of Kurrus began screaming for help that the situation began to clear up.

Even then, it didn't make any sense.

IN CENTRAL ALLOS, a gray-shirted Kapar airman carefully raised a trapdoor covering a spy hole leading down to the city of Jorros. The bombing had stopped but the sound detectors reported hundreds of bluecoat aircraft overhead. Someone had to kick the shadow wolf to see if it was really dead and he had been chosen.

As he was lifting the trapdoor, it was suddenly jerked away from him. Two blue-clad ogres seized him by the arms and yanked him upward. A third slapped a hand over his mouth and threatened him with a sword. A very sharp sword.

"Surrender or die, Kapar. If you surrender, blink." The singsong voice's command of the Kapar language was less than perfect but the sword point in front of his eyes corrected the grammar wonderfully. The captive airman blinked. Rapidly.

Blue-clad hands relieved him of his weapons and telephone. They lifted him out of his hole and swiftly gagged and bound him. Within a surprisingly short time, he was on his way to a prisoner of war camp hidden in the forests of Allos.

With him out of the way, I gestured. One soldier handed me the Kapar telephone. Another soldier looked down the hole and jumped in. He was followed by others. I spoke into the telephone, reporting the post number thoughtfully written on the hole's walls and "All clear. The sound detectors must be mistaken." I listened like a good little Kapar and said "Yes, Most High" several times before hanging up. The advantages of an education at the Sellon Sura School of Manners.

Silent signals sent more troops down the hole. Other signals brought a line of soldiers and motor vehicles out of the woods. The machines were blue and so were the uniforms of most of the soldiers. But not all. A handful of men wore red plastic and brown boots and another handful wore grey spangles and black boots. Vollor's Sword had returned to Allos. And the True Men of Zurris had come with them. I waved Gillan Alle and Honnol Jannam forward.

The ground split open along a rectangle a hundred feet long in its shorter dimension. The gigantic hatch of a subterranean runway cranked open. Another paratrooper gestured forcefully. Machines and men ran forward to the lip of the expanding opening and peered downward. The hatch clanged to a stop. The underground airfield was ready to spit warplanes into the sky. A bluecoat peering down the tunnel shouted orders and flapped his arms frantically. The armored cars rolled over the lip and braked to a halt. They fired downward in unison.

There was a second – or an eternity – of silence followed by a shattering thunderclap. Flame spewed forth like one of eastern Unis' active volcanoes. Pieces of black-winged aircraft shot out of the tunnel and crashed down on the already battered countryside.

More explosions rocked the landscape as engineers blasted open other trapdoors. Allied soldiers dropped grenades into the revealed holes and stepped back. Vicious thuds sounded. Unisans, Allosans and Zurrisans launched themselves into the underworld.

We raced onward and downward. Most Kapar cities were built to the same, centralized plan. We had trained hard. We were prepared for war in the underworld. Uvala! I was proud of these men.

Kapars understood green shirts waving guns in their faces. But they had no idea that a Unisan or free Allosan or Zurrisan might appear out of nowhere and do the same. When blue, red or gray devils burst upon them, they froze in fear. Paralyzed, and conditioned by a century of obedience to be sheep, they quickly submitted to orders barked in accented Kapar. Even hardened airmen and police thugs were caught off guard by an invasion completely inconceivable in modern history.

Some gray shirts and green shirts did have the opportunity, the will and the guns to resist. They took a toll. But most were mowed down where they stood. Unisan plastic resisted bullets and flying grenade fragments far better than Kapar cloth did. Rifles reached further than pistols. Cannon mounted in trapped airplanes did their former owners no good at all.

Most importantly, we had spent two years training for this day. My guys ducked, they dodged, they took cover while Kapar thugs unthinkingly stood in place — easy targets for the veterans of two devastated countries and a hundred bombed cities.

Soon, long lines of numbed Kapars of all shirt colors were marching into central spaces. The assembled Kapars heard their returned countrymen explaining the ideals of ancient Allos and the new alliance, the ability of allied technology to feed and house thousands in civilized style, and a temporary military government. Led by Gillan, the speakers punctuated their words with their swords. While there was only one Sword of Vollor, each flashing blade, each rousing speech, stirred long-suppressed emotions. Here and there in the crowds, stunned but thoughtful Kapars listened. And remembered that they were Allosans.

A RUNNER REPORTED. "Sir, Tenth Squadron has captured the central train station. They say that we can ride into the bottom of Kurrus and other cities like gentlemen and catch the Kapars there off guard."

I smiled. I must have looked like a hungry shark. "Good idea but wait until we have enough people on hand to hold the cities."

REPORTS REACHING THE Kapar Military High Command funneled into the operations center. There they jammed up as the airmen struggled to understand the unprecedented situation. Those with the true Kapar spirit were arrogantly ignorant of millennia of history and therefore of even the concept of land warfare. The finest military minds on the eastern half of the planet simply froze up – unable to comprehend what they were hearing.

Aerial scouts from northern Epris attempted to reconnoiter the battlefields but reported little. The long war had produced generations of Polodans skilled at hiding in even the most inhospitable terrain. The lush forests and rugged mountains of Allos were a natural terrain to the guerrillas, whose camouflaged snipers made short work of any overly enthusiastic Kapar scouts. The surviving scouts kept their distance, and the quality of reports flowing into the High Command deteriorated.

And the air above the concealing land was rapidly becoming even more inhospitable to the Kapar air force. The airmen of Unis were back and fiercer than ever.

They scented blood.

KAPAR FIGHTER SQUADRON F964 took off from Umars and climbed swiftly to cruising altitude. High overhead, black-winged defenders dueled with sky blue aggressors. The corpses of men and machines rained down on the battered landscape like overripe apples. The aircraft of F964 swung east, out over the tropical Karagan Ocean.

The squadron leader's interphone buzzed. He had expected a question and answered it readily. "Most High Squadron Leader, I respectfully ask why we are headed to the east rather than to the southeast where the fighting is," queried his belly gunner.

"A good question, Kapar. The bluecoats will expect us to attack them from their northwest as our other squadrons are. Instead, I propose to surprise them by swinging east and then south over the ocean."

"Ah, I understand, Most High Squadron Leader. I obey."

"You have the true Kapar spirit," affirmed the leader. He disconnected the interphone and concentrated on flying his fighter.

Some hours later, the pilots of Squadron F964 sighted masses of black dots twisting and dodging over northern Punos. The thickest concentration seemed to be a mile above the site of a captured sound detection station. The squadron leader issued orders to descend and prepare to attack.

The interphone buzzed again. "Most High, what are those things ahead of us on the water?"

The leader looked. A cluster of dots was visible ahead, moving slowly across the ocean surface. Lights flickered on their southern sides, opposite the oncoming squadron. He recognized them from previous assignments attacking pirates and smugglers in the Karagan Ocean.

"They're watercraft called *ships*," explained the leader. "They transport cargos and sometimes people. The bluecoats must be transporting supplies to the battle using those ships." He grinned cruelly. "We'll destroy them first and then join the air battle."

His crew acknowledged and began their final weapons checks. He signaled his intent to his wingmen. They acknowledged and passed the command to the other air crews. Fighter Squadron F964 dove at their targets, the sky blue ships becoming larger with each passing second.

Cylinders mounted on the strange waterborne vessels became visible. Several of them rotated to face the diving squadron. When the two largest pipes faced directly towards the aircraft, lights flashed.

"Omys!" screamed the belly gunner over the interphone. "Those are air defense cannon…!!"

The squadron leader's airplane flew directly into the first airburst. One second a black-winged aircraft cut the skies above the Karagan; the next instant a pink-gray mist obscured vision.

The other aircraft were not as lucky. Shrapnel flayed planes and pilots alive. Bursting metal teeth dismounted propellers, savaged engines, shredded bodies of men and machines....

Dying, Fighter Squadron F964 began its long fall into the unforgiving sea.

The Kapar counterattack on the northern flank of the invasion disintegrated. The last attacker got close enough to spray the warships with machine gun fire. The bullets hammered the vessels' metal armor spectacularly but futilely

The antiaircraft cruiser *Hagar* and its escorts rotated their primary weapons to the west and continued clawing Kapar aircraft from the sky.

KALDUR JAN stood in the entrance of his home and surveyed his farm in the early evening dusk. The cool wind ruffled his thin hair but he barely noticed either wind or hair. In the bluish light of Antos and Rovos, he could see the ripening produce stretching across the valley. And smell its sweet goodness as well. A thousand acres of garden vegetables destined for the tables of the cities of Tuldros, Polan and Orvis.

Provided the accursed Kapars would allow him to harvest his crops. There were three craters in the northwest quarter still to be filled in, replowed and replanted. Well, they would keep until morning. His hired hands would be back from their weekly day of rest in Tuldros. Young Soran Zan was working out well. However foolish he had been once, Kaldur Jan approved of him now.

As satisfied as he would ever allow himself to be, Jan clumped down the steps until he could lower the splinter proof trapdoor into position without banging his own head. Once it was properly seated, he bolted it and turned on the light. He could walk anywhere in his home without a light if need be but preferred the convenience of seeing his path. He walked down a flight of steps and into a long tunnel with heavy blast doors set in the walls. If the Kapars landed a bomb squarely on his front door as they had with his late cousin Tori, the explosive force would dissipate down the tunnel and out an emergency exit at the far end.

He opened the nearest blast door, stepped through, and locked it behind him. He paused before passing through the neat room with doors in each wall. Two of them led into the equipment and crop storage rooms. Jan checked the duplicate telltales to be sure nothing was amiss. Satisfied, he rapped a signal on the remaining door to alert Maro that a stranger had not infiltrated the family home.

His wife called a greeting as he entered the family quarters and bolted the inner door shut. Jan answered as he double-checked the master telltales in their alcove. There was nothing wrong. There never was with Maro in their home. Satisfied that no one — Kapar infiltrator or other animal — could get in without a fight, he racked his machine pistol.

Jan stepped into the kitchen where Maro was frying something — it smelled like fish — on the stove. With the hired hands in town, the house was empty except for them.

Maro looked up. A smile died on her lips. "Jan, is something wrong?"

Jan didn't ask how she could tell that he was annoyed. She just knew. "Maro, something mighty strange happened today."

"What was that?"

"The Kapars didn't bomb the farm today. Bombed it yesterday and the day before. Not today."

Maro was silent for a time. She shook her head and began scooping delicately browned fish onto plates. Vegetables, fruits and bread were already on the table. "That is strange," she confirmed.

Jan took the plates and set them on the table. "In fact, I didn't see any blackwings today. And I didn't hear any alerts, either."

"Neither did I. That is strange. What do you suppose it means?"

Jan shook his head. "I don't know."

"Maybe the Eljanhai took your advice and shot down more blackwings. Over the ocean."

Jan sniffed. "The Eljanhai took my advice? That's even stranger."

A SPRIGHTLY MAN in the black spangles of retired service stopped abruptly. A large crowd was standing quietly in the corridor that he wished to enter. He slapped his hands together lightly to attract attention. Two men turned around to face him.

Well, one and a half men. The family resemblance was obvious but there was at least five years age difference between the two. The older man was wearing the brown of civilian service while the younger was still wearing the yellow of youth.

"Excuse me, honorable Unisans. Why is there a crowd here?"

The older man started to speak but the younger piped up first. "Honorable sir, we are waiting for the military recruitment office to open. We wish to join the Fighting Corps and destroy the Pom Da."

The black-clad newcomer studied at the assembled crowd. "I am certainly glad to see so many volunteers. However, since I am the recruitment officer, no one here will be joining the Corps until I reach my office."

The young man's face lit up. He made an energetic if sloppy military salute. "Sir, we are very glad to meet you. This is my brother Dardan Chol and I am Dardan Vol. We wish to join the parachute division fighting in Epris."

The recruitment officer looked at the eager young volunteer skeptically. "Ah, yes, honorable sir. However, the Fighting Corps does not accept volunteers less than twenty years old. Are you sure that you are old enough?"

The volunteer's face darkened. Again his older brother attempted to speak but, again, the youngster interrupted. "Most honorable sir, three years ago my school was attacked by Kapar infiltrators. If I am old enough to be attacked, I am old enough to defend myself. And others." His young body radiated defiance.

Dardan Chol finally got a word in. "Vol's teacher Loris Kiri defended her class from the attackers. She was kidnapped to Kapara but her sacrifice allowed her students to escape." He finished solemnly, "Vol would like to rescue her if possible." Vol nodded fiercely.

The recruitment officer absorbed this information and then nodded in sympathy. "I recall the incident and the honorable Loris' sacrifice. Honorable Vol, I will take your application but I cannot guarantee that it will be accepted. In the mean time, our first priority is to open my office. Will you assist me with asking this crowd to form lines so that I can reach the door?" Vol swelled with pride and nodded energetically. The recruitment officer winked at Chol when the happy young man's face was turned.

Guards in orange military coats saluted the gray-uniformed Unisan ambassador as he entered the domed Capitol of Karis. The continent of Karis was a splotch of ice and rock hugging Poloda's Northern Pole. Perhaps a million people scratched out a living fishing, farming lichen, and hunting *muthluqs*. The real attraction of the land was the fact that it had no resources that the Kapars (or anyone else) wanted. As a result, the Kapars bombed Karis infrequently and the Unisans not at all.

While being bombed infrequently was not a pleasant experience, the Karisans could easily imagine worse. As a result, the Thaqung, or ruling council, of Karis loudly maintained its official neutrality in The War savaging the southern nations. Communiqués from Ergos received effusive responses while messages from Orvis received businesslike replies. Unofficially, however, Unisan citizens were welcome "from shore to shore" while Kapar agents learned to keep a low profile.

The ambassador expected to be escorted to the cozy personal office of the Aqunq, or Speaker for the Thaqung. Instead, he was led to the grand ballroom. There he was surprised to see the rotund Aqunq and the entire Thaqung waiting for him. He masked his astonishment with a delighted smile.

The Aqunq came to the point with typical Karisan directness. "Is the Polodan League of Nations open to all nations? Nations such as Karis?"

The ambassador responded, "Definitely." He then started to diplomatically caution his host that membership implied war with the Kapar regime.

The Karisan cut him off with a forceful gesture. He paused, gathered himself, and deliberately declared, "The Thaqung of Karis wishes to join the League of Nations."

He paused again and continued, his voice now quavering just a bit. "And to request Unisan assistance in defending Karis against Kapar reprisals."

The ambassador nodded solemnly in return. "The Republic of Unis is honored to welcome the Thaqung of Karis to the League. We offer you five fighter squadrons to patrol your coastline on a rotating basis and a division of engineers and their equipment to improve your existing airfields and to construct new ones. We ask that you contribute a group of soldiers to the battle in Epris."

Most of the assembled Thaqung members nodded approvingly. Unis' request for soldiers — even a token number compared to what it was contributing — made the alliance psychologically one of equals. Such agreements were very Karisan.

The new allies toasted each other in *vosht*, a fiery liquor distilled from lichen. The ambassador had often thought that a hundred barrels of vosht poured down an Ergosan air hole would bring the entire Kapar empire to its knees. He said so aloud and the assembled Karisans roared with laughter.

A SHARP KNOCK sounded through the door of the Commissioner of War's spartan office. He looked up and was about to give permission to enter when the door opened. His eyebrow cocked at the impertinence.

A not-so-young man with the insignia of a squadron commander marched into the office, a beatific smile on his face and an official report in his left hand. He carefully laid the report on the Commissioner's desk and saluted smartly, his prosthetic right hand touching the center of his chest.

"Most Honorable Commissioner, the staff presents the morning report on yesterday's military actions."

Palden Zar eyed his staff assistant carefully. He leaned back in his hard plastic chair without touching the report. The report was due at this time of day and the not-so-young man's actions were punctilious military courtesy. But the degree of formality was most unusual and his smile was big enough to swallow a Kapar fighter plane; sideways.

"Squadron Commander, you obviously have something on your mind. What is it?"

"Most Hon...."

"'Commissioner' will do. Tell me the key points."

"Commissioner, yesterday *no* Kapar bombs fell anywhere on Unisan soil. Several relatively small raids were launched from Auris but they were driven off with minimal casualties. No raids were launched from Epris or the other continents. There were *no* civilian casualties during the last day. *None!*" Now, the not-so-young man's grin could swallow a Kapar *bomber*, propellers and all! There was a moment of silence in the room.

The staid, reliable Commissioner exploded in joy. He whooped; he hollered; he pounded his desk as if he intended to break it. Stacks of paperwork jumped in response and fell to the floor. His junior joined him in his glee.

Then, lightning-like, the Commissioner sobered up. In a businesslike voice, he remarked, "The Eljanhai will be glad to hear the news. I imagine that she will announce it to the nation this morning. I imagine that both soldiers and civilians will be glad to hear the news as well."

"However, in Epris...," the not-so-young man continued.

"What about our men and women in Epris?"

Chapter 17   *IT SEEMED LIKE A GOOD IDEA AT THE TIME*

THE EARTHQUAKE roll of the Ithrisan countryside died away. The ground stabilized. A last bomb blast thundered; the last shock rippled the soil; the last fountain of dirt and rocks hurled skyward and then earthward.

Cautiously, brown-coated soldiers raised their heads from their fighting holes and peered skyward and landward. Their uniforms were blue plastic but each man was covered in enough dirt to provide natural camouflage.

From the tortured ground to perhaps a hundred yards overhead, the air was filled with dust and occasional falling rocks. But, beyond that, the sky appeared clear. Both black-winged and bluecoated aircraft had withdrawn for the moment. Their corpses littered the ground. Sections of bluecoats ran to check the smashed aircraft for bodies and possible survivors. Otherwise, the Unisan land army remained still, quietly watching the trapdoor covers leading into the city of Umars.

A long hour passed. "All right, boys. We unlock Umars the hard way," directed a division commander. His staff passed the word. Engineers moved forward and set demolition charges. Fighting men assembled into files ready to enter the resulting holes.

Explosions rocked the battlefield. Hatch covers popped. Grenades dropped downward and exploded. Men entered the new underworld, either leaping downward or climbing ladders. They entered the labyrinth of corridors, fanning outward and downward as they had done in tens of Allosan cities. Now they were beginning the liberation of the captive nation of Ithris. Forward and downward…!

The bluecoated invaders overran observation posts manned by armed airmen. Once again, the gray shirts' lack of training, preparation and equipment weighed heavily against them. Airmen jumped out into corridors, braced themselves, and fired. Rifles cut them down. When gray shirts tried to hide in rooms and crawlspaces, grenades flushed them out. Scents of blood and cordite mingled with the petroleum stench endemic to Umars. Lines of Kapar airmen began marching to captivity in their own hangars.

The invaders broke through the military facilities on the upper levels and entered the midlevel industrial districts. Troops of red-shirted engineers and black-shirted prisoners labored to restore Umars' food factories to full production. Both worked under the supervision of squads of green-shirted guards.

The invaders blasted their way into the uppermost factory. Relatively little-damaged by the riots, it was almost ready to begin processing petroleum into the synthetic foods that sustained red shirted life. Bluecoats shouted commands to surrender and drop to the ground. Startled, the red and black shirts complied. Confident invaders stalked forward to secure first the prisoners and then the remainder of the huge facility.

Pistols barked in unison, and the front ranks of blue collapsed. Ahead of the invaders was a skirmish line of green shirts. Unlike their gray-shirted rivals, the police were behind cover. Tens of huge processing tanks obscured the view.

Both sides went to ground. The thunder of gunfire escalated rapidly. Ricochets killed as many men as straight shots. Grenades flew – and bounced off the maze of piping filling the factory.

Both green and blue fighters struggled to gain ground. They rushed, and shot, and stabbed. Blood soaked the metallic floor mingling with weirdly colored sludges.

More green shirts began appearing here and there in the vast manufacturing room. Some rode elevators like gentlemen. Others oozed upward through the myriad of tunnels, airways and chimneys threading the city and factory. Pockets of green began condensing, seemingly out of the rancid air, behind the blue lines. They came forward in short rushes, cutting down invaders from behind. The Unisan lines began to crumple.

A full section of green troopers entered the factory from an undamaged elevator. They carried heavy equipment on their backs. They worked their way forward. When the nearest knot of blue resistance was only a few tens of feet away, they paused. They gave each other final checks. Their machines hissed. The special police ignited the jets of gas.

Dragons' tongues roared out from the police flame-throwers and touched a section of Unisan paratroopers. One young man with quicker reflexes than his fellow soldiers lived. He jerked his entire body backward, out of the path of the flames. He leaped to his feet and fled. His rifle clattered to the floor.

His brothers died. The plastic uniforms of Unisan fighting men were designed to resist flame as well as fragments. But concentrated jets of devil's fire melted the plastic. The resulting jell ate deeply into human flesh. Each man received a foretaste of Omys before — mercifully — he died.

The flamethrower troops advanced protected by their fellows. The Unisans fought on. But they faced fire to their front and bullets to their rear. The blue perimeter shrank inward. A Unisan officer trumpeted, "Retreat!" over the crackling flames, the clanging gunfire, and the screaming men. His troops leaped to their feet and charged the entrance to the factory.

Squads of infiltrating green shirts guarded the door. They fired until their guns ran dry. A handful of blues burst past them while they were reloading. The senior police leader shouted for one section to search the bluecoated bodies for prisoners. The rest were ordered in pursuit like shadow wolves running down fleeing antelopes.

Despite their surprise, the invaders gave ground grudgingly. It took a week for the Kapar police to force their way to the surface, freeing the captive gray shirts en route. But numbers told. When training matched training, numbers told.

The remaining Unisans were forced out of Umars and back to the surface where they found the vengeful Kapar air force waiting for them. Despite the best efforts of the blue-coated fighter pilots, bombs rained down on the land army for a solid week without a pause. When the Kapar Military High Command called off the bombardment, it was because neither air spotters nor land scouts could find a live Unsian anywhere in Ithris.

I DROPPED the report on the Umars disaster on my field desk. Unisan is not a good language for cursing so I vented myself in English and French. My chief of staff and Varima looked at me quizzically.

I changed back to Unisan. "In retrospect, I should have realized that the Kapar police would be good ground fighters. They control the cities and the settled portions of the land surface. By necessity, they would learn how to fight effectively on the land. And there are a lot of them. Now a lot of good men are dead because I didn't foresee that."

My chief of staff shook his head. "Not your fault, sir. No one saw that one coming, including intelligence officers who have been studying the Kapars since you were in diapers. Or whatever mothers put children in on planet Urtha. Now we know better."

"Still...."

"Buck up, sir. According to your friend Tangor, even the adepts of Tonos cannot predict the future perfectly. You have accomplished more for Unis and our allies than half of our Fighting Corps has done in a hundred years. That far outweighs any imaginary failings at Umars.

"And speaking of which, the paratroops are rested, re-equipped and ready to go. Do we send them to Ergos or Umars?"

I laughed at the change of subject. The chief was right. Those brave men in Umars had given their lives for Unis and Poloda. It was up to me to ensure that their sacrifices meant something. "Neither. I want to send them to Auris. After our air force donates some super bombs to Umars."

"Auris?!" The chief's face clouded up. "Sir, please explain your thinking. The paratroops are our best ground fighters but I doubt that they can conquer Auris by themselves."

"I don't expect them to conquer the continent although that would be nice. I want to convince the Pom Da that we are about to invade Auris and therefore cause him to shift forces north from Epris. That will weaken the Kapara defenses and improve our chances to crush them and occupy Ergos. But to convince the Pom Da, we need a strong raid and that requires our best men to take ground and seem to hold it for reinforcements. If the Aurisans rose against the Kapars, we might be able to hold the continent but I am not betting the farm on that. I'll be satisfied to raid northern Auris and to withdraw our men when the Kapars counterattack.

"Our real target is the mind of the Pom Da. If nothing else, a giant raid ought to make him nervous about our overall strength and strategy. Nervous people seldom make good decisions. The Kapars still outnumber us three-to-one so our immediate goal is to cause them to waste their strength fighting shadows."

"Ah, now I understand. I will have the staff work up a plan. We will call it 'Bet The Farm' in case any English-speaking Kapars steal it." We laughed but I said to give the final plans more serious names.

The chief reminded me of something I was trying to forget. "Sir, have you seen the recommendation on page six of the Umars report?"

"Yes, chief. Frankly, I don't want to sign the poor kid's death warrant."

"Sir, cowardice in the face of the enemy merits the death penalty."

"You're legally correct but I would like to salvage the kid if possible."

"'Salvage', sir? How?"

"Ask Squadron Commander Morga if the Second Chancers will take him. If he dies for the honor and glory of Unis, we can overlook his running away from a flamethrower."

ONCE AGAIN THE Pom Da sat in the command chair of the great map room. Once again the commander of the Operations Center Night Shift stood before him. The command balcony was again crowded with both military and Zabo officers and the normal sounds of the supreme headquarters were hushed. And down on the great map floor, technicians were quietly moving cleaning supplies to a position under the command balcony.

"So, War Leader Terro, it appears that you can do some things right." The sarcasm was thick enough to stop a direct hit by a Unisan super bomb.

"Thank you, Highest Most High."

"At least you can do some things right when the police do the hard work for you," hissed the supreme leader.

The still new War Leader winced. "Most High, the Kapar air force destroyed the Unisan invasion of Ithris."

"At the cost of much of our remaining air fleet. *After* the police routed the invaders from the city. Which occurred *after* the *Kapar* air force *surrendered* their hangars and other facilities." The emphasis on the word "Kapar" reminded anyone who needed reminding that all Kapars were supposed to be ruthless and invincible fighters.

"Most High, our airmen fought the invaders fiercely. Our casualty lists prove...."

"Your casualty lists prove nothing! If your airmen fought so bravely, then why were so many *rescued* by the police counteroffensive?!!"

The War Leader flinched. He attempted to recover. "Most High, I believe that a break down occurred in the Umars Military Command. We are investigating and will report to you when we have identified the problem."

"The problem, *ikhurr*, is that the Kapar air force lacks the true Kapar spirit! You lost control of Umars and had to be rescued by the police! You lost control of Allos and Punos and have not recovered either of those colonies!! And you have lost control of the sky over Epris!!! Perhaps I should name that competent technician to be the new War Leader!!! What do you think of that, *Kapar*???!!!" The sarcasm was, if possible, even thicker. Under the command balcony, the technician in question blanched. Junior technicians began edging away from him.

The War Leader choked back his fear and anger. "Most High, I obey. If you wish to promote that technician I will locate him...."

The Pom Da exploded. "No, you idiot! You understand nothing!! You are...!!!" The supreme leader suddenly cut off his words. His hand had been moving toward his holster. But he suddenly realized that every military officer on the balcony was now armed. Perhaps this was not a good time for a military reorganization.

The Pom Da glared at his new War Leader for an eternity. Everyone on the balcony was frozen in place. Eventually, the Pom Da broke the silence. "Kapar, I wish to see the results of your investigation into the failure of the Umars command as soon as possible. If you are unable to discover the guilty parties, perhaps the Zabo can assist you. I also wish you to develop new plans to destroy the Unisan invaders of Epris and to conquer both Unis and Karis. Am I clear?"

"Yes, Most High. I obey!"

"Very good, Kapar. I will now return to the palace and await your reports." The assembled military officers made fists in unison as the Pom Da and his disappointed bodyguards departed.

Newly promoted War Leader Terro Garr died a few days later as the result of a tragic traffic accident. His replacement was a planning officer who had been recommended for the position by the Chief of the Zabo. There were a lot of traffic accidents in Ergos that year. The newspapers reported very few of them.

TWO KAPAR military officers met in a secure room in the Military High Command headquarters. Both were tired from nights of sleepless work.

"What is your proposed plan, Kapar?" grunted one.

"Most High, the plan has three elements. First, we continue to hold in place in Kapara and Ithris. Our forces have stabilized the battle front for now." Left unsaid was the fact that "our forces" now included significant numbers of police troops performing *military* tasks.

The junior officer continued, "To regain the offensive, we create our own parachute land army and drop them into northern Punos behind the bluecoat air over Allos. Once in northern Punos, our land army will cut their supply lines and cause their fighters to collapse."

The senior gray shirt nodded. "Good thinking. We use the Unisans' tricks against them. Continue."

"Second, we activate our sleeper agents in Unis and have them create as much mayhem as possible. The bluecoats may be bold but they lack our inner strength. A few fires, bombings and assassinations in Orvis and their other cities and they will crack. At the very least, we will destroy a good deal of their military production. The weakness is that we will expend our sleeper network in the process. Some might escape."

The senior officer pursed his lips and decided, "Acceptable losses. The sleepers are there to be used and now is the time to use them. Continue."

"Third, we use our parachute infiltrator division and have them kidnap selected bluecoat leaders and otherwise create mayhem that our sleepers cannot do by themselves. Showing the bluecosts that they are not safe in their own beds will strike fear and generally cause chaos. Again, the weakness is that we will expend most if not all of our infiltrators. Since they are trained to escape and evade bluecoat police and military, we can expect a fair number to return safely to Kapara."

"Again, acceptable losses. We urgently need to show the Pom Da that we are the defenders of the Kapar empire, not those —" He double-checked the room for possible listening posts and microphones. "— Not those green-shirted thugs." His junior nodded curtly.

The senior resumed, "Kapar, include the kidnapping of the daughter of their Commissioner of War on the infiltrators' task list. He may be the sharpest sword in their arsenal but all swords have their breaking points." He grinned satanically.

"Yes, Most High."

"And Kapar...."

"Most High?"

"Tell the infiltrators to grab the *right* school teacher this time. Kidnapping the wrong woman three years ago was embarrassing. I do not care that all Unisans look alike; get the right woman this time."

"Yes, Most High."

A FAST Kapar scout plane orbited over the dense forests of northern Punos about a hundred miles west of a former sound detector base tenaciously occupied by the accursed bluecoats. The sky in that direction was gray-black with swarming aircraft and nearly continuous air defense artillery bursts. An entire wing of Kapar bombers and fighters was attacking the base and the bluecoats were not making things easy.

However, that operation concerned the spotter only indirectly. One of the side effects of the bombing attack was that it drew enemy fighters away from this point and Operation Jugular.

On schedule, a division-sized task force appeared overhead. The force maneuvered carefully, staying well west of the battle above the occupied base. The spotter could see the planes shifting positions to maintain their proper alignments. It was Kapar planning and efficiency at its best. He nodded his head in unconscious pride.

On cue, the converted cargo planes opened their doors and gray specks filled the sky. Ranks and files of gray-shirted paratroopers descended on the Kapar colony of Punos that was *temporarily* occupied by the bluecoats.

The spotter maneuvered his plane to allow the paratroopers to pass. He shuddered at the thought of a parachute entangling his propellers or obscuring his windshield. He heeled over slightly to watch the airmen of Kapara as they approached the great trees of Punos.

Thousands of tiny lights were sparkling among the trees of Punos. Was this some strange Punosan insect swarm disturbed by the first wave of descending gray shirts? The spotter moved closer.

Suddenly, he realized that the descending paratroopers were jerking and thrashing in their harnesses! The points of light were the flashes of guns being fired upward! By hidden bluecoats!! Helpless in their parachutes, Kapars died by the hundreds. An entire division entered the woods — and disappeared.

Duty demanded that the spotter observe and report. Instead, he began to strafe the wooden fortress below. The trees did not reveal if his bullets found any bluecoat targets. Eventually a sniper nailed his engines.

THE ANCIENT GOD OF WAR had smiled on a gaggle of perhaps twenty Kapar paratroopers. They had survived the gauntlet of fire, landed safely, and avoided being captured by blue-uniformed soldiers combing the woods for them. They formed up and decided their best option was to escape and report back to Ergos.

Unfortunately, unaccustomed to operating in dense woods, they became disoriented and marched east rather than west. After several days of exhausting travel, they came to a point ten miles from the captured sound detector base. They broke out of the woods into a strange clearing.

Someone had razed trees and bushes in a swath a hundred yards across and miles wide. Ahead of them reared a long ridge of freshly turned earth. And above them overlapping camouflage nets were suspended on a thick network of plastic cables. Trained ground troops would have muttered "Trap" and backpedaled. Airmen drafted into land warfare marched unthinkingly forward.

A feminine voice shouted a demand "Surrender or die!" The Kapars paused and charged forward, pistols blazing. No woman was going to intimidate airmen possessing the true Kapar spirit!

Rifles cracked repeatedly. The entrenched purple-uniformed defenders left no survivors. Their commander criticized "her girls" for that, but not very harshly.

One guard outside the Eljanhai's office frowned as he saw a messenger approach. "Honorable Unisan, are you well?"

A sad smile flickered across the messenger's face. "War wounds. The doctors say that I am fortunate to be alive. But I can still move and I do my part." He held up the message case chained to his body for their inspection. Each movement was stiff with repressed pain. He also showed his credentials.

Both guards nodded in sympathy. Still, they inspected the messenger carefully. Satisfied that he carried no weapons, one knocked on the door and opened it when he heard the command "Enter."

The messenger entered the Eljanhai's modest office. A golden sunburst in the center of one pale blue wall was the only sign that the resident was the most powerful woman in Unis.

Tondul Misema looked kindly at the messenger as he approached. "More paperwork?" she asked semi-humorously.

The messenger smiled politely. "I do not know, Most Honorable Eljanhai. I merely deliver the messages, not write them. Please use key 14 to unchain the case and then use key 23 to unlock it." Tondul nodded and turned to get the necessary keys from a desk drawer.

"And the message that I am delivering, you accursed she-*ikhurr*, is that you will never prevail against the true Kapar spirit!!!" Tondul started and stared at the infiltrator. Her hand darted toward another desk drawer....

He bent his arms behind his back in a posture no human assumes without risk of crippling injury and pulled them together. There was an unnatural snapping sound and the bomb implanted in his body exploded.

THE TELEPHONE BUZZED and its attention light went directly to red. Palden Zar picked up the instrument and identified himself. His caller was the Commissioner of Justice.

"Eljanhai Tondul Misema has just been assassinated. The suspect is dead. We suspect another traitor but do not know his motives yet. In addition, we are receiving widespread reports of sabotage directed against military and manufacturing facilities as well as general terrorism directed against the civilian population."

Palden bit his tongue. "Do you need any support from the Department of War?"

"Thank you, but not at this time." The Commissioner of Justice sighed loudly. "It appears to be a security matter at present. I have ordered a full police mobilization. That should give us the manpower to defend critical facilities and catch these criminals."

"Good. I will place our people and installations on defensive alert and place the Home Guard on stand-by alert. If you need help, ask."

"Thank you, Commissioner."

"One other thing. We need a new Eljanhai. I would appreciate your support."

"Two years ago, you refused the nomination."

"Things have changed in two years. I want to show the Kapars that they will never terrorize us into surrendering."

"You have my support."

Thirty middle school children and one teacher faced a world map and recited, "For the honor and glory of Unis" in unison. The patriotic recitation was more energetic than it had been in recent years.

Following the chorus, everyone sat and opened their notebooks. Their teacher smiled and asked someone to explain why Unis was the richest country on Poloda. Twenty or so hands shot up. The teacher selected one girl who stood and began contrasting Unisan free enterprise with the Kapar command economy.

A booming sound resounded through the school. The classroom door quivered. Eyes turned to the door and then to an alarm light. The latter remained a serene green. The teacher shouted "Duck!" despite the All Clear signal. The students dropped to the floor and scrambled under their desks. Their teacher reached for a telephone on the wall....

Running footsteps sounded in the corridor outside the classroom. They halted at the doorway. Indistinct voices grunted and barked outside. The teacher paled, her hand frozen before it could hit the telephone's power button.

Heavy machine pistols smashed the door's lock and hinges into ruin. The plastic panel flew inward, propelled by a black boot. The door crashed to rest on the floor in front of the teacher's desk. Two Kapar fighters stepped through the doorway, guns ready.

"Quiet! Listen! For Palden Zinova we are looking!" one shouted in heavily accented Unisan. "With us she must come! Or your whelps we will shoot!"

The teacher stood up, her back rigid, her face a storm cloud. "Bazhulan!" she hissed contemptuously in Unisan. "I am Palden Zinova. Give me a minute to give my children safety instructions."

The Kapar seemed to appreciate that concept. "Yes! You obey! One minute you have!"

Palden Zinova nodded and sang to her children. Teen-aged faces peered from behind desks and chairs. "Honorable Unisans, I must go with these... these fighters. You must remain here until the schoolmaster...."

"No!" Dardan Vol stood bolt upright. "Not again!!" He hurled himself forward.

He almost reached the invaders before the second Kapar emptied his pistol into the young patriot. Vol collapsed on the dismounted door, a Spartan warrior lying on his shield.

There was a moment of shocked silence. The second Kapar automatically began to reload his weapon.

"Well, there was one Unisan in this class," sang an angry voice. The speaker was the girl whose answer had been interrupted. She launched herself at Vol's murderers.

Taken aback, the Kapars lost precious seconds before their guns roared death. They were beaten into pulp by children who would not be slaves.

I WAS LYING on a hill overlooking the Kaparan city of Ilgros when the clear sky began raining death. Varima was

"*They were beaten into pulp by children who would not be slaves.*"

with me to record my observations and orders. We were surrounded by ten guards in one division's forward command post.

Our guys were moving carefully forward across the
muddy ground that marked the site of Ilgros and its plastic
ware and plastic sheet factories. The Kapars were on to our
trick of using their underground motor highway and railroads
against them so we had to attack overland. Since our bombers
had long since blasted the landscape over the roof of Ilgros into
mud and dust, it was slow going.

Suddenly Death began walking across the land in a
grumpy mood; bomb blasts erupted all around us. Geysers of
rock and slime leapt into the air. My guys grabbed the ground.
Some were too late. They flew into the air like Superman but
landed like Clark Kent.

The division commander shouted for his air force liaison
officer to find out why our fighter aircraft weren't keeping the
enemy bombers off us. I rolled over and scanned the sky with
my binoculars. There were no blackwings overhead. I could
see occasional flickers of blue as Unisan aircraft passed by on
patrol but no bad guys. Where were the shells coming from?

Upside down, I saw a shell arching in from Ilgros. It
smashed into a company of Unisan soldiers behind a slight rise.
Light dawned. I rolled upright. "Division Commander," I
barked. "There are no Kapar aircraft up there."

"Are we being bombed by our own planes?" In the
words of one of my OSS instructors, friendly fire isn't.

"No, the Kapars are using the Ilgros air defense artillery
as field artillery."

His face was a giant question mark. "Division Commander, have everyone fall back. Now."

He nodded sharply and began giving orders despite
the roaring thunder of shells bursting over the battle zone.
Runners raced outward and flagmen signaled. For the millionth
time, I wished that we had radio communications on Poloda.
When in Rome....

Slowly, the retreat became general. Lines of blue uniforms reversed course and rippled backward, leaving Ilgros for
another day.

I smiled faintly at the professionalism of the retrograde
movement. We'd practiced this maneuver in Unis and the men
handled themselves well. They moved out of the target area,
headed back to their designated rally points.

No sooner had I congratulated the Division Commander than the bombardment stopped. He gawped at the
sudden silence.

"Keep them moving," I snapped. He nodded again and
issued more commands. Our bluecoats continued to move out
of the killing zone.

Holes popped open in the ground and green shirts
vomited forth. Lots of holes and lots and lots of green shirts.
They looked around like frat boys who went to the wrong address
for the beer bust. Ah, hah! They had expected to ambush us…!

My mouth lives a life of its own. "Fire!!!" I shouted at
the top of my lungs. Some of the green shirts oriented on my
big mouth and pointed.

My guys got the message. Rifles cracked in a colossal
roll of thunder. Death ran through the green horde on lightning
feet. As many fell, some of them tried to attack. Another OSS
instructor cautioned that there are old soldiers and bold soldiers
but no old, bold soldiers. That was true at least for the first
battle of Ilgros. Other green shirts adopted a more sensible
strategy. They died tired.

After a while, the guns of Ilgros roared again, and
explosions tossed up mud and fire and bodies in the original
killing zone. They murdered a lot of their own wounded.

The Division Commander remembered to breathe as
he stared across the blood-soaked terrain. "Uvala. Sir. They
had planned to trap us between their guns and their soldiers.
If you had not ordered a retreat when you did, they would have

killed thousands of us." He was looking at me as if I were
George Washington or King Ulandu.

I shook my head. "Thank you, Division Commander,
but you would have gotten our guys out if I hadn't been here.
Have the men pick up our wounded and dead. Then fall back
to our jump off positions. 'We'll lick 'em tomorrow.'"

One of the advantages of dying and teleporting to a
distant planet is that you can quote better men than yourself
— in this case U.S. Grant — and everyone thinks you're brilliant. The Division Commander glowed like Omos and continued moving his men backward. His staff packed up and left.

Varima, my guards and I should have moved out with
the division. But I stayed too long trying to think of something
clever. The worst thing about a reputation as a miracle worker
is when you start believing it yourself.

Out of the corner of my eye, I saw one of my guards
survey the landscape. He sat up a little too far and his head
exploded.

There was an instant of silence and then a fusillade of
lead erupted on the *back* of our position.

I whipped my head around. There was a company of
green shirts *behind* us! In the near distance, I saw an open
bolthole and my withdrawing bluecoats *beyond* the bad guys!

"Guys!" I whispered forcefully. "That way. Towards
Ilgros." Varima led the way.

I looked back and saw the withdrawing Unisans turning
around to see what the fuss was about. They would catch the
green shirts in the rear. Time to leave.

My guards and I crawled away, dignity forgotten. I
pointed towards the slight ridge that had failed to protect other
Unisans and we angled towards it. Bullets tore up the ground
around us. One guard made a funny sound and laid down,
blood welling up from a sudden cavity in his back. I hoped
that he made it to Uvala.

We didn't make it over the ridge but we did reach the crater that had once been a company of paratroopers and was now an annex to Hell. Bullets were passing inches above our heads but we were relatively safe for the moment.

I stuck my head up to study the situation when I heard my name. I looked to my right.

Varima and other guards had headed directly towards Ilgros. When she realized that I wasn't following her, she turned and crawled for the crater. Her left arm was towards me except that it mostly wasn't there. She looked at me like a kitten pleading for its mother.

My mouth lives a life of its own. I shouted, "Hold on; I'm coming."

I leapt up and ran to her. Bullets snapped and rattled around me. A lunatic part of my mind wondered if Tangor's theory that Earthman who died on Earth can't die on Poloda was correct.

There was no time to be gentle. I grabbed Varima up and fireman carried her to our refuge.

More or less.

I was almost there when a bullet hit me in the leg. I collapsed to a kneeling position. My guards were using the crater wall as a firing position and emptying their guns at the oncoming green shirts. The nearest one looked at me with eyes as big as saucers.

I threw Varima into his arms. "Tourniquet!" I screamed. He knelt and started to work....

"Withdraw! Over the ridge, guys!! That's an order!!!" They started to move. The first one out of the crater took a bullet in the center of his back. I focused on the bad guys. Omys! They were too close!! My guys needed covering fire.

I emptied both guns at the green menaces. Out of the corner of my eye, I saw my guys getting the Omys out of Dodge. Two of them were carrying Varima between them.

Then, something hit me in the head and I put Tangor's theory to the test.

THE NOT-SO-YOUNG squadron commander nodded grimly. "Yes, Eljanhai, our land forces have confirmed that Wing Commander Tomas Ran is dead. Witnesses saw him shot and his body carried off by the Kapar raiding party. He died rescuing the honorable Vondol Varima and buying time for his guards to escape."

Palden Zar scowled and bit his tongue. It was too late to say "I told you so" to the insanely confident Earthman. Hopefully he had gone to Uvala rather than Omys.

That thought inspired another.

"What we really need to command the land army is another Earthman. Have we located one?"

"No sir. The Department of Justice reviewed the entire population of alleged aliens as you requested. They concluded that Harkas Tangor and Tomas Ran are the only authentic Earthmen in Unis. Or *were* the only authen...."

"What is Tangor's current assignment?"

"Sir, Wing Commander Harkas is leading our air offensive over Epris. He reports that the Kapar air force is almost completely destroyed. I recommend we allow him time to finish the job."

"Very well, promote Deputy Wing Commander Manchan to Wing Commander. I order him to continue our land offensive until we capture Ergos and the Pom Da."

BOOK FOUR:
INSIDE ERGOS

Chapter 18 *A CHANGE OF PLANS*

WING COMMANDER Manchan was a rarity among Polodans: a man with a beard. True, it was small and wispy by comparison with an Earthman's facial hair but on his native planet, it gave him the appearance of distinguished age and therefore great wisdom. He stroked it often when he was thinking; such as now. He was listening to his staff's complex plan to attack the Kapar empire from every direction. The more he heard, the less he liked it.

After the briefers were finished, there was a long pause. All eyes turned to Manchan. "Honorable members of the staff, I thank you for this plan. However, I do not approve it."

An unprofessionally loud sigh echoed through the bunker. Manchan ignored the opinion and continued to speak. "My primary concern is that we need to focus on our overarching goal of conquering Ergos and capturing or destroying the Pom Da and his counselors. This plan diffuses *our* efforts over all five continents rather than concentrating them on our goal. I very much doubt that we can dance the Pom Da into surrendering. It will be necessary to capture or kill him. The best time to do that is now. We have substantial forces here in Epris. We need to use them for maximum effect.

"Therefore, I request that you develop a new plan to drop our paratroopers and engineers on the roof of Ergos while our air force provides cover. The paratroopers will establish an airhead, and the engineers will drill down into the enemy capital." He nodded at the allied commanders. "We will enter the city and finish The War the way that it must be finished."

There was a great deal of debate about the commander's guidance but, ultimately, Manchan insisted and the Unisans saluted and executed. The allies went along with their giant partner.

OPERATION KNOCKOUT began well enough. The crater where the old city of Ergos had once been was now perhaps a hundred square miles of Hell. From above, the effect was a gigantic bull's eye.

The crater was filled with a horrid soup of dirt, water and less identifiable substances. The stench was awful and some of the newer soldiers had donated their breakfasts to the vile stew.

"The underground hydraulic flow must have broken down. Even super bombs are just stirring the slime. No Kapar will exit through that," stated engineer Dardan Chol, half to himself. He turned to Group Commander Morga Sal. "Keep everyone back from the slope unless they are engaged in rescue operations." Sal nodded and issued the necessary orders.

The paratroopers had landed in a circle around the crater. Inevitably, some of them had drifted into the mess. Most, however, had landed safely in the barren ground outside the crater and formed up promptly. Unit commanders had established strong points in the crater wall and pushed their perimeters outward to the surviving forests. Even with the massive destruction inflicted on the Kapar air force, Polodans felt safer when they could hide from overhead observation. Scouts hunted for signs of enemy activity on the roof of the capital city – the very center of Kapara. Overhead bluecoat fighters and bombers patrolled.

Engineers located firm patches of ground away from the central quagmire and began digging. Portable electric augers whined and ejected dirt was drawn into serpentine tubes. Small mountains developed here and there across the eerie landscape. When possible, the engineers dumped their spoil into the great wound in Poloda's surface.

Holes appeared and extended rapidly. Engineers entered the excavations and continued carving ever-deepening tunnels. Behind them, other workers set plastic panels and steel reinforcements. If an earthen tunnel collapsed, the men would be safe behind the barriers lining the walls in theory.

Units of paratroopers patrolled the foothold. Some threw up tents for hospitals, food, water, and the storage of the thousand requirements of warfare…. Others were formed and waiting for the engineers to break through into Ergos. Intelligence reports suggested that the smashed upper levels of the city formed a vertical barricade a thousand feet deep. The drills chewed their way downward.

One Second Chancer patrol found a shattered air defense cannon turret and began exploring its mangled structure. Sal left his group command post and went over to see what was going on. He took guards with him.

"Sir, we might have found a back door into Ergos," reported the patrol commander. In the darkness visible through the rents in the armored turret, blue flashlights were winking on.

"Good job. Keep going." Sal emphasized his order by pointing with his elbow. "If you find anything or need more men, ask your company commander for support."

The commander acknowledged his orders and disappeared underground. Sal gave the necessary orders to the company commander. The latter nodded and moved his own command post to the meager shadow of the ruined turret. They were discussing possible operations when, ever so quietly, Hell broke loose.

Tangor was looking at the ghostly sphere of Antos when the devils of Poloda came calling.

Once again, he was seated in the co-pilot's chair of a fast scout/pursuit plane. Once again, Fontan Ianami was his pilot. So far, the mission had been a breeze, more of a training exercise than an actual wartime maneuver. So he was speculating on what might have happened if he and Handon Gar had flown to Antos instead of Tonos years ago. *To start with, Gar might be here now....*

With his eyes high in the sky, Tangor spotted the new threat before his men did. A flight of black dots was passing in front of Antos. As he watched, they changed angle, aiming at his fleet. He quickly estimated their heights... and then re-calculated as his first estimate made no sense. The black dots grew closer — rapidly.

Tangor began issuing orders, speaking aloud to Ianami but also signaling the other aircraft commanders in the patrol. "Signal all planes: Urgent. Kapar aircraft approaching from the north at extreme high altitude. Fighter Squadrons Seven and Eight rise and engage." The commands jumped from airplane to airplane and the designated squadrons tilted upward. "Signal same to ground forces."

The incoming blackwings blazed past the interposing blue planes. Within seconds, they were passing through the layers of the main body. Startled at the unbelievable speeds, and cautious about hitting their fellows, the Unisan pilots and gunners mostly held their fire.

"What are those?" muttered Ianami. "Nothing can move that quickly."

Tangor's handsome face paled. "These can. Someone reinvented Horthal Wend's power amplifier.

"Signal all planes: Urgent. Priority attack on the Kapar fast movers. And look out for other planes."

The fast movers rocketed through the bluecoat air patrols and flashed over the barren patch marking Ergos and the Knockout landing zone. They strafed the diverse allied troops enthusiastically.

Then, as quickly as the came, they were gone – climbing for altitude through the sky blue airplanes. Squadrons Seven and Eight followed, falling further behind each moment. As Unisan eyes followed the new threat upward, Tangor scanned the remainder of the sky. He grimaced as he looked north.

He signaled again. "Urgent. Mixed Kapar aircraft attacking from north. Reaction force fighters engage." Previously designated fighters peeled off. The orbiting bombers automatically tightened their formation into a mutually supporting fighting box. The new air battle of Ergos was on.

Tangor's warning had bought precious seconds for the ground soldiers to take cover. The strafing had hurt but not as badly as it might have. Morga Sal barked an order for his company commander to continue exploring the turret and ran back to his group strong point.

His chief of staff spat out a situation report. Green-shirted Kapar ground fighters had materialized in the forests all around the Allied landing zone. Unisan patrols had uncovered recently excavated air and access holes in a wide arc around the central crater. When they had probed the holes, they had run into strong resistance from green shirts. Once the fighting had begun, other exits had released additional hordes of Kapar police.

Obviously the Kapar engineers had not waited for Allied permission to begin rebuilding Ergos. They had tunneled outside the devastated zone and then cut their way upward to create the new entrances and exits.

The Second Chancers' outermost squadron reported contact with the enemy in the woods. Sal reviewed his arrangements and ordered, "Cease advancing and hold in place. Use explosives to drop trees and form barriers. Then place blue panels on the barriers. Signal the light bombers to plaster the areas beyond the panels. Repeat, beyond the blue panels." Signalmen acknowledged and passed the orders. Trees began falling in the woods. Clearings appeared.

Overhead, signals flashed back and forth among the bombers and ground combatants. Light bombers peeled off and began hammering the woods outside of the thin blue lines.

The air battle had become a gigantic free-for-all. Kapar bombers tried to get close and bomb the roof of their own capital city. Unisan fighters counterattacked and Kapar fighters counter-counterattacked. It was the kind of war that Polodans had been fighting for 110 years.

The wild card was the squadron of fast movers. They stayed out of the main battle and sniped around the edges, devastatingly. Each slashing attack knocked ten or twenty Unisan planes out of the sky. Their speed made blocking or counterattacks nearly impossible.

But not completely impossible; Tangor watched the enemy speed demons carefully. The airmen of Unis had mauled the Kapar air fleets for a century; they could handle the main battle without him micromanaging things. Patterns emerged. Ideas clicked.

Tangor signaled. "Fighter Squadrons Seven and Eight remain above the battle. We will pull them to you. All bomber squadrons with expended loads return to base. Maintain unit fighting boxes. Fighter squadrons 14 and 15 escort the bombers." The Unisans began their maneuvers. Tangor's plane surged upward.

The fast movers saw the lumbering bombers returning to Allos. As the latter broke free from the grand melee's eastern edge, they became vulnerable. Signals flickered high above the Unisans. The fast movers heeled over, diving for the withdrawing bombers.

Unisan signals flashed back and forth. Squadrons 14 and 15 began a vertical turn and climb, abandoning their charges. The bombers closed up their ranks as they continued their retreat. Aboard the withdrawing bombers, gunners checked their defensive weapons. Down slashed the fast movers.

They saw Squadrons Seven and Eight laboring upward…
and sneered. They had the speed, the guns, and the true Kapar
spirit. But the true Kapar spirit had not subdued the glory of
Unis.

Power-amplified airplanes were still airplanes. The
Unisan pilots had fought Kapars for years and had learned from
this day's attacks. They adjusted their aim, leading the blackwings
more than usual. Squadrons Seven and Eight emptied their
forward weapons at their enemies. Dry, they began to heel over.

The fast movers ran into a wall of lead. Many bullets
simply missed. Perhaps a quarter hammered the black plastic
bodies of the Kapars, shaking them and deflecting their aim.
Another tithe of slugs smashed into propellers and engines.
Circuits arced and motors died.

Tens of fast movers began the long fall to the war torn
roof of Ergos. The remaining Kapar formation was noticeably
more ragged than before. Squadrons 14 and 15 ripped into the
survivors. More fast movers headed towards the landscape
rather than their intended targets.

Some Kapars survived to attack the retreating box of
bombers. The bluecoats were out of bombs but not out of
machine gun bullets. Another wall of lead appeared in the
Eprisan sky. Bombers fell, but so did the smaller, more vulnerable fighters.

As the surviving fast movers turned to leave the fight
and regroup, new squadrons of bluecoats appeared on each side.
From above them came the avenging angels of four veteran
squadrons, belly guns blazing. The fast mover squadron disintegrated.

After that point, the fight was a straightforward air
battle. The kind that Unisans had been winning for a hundred
years.

Ten days later, Tangor's command plane orbited slowly
over the savaged battlefield. Above him twenty thousand Unisan
fighters and bombers awaited his orders. Uncounted thousands

of new craters had devastated the surface once more. A layer of dirt and stones covered everything, tinting formerly bright colors an ugly brown. Smoke rose from burning trees, machines, tents, boxes, and, of course, bodies. Everywhere blue and green clad bodies littered the land. Most of them were still. Some crept slowly forward, still fighting. Others writhed in agony.

Tangor's face was a mask of ice. If he allowed himself to express his true feelings, he would cry for a year. Even Ianami's cheerful nature was subdued by the scope of the slaughter. *Two hundred thousand Unisans and allies known dead; others nearly so. Their bodies in danger of being hauled into Ergos to feed the living zombies who slave for the Kapar empire. And the ghouls who rule it. A few thousand wounded and high value personnel, including our remaining allies, had been evacuated by transport pilots brave to the point of insanity. A few thousand out of all those men who wanted nothing less than freedom for Poloda.*

God alone knew how many Kapars died for the perverted dreams of the Pom Da. Some estimates ran as high as a million. Some even more. Including every black-winged airman who dared come near the scene of their "victory."

Allied flags were draped on a ruined air defense artillery turret marking it as the final strongpoint of Task Force Knockout. A continuous coruscation of lights sparkling on its armored walls showed the Kapars' efforts to destroy it with personal weapons.

Despite the gunfire, a blue-coated officer stood calmly in the gaping tear in the armor that had allowed an unknown number of soldiers to escape underground. He signaled his report as if days of slaughter were all a training exercise and everyone was firing blanks.

"Initial attack on Ergos failed. Men fought heroically but overwhelmed by superior numbers green shirts. Now beginning second attack. Break. Give us five minutes and pulverize surface behind us. Break. To the honor and glory of Unis and our allies. Morga Sal, acting commander, Task Force Knockout. Out."

Tangor flashed an acknowledgement. Sal saluted and disappeared. The Earthman said something in English and then switched back to Unisan. "Urgent. Odd numbered fighter squadrons strafe the ground around the turret in numerical order beginning immediately. Even numbered fighting squadrons maintain patrol. Light bombing squadrons orbit until fighters are finished; then pulverize battlefield. Heavy bombing squadrons begin pulverizing forests immediately...."

THE ADMINISTRATIVE ASSISTANT put down her telephone and announced, "You may enter immediately." The not-so-young military staff assistant thanked her and entered the Eljanhai's new office, plastic message form in his left hand. The only thing in the office with personality was the occupant.

Palden Zar looked up from the mountain of paperwork that he had been methodically demolishing. "It is not time for the regular reports. Therefore, there must be a problem."

His staff assistant saluted. "Yes, Most Honorable Eljanhai. We have just received a report from the land army." He outlined the results of Operation Knockout.

Palden's face reddened but he bit his tongue. "Send a message to Wing Commander Manchan that I want to see him in Orvis as soon as possible. Have his chief of staff take over operations in southern Epris for now."

"Sir, this report was from the chief of staff who signed it as acting commander. He says that Manchan committed suicide." Palden stared at the ceiling for a lifetime.

"Promote the chief to Wing Commander of the land army. Tell him to stabilize the battlefront. Then, give me a full report. And then provide recommendations for future courses of action; if there is one."

"Sir? I do not understand your last comment."

"Son, we are running low on manpower. I am not going to just throw bodies at a problem as the Pom Da would. We might not be able to continue the land war."

A MAN IN A Unisan uniform lay on the floor of a maintenance closet somewhere inside Ergos. Two of his countrymen knelt over him while a fourth man, this one in Zurrisan gray and black, peered through a ventilation grill in the closet door.

One of the kneeling men felt for a pulse. After a long minute, he shook his head. "Sir, he is dead. Task Force Knockout is now down to three soldiers." The speaker used Kapar or Zurrisan as a convenience to their ally.

Morga Sal mused. "That means that each one of us will have to kill an average of 100,000 grey shirts and green shirts before we liberate Ergos. Well, they would have killed us sooner if we had stayed on the surface. As it is, we got several hundred of them as a bonus and terrorized more."

The young man smiled faintly.

A low whistle came from their ally now looking out the door. The Zurrisan's body language was tense. He hissed, "The Pom Da!" He remembered to hiss quietly.

"What about the Pom Da?" queried the young man.

"He is out there. Inspecting the engineers bracing the cavern ceiling." His comrades joined him. Taking turns at the grill, they surveyed the scene beyond the door.

The maintenance closet opened onto a wide balcony overlooking a vast cavern. The floor below the balcony had once been a factory of some kind. But all of the original machines had been removed. The working floor was now given over to squadrons of red-shirted engineers and their equipment, including huge floodlights. They were working steadily to erect gigantic steel columns from floor to ceiling and huge sheets of armor plate atop the columns.

A gaggle of green shirts heavily-encrusted with gold braid and medals plus a few red and gray shirts was standing at the edge of the balcony. Some red shirt was speaking, apparently explaining the engineers' progress to the gaggle; or, more accurately, to someone within the gaggle.

"I do not see the Pom Da. Are you sure?" breathed the young man.

"Definitely; he is standing behind that statuesque woman with the jet black hair."

"Well, I see her. I would not mind.... What are you doing?"

"I am going to walk out there and kill the Pom Da." The Zurrisan's voice was completely sincere. He was checking and adjusting his pistol and sword as he spoke.

"That is insane!" The young man's voice was rising rapidly and Morga Sal put his hand on the man's arm.

"I am a True Man of Zurris. I will kill the Pom Da." The Zurrisan looked around the small room to see if he had missed anything useful. He seized a clipboard hanging on a hook on the wall.

"You True Men of Unis stay here. This is my country and my fight. In addition, I am wearing a gray uniform so I can pretend to be a Kapar airman delivering a message to the Pom Da." He waved the clipboard slightly in the dim light of the closet to emphasize his idea.

Morga Sal attempted to dissuade him but the Zurrisan was resolute. Finally, the senior Unisan clasped his ally on the shoulder and whispered, "For the honor and glory of Zurris." The young man duplicated the gesture.

The Zurrisan nodded and responded, "And for our own." He squared his shoulders and opened the door. He closed it behind him and marched across the broad balcony as if he were escorted by 100,000 soldiers.

His companions watched through the grill. They saw and heard him bluff his way past one gold-encrusted green-shirted guard, waving the stolen clipboard. A second guard was more suspicious and attempted to take the clipboard from the assassin. An argument ensued. The black-maned beauty turned to see what the problem was....

She suddenly tensed up. Her hand dove to her holster while she screamed, "Idiot! He is wearing a Unisan uniform!!" Her gun came up....

As did the Zurrisan's. He fired methodically into the crowd, knocking down the Pom Da's protectors. Green shirts and gray shirts were flung about like toys in the hands of a destructive child.

The woman fired a short burst straight into the True Man's chest. He folded up and collapsed, his remaining bullets hammering the balcony floor. Pandemonium reigned on the balcony. Belatedly, green-shirted guards leaped to form a shield around the Pom Da.

Shrill commands imposed order on the chaos. The watching Unisans heard a malevolent voice demand to know where the assassin had come from. They tensed. A guard pointed to the maintenance closet door. More orders and at least ten green shirts advanced rapidly on the door.

Morga Sal stood erect and said quietly, "I would rather die fighting than in a Kapar question box."

"And I as well," echoed his young companion. They checked their weapons.

"I will go first. For the honor and glory of Unis," breathed Sal.

"And for our own," responded the young man. He pushed the door open and raced through it before Sal realized what he was doing. The acting commander of Task Force Knockout followed his man.

Despite their suspicions, the approaching guards were taken by surprise. The first fusillade of lead dropped most of them. The young man ran forward in great bounds, vaulting over the bodies groaning on the balcony floor. As he approached the Pom Da's elite guards, he fired his gun dry and threw it away. He yanked his sword from its holster and hacked a guard's gun arm off. He pushed the screaming guard's body aside....

And collapsed as five or more guns shredded his body; Kapars stared at his sky blue uniform in disbelief.

Morga Sal ran forward as quickly as he could. The young man's sacrifice had created a rare opportunity. He saw the Pom Da ahead of him, the elite guards dead, dying or in disarray and distracted by the courage of the young man who had joined the Second Chancers after the battle of Umars. The acting commander already had both gun and sword out. He hurled himself forward toward the narrow corridor leading to the supreme Kapar.

Guards began reacting. He shot them down. The way was open. All he had to do was keep it open for a few more seconds....

The Pom Da was ahead of him! Guards to either side but none between hunter and prey!

Suddenly, a red-shirted man jerked forward, arms flailing wildly, blocking Sal's path. The Unisan fired, bullets ripping into the red shirt's chest. The body collapsed. As it fell, Sal noted that it had a series of entry wounds in its back.

Sal jerked to one side to avoid the falling corpse. He moved his gun to aim at the Pom Da. His finger tightened on the trigger as the gun came to bear....

The black-maned woman was standing before him, legs braced, a heavy machine pistol held in both hands. Her finger squeezed....

A sledgehammer smashed Morga Sal's guts and gun arm into red ruin. He fired, desperately trying to nail the Pom Da. One bullet sliced through the dictator's ornate jacket sleeve. Other slugs sent a hulking guard on his way to Omys.

Sal's momentum had been checked by the impact of the bullets. For a moment, he was still erect, more or less standing before his executioner. Then the woman hit him with her fist —— a good solid haymaker — and he fell to the floor. He rolled and came to rest eyes on the distant ceiling.

She kicked his pistol from his hand. And spit in his face. Danger over, Kapars gathered around, staring at the man who had almost killed the Pom Da.

Morga Sal was bleeding out. He sang, "For the honor and glory of Unis" at the looming circle of hostile faces. His listeners scowled as they recognized the salute.

He had time to say a great deal more but he decided that he had said everything that he needed to say. He relaxed, smiling in deep satisfaction. Seeing his smile, several Kapars frowned. After several minutes, Morga Sal left Poloda to search for his sister.

Chapter 19   *A JOB INTERVIEW IN ERGOS*

MY FIRST THOUGHT when I came to was that the Uvalans had their theology wrong because Paradise seemed to be caverns and cages full of Kapars. A couple of kicks in the ribs later I realized that I wasn't in Paradise. I was in Hell. More precisely, I was in downtown Ergos, capital of Kapara and the Kapar empire. Well... that *was* close enough for government work.

The torture this time around made the Gerrisan question box seem like a sauna. First, in any given dictatorship, The Leader has the best of everything, including torturers. The goons in Gerris were amateurs compared to the Ergosan elite. Second, as a general officer in the Unisan Fighting Corps, I now had real secrets to protect. And third, the Ergosans seemed to accept that I was from a real place called Earth.

The insanity defense wasn't going to work this time. I held out as long as I could and then spilled my guts. That bought me a week's relief while their intelligence officers were poring over the Order of Battle that I revealed.

Of course, they were madder than hornets soaked in skunk oil when they realized that I had been describing the American Army in Normandy instead of the Unisan Fighting Corps in Allos. Offering to reveal the secrets of the British, Canadian, French and Polish armies earned me screamed insults, threats, slaps and a truncheon massage respectively.

243

Some people can't take "Yes" for an answer. I blacked out after the truncheon massage. I supposed that being beaten unconscious is one way of keeping a secret but I wasn't anxious to find out how much damage my skull could take before I went to Uvala.

I came slowly back to consciousness to find myself lying on a steel table with about fifty pounds of chains restraining my movements. Otherwise, I was naked. Adding insult to injury, one hand was soaking in a pan of warm water. That hand didn't hurt, but everything else did.

A couple of green-shirted comedians were discussing some ideas for more entertainment at my expense that would have horrified Dr. Moreau. Once again, I tried *really hard* to teleport back to Earth.

Once again, it didn't work. Apparently you needed a German to fire a bullet into your heart. Just my luck; there were no Germans on Poloda. And once again, we were interrupted by a visitor.

At first, I thought I was reliving my memory of when City Governor Virrul had dropped by the Gerrisan question box. A couple of gold-encrusted green shirts entered the room and looked around in case the Eljanhai was here stealing pens. Satisfied that she wasn't, they signaled Someone that it was safe to enter. Then Someone entered.

He was a small man, made smaller by his nervous, birdlike movements. His expression was a mixture of fear, suspicion and arrogance. If he ever smiled, his face would have broken.

More green shirts crowded into the question box behind him. All of them had several pounds of gold braid and medals on their uniforms. Everyone paid more attention to Someone than to me.

To my surprise, I thought that I recognized two green shirts: Sellon Sura and Loris Kiri. Sura was her Amazonian glamour girl self, tight-fitting green shirt and coverall and all.

She had at least a pound of gold braid on her shirt now. Her eyes narrowed in concentration when she saw me. Kiri was now playing secretary with a writing tablet in her hands. She was wearing prisoner's basic black again — which complimented her face and hair. Her eyes widened in shock. Her lips moved but I couldn't hear what she was saying.

Now I knew that I was either dreaming or hallucinating. Kiri was dead and Sura should be dead. I did my best to roll over and dream a better dream. Perhaps one in which Kiri and I were watching the Red Sox shut out the Yankees. I closed my eyes.

"Why is this man ignoring me?" demanded Someone. His voice was a sort of loud squeal.

"I will teach him some manners, Highest Most High," answered one of the comedians.

I was puzzling over the title "Highest Most High" when something stabbed me and lightning shot through my nerves. My muscles spasmed painfully against my restraints. At least one of my interrogators thought he was Luigi Galvani making frogs' muscles jump. The assembled Kapars barked laughter.

I twisted around and eyed Professor Galvani. He was standing arrogantly next to my table, hands on hips, electric wand in his right hand. It was still sparking. The power cord ran to his waist and then to some source behind him.

The hand soaking in the pan of water was partly free. I threw the water at him. Water splashed on the wand and down the Professor's leg. When it completed the circuit, lightning arced.

The Professor screamed and collapsed on the floor. Lying as he was in a puddle of water, electricity continued to torment him. His partner in slime goggled.

"Now *that's* entertainment!" I declared.

The Kapars stood in stunned silence. Kiri smiled ever so slightly at the Professor's comeuppance. She smoothed her face into a common Kapar nonexpression. Perhaps....

"I threw the water at him. Water splashed on the wand and down the Professor's leg. When it completed the circuit, lightning arced. The Professor screamed and collapsed on the floor.

246

Sura smiled as well. Only her smile was more like a shark smelling blood. Her contralto voice overrode the Professor's agonized grunting. "Most High Pom Da, I said that this man was Tomas Ran. This proves it."

"So you did," mused the small man.

Uh oh! The Pom Da. The Adolf Hitler of Poloda. There was only one thing to do.

I put a sincere expression on my face that I learned in Business School. It's not a smile but it looks like one. "Boy! Most Honorable Pom Da, am I glad to see you!" I gushed.

And I was, too. Dad frequently said that you always want to negotiate against the other team's top man because he has the power to give away the store. The Pom Da was taken aback by the idea of someone actually being glad to see him instead of quaking in fear.

While he was frowning his thoughts, the standing guard snapped, "The proper address for the Pom Da is 'Highest Most High.'" I noticed that Miss Manners didn't try to stab me with his wand. This was a good thing because I was out of water. I rolled my eyes and looked at him as if he were an obnoxious schoolboy interrupting his betters. Then I returned my again respectful gaze to the Pom Da.

"Highest Most High, this is one of the things that I need to speak to you about. I originally asked for an appointment to discuss a job in your administration but we also need to talk about your staff. For example, this lout didn't tell me that you were here or teach me proper manners or allow me a chance to clean up before our appointment." I ruefully gestured at my chains to indicate that they weren't proper business attire.

The guard's face dropped. He couldn't figure out how he had suddenly become the bad guy. He started to say something but the boss cut him off.

"You asked for an appointment with me?" He seemed to be genuinely puzzled. Good.

"Of course... Didn't you receive my request...? Isn't that why you're here now...?" I spoke haltingly as if I was just now realizing that something might be wrong.

"No," he snapped. "My interrogators...."

"...are idiots," I finished for him. "I make a simple request to speak to you and they take it upon themselves to deny you information of the utmost importance to your administration...."

A rainbow of emotions — all ugly — raced across the Pom Da's face: disbelief that anyone would interrupt him, curiosity at the 'information of the utmost importance' and anger at *someone*. He closed his mouth and then opened it again....

It was a delicate moment but the guard bailed me out by shouting at me. "Ikhurr! You lie! We obey the Pom Da and his officers!" He gestured dramatically with his wand.

I turned on him in my best Adolf Hitler imitation. "Silence, you buffoon! The Highest Most High was about to speak! And you dared to interrupt him!" His jaw metaphorically hit the floor. He paled and began stuttering.

I quickly turned back to the dictator, my face apologetic. "Highest Most High, you see the problem here. Your staff is poorly trained and incapable of carrying out your orders properly. That's one of the things that I can help you with."

The tyrant was still choking mentally on the idea that anyone would interrupt him. Since I seemed to be on his side, he wasn't sure whether he should scream at me or Miss Manners.

A Zabo agent attempted clarify the situation. "Highest Most High, this prisoner is insolent vermin. I respectfully suggest that he be returned to the question box until he provides us with the Unisan Order of Battle and other answers."

"Ah, hah," I said archly. "Yet *another* person who is *anxious* to prevent me from *helping* the Pom Da with *the most critical problems of his administration*. Why are *you* interfering with the execution of the Pom Da's policies?" I accused, glowering at the green shirt as if our positions were reversed.

He cursed and denied everything. "You lie! We obey the Pom Da's policies!!"

"Is that why you green-shirted ozmonkeys are losing The War?" I asked sweetly. I used the Allosan word for 'ozmonkeys.'

That produced an explosion of incoherent sound. Everyone (except Kiri and me) was shouting and screaming at the top of his lungs. The city of Babel must have sounded like this about an hour after the Confounding of the Language.

I waited impassively like an adult unimpressed by a child's temper tantrum. The green shirts were outraged. The two gray shirts present smirked. Kiri was struggling to avoid laughing out loud. Sellon Sura said something that no one heard and stopped, alternatively watching her tyrant and me. The Pom Da turned a truly beautiful shade of purple.

Finally, the dictator screamed, "Silence!" at the top of his lungs. Everyone shut up instantly.

I jumped back in. I pointed at the aggressive Zabo agent and demanded, "You haven't answered the question, *Kapar*." I made the word as sarcastic as possible. "If you are loyal to the Pom Da and obey his policies faithfully, why are you losing The War?"

"Yes, Kapar, why?" echoed a sardonic gray shirt.

"Unlike the army, the Zabo is not losing The War!!" screamed the green shirt. He was turning a pretty impressive shade of purple as well.

The Pom Da took his pistol out of his holster and shot both of them without further ado. There are no long drawn-out trials in Kapara.

That produced another deathly silence. The remaining gray shirt attempted to turn invisible. The Pom Da turned to me, gun in hand, and demanded, "Explain to me why I should not just execute you now?" The ferocious whine of his normal voice was almost silky smooth.

I looked him squarely in the eye and played my ace. "Because I can win The War for you, Highest Most High."

Sellon Sura sucked in her breath. Kiri turned chalk white. Her writing tablet crashed to the floor. Several Zabo agents muttered incomprehensible noises.

"How?" the Pom Da snapped.

"I would form a land army for you and defeat the Unisan land army in glorious battle." I paused for effect. "I will need your permission and authority to do so, of course." My words were utterly sincere.

"Why do I need you?"

"Because none of your other people can do this. If they could, they would have done so by now, Highest Most High."

"One 'Highest Most High' is sufficient," said the Pom Da wearily. "Where would you get this land army from?"

"From several sources, Most High. From Zabo and military troops already fighting land warfare. From underused military troops such as aircraft mechanics who have no airplanes to work on. And from your worker and prisoner populations. Many prisoners will fight for Kapara if offered freedom at the end of The War."

The Pom Da paused to think about the idea. Another Zabo agent diffidently brought up Montar Ban's point about prisoners loose in Kapar society. I reminded him about military discipline and predicted that most of them would die gloriously for the Pom Da. There would always be meat in the slop.

Finally, the Pom Da asked, "How can I trust you, Tomas Ran?" He drew out the 'm' in my name. "Earthmen are notoriously untrustworthy."

I nodded my head sadly. "Most High, I understand your suspicions...."

"I am never wrong!"

"Of course not," I agreed quickly. "That's how I know that the recent setbacks in The War are the result of your underlings not following your orders. The reason why you are suspicious of me is that the arch-spy Tangor deceived your underlings and then stole your power amplifier. However, I am no traitor like Tangor. He demanded freedom to work in his own way, which of course, was a cover for his betrayal of your trust. I, on the other hand, have nothing to hide. I volunteer to be an army officer subject to regular military discipline and control. Moreover, I suggest that you assign a detail of Zabo agents to both guard me and ensure that I do not return to Unis."

The Pom Da's eyes narrowed. "You say that you are not a traitor but you are obviously betraying Unis."

"I am not a Unisan and I never have been," I said smoothly. Kiri flushed. Her body shook with suppressed emotion. Sellon Sura looked at me with new eyes.

"Unis took me in and gave me a job. I did that job: I conquered Punos and Allos for the Eljanhai. If you give me the job of conquering Punos and Allos —" I paused for effect, "— and Unis for you, I will do that job." The Pom Da began nodding his head thoughtfully.

Sura opened her mouth and then closed it. There was an ominous gleam in her eye. Then she made her face bland. Or as bland as a Kapar can be.

"You have the true Kapar spirit, Tomas Ran."

Ouch. I smiled in appreciation.

"Very well. Since my other officers have not won The War, I will give you a chance." He pointed to two Zabo agents. "You and you, release this man and escort him to the palace for more detailed instructions."

The Zabo agents passed the orders to Professor Galvani and Miss Manners, both of whom looked at me as if I were King Kong. I smiled benevolently as they unshackled me. For some reason, that made them even more nervous.

"By the way, Most High, there is the matter of my rank in the Kapar army. I am already a Wing Commander in the Unisan Fighting Corps." I kept my face as expressionless as possible.

The Pom Da nodded. "You are promoted to the rank of Force Leader of the new Kapar land army."

I thanked the Pom Da loudly and sincerely. In Polodan militaries, force leaders were the equivalents of US Army generals of the army. I was coming up in the world. "And one more thing, Most High."

He frowned. I was getting close to the edge here.

"I would like that woman to be my Special Assistant."

Sellon Sura looked at me thoughtfully. I pointed to Kiri. She blushed and lowered her head modestly.

Sura scowled and objected. The Pom Da waved her off with an airy gesture. "You have enjoyed her long enough, Special Assistant. Let him have her." Sura submitted with poor grace.

The job interview was over. My guards escorted me to the palace for the new employee orientation lecture. I limped for the rest of my life after leaving the Ergos question box.

AFTERWARD, I was back in the army with a vengeance. The gray shirts produced a Kapar uniform in short order and a temporary office by the end of the day; neither fitted properly.

When I went to check my office out, Kiri was there. I remembered to close the door on the outside world and rushed over to her. I clasped her in my arms. I rubbed her cheek with mine.

She made a strangling sound and pushed against my shoulders with both hands. "You are squeezing me to death!" she choked out. She made the Kapar syllables sound like an angel's blessing.

I relaxed my grip. I looked her full in the face. "I thought you were dead."

"And I you. I am so glad that you are actually alive. I could not believe Special Assistant Sellon when she announced that you were alive."

I shrugged. "'The rumors of my death have been greatly exaggerated.'"

She smiled at my quotation. We had discussed Mark Twain on our long walk from Gerris to Nira. "And now you are alive – to serve the Pom Da." She spoke earnestly.

I frowned and shook my head. "That was a ru...." I began.

She thrust her hand into my mouth and held it there. Startled by the unexpected (although not entirely unpleasant) action, I froze in place. She leaned forward and whispered into my ear. "There are hidden listeners."

I wanted to nod but couldn't. I gently took her hand and removed it from my mouth. I held it longer than necessary before I dropped it. "I understand," I said aloud. "We are both alive to serve the Pom Da."

By unspoken agreement, we stepped back from each other. My eyes feasted on her beauty and, I fancied, her eyes complimented me. But we quickly began looking around the bare office. We saw nothing out of the ordinary. In Kapara, that meant nothing.

Finally, I broke the awkward silence. "Well, I suppose that we should get to work. Your title will be Special Assistant. Your initial duties will be those of my administrative assistant."

"Yes, Force Leader. I understand."

"Very good, Special Assistant." It was all very formal, very horrible, and all very necessary.

The Zabo surely suspected my feelings already. If they decided that Kiri was anything but ambulatory furniture, each of us would be a hostage to the other's good behavior.

"Force Leader, may I ask a personal question?"

"Yes, Special Assistant."

"Who is your favorite Pom Da of the United States of America?" Butter would not have melted in her mouth. Ah, hah! Loris Kiri might not have learned conspiracy at her mother's knee as Sellon Sura obviously had, but my little redhead was catching up fast.

"My favorite is George Washington and my second favorite is Abraham Lincoln," I replied honestly. The school teacher of Unis nodded decisively and amplified for the benefit of our listeners.

"George Washington because he defeated the British monarchy and founded the United States. He persevered against incredible odds and emerged victorious. Abraham Lincoln because he guided his country through the worst war in your history. Pom Da Lincoln was ill served by his military officers early in the war but he emerged victorious when he found and promoted able men."

"Exactly right," I confirmed. I nodded my head sagely for emphasis.

"Well, Force Leader Tomas." She gave my Polodan name the Kapar pronunciation. "I believe that we should get to work. We have a war to win."

Chapter 20 *LENI RIEFENSTAHL*
        WOULD HAVE BEEN PROUD

T HE NEXT YEAR and a half passed in a blur of work
— organizational and training work that was *generally* similar to the equivalent processes in Unis.

Aided by the bureaucratic nature of the Kapar tyranny,
the new Thirteenth Force and its subordinate units took shape
rapidly. At first, people cooperated grudgingly because I was
obviously the Pom Da's latest pet and no one wanted to be on
his bad side despite my diversion of resources. As time passed,
I became aware of changing emotions and more enthusiastic
cooperation. The Kapars wanted me to win The War for them…!

The Kapar Department of Education and Propaganda
painted every little military action as a glorious victory. But
my new peers among the Kapar elite were privy to reality.

The land war had bogged down into a stalemate similar
to the Western Front in Earth's puny World War I. Battle lines
followed the western border of Allos from Ithris down to the
Southern Pole. There was constant raiding back and forth and
occasional incidents such as the Karisans planting their flag on
that Pole, but no great progress in either direction. Both sides
were conserving their strength and building up their manpower.

The air war was an ongoing and expanding disaster.
Tangor had pointed out that Unisan flyboys killed Kapar airmen
at a ratio of at least two-to-one and sometimes as high as five-

to-one. Until recently, the larger Kapar population had supplied enough manpower to balance superior Unisan equipment and training. But the vicious air battles that had accompanied the liberation of Allos and Punos had devastated the black-winged fleets. Five years ago, two million Kapar airplanes darkened Poloda's skies. Now a tenth of that number struggled to survive. In contrast, the Unisans had started with a million planes. Now they were down to four or five hundred thousand. The Soviet Pom Da Vladimir Lenin had said that quantity had a quality all its own. The Kapar air force was still fighting to keep Unisan bombers away from Auris and Heris but the skies over Epris were a lost cause.

And each day seemed to bring a new report of another Eprisan city cracked open and gutted by massed super bombs. Nonetheless, any open talk of peace could lead to a quick trip to the nearest question box.

The Kapar elite knew my role in the Unisan air, land and sea offensive. What I was doing would never work in the United States. No defector would ever be allowed the kind of power that the Pom Da had awarded me. But his unlimited power and the resulting brutal political maneuvering and in-sensitivity to bloodshed or friendship meant that bitter enemies one day had to be ready to cooperate against common foes the next day. I was simply an extreme example of established lack-of-principles. Now the Kapar elite were hoping that I would undo what I had done. No *other* Kapar had been able to repel the Unisan invasion; perhaps I could.

I assured them that I could. Always tell the truth whenever possible.

It was startling enough to find the gray shirts looking at me as if I were George Washington or the first Pom Da Kapar Ov. It was truly amazing when I realized that some green shirts were doing the same thing.

Things soon became clear. The green shirts' defensive victories at Ilgros and Ergos had boosted their stock enormously with the only man whose opinion counted. But it had come at an unprecedented cost in lives. The Kapar police force was huge in comparison to any Earthly or Polodan counterpart. But, as gigantic as it was, it was stretched to the breaking point by the requirements of governing a population of 400 million, maintaining order among restive peoples, fighting a war that they had never trained for, and keeping an eye on the military that hated them. If I could crush the Unisans, things would settle down and they could exploit their new prestige.

The fact that I was recruiting heavily from their criminal population to form the Black Legion was a bonus in the Zabo's eyes especially since I quietly promised to kill most of them off in battle. Always tell the truth whenever possible.

Even so, the Zabo maintained the "guard force" that I had requested from the Pom Da close to me ten Polodan hours a day and ten Polodan days a week. They were respectful of my rank and didn't find it necessary to follow me into the bathroom. But they checked everyone I came in contact with and no one forgot who was working for whom.

The Thirteenth Force was a hodgepodge of units including green and gray shirts already fighting the land war. The Ironheart Division was composed of Kapar fanatics. Teach them to speak German and they would fit right into the Waffen SS. Other divisions had equally ferocious names.

The Black Legion was composed of prisoners who volunteered to fight for freedom. Well, for *their* freedom once The War was over. Many of them were the petty offenders of the Kapar injustice system — men like Oundurun Tod and Garrud Kun, both of whom I requested by name. Most of them didn't like military discipline but liked the alternative less.

Others were real hard cases, especially the robbers and murderers that we snatched out of the hands of the Zabo executioners. These were people who couldn't act in a civilized manner even by Kapar standards. However, most of them shaped up once we handed some of the real scumbags back to the green-shirted headsman. There's nothing like watching a troublemaker's head rolling around on the floor to encourage good behavior. Especially when the lesson is reinforced with rewards for good behavior.

KIRI AND I were studying a map of Ergos one night when Garrud knocked on the office door. I gave permission; he entered, saluted and reported. "Most High, we caught another spy snooping around headquarters." He seemed puzzled by the event.

"Good. Bring him in and sit him down there." I pointed to a spot in front of my new desk. The expansion of the Thirteenth Force into a real army had included our being assigned a new building deep inside Ergos. We could barely hear the Unisans pounding on the roof of the city. "You know the good cop/bad cop routine."

"Yes, Most High." Garrud departed. He returned less than two minutes later with a relatively young red-shirted fellow with his hands tied behind his back. He was accompanied by Section Leader and five gray-shirted guards.

In the interval, Kiri had cleaned off my desk and sat down beside it like a court reporter. I had placed a chair where I had indicated and settled myself behind my desk like a judge. The huge, flattering portrait of the Pom Da on the wall behind me reinforced the courtroom atmosphere.

Our visitor insisted that he was a maintenance man here to inspect the air conditioning system. Section Leader called him a liar, saying that the system had been inspected last week.

That was more or less true. We had found a red-shirted Zabo agent trying to hide microphones in the system. He had had an unfortunate traffic accident on his way out of the building. The newspapers had mentioned that briefly. I suspected that our ersatz maintenance man was the second team.

Kiri telephoned the ace of spies' alleged place of work. She listened for a few minutes and shook her head. Garrud urged the ace to cooperate while Section Leader reminded him of what the victims of traffic accidents looked like. He went into revolting detail.

Finally Ace broke down and confessed that he was a Zabo agent. Section Leader laughed at him, pointing out that there was an entire team of green shirts lounging in the outer office. Clearly this false maintenance man was a burglar trying to intimidate honest Kapars. Garrud gently asked if he had any identification to prove that he was an agent. He shook his head. Section Leader commented that late night traffic was still dangerous.

At this point, I mildly asked the young fellow if he really was a Zabo agent. He nodded his head energetically. "Then prove it. Where is your office and who is your superior officer?" He paused and Section Leader asked me for permission to "remove" the prisoner.

The young fellow broke down and began babbling. By midnight, he had given us the names, jobs, and assignments of an entire station of Zabo agents in our neighborhood plus scattered agents from around the area. We continued questioning and dug out details about his fellow agents' personal relationships, homes, habits, weaknesses....

As he cooperated, Section Leader faded into the background while Garrud beamed approval and encouraged further revelations. A couple of my guys brought food from the building cafeteria and pretty soon we were having a picnic in my office including plenty of wine. The Kapar elite lives extremely well in contrast to their population and even dedicated Zabo agents relish a good feed. Kiri drew a picture of the festivities and Ace signed and dated it.

Close to dawn, the party broke up. We were now all best buddies. Ace was welcome to come and go as his bosses required, provided he checked in with headquarters security.

We gave him a Thirteenth Force organization chart as a parting gift. When the night shift left the building, Ace went with them like a gentleman. He was still a little tipsy from the wine so a couple of my guys escorted him home. That way, he didn't run into any nasty traffic accidents and my guys got to look at the inside of his apartment.

Afterward, Garrud Kun asked to see me in private and expressed his amazement. "Most High, why did we treat last night's spy to a party instead of a traffic accident?"

"Counterespionage, Group Commander. We turned a low level Zabo agent into one of our agents inside the Zabo. First, he told us a lot about the Zabo in our area and he will tell us more when he gets deeper into our pocket. Second, as long as he's producing quality results, his leaders are less likely to send in spies that we don't catch. Both factors make it easier for us to build the Thirteenth Force without police interference."

Garrud grunted. As far as he was concerned, the entire police apparatus was a gigantic waste of time and diversion of resources from the true guardians of the Kapar regime. Perhaps a few clerks did useful work but otherwise.... "What if he betrays us to the Zabo?"

"He betrays himself as well. It will be hard for him to explain that signed picture of him partying with us unless he's a corrupt wastrel as well. If we continue to feed him high quality food and low quality information, he's ours."

Garrud Kun shook his head in puritanical disbelief but Ace was back the next week. He timed his arrival so that lunch was being served just when we finished swapping information.

OTHER CHALLENGES WERE SUBTLER. Sellon Sura slithered up to me at a wine tasting party for the Kapar elite. I was raiding the food bar while most of the guests were getting smashed on the other side of the room. Eating right helps you keep your head on your shoulders – a fact that I appreciated all the more that evening. The universal shirt and coverall outfit made most Kapar women look like boys if not bags of suet. Sura's tight fitting clothes reminded everyone other than Helen Keller that she was all woman. Just like Mata Hari.

After some pleasantries, she shooed a waiter away so that we could speak privately. She offered me some a Polodan apple and a smile. "Congratulations on your promotion, Force Leader."

"Thank you, Special Assistant Sellon." I accepted the apple and offered her a fruit dish. The liberation of Allos had cut off the garan supplies but the elite still ate well.

"Call me Sura. It is my *personal* name, Ran." She tried to be kittenish and failed.

"Of course. What do you wish to speak about?"

"Oh, I was wondering what the Pom Da would say if he knew that you destroyed the city of Gerris?" Her smile developed shark-like qualities.

Uh, oh. "Probably that you are a traitor trying to hinder The War effort by making false accusations against a loyal servant of the Kapar regime. Your motive is to cover up your own failings in handling my initial arrival on Poloda. If you hadn't tortured me and thrown me into the prison system without a trial, I could have started working for Kapara three years ago and the Pom Da would be celebrating the conquest of Unis by now. You do remember Unis, don't you? It is the country that you wanted to be continental governor of. Care for one of these little sandwiches? I think the mystery meat is real horse."

Sura's face turned as white as a cloud and then as red as a sunset. She jerked backward a step. Her eyes flashed lightning. Her hand came up to slap my face... but I caught it with my off hand. I didn't let it go until I was ready.

I leaned forward to share a confidence. "You don't have a thug ready to dent my skull tonight, Sura," I hissed. "This is obviously a shakedown of some sort. What do you want?"

She ignored the question and tried to get her wrist out of my grasp. She was a big woman and she almost succeeded. Finally she stopped. She looked into my eyes with her baby blues. The hint of madness had returned. "I have evidence of your crimes in Gerris. It is…."

"…. in a safe place where I will never find it. A colleague of yours will send it to the proper authorities if anything happens to you," I finished for her.

Her face twisted in confusion. "How did you know that?"

Now I ignored her question. "Skip the theatrics. Describe my alleged crimes."

As Grandmother Randolph would have said, Sura was clearly "saving up spit." However, she obliged with a concise description of many of my good deeds in Gerris. She missed a number of points including putting Virrul out of Kiri's misery but, overall, Sura would have made a good detective. So, I laughed at her, out loud; as if she had been telling a funny story. No one else took more than momentary interest.

Naturally, she was outraged by my failure to fall on my knees and beg forgiveness. But I cut her off before she could say something that I would have to make both of us regret.

"Your overall theory is weak and your witnesses are all hysterical people who panicked when the Unisans destroyed Gerris. Seriously, which is more logical: a lone man with no weapons and in police custody destroyed an entire fortress city, or that the Unisan air force did the job, possibly using their experimental super bombs? I distinctly recall hearing people blame the Unisans at the time, not me.

"And assuming that I did destroy Gerris after you tortured me for no reason, doesn't that mean that the Gerris police are a pack of incompetent morons? And who is the highest-ranking police officer that survived the disaster? I believe that would be you, Sura. Seriously. I saw you taking charge of the city after the disaster so that makes you responsible for the previous failings of the police including the disaster.

"And speaking of you taking charge, I saw you ordering the execution of dozens if not hundreds of people. How many people did you execute to cover up your failures of command? And assuming that a lone agent destroyed Gerris, your own story says that he sounded the emergency siren and gave people time to evacuate. Your theoretical lone agent saved a lot of Kapar lives that you gunned down, Suurraah." I slurred her name on purpose. Anger makes people do stupid things.

"So, Suurraah, do you really want to make these false charges and to face the resulting investigation of *your* actions in Gerris? Hmmmm?" I arched my eyebrows to emphasize the question.

Sellon Sura was still standing in front of me but the valkyrie of Gerris was gone. In her place was a deeply hurt little girl; a little girl whose pet puppy had just been kicked to death. For a moment, I wanted to take her in my arms and comfort her....

She looked into my eyes and breathed very deeply – a dual movement as spontaneous as a political party drafting a president for a third term in office. "I thought that we could be friends. I thought that we could help each other."

Until the day I'm of no further use to you and I wake up with a knife in my ribs.

"I think that we can help each other," I said judiciously. Always tell the truth whenever possible.

Hope broke out on Sura's face like sunshine after a rainstorm. "What will you give me?" I asked.

"Anything," she replied in a little girl voice. She stepped forward, looking up into my face. Just at that moment, I think she was completely sincere.

"I accept. The first thing that I want from you is all of the evidence that you gathered about the disaster at Gerris. All Of It." She flinched but reluctantly agreed.

"Second, you should inspect the Thirteenth Force headquarters and military-police cooperation arrangements. While you are visiting our headquarters, you and I will discuss the Zabo and ways to improve its leadership."

Her eyes bulged like a cartoon character. Her face was filled with a radiant vision. "Do you mean...?" She whispered, partly for fear of being overhead, mostly because she could not believe the implications.

"Of course," I replied confidently. "Friends help each other." She nodded vigorously, her face still glowing.

"And at that time, we will discuss your future career plans. I cannot promise the continental governorship of Unis but that job will be open upon the successful conclusion of The War." I paused and smiled warmly. "I believe that the Pom Da will consider my recommendation very seriously."

"Yes, Ran, I will." She lowered her face with apparent modesty. Again, the tiger was trying to play a kitten. We were now best buddies. But as soon as the evening was over, I went back to headquarters and doubled our security arrangements. And, after that, I made sure to have Kiri on my arm when I attended wine tasting parties.

MY POWER AS a leader, even with the Pom Da's blessing, only extended so far. Neither the Zabo nor the army wanted the Black Legion to have guns. The Legion didn't even have regular gray-shirted uniforms. They had to settle for black coveralls and gray shirts and jackets. The police and military leadership did allow us to train with real weapons but every gun and unused bullet was confiscated afterwards. When I complained, I was told that weapons would be issued when needed. I pretended to believe that.

The other divisions in the Thirteenth Force were properly equipped but the Legion was a significant fraction of our total manpower. The Legionnaires needed weapons.

The obvious answer was a parade.

SURPRISINGLY, the militaristic Kapars had no large-scale parades or even any military bands. I thought that all dictatorships loved marching troops but this was clearly a difference between Earth and Poloda.

We staged our show in a huge cavern large enough for a game of American rules football. Everyone of any importance attended if only for the novelty; that and the chance to bask in the Pom Da's favor. I slipped him a schedule of events with cues beforehand so that he was never at a loss for words.

My Legionnaires marched back and forth and formally presented themselves to the Pom Da for approval. A women's chorus sang the old Kapar marching song, "Hearts of Iron, Eyes of Fire," and other favorites. Pretty soon, the entire audience was pounding its fists in Kapar applause.

We also staged a play in which a Pom Da impersonator and some representative Kapars (including Legionnaires) repelled a Unisan attack. The victorious Kapars escorted two "prisoners" to the dais. One was a blonde man dressed in Unisan Fighting Corps blue while the other was a redheaded woman dressed in gold spangles and red boots.

The man formally surrendered the land of Unis to the Kapar empire and the woman surrendered the people to his mastery. If she had fluttered her eyelashes any harder at the Pom Da, the entire audience would have been blown to Oz by the resulting tornado.

The dictator of an empire greater than anything that Adolf Hitler or Genghis Khan had ever achieved stood up (on a box that I had positioned while other people were watching the show). He formally accepted the service of the Black Legion. I began applauding as loudly as I could. The Legion followed my lead. The audience joined in. The huge cavern was filled with thunder for many minutes. I got a gold medal large enough to serve soup from and the Black Legion got its guns. Leni Riefenstahl would have been proud.

Chapter 21 GO TO THE HEAD OF
THE CLASS

I T CAME TIME for the Thirteenth Force to officially present our plans to win The War to the Pom Da. Naturally, some second lieutenant almost messed everything up.

I was chauffeured to the Pom Da's palace on the bottom level of Ergos like a gentleman. (The city water treatment plant was five levels *above* the palace. Apparently, if you have enough rank, you *can* ignore the laws of physics.) My iron-gray motor car was followed by a cavalcade of trucks carrying a representative unit of the Force. We entered a gigantic cavern next to the palace where public ceremonies were held. The traffic cops had been alerted to our coming and they directed us into a multistory garage opening off the square. We parked, got out and formed up. I gave my guys a quick inspection with Kiri trailing behind me.

Then we marched across the square and up to the stupendously ugly building that housed the Pom Da, signal flags flying in the breeze of the executive air conditioning and the glare of massed electrical curlicues high overhead. The important Kapars who had reasons to be in the vicinity of the palace stopped to watch. Some of them made fists in salute and I carefully returned every salute we received.

Some green-shirted platoon leader stopped us at the gates and inspected our credentials. Those were in order but he almost had a heart attack when he saw that we were armed with our hard-won guns and swords. After a short argument,

266

I told him to have his men fetch a box. He did and we stacked our guns and swords in the box. Each member of the platoon representing the entire Thirteenth Force saluted the pipsqueak before disarming. Naturally, he swelled up like a puffer fish. His men stowed the weapons inside the front door where we could pick them up on the way out.

The Pom Da's public office is a huge room with a dais at one end topped by a desk large enough to land small airplanes on. Behind the desk was the only chair in the room. Seated in the chair was the supreme Kapar himself, his hideous face glowing with pride. Everyone else in the room stood the entire time they were there.

The Pom Da's new administrative assistant got to stand beside the desk, writing tablet in hand. She was Heze Salis, the woman who had played the female Unisan prisoner in our parade. The Pom Da had liked her performance. The elite Zabo and military officers as well as some honored red shirts present for the ceremony stood in ranks on the main floor near the dais. Assorted Zabo agents clustered near the main door to ensure that the Eljanhai didn't sneak in and tie their bootlaces together. They also escorted guests from the door to the throne and back again. The latter checked us all for concealed weapons and reluctantly passed us into the Presence.

We staged another short parade and show. Since we only had a platoon of troops this time, we emphasized waving colorful signal flags, which contrasted nicely with our black and gray uniforms. The Pom Da sort of smiled and the assembled bigwigs pounded their fists in applause.

Finally, we got down to business. Kiri and I advanced to the imperial desk where I pompously announced the submission of the high-level war plan Operation Grand Sweep, and its subordinate operations to recapture eastern Epris and then conquer Unis. Kiri unrolled the elaborate map on the desk. Nothing improves a presentation like including a pretty girl.

The trouble was the map rolled right back up after Kiri released it. Not a good start. I apologized to the Pom Da before he could explode and borrowed knickknacks from his desk to anchor the four corners of the stubborn roll of plastic.

As the dictator was drinking in the confident gray arrows cutting across eastern Epris and Unis, I borrowed a pen from his desk and stabbed him in the soft spot under his right ear. He convulsed as if electrocuted and Omys was a brighter place.

I shouted "Air Maiden!" and yanked his body upright so I could grab his pistol.

My guys reacted instantly, splitting into two teams and charging their green- and gray-shirted tormentors. They had no weapons except for their signal flags — and their hearts and hands.

The Kapar elite were stunned speechless by the assassination and the charge of the Black Legion. We gained valuable seconds before they reacted. They woke up when I started systematically gunning down green shirts starting with the Chief of the Zabo. A number of my guys had requested the privilege of killing him slowly but, as Dad always said, business before pleasure.

Two gray shirts tried to charge me by going through Loris Kiri. She dropped to the floor and they tripped over her. While they were trying to figure out how the floor jumped up and slapped them silly, she rolled, came to her feet, and kicked them unconscious.

Four lines of fighters collided, Black Legionnaires against the grays and greens. The Zabo agents had more than decimated the apparently unarmed rebels but my guys reached their foes. Stiff hand blows shattered necks and wrists; savate kicks broke legs and crushed stomachs. The defenders of the Kapar regime collapsed under the unprecedented attack. Even so, it was only a forlorn hope left standing when the last of the

"I shouted 'Air Maiden!' and yanked his body upright so I could grab his pistol."

Kapar elite died or surrendered. But all of us were grinning from ear to ear.

"Well done, men!" I shouted as I gestured. "You four stand guard here! The rest of you, get our weapons from the front hall and signal the reinforcements! Kiri, shut that woman up!"

I had tossed the former Pom Da's body on the desk to get it out of my way. Salis was screaming and crying simultaneously over the death of her boss. Kiri stepped over to the larger woman and shook her vigorously. When that didn't staunch the noise, Kiri slapped her in the face. Salis fell silent. Kiri said something that I didn't catch and pointed to me. Salis stared and a smile broke out on her face. What had Kiri said?

Our four guards herded the merely stunned or wounded Kapars into a gaggle in front of the desk. Most of them were shocked speechless. One green shirt began a harangue. I signaled and a Legionnaire cut him off with a fist.

I began going through the former Pom Da's pockets and then his desk. Salis stepped over to me and asked, "Highest Most High Pom Da, are you looking for the executive notebook?"

I froze momentarily when she called me Pom Da but figured that I had better get used to it. "Yes, I need his telephone numbers."

She pulled a drawer open and handed me a battered notebook. Inside were lists of names, organizations and telephone numbers. Jackpot!

"Thank you. Heze Salis, you are confirmed as administrative assistant to the Pom Da." I paused and clarified, "Myself. You will report to Special Assistant Loris Kiri."

"Yes, Most High," she said in a husky voice.

Gunfire erupted from the front lobby. Every eye jerked to the doors separating the Pom Da's office from the outer rooms of the building. Our prisoners began babbling. I sucked in half the air in Omos' atmosphere belt.

"Kapars!" I thundered. "I hereby proclaim myself to be the new Pom Da of Kapara. The nation is hereby renamed the United States of Poloda and the several colonies are raised to the status of states co-equal with the state of Zurris (formerly Kapara). I also assume the title of *President* of the United States of Poloda. I request the approval of the Council of Five."

Three counselors were still alive, all red shirts. They were in charge of philosophy, education and propaganda; war production; and general production, respectively. The philosopher tried to make a speech but my parliamentarian slapped him soundly and he moved the question. The two economists quickly got on board the railroad. The Chiefs of the Zabo and the Army were both dead but I appointed substitutes and that was that.

The philosopher started another speech but he yielded the floor when Black Legionnaires began pouring into the huge office, guns in their hands and fire in their hearts. Their commander was Division Leader Oundurun Tod. Behind them, I could see other Legionnaires sprinting out of the garage, across the great square, and into my palace.

The old Pom Da had authorized a platoon for the occasion. I had authorized the other 24 platoons myself. We had the palace. I sat down at the executive desk and began capturing the new United States.

First, I called Police Command Headquarters and told the officer of the day that the military had just assassinated the Pom Da and the Chief of the Zabo. I was now the new Pom Da and my appointee was the new chief of police. Always tell the truth whenever possible. In the meantime, the officer of the day was in charge. I ordered him to mobilize his entire force and take the military into custody. The code name for this operation was Round Up. He gulped and announced, "I obey!" I congratulated him on having the true Kapar spirit.

Then I called Thirteenth Force headquarters and spoke to Garrud Kun. I told him that the Zabo was on their way to arrest him, the Force and the rest of the military. He and the Ironheart Division should seize vital communications facilities in accordance with Operation Air Maiden at once. His "I obey!" was positively gleeful.

And then I called Military Command Headquarters and warned them that the Zabo was attempting a coup. I ordered the military to capture or kill every green shirt in the three continents. The code name for this operation was Fortitude.

The War Leader on duty paused noticeably before answering. "Highest Most High, I am not sure that we have sufficient manpower to capture all of the police. Our surviving airpower is engaged in defending the three continents from the bluecoats. And our airmen have not been trained for warfare inside our cities."

"Good analysis, War Leader," I responded. "I want you to ground three-tenths of our air fleet. I will get the Unisans out of our skies. Then you will land another six-tenths in two phases. That will provide you with the necessary manpower. The remaining one-tenth of our air fleet will be sufficient for patrols once the Unisans are gone. In addition, arm every mechanic and supply clerk in the army. Do you understand?"

There was a *very* long silence on the line. I barked "Is anyone there?" several times before the War Leader responded. His voice was very strange.

"Please excuse me, Highest Most High. Did I understand you to say that you will clear the Unisans from our skies?" Clearly he did not believe what he was hearing. That blasted lobster again.

"Yes, I'll do that."

There was another lengthy silence. When he spoke again, he sounded like a little boy rather than a professional field marshal. "Highest Most High…."

"One 'Highest Most High' is sufficient." Omys! I was even beginning to sound like the Pom… the former Pom Da.

"Yes, Most High. I obey! However, the bluecoats have attacked us almost daily for over 100 years and never more fiercely than in the last year. With respect, it seems impossible for any one person to rid us of the Blue Threat." You could hear the shock and awe in his voice.

I forced myself to smile. Mama always said that people can hear a genuine smile over the telephone. I adopted a "just between us girls" tone.

"War Leader, I am your Pom Da. I have never failed you. Begin grounding the air fleet. Secure our bases against Zabo attacks and then counterattack their police stations. I guarantee that I will get the Unisans to leave. Do you understand?"

"Yes, Most High! I obey!"

"You also stated a concern that our airmen have not been trained to fight inside cities. This is true. But, unlike the traitors who are even now attacking our airmen and facilities, we possess the true Kapar spirit! We cannot be defeated!"

"Yes, Most High!! I obey!!" We concluded our conversation with mutual congratulations.

The next phone call was the most difficult to connect. I demanded that the Kapar Foreign Office — yes, there actually was one — connect me with the Eljanhai of Unis.

While I was waiting for the call to go through, Salis raided the former Pom Da's personal food bar for us. I directed both sides of the Kapar civil war between bites. Kiri took notes and wrote orders. Messengers dashed to and fro. The inevitable staff officers set up charts, maps and lists. Change the black and gray uniforms to American brown or British khaki and we could have been in Fort Benning or Aldershot.

With the palace secure, I sent Tod off to muster the remainder of the Black Legion and to execute Operation Dragoon. "Dragoon" is a Kapar word for coercing or browbeating someone. He grinned, saluted, and raced off.

My telephone rang and the attention light went immediately to red. I answered in Unisan, "Tomas Ran, Pom Da and President of the United States of Poloda, formerly known as Kapara."

The man's voice on the other end of the line exploded, "What?! Is this a joke? Tomas Ran is dead."

"I was, but I got better. Twice," I responded airily and accurately. "Is this Palden Zar? I asked to speak to Eljanhai Tondul Misema."

"Misema was assassinated two years ago by a Kapar infiltrator. I am the Eljanhai of the Republic of Unis. If this is really Tomas Ran the American, why did you speak French at home?"

"Because Mama was a French war bride. If this is Palden Zar, who is the princess of Unis?"

"Fontan Ianami. Uvala! It really is you, Ran!" The old war dog's voice was filled with astonishment and wonder.

"Yes, Zar. However, at the moment we seem to have a war on that I would like to end. The United States of Poloda, as successor to the Kapar empire, formally accepts Unis' most recent offer of an honorable peace. Hold your land forces in place along the Allosan western border and we will do the same. Cease your aerial attacks and get your planes out of our airspace. That is defined as all of Auris and Heris plus all of Epris excluding Allos and Punos. In return, we will cease attacking Allos, Punos, Karis and Unis. Both sides can fly patrols over the oceans to prevent sneak attacks but neither side will fire on the other. Deal?"

Zar snorted half derisively, half humorously. "Are you going to be running both sides of The War now?"

I sort of waggled my head in amusement but remembered that he couldn't see me. "If I have to; it would certainly save a lot of work on both sides."

"True. How long will this truce run?"

"What did your last offer say?"

Zar made a humming sound before answering. "I do not remember. I have not taken the offers very seriously for many years now."

"It'll take time to get the orders to the pilots. Let's get the orders issued as soon as we can. We'll land three-tenths of our air fleets today as a sign of good faith. The truce goes into full effect at noon Ergos time three days from now and remains in effect for one year. After that, it will be renewable by mutual consent. Deal?"

"Yes; deal. Ran, what about the future?"

"Zar, my long-range goal is the same as yours: an honorable peace for all of Poloda. There are a great many details to be worked out but Polodans created The War and Polodans can end it."

"With a little help from some Earthmen. One more question, Ran. Have you been to Uvala?" Zar's voice was again filled with wonder but also trepidation as if he was not sure that he could handle the answer.

"Not yet." We exchanged pleasantries and hung up.

As soon as I finished with Palden Zar, I called Military Command again and told them the details of the truce. The War Leader was so effusive in his praise that I seriously thought of sending Section Leader over there to slap him sober. I didn't, though; he still had the police war to run.

Then I announced the truce with Unis to my staff and had Garrud Kun's men send a few Education & Propaganda boys over to hear the word first hand. The whole nation would hear it soon enough.

I noticed that everyone was looking at me as if I was a combination of Charles Lindbergh and Errol Flynn. I tried to ignore it even though it was more than a little creepy. After that I called....

And after that I called....

And after *that* I called....

And finally I called Police Command Headquarters again. It was time to bring an end to the civil war and to incorporate the green shirts into the new United States. No one answered the phone.

I SAID THAT I was not present for all the changes that occurred in The War. Some things I only learned about when it was too late.

THE ZABO OFFICER of the day was in his office trying to make sense of the situation. His men and women were fighting the army on three continents as well as the Unisans in southern Epris. So far, they seemed to be doing well. The army was expert in aerial combat but still ignorant of land warfare. In Earthly terms, the police *were* the government and so all they had to do was defend the centers of administration and the factories and engineering centers that sustained life in the underground world of Kapara. In some cases, the army had seized control of administrative and industrial centers but, for the most part, they were penned up in their upper level bases.

The Zabo officer nodded in self-satisfaction and reached for his telephone to report to the new Pom Da. He worked the planchette and pressed the power button. Nothing happened. He was still trying to get the recalcitrant instrument to function when his office door burst open. He looked up to see....

"Sellon Sura! What is the meaning of this intrusion?" he growled.

"Traitor!" she answered and shot him in the head. Satisfied that he would commit no further treasons, she turned on her heel and marched to the police operations center. She was accompanied by a double section of guards, each with his gun out, each with a locket of black hair fastened to his uniform to identify himself to others.

The police operations center was arranged differently from its military counterpart but many elements were very similar. Sura and her thugs marched onto the command balcony; the black-maned valkyrie fired a burst of bullets into the stone ceiling. Every voice stopped; every eye jerked to the command balcony and the warrior woman mounted there.

"I am Sellon Sura, Special Assistant to the true Chief of the Zabo. As you know, there has been an attempted coup d'état by the army led by Force Leader Tomas Ran. He has assassinated the true Pom Da as well as our Chief and directed the army to kill or capture every Zabo agent in Kapara. That means that we are all under sentence of death unless we destroy Tomas and his fellow traitors.

"As the Special Assistant to the true Chief, I now assume the authority of acting Chief of the Zabo. I have just executed the officer of the day who had accepted the orders of the traitor Tomas Ran and therefore was a traitor himself. In addition, I have executed Tomas' pretended new Chief. If anyone wishes to survive, you will accept my orders and fight Tomas and his military co-conspirators."

She paused. No one spoke. Every Kapar had been educated since birth to revere ruthless power and to despise treason. To them, Sura's revelations were the epitome of the true Kapar spirit. Were they true? Who knew… or cared?

"Our goal must be to seize the palace and depose the false Pom Da Tomas Ran. Once that is done, the Zabo will regain its proper power as the leaders of the Kapar empire and will win The War that the treacherous army was unable to do."

Fists began to pound in Kapar applause. Until now, the Zabo (and many other Kapars) could not understand why the army had been unable to win The War. Now they had been given a reason that they understood!

"Therefore, my loyal Kapars, mobilize at least two full wings of police storm troopers here in Ergos. Since the military bases above us were destroyed by the gargoyles of Unis, we will not have to fight those traitors at this time. Once we have fully mobilized, we can easily restore true order to the capital city —" She paused for effect. "— And capture the palace." The room exploded in Kapar applause.

EVERY UNDERGROUND RAIL STATION in Ergos was packed. The trains ran on emergency schedules night and day. Each outgoing car was jammed with red shirts who were allowed to leave. Nine out of ten shirts were turned back. Their skills and labor were needed to keep the deeply injured metropolis functioning.

Each incoming vehicle was stuffed to the walls with green-shirted police and green painted equipment stripped from the other cities of Kapara and northern Epris. Despite the urgency of acting Chief Sellon's orders, her decapitating task force was slow to build up. Military forces previously penned up in other cities were quick to notice the reduced police presence. So were the criminal organizations that officially did not exist in Kapara. Gray-shirted strike forces stalked green-shirted patrols through the urban mazes below three continents. The green shirts often knew their cities better than the airmen did, but casualties mounted, and grew exponentially. Some cities fell out of communication with Police Command. Green shirts transferred to Ergos began to worry who was watching their backs. Finally, the acting Chief decided that she had enough men in place. She ordered them forward.

"Forward" in a three-dimensional city was complicated. A wall of green moved outward to secure the 50th level. Once they had covered the horizontal expanse, sections and platoons began moving downward through the executive levels. Every housing or food distribution center was occupied by at least a section.

Their first check came at the 55th level. The city waterworks was a priority target for the former Special Assistant of Gerris but the Ergosan works were heavily armored. Every level of lower Ergos was armored with layer upon layer of steel and concrete to protect the Pom Da and his favorites. The police advance stopped. The call went out for engineers and digging equipment.

But the red-shirted engineers seemed to have disappeared from their homes. When questioned, their neighbors said that they had been taken away by the army several days ago. No one knew where.

Sniping began in the police rear areas. Black and gray ghosts fired as patrols passed and disappeared when counterattacked. Zabo leaders poured more police into the rear areas and the ghosts vanished. No one noticed that a significant fraction of the available manpower had been diverted from the front lines and that forward momentum had been lost.

More reports came in of cities falling out of communication with Police Command. Information was sketchy. Apparently, the army was not only gaining manpower from somewhere but they were inserting patrols well behind the police lines. Intelligence officers in Ergos worked their sources and spies in the hinterlands as hard as they could but no one seemed to have answers.

One intelligence officer investigated the idea that the Unisans were slipping infiltrators into Kapara but found no evidence.

Police thrashing around the 50th through 55th levels of Ergos began reporting mysterious illnesses. Symptoms included shortness of breath, dizziness and lack of energy; nothing fatal, but debilitating and frightening.

The grand offensive to retake the Pom Da's palace and staff stalled out. Two wings of police were milling around accomplishing little except for losing their tempers.

A red-shirted engineer showed up at an underground train station. Unlike so many potential refugees, he had work to do and the papers to prove it. He began changing the electric lights over the passenger platform. Soon, the station lighting was a quarter of its normal value.

Thus, it required long seconds for the green shirts monitoring the ebb and flow of people and things to realize that the latest arrivals from northern Epris were wearing gray uniforms rather than green. The gray shirts charged forward, guns blazing. They overran the startled police and captured the station. Red shirted workers panicked. Shouting military policemen directed them into the city. Much the same thing was happening at every train station in the city.

Trains continued to pour gray shirts into Ergos' middle levels. The few observers left realized that well over half of the gray shirts were wearing black coveralls. Red shirts materialized to guide both the conventional military and the Black Legion through the metropolitan mazes.

The slaves had risen for freedom.

Many black and red shirts had volunteered for the Black Legion only to be assigned to hide among the general population until the code word "Dragoon" was given. On signal, they came forth to overturn their green-shirted oppressors.

The black and gray military spread out through the middle levels, duplicating the original police dragnet. The massive police attack force was trapped between the armored walls of the Pom Da's inner fortress and the guns of the aveng-ing army. Trapdoors slammed shut and were barricaded from above.

Meanwhile, the black and gray ghost units evacuated the air conditioning ducts that had been their secret highways and fortresses. Above them red-shirted engineers began closing down the vast network of breathing tubes that supported life in levels 50 through 55, as well as the jury-rigged system that they had used to feed carbon monoxide and ozone into the enemy-held levels.

The silence of the air conditioning system panicked the green shirts. They had lived underground all their lives;

they knew that that particular silence meant death on the installment plan. Discipline broke; the masters of fear fled upward in terror.

They were met with sealed doors and hungry guns. Many of the trapped green shirts managed to surrender. Others fought to the bitter end — mostly theirs.

The Department of Education & Propaganda publicized the destruction of the great decapitating task force from southern Epris to northern Heris. Police morale collapsed. Green-shirted officers fearfully sought out their gray-shirted counterparts to arrange surrenders. As for those who chose not to surrender....

Green shirts were soon being hunted through every room and corridor in Kapara. Some escaped.

Meanwhile, high overhead.... Black-winged aircraft landed for orders and ammunition. Most of them were grounded and their pilots reassigned to the street fighting. The others were told to stay inside the borders of the new United States of Poloda. Defend the homeland but do not push east of the lines.

It took longer for the dispersed Unisan planes to receive the new orders. Until they did, firefights blooded the sky and land. But, slowly, the word spread. Bluecoats crossed the United States borders heading outward and did not return.

The two air forces patrolled their respective zones. They eyed each other with all the hatred and suspicion accumulated in a century of spilled blood. But they did so with the agreed upon separation between them.

They patrolled – but did not fight. Bomb doors remained closed. Guns remained silent.

Peace had come to the planet of perpetual war.

EPILOGUE: TRUCE

Chapter 22 *BEAUTY AND THE BEAST*

"Not if I can help it," hissed Sellon Sura.

"Most High Special Assistant?" queried a haggard green shirt.

"I am now the Chief of the Zabo," responded Sura, turning her gorgon stare on the questioner. She bit each word off as sharply as if she had cut them with a knife.

The green shirt's mouth dropped open. He closed it and then opened it again. "Yes, Most High." No one argued with her self promotion.

Sura nodded in acknowledgement. Her audience was a handful of high-ranking police. The slaves' final assault on Zabo headquarters had not left many survivors. Those that had escaped had regrouped in a secret police command post. Her chief officers were gathered in a cramped conference room wondering if they could escape from Ergos with their skins intact. They had seen terrible vengeance wreaked on gold-braided Zabo officers and low ranking clerks alike. The air conditioning system labored to clear the atmosphere of the stink of fear.

Sura seemed not to notice these problems. Her officers were collapsed in their chairs. Many were panting for breath, exhausted after their bloody defeat. She paced back and forth across the narrow space available, her energy seemingly undiminished by the recent battles.

"The problem is Tomas Ran. He assassinated the Pom Da, took control of the army, and turned both army and slaves against us. Tomas Ran is the key to controlling Ergos and Ergos is the key to controlling Kapara. We must capture Tomas Ran," the new Chief thought aloud.

"Most High Chief, we lack the strength to assault the palace and capture Tomas. May I suggest..." began one Zabo officer diffidently. His poison ivy green uniform was still clean, his gold braid still gleaming.

"Be quiet," snapped Sura. The diffident officer closed his mouth. "Tomas has two armies protecting him. Another army would accomplish nothing."

She paused for a long time and then smiled like a kalidah ready to feed, "But the right woman might." Her smoke-dirtied face flashed into a brilliant smile. Her men stirred in anticipation. Exactly what they anticipated, they could not define.

She snapped orders. "Find me a gray jacket. Kill one of our prisoners if you have to. I will go to the palace and negotiate an agreement with Tomas Ran. In the meantime, continue contacting all of the Zabo agents you can. Get them into hiding. We need to deal with the army with as much strength as we can muster."

Her men began to obey. Before she left the hidden command post, Sura carefully unbuttoned her shirt.

"So, you won The War." Kiri was dead-tired, but her voice was filled with wonder; and something else. She was looking at me as if I were a combination of George Washington, King Ulandu and Clark Gable.

"No, *we* won. You won. The slaves won. Even a million gray shirts that fought for their Pom Da won. We won The War," I corrected. I was dead-tired, too, but neither of us could rest just yet. We were seated....

No. We were sprawled in chairs in the Pom Da's...

No. We were collapsed in chairs in my private office. The one with a desk proportioned for human beings rather than aircraft landings. There were telephones and knickknacks on the desk. And a food and wine bar that could feed ten Kap... that could feed ten Eprisans for a week. Nothing else. No books, no newspapers, no government reports, nothing but pale green walls. There had been a portrait of the former dictator on one wall but Kiri had torn it down when we moved in.

Heze Salis was guarding the door, rebuffing all calls until we had a chance to catch our breaths. She was a good person. I was planning on making her my permanent administrative assistant, along with a thousand other things on a list in my head.

The list had to be in my head. We had not dared write down any part of Air Maiden that could not be explained as some part of Operation Grand Sweep.

And what I couldn't remember, we had made up on the spot. It had been a very, very long and very, very exhausting week. If either of us had slept for more than an hour at a time, I couldn't remember it. So far, it had worked.

Kiri closed her green eyes and whispered, "And now we can go home."

I winced. I wished that there was some other way to say what had to be said but there wasn't. That's why Pom Das get paid the big money. "Home to Unis?" I asked gently.

"Of course," she breathed contentedly. Another minute and she would be asleep.

"You can go home to Unis any time now. It'll be easy to pass you through the lines or to fly you around the war zone.

"But I am staying in Ergos...." I continued. "For the rest of my life."

There was a moment of silence. Even the omnipresent air conditioning seemed quiet. Then, Kiri jerked herself bolt upright, eyes as wide as dinner plates. The lobster that lived in my ear had made a final appearance. This time he was juggling dinner plates with both claws.

"What do you mean?" she shrieked. "I thought we were both going home… home to Unis. I thought we could… could…."

"Be husband and wife?" I finished for her.

She blushed and then nodded vigorously. Her hair was a halo of red fire in the harsh electric lighting.

I think that my face was a picture of sincere sympathy. After so much lying to save our skins from the Kapars, I was no longer sure what my face said. But I spoke from the bottom of my heart.

"Kiri, I love you with all my soul. I want you to be my wife. I've probably wanted you since I first saw you fighting tooth and nail against your kidnappers (although I didn't realize it until I thought I had lost you). I want you to have all the happiness that you deserve. And if your happiness means that you go to Unis and I never see you again, well, so be it. Your happiness is more important to me than mine is."

"But I *have* to stay in Epris."

"Why?" she wailed.

"Because I'm the Pom Da of the Kapar Nation. So far, the United States of Poloda is just a name. We've conquered a nation; now we, or I, have to lead it to freedom. Otherwise, The War will simply begin again."

Her beautiful, beautiful face twisted in misery and confusion. "I do not understand," she choked out.

"Kiri, dear Kiri, there are 400 million people on three continents who have never known anything but war all their lives. You can't change their minds overnight. Every one of them has been taught since birth that war is the natural state of humanity. Some want real peace but more will want the exaltation of victory and the loot of Unis. They'll see the present truce not as an opportunity to build peace and prosperity for all Polodans but as a lull to rearm and renew the fighting as they saw the previous lulls in The War. If we leave together, some Kapar will say that the filthy Earthmen stabbed Kapara in the back. That's exactly how the Pom Da Adolf Hitler rose to power on Earth. The only thing that will stop that is if the current Pom Da has a vision of genuine peace on our planet and the will to enforce that vision.

"That Means Me." I said that sentence slowly. I did so partly to emphasize its importance — and partly because I hated saying it.

"There must be others you can give the job to. Ourundun Tod for example. He is a good man."

"Yes. And the Kapar ironhearts would drive him out of office and murder him within a year. Besides, I want to make him continental governor of Auris. With my help, he can lead his people to freedom."

"Garrud Kun?"

"He's the ironheart that I worry about most. He would murder half of the surviving police without trials and absorb the rest into the army. The Earthly Pom Da Napoleon Bonaparte said that you can do anything with a bayonet except sit on it. Garrud doesn't understand that. Within five years, he would restart The War and possibly reconquer Allos and Punos. I don't want our children to be fighting his children for the rest of their lives.

"The War needs to stop now and stay stopped. We have a truce; now we need peace."

Kiri was as brave as anyone on two planets but tears were flowing down her face. Her body was wracked with silent sobbing.

The moment was interrupted by the interphone buzzing. It was Salis announcing that Chief of the Zabo Sellon Sura had arrived at the palace under flag of truce and wanted to see me.

Sellon Sura swept into my office as if she owned it. Perhaps she thought that she did. She stopped cold when she saw Kiri sniffling beside my desk.

"Highest Most High, I wish to be alone with you," Sura purred loudly.

I buzzed Salis on the interphone. "Has Special Assistant Sellon Sura been searched for weapons?"

"Yes, Most High. Twice; once at the palace gate and once at the office area gate."

I knew how well that had worked last week. "Come in here and search her again."

"Yes, Most High."

The three of them stepped into a private room and came back in about a quarter of an hour later. I used the time to write a proclamation or two and then file them. When the trio returned, Kiri shook her head briefly and I thanked them. I had Salis pour Sura and me cups of wine and then my redheads left me alone with the man-eater.

I waved my hand at a chair in front of my desk and invited Sura to sit down. Instead, she swirled her wine in her cup and walked over to me. Even Helen Keller could see what she was up to. And why she thought that she would succeed.

"That was not very nice," she declared loftily.

"Sorry but my predecessor was assassinated recently. I'd like to avoid his fate." I smiled knowingly.

"I see," Sura said thoughtfully. She smiled invitingly. "You could have searched me yourself."

"A good leader knows when to delegate responsibilities. Speaking of which, I see that you are now the Chief of the Zabo. Congratulations."

She shrugged with apparent modesty. "It is a working title only. I took the job in order to bring the police into your new administration."

"Ahhh. Thank you. If the police surrender, they will be treated humanely."

"And what will the role of the police be in your new 'United States of Poloda'?"

"I am planning a complete overhaul of the national economy and administration. There will be a new code of laws and a professional crime-fighting organization to enforce them. But the new police force will be detached from the ordinary administration of the country. Police of the old regime who loyally serve our new nation will not only be treated humanely but can expect honorable rewarding careers in the future."

"I see," Sura repeated. "So the new police will not have the power that the Zabo hav... the Zabo had."

"No, they won't. Is that important?" I was teasing her. I was pretty sure what her response would be.

"It might be," she drawled languidly. "What is the 'honorable rewarding career' for a woman who risked her life to bring the police out of hiding and into your administration?"

Ah, hah. "A person of such loyalty and executive skills deserves a promotion," I said smoothly.

Sura kept her face bland but her body language shouted "Yes! Yes! Yes!"

"Since the future police force will be too small to fully use your talents, and since the continental governorship of Unis is off the table for the immediate future, I was thinking of naming you continental governor of Auris."

She was quivering with excitement. She tried to hide it and I pretended not to notice. "Auris? The smallest continent on Poloda? And hot, sweaty and stinky as well. That is a very small reward for someone who can end the police war for you." She gazed invitingly into my eyes. I returned her attention as blandly as I could. "How about Heris?"

I nodded my head as I pretended to consider her counteroffer. "Very well. If you can make the entire remaining police force surrender without further violence, I will name you continental governor of Heris."

Her face lit up like Omos coming over the horizon. She leaned close to me. She promised, "You will never regret this decision, my leader. My powerful, handsome leader."

It took all my strength to press the interphone button to summon Salis. And Kiri. While Kiri was escorting the new princess of Heris back to the palace gate, I took Sura's death warrant out of my private file and reviewed it. I had written it while Kiri and Salis were searching the man-eater. I sighed, and returned it to its hiding place. Unsigned. Abraham Lincoln would have approved.

I called Kiri back into my office and started dictating Sura's appointment as continental governor. Kiri finished taking the dictation and then remarked, "You should kill her instead."

I sighed. "Possibly. But if she can bring the surviving police over to our side without further fighting, she's worth her price."

"Well, then, kill her once that job is finished."

Wow! How Loris Kiri had changed...! She had always been a strong woman; now she was a.... Now she was different. I understood the change but wasn't entirely comfortable with it. Well, Dad and Mama had set a pretty good example of people from different backgrounds meeting each other halfway.

"The old Pom Da would probably do just that. And I'm deeply suspicious of her for many reasons. But I have no proof. Until we develop proof that Sellon Sura betrayed our new nation, she gets the benefit of the doubt; and her promotion."

Kiri made a face but she turned the page on her writing tablet. She looked at me with professional aplomb, ready for the next dictation.

"Now that that's done, I have another promotion in mind. I wish to promote you from special assistant to wife." I smiled as sincerely and tenderly as I could.

Her face exploded in joy. Then it collapsed. "Kapar men do not marry their women," she said in a very small voice.

"That's another custom that I... I think we should change." I stood up and walked around my desk. I picked her up and sat her down on the edge of the desk. Then I knelt down and proposed.

For a woman only half my size who never saw a game of American rules football, Loris Kiri tackled me like a pro. We were still on the floor when Heze Salis knocked on the door to see if we needed anything.

Appendix

A Polodan Glossary

Allos: Formerly an independent kingdom in southern Epris and later the first Kapar colony.

André: Member of the French Resistance in Nazi-Occupied France.

Ang, Don and Gar: Overworked Unisan citizens.

Antos: Omosan planet immediately adjacent to Poloda. The "evening star" of Poloda.

Aqunq: Speaker for the ruling council of Karis (the Thaqung) and effective chief executive of Karis. "The-speaker" in Karisan.

Auris: Small tropical continent in the central portion of Poloda's Eastern Hemisphere and a Kapar colony. The native name is "Aud."

Balzo Jan: Unisan airman and brother of Balzo Maro. Tangor rescued him from a crash landing near Bhon in Punos.

Balzo Maro: Unisan botanist and sister of Balzo Jan. She was the first Polodan to meet Tangor.

Bantor Han: Unisan airman.

Bazhulan: "Cowards" in Unisan. One coward is a "bazhul."

Bhon: Hidden village of Punosans resisting the Kapar conquest of their nation. Tomas Ran promoted the village to be the capital of Punos for the duration of The War.

Black Legion: Military organization recruited by Tomas Ran from the Kapar prison population and trained to fight against the enemies of the empire. The name was inspired by the color of their uniforms and the French Foreign Legion.

Cave of the Winds: Large cavern system in the Hallas Mountains of eastern Allos. The entrance was a royal Allosan national park and the last refuge of Zurrya and Vollor.

Chendin Dol: Unisan Commissioner of the Interior and

Eljanhai of the technocratic republic of Unis when Tomas Ran met the Janhai.

Churor: Zebra-striped lion-like creature native to the tropical plains of Unis. Hunts by stalking prey.

Commission of Unis: See "Janhai."

Council of Five: Kapar executive body theoretically similar to the British Cabinet. One of their corporate duties is the election and certification of a new Pom Da when that office is vacant. Oudurun Tod used the term to sarcastically refer to a group of five disgraced police prisoners in the Gerris city slave pens.

Danul: Manservant in Ergos and a loyal Kapar.

Dardan Chol: Hydraulic engineer in Tuldros and later a Unisan fighting man in northern Punos. The older brother of Dardan Vol.

Dardan Vol: Middle school student in Tuldros. His teachers included Loris Kiri and Palden Zinova. Younger brother of Dardan Chol.

Denbol: Unisan Commissioner of Education. His personal name is unknown.

Despair, Island of: Large Unisan island in the Talan Strait and the Unisan territory closest to Kapar-controlled Epris. The name refers to the large prison population.

Doc: Earthly psychiatrist.

Ed: Earthly author. His psychic abilities enabled him to telepathically receive Tangor's and Tomas Ran's accounts of their experiences beyond the farthest star known to Earthly science.

Eljanhai: Chief executive of Unis. "High-seven-elect" in Unisan.

Epris: Large crescent-shaped continent overlapping Poloda's Eastern and Western Hemispheres, Epris extends from the Equator to the Southern Pole. The continent is the heartland and stronghold of the Kapar empire.

Eprisan: Adjective meaning "of the continent of Epris." Frequently used as a common term for Allosans, Punosans and Zurrisans in contrast to Kapars.

Ergos: Capital city of Kapara, Epris and the Kapar empire.

Five Daughters and a Crown: Classic Unisan play; a historical comedy. The story incorporates several songs including the popular *Maidens Rejoice* and *Gentlemen Come Calling*.

Fontan Ianami: Courier airplane pilot and princess of the old Unisan nobility.

Frink: Kapar secret agent in Pud.

Garan: Extremely sweet fruit grown in Epris and especially in the valley of Gerris.

Garrud Kun: Disgraced Kapar military officer. Tomas Ran chose him to command the Ironheart Division of the Black Legion.

Gerris: Allosan city noted for growing garan fruit. The original Allosan name was Gellis. Tomas Ran appeared on Poloda in Gerris.

Gillan Alle: Hereditary Prime Minister to His Majesty, Vollor, King of Allos, and the commander of various Allosan military units.

Gimmel Gora: Grunge's woman.

Globular Cluster NGC 7006: Star cluster in the Milky Way Galaxy and the constellation Delphinus as seen from Earth. The Unisan name is Kanapa.

Gompth: Kapar secret agent in Gorvas.

Gorvas: Capital city of Karis. The native name is "Gorvasht."

Grunge: Loyal Kapar with no visible means of support, and Gimmel Gora's man.

Gurrul: Chief of the Zabo during the 101st year of The War. Liquidated following the events of *Beyond The Farthest Star*.

Hagar: Unisan city bombed out of existence by the Kapar air offensive.

Hagar: Flagship of the Unisan Ocean Fighting Corps (navy).

Hagar, Bay of: Large gulf indenting the west coast of the Unisan continent.

Hallas Mountains: Range separating Allos and Punos.

Haka Gera: Horthal Wend's woman and mother of Horthal Gyl.

Harkas Don: Unisan airman, son of Harkas Yen, and close friend of Tangor.

Harkas Juniri (Jun): Unisan housewife and wife of Harkas Yen.

Harkas Tangor: See "Tangor."

Harkas Yamoda: Unisan housewife, daughter of Harkas Yen and Jun, and wife of Tangor.

Harkas Yen: Unisan psychiatrist and leading expert on real and alleged visitors from other planets. Husband of Harkas Juniri and father of Harkas Don and Yamoda.

Handon Gar: Unisan airman and Tangor's co-pilot on the first Polodan expedition to Tonos. He did not return from Tonos.

Hearts of Iron, Eyes of Fire: Kapar marching song celebrating physical power and ruthlessness.

Heris: Large tropical continent in Poloda's Eastern Hemisphere and a Kapar colony. The native name is "Heru."

Heze Salis: Kapar prisoner condemned for unspecified crimes and later a member of the Black Legion. Later she was the personal secretary for two Pom Das.

Honnol Jannam: Baron and acting Prime Minister of the True Kingdom of Zurris in exile.

Horthal Gyl: Young Kapar bully, Zabo agent, and son of Horthal Wend.

Horthal Wend: Kapar scientist-inventor and the father of Horthal Gyl. Died under mysterious circumstances in Ergos.

Ikhurr: Rat-like creature native to Epris. Ikhurr skins are smooth and pig-like rather than hairy. Also an insulting term for anyone whom the speaker dislikes.

Ilgros: Kapar city noted for manufacturing the Polodan equivalents of paper products. Ilgros is located inside Kapara a short distance from the border with Allos.

Is: "Land" in Unisan.

Ithris: Formerly an independent monocracy in central eastern Epris north of Allos and Kapara, and later a Kapar colony.

J: Mysterious revolutionary figure dedicated to the overthrow of the Kapar regime.

Janhai: Executive and legislative commission ruling Unis. Unisan voters elect seven functional department heads (commissioners) who form the council, which then chooses the Eljanhai and all major Unisan governmental officials. "Seven-elect" in Unisan.

Jorros: Central Allosan city noted for manufacturing air conditioning and plumbing equipment; the first Kapar city liberated by the allied counteroffensive. The Allosan name was Jollis.

Juthi: Antelope native to Punos. It resembles Earth's mythical unicorn.

Kaldur Jan: Unisan farmer and husband of Kaldur Maro.

Kaldur Maro: Unisan farmer and wife of Kaldur Jan.

Kaldur Ron: Unisan intelligence officer and son of Kaldur Jan and Maro.

Kaldur Tori: Kaldur Jan's unlucky cousin.

Kalidah: Green furred bear-like creature native to Allos. Tomas Ran gave the "bear of Poloda" a name from the Oz books by L. Frank Baum.

Kanapa: Unisan term for Globular Cluster NGC 7006 outside the Milky Way Galaxy. Spelled "Canapa" in Kapar.

Kapar: Member of a political movement — Zurrisan in origin — whose program of government is characterized by extreme militarism and totalitarian direction of all political, economic and cultural activity. The word was coined from the name of the movement's first leader, Kapar Ov. "Kapar" later became a general purpose adjective and noun for all aspects of the resulting empire, including its citizens and language. Equivalent to "Nazi" in German history and "Soviet" in Russian history.

Kapar Ov: Egomaniacal founder of Kaparism and the Kapar empire. He organized a mass movement based on an ultra-militarist philosophy, converted airplanes to weapons of war, overthrew the Zurrisan royal government, and conquered much of the continent of Epris.

Kapara: Kapar homeland located in southwestern Epris west of Allos and Ithris. Kapara was originally the kingdom of Zurris. The term is also used to mean the entire Kapar empire and its government.

Kapars: Tomas Ran met a number of unnamed Kapars during his adventures including the Kareless Kraut, Herr Slugger, The Sideman, the Laughing Hyena, Larry, Curly, Moe, Silver Trim, Gold Trim, More Silver Trim, Punxsutaw-ney Phil, Goggle Eyes, Buddy, Numbers One through Ten, Professor Galvani, Miss Manners and Ace.

Karagan Ocean: Tropical-temperate ocean in the northern part of Poloda's Western Hemisphere. The Karagan separates the continents of Epris and Unis.

Karis: Arctic continent with few natural resources and the republic representing the united tribes of the continent. The native name is "Karsh."

Khaparh: Punosan pronunciation of "Kapar."

Kishkin: Unisan party game in which players alternately guess words from a source book and clues provided by the opposing player.

Korvan Don: Tangor's *nom de guerre* during his spy mission in Ergos.

Kuikol: Monkey-like creature native to the tropical forests of Unis. Kuikols have powerful rear legs and leap from tree branch to tree branch.

Kurrus: Allosan city noted for production of clothes, includ-ing boots. The original Allosan name was Kullos.

League of Nations: Earthly organization for international cooperation, 1919-46. Merged into the United Nations Organization, 1946.

Loras, Mountains of: Range in southwestern Unis.

Loris Kiri: Unisan school teacher kidnapped and taken to Gerris by Kapar scout-infiltrators. She was subsequently forced to be a slave to City Governor Virrul and Special Assistant Sellon Sura.

Lotar Canl: Lotar Kan's *nom de guerre* during his spy mission in Ergos.

Lotar Kan: Unisan spy in Ergos and later a commander of Unisan intelligence operations.

Maidens Rejoice: Popular Unisan song sung by young women celebrating life and romance. The lively tune was first written for the play *Five Daughters and a Crown*.

Manchan: Tomas Ran's Deputy Wing Commander. An old school commander who did not understand Tomas' methods of warfare.

Mandan Ocean: Tropical ocean in Poloda's Eastern Hemisphere. The Mandan separates the continents of Auris, Epris and Heris.

Marran Kun: Kapar military War Leader (equivalent to a seven star field marshal). Murdered by the Pom Da for failing to prevent the Unisan invasion of Punos.

Mekarru: Historical Chief of State of Punos during the early phases of the Kapar War.

Military Organization and Ranks: Polodan military units are not directly equivalent to US or NATO units. The table below should only be used as an approximate guide. Unisan ranks are formed by adding the word "Commander" to the unit name. Thus, Tomas Ran reached the rank of Wing Commander in the Unisan Fighting Corps. Kapar ranks are formed by adding the word "Leader" to the unit name. In addition, the Kapar military includes the ranks of War Leader and Battle Leader, which are roughly equivalent to seven and six star field marshals.

Polodan Unit	Enlisted Manpower	US Equivalent Unit	US Commander
Force Group	3,906,250	Theater Command	General of the Army/AF (5 stars)
Force	781,250	Army Group	General of the Army/AF (5 stars)
Wing	156,250	Army/Air Force	General (4 stars)
Division	31,250	2 Divisions/1 Corps	Major General or Lieutenant General
Group	6,250	Brigade	Colonel or Brigadier General
Squadron	1,250	Battalion	Lieutenant Colonel
Company	250	Company	Captain
Platoon	50	Platoon	Lieutenant
Section	10	Squad	Staff Sergeant

Montar Ban: Unisan Commissioner of Justice and later Special Assistant to the Commissioner of War.

Morga Sagra: Unisan traitor and older sister of Morga Sal. She defected to Kapara out of a misguided admiration for strength of character and militarism. Executed by Gurrul as a traitor to Kapara.

Morga Sal: Younger brother of Morga Sagra and a paratrooper in the invasions of Allos and Kapara.

Mula Mountains: Range running east-west through central Punos.

Murrs: Kapar city in northern Epris noted for production of motor vehicles, equipment and supplies.

Muthluq: Whale-like land creature native to Karis.

Nangan Don: Retired Unisan airman and air conditioning engineer; later a professor of history; and still later an advisor to the Unisan Department of War on land warfare.

Nayon: Unisan city noted for manufacturing military equipment.

Nira: Former capital city of Punos destroyed by the Kapar air offensive.

Niros: Former Kapar city built on the ruins of Nira but destroyed by the Unisan air counteroffensive; and later a secret Kapar military fortress under the ruins of Nira.

Omos: Yellow dwarf star in the ultra faint Hercules Dwarf Galaxy 450,000 light years from Earth. The Omos solar system includes 11 Earthlike co-orbital planets and a common atmosphere belt. The planets are Poloda, Antos, Rovos, Vanada, Sanada, Uvala, Zandar, Wunos, Banos, Yonda, and Tonos.

Omys: Archaic pronunciation of "Omos" now used as a curse word by most Polodans.

Oomm: Mildly stimulating drink similar to chocolate. Also the sound that most Polodans make after their first swallow.

Opros: Formerly an independent regency in central Epris north of Kapar and west of Ithris.

Orondo: Legendary king of Unis and the father of *Five Daughters and a Crown*.

Orvis: Capital city of Unis. Tangor appeared on Poloda in Orvis.

Oundurun Tod: Aurisan citizen of the Kapar regime and a distinguished architect; later a prisoner. Tomas Ran chose him to command the Black Legion.

Ozmonkey: Monkey-like creature native to Allos. Ozmonkeys glide among trees on flaps of skin similar to Earthly flying squirrels. Tomas Ran invented the name based on the movie *The Wizard of Oz*.

Palden Zar: Unisan Commissioner of War and later Eljanhai.

Palden Zina (Palden Zinova): Unisan middle school teacher in Tuldros and daughter of Palden Zar. Her class included Dardan Vol.

Path of the Sun: Super-highway built by the pre-War nations of Allos, Punos and Zurris to improve commerce and peaceful international relations. The main route ran east to west. Partially destroyed by the Kapars.

Pierre: Member of the French Resistance in Nazi-Occupied France.

Polan: Unisan city on the Yalivis River noted for manufacturing plastic products.

Poloda: Earthlike planet of the Omos solar system. Home to a race of human beings who attained high levels of science and culture before the Kapar War. At least two Earthmen were mysteriously transported to Poloda after dying in Earth's comparatively small scale World War II.

Pom Da: Title of the dictator of Kapara. Literally, "[the] Great I" in Kapar.

Pud: City on the continent of Auris.

Punxsutawney Phil: Famous long-range weather forecaster living in Punxsutawney, Pennsylvania.

Punos: Formerly an independent republic in eastern Epris and then a Kapar colony. The native name is Punha.

Puntha: Punosan name for the Punosan language.

Rondor Chan: Mechanic in the Unisan Fighting Corps.

The Rufus T. Firefly Rules of Order: The source authority for parliamentary procedure in the nation of Freedonia.

Rupert von Hentzau: Character in the novel *The Prisoner of Zenda*. Tomas Ran used the name as a cover identity when spying on German activities in Occupied France.

Sangor Maro: Unisan Commissioner for Foreign Affairs.

Sathis: Herisan Kapar city noted for manufacturing electrical equipment. Destroyed by new weapons and techniques introduced by Tomas Ran.

Second Chancers: Unisan paratroop division formed from patriotic prisoners anxious to redeem themselves. Morga Sal commanded the division in the invasion of the Valley of the Sun and the Battle of Ergos.

Sellon Sura: Special Assistant to the City Governor of Gerris and later Special Assistant to the Chief of the Zabo. She had the true Kapar spirit.

Shadow wolf: A wolf-like or cat-like creature native to Allos. Shadow wolves ambush prey by concealing themselves as shadows on the forest floor. Tomas Ran named the creature for its appearance.

Siron: Unisan university city destroyed by the Kapars.

Soran Zan: Unisan prisoner in Prison 116 and later a farmer.

Suzette: Member of the French Resistance in Nazi-Occupied France.

Talan Strait: Oceanic body of water separating the Eprisan and Unisan continents and connecting the Karagan and Wudan Oceans.

Tangor (Harkas Tangor): First Earthman to be mysteriously transported to Poloda. His experiences are described in *Beyond the Farthest Star* by Edgar Rice Burroughs.

Terro Gar: Kapar War Leader and Marran Kun's replacement.

Thaqung: Ruling council of Karis. "High-speak-several" in Karisan.

Time of Legends: Semi-mythical historical period roughly 10,000 to 5,000 years before the start of the common Polodan calendar.

Tomas Ran (Thomas Randolph): Second Earthman to be transported to Poloda. His experiences are described in *A Soldier of Poloda*.

Tondul Misema: Unisan Commissioner of the Treasury and later Eljanhai.

Tonos: Omosan planet immediately adjacent to Poloda opposite Antos. The "morning star" of Poloda.

Tukarr Derru: Chief of the village of Bhon. Tomas Ran promoted him to be Chief of State of the Punosan nation resisting the Kapar conquest.

Tuldros: Unisan city on the Yalivis River noted as an agricultural center. The original home of Loris Kiri.

Tunzo Bor: A prisoner of the Kapars in the city of Ergos.

Tunzo Pal: A counterfeiter and forger.

Two Moon Planet: Tomas Ran's name for Poloda before he learned that the "moons" were actually the adjacent planets Antos and Rovos. None of the planets in the Omosan solar system has a moon.

Ulandu: Heroic Unisan historical figure. The last king of the former monarchy of Unis, he decreed strict eugenic laws to protect the health of the Unisan race and, having no heir, vested his royal authority in his cabinet, which subsequently evolved into the Janhai.

Ulandu's Godchildren: Unisan term for the physically handicapped. The term derives from Ulandu's legislation providing humane treatment of the handicapped.

Umars: Kapar city in southern Ithris most noted for its petrochemical industry including the production of synthetic foods. Smugglers often used Umars as their Kapar port of call.

Unis: Medium sized tropical continent in Poloda's Western Hemisphere and the technocratic republic that occupies the entire continent. By the 101st year of the Kapar War, Unis was the only free nation on Poloda.

Urtha: Most common Polodan pronunciation of "Earth."

Uvala: Planet in the Omos solar system and the heaven of a Polodan religion.

Uvalan: Adjective meaning "of the planet Uvala." Also a member of a religion that preaches that that good souls teleport to Uvala upon death.

Virrul: Kapar City Governor of Gerris.

Voldan Ocean: Arctic ocean in the northern part of Poloda's Eastern Hemisphere. The Voldan separates Auris, Heris, Karis and Unis.

Vollor, Sword of: Ancient weapon symbolizing Allosan independence, honor and justice.

Vollor, the Lost King of Allos: Tragic historical figure.

Vondol Rima (Vondol Varima): Secretary to the Janhai and later Tomas Ran's administrative assistant in Punos.

Vornan Tomi (Vornan Tomada): Unisan parachute maker and emotional heart of the Polan Parachute Company.

Vosht: Fiery liquor brewed in Karis.

War, The, or The Kapar War: War of conquest begun by Kapar Ov and continued by his successors with the goal of reducing all peoples on Poloda to slavery of various degrees.

Warden: Administrator of Prison 116 on the Island of Despair.

Wudan Ocean: Tropical and subarctic ocean overlapping Poloda's Eastern and Western Hemispheres. The northern portion separates Heris and Unis while the southern portion washes Punos on the west and Kapara on the east.

Yalivis River: River in southwestern Unis east of the Mountains of Loras.

Zabo: Elite police force of the Kapar regime. Since the Kapar tyranny regards all national issues as security issues, the Zabo is the actual government of Kapara.

Zondor Von: Unisan Commissioner of Commerce and former Eljanhai. He advocated evacuating the Unisan population to another planet in order to escape the Kapar War.

Zurris: Former kingdom in southwestern Epris later renamed Kapara.

Zurrya, the Last Princess of Zurris: Tragic historical figure.

AFTERWORD

Who is The Man From Nothing?

Who is Harkas Tangor?

Who is the man "from nothing" whose deeds struck fear into the hearts of Kapars across Poloda and gave hope to Polodans from Pole to Pole?

An American pilot and champion of liberty, Tangor volunteered to fly for France in the early days of World War II. Apparently killed in action, he lived again to fight for freedom on the Planet of Perpetual War!

Freedom fighter on two planets, humanitarian, secret agent in the heart of the Kapar empire, developer of revolutionary new technology, and bold explorer of the Omos system, Tangor is all of these and more!

Read the story of the first Earthman on Poloda in Edgar Rice Burroughs' classic novels of intergalactic adventure *Beyond the Farthest Star!* and *Tangor Returns!*

THE WILD ADVENTURES OF

EDGAR RICE BURROUGHS® SERIES

1 Tarzan: Return to Pal-ul-don

2 Tarzan on the Precipice

3 Tarzan Trilogy

4 Tarzan: The Greystoke Legacy Under Siege

5. A Soldier of Poloda
    Further Adventures Beyond the Farthest Star

About Edgar Rice Burroughs, Inc.

Founded in 1923 by Edgar Rice Burroughs, as one of the first authors to incorporate himself, Edgar Rice Burroughs, Inc. holds numerous trademarks and the rights to all literary works of the author still protected by copyright, including stories of Tarzan of the Apes and John Carter of Mars. The company has overseen every adaptation of his literary works in film, television, radio, publishing, theatrical stage productions, licensing and merchandising. The company is still a very active enterprise and manages and licenses the vast archive of Mr. Burroughs' literary works, fictional characters and corresponding artworks that have grown for over a century. The company continues to be owned by the Burroughs family and remains headquartered in Tarzana, California, the town named after the Tarzana Ranch Mr. Burroughs purchased there in 1918 which led to the town's future development.

www.edgarriceburroughs.com
www.tarzan.com

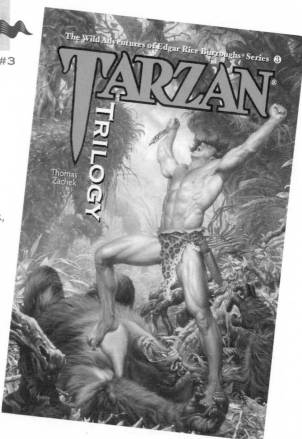